NO QUARTER

The major laid out their attack plan. It was to be a quick raid, their force split into three segments: a special task group to take out the enemy scouts and perimeter; the main action group to initiate the heaviest fire into the killing zone; and the security group to cover the approach and withdrawal.

"We'll use the *mang* bowmen to open," Hannon said to Red Parnell. "I want *your* men there to direct fire since they're combat savvy. You take the rest of the guns and set up security." He paused to glass the target area. "The approach is on the upside of the village hill. We'll work our way down between the paddy ridges, then cross through the woods and set up a firing line in the grove. Afterward, continue heading northeast. Here." He handed Red a small compass with a flip top. "Hold on zero-two-zero. We'll stay with our group till we're at least a mile out."

"Yes, sir."

"Warn your men, Parnell, this'll be close-in fighting. Once the Nips react, they'll charge straight for the center of the firing line. An' they'll scream. Ignore it or it'll rattle the bollocks off ya. They'll come at you out of the brush quick as a gnat's blink, bayonets first. So keep your blades handy and be positioned to parry and counterthrust."

The Aussie looked straight into his eyes, said quietly, "Kill every one of 'em, Parnell. No quarter. *Nobody* left alive. That's an order. You understand?"

"Yes, sir," Red answered quietly.

TYPHOON

CHARLES RYAN

PINNACLE BOOKS
Kensington Publishing Corp.
http://www.kensingtonbooks.com

PINNACLE BOOKS are published by

Kensington Publishing Corp.
850 Third Avenue
New York, NY 10022

All Kensington Titles, Imprints, and Distributed Lines are avail-
able at special quantity discounts for bulk purchases for sales
promotions, premiums, fund-raising, and educational or insti-
tutional use. Special book excerpts or customized printings can
also be created to fit specific needs. For details, write or phone
the office of the Kensington special sales manager: Kensington
Publishing Corp., 850 Third Avenue, New York, NY 10022,
attn: Special Sales Department, Phone: 1-800-221-2647.

Pinnacle and the P logo Reg. U.S. Pat. & TM Off.

First Pinnacle Books Printing: June 2006

10 9 8 7 6 5 4 3 2 1

Printed in the United States of America

To Private James Miles and, by extension, all who served in World War II. Some died, many bled, but all were scarred by its chaos.

O that a man might know
The end of this day's business ere it come!
But it sufficeth that the day will end,
And then the end is known.

Julius Caesar
William Shakespeare

DILLON

Chapter One

Honolulu, Hawaii
14 January 1945
0355 hours

They looked like a squad of Marine Marauders, sitting on their battle gear in the dark, everyone in new jungle-camo fatigues, soft-soled jungle boots, and floppy boonie caps. Close by were the darkened Quonsets of the 109th Air/Sea Rescue Squadron. The only lights came from the unit's operations building and from the string of red and white bulbs on the facility's landing wharf.

The wharf protruded out into Kiehi Lagoon, a shallow-water bay located slightly north of the city of Honolulu. Tied up to it was an old Elco PT boat, its guns and upgear under canvas, and a recommissioned coast guard MTF Cutter named USS *Piute*. Anchored out in the channel were two PBY Catalina patrol seaplanes, their hulls painted blue white.

Back of the station stretched the matrix of runways and taxi lanes of Hickam Air Force Base, their multicolored side lights and tower strobes looking oddly lonely out there in the darkness, like distant campfires on a plain. Across the lagoon were the dimmer lights of Fort Armstrong, nearly lost in the brighter glow from Kapalama Basin and the city beyond.

Lieutenant John "Red" Parnell, team leader of a small commando unit designated Blue Team, settled himself back against his pack and lit a cigarette. A cool onshore breeze drifted in off the channel, smelling of ocean and the sourness of mudflats. The others had already fallen back to sleep, curled on their gear bags, everybody badly hungover.

He'd rousted them from bed at 0200 hours. They were all staying at the EM quarters in Fort DeRussy, a military recreational facility near Waikiki. Afterward, the team was driven to the 109th by Lieutenant Commander Sam "Woody" Chestnut, a naval intelligence officer who had acted as their liaison during their seven-day leave in Honolulu. He'd also invited Parnell to stay with him and his family in their home in Kahala, an upscale, beachside neighborhood located at the eastern foot of famous Diamond Head Crater.

Blue Team was part of an elite army unit officially known as the Mohawkers. Created by Colonel James Dunmore, a senior officer with General George Patton's staff, it had originally been composed of eight separate teams, all volunteers and highly trained in reconnaissance and commando tactics for conducting operations behind enemy lines in the Mediterranean and Europe.

But in late 1944, Army Command Headquarters in Washington had ordered Dunmore to disband the Mohawkers. It was part of a military force reduction since it was obvious Germany was near unconditional surrender. All the other teams had already been recycled back to the States, each member returning to his old unit or being assigned to new ones.

Still, Parnell and his men had always been the colonel's favorites. He hated to see them separate now. Blue Team was the first Mohawker unit to see combat. They'd fought in Morocco, Algeria, and Tunisia and had performed so admirably they had won official recognition for the entire Mohawker unit. After Africa, they were sent into Sicily and Italy and then dropped into France ahead of the D-day invasion, fighting all the way across Normandy and eventually in the great Battle of the Bulge in Belgium.

Just after Christmas, Dunmore came to offer them the choice of remaining intact as an operational team or getting reassigned to other units as instructors back in the States. All of them voted to remain as members of Blue Team. With Patton's help, the colonel got ACHQ's clearance for them to be kept in the official logs as an active operational unit of the United States Army. Now they were headed for the Philippines to go into jungle training for a highly secret operation on the island of Luzon.

Parnell quietly smoked, listening to the surge and fade of aircraft engines as military planes transited in and out of Hickam AFB, and watching the light reflections dance and shimmer on the surface of the lagoon. He was still half drunk, his head throbbing, his stomach sour and noisy. He and Beth Jennings had tied a heavy one on earlier that night.

Beth was Woody Chestnut's sister-in-law, temporarily living with them while she waited for employment with the Hawaiian Board of Health as a testing nurse for VD among the brothel prostitutes of Honolulu and the outer islands. She was twenty-four with a nursing degree from Stanford, a vivacious blonde who resembled Carole Lombard.

She and Parnell had hit it off immediately, spent all their time together covering ground in Beth's beat-up '39 Ford coupe, body-surfing at Makapuu, or skin-diving off Kaena Point where the water was as clear as gin and they could see the shadowy shapes of sharks moving just at the blue-green edge of their vision. They often slept on the beach and got roaring drunk on Primo beer and once even hiked up to Sacred Falls and went swimming naked in the dark, frigid water.

Red enjoyed Beth's bright, funny, adventurous personality. And she found his quiet, combat-vet lethality heroically attractive, his big-shouldered physicality deliciously arousing. From the first, she had blatantly tempted him into bed. Yet Parnell found himself uncomfortable at having another woman just yet. It was too soon. He tactfully managed to hold her off.

Until last night. Recalling it now, he chuckled to himself. A bittersweet thing. They'd started out the evening with an early dinner at *Lau Yee Chai's* in Waikiki, then walked down to the *Moana* Hotel to see its Banyan Court floor show. Afterward, they hit the *Waikiki Tavern* and then the *Aloha Lounge*. By eleven o'clock both were decently sozzled.

They headed back for Kahala, drunkenly singing football fight songs as they skirted Diamond Head. On a sudden whim, Beth swung the Ford down onto a side road that branched off to a coast guard lighthouse and also down to a tiny strip of beach lined with Samoan dwarf palms and wild mangroves.

They sat on a stone water break and Beth pointed to a series of tiny blue lights that formed a slanted line up a nearby cliff face. "You know where those go?" she asked him.

"Where?"

"To Doris Duke's summer house."

"Who the hell's Doris Duke?"

"You know, the tobacco heiress? You should see it. Damn thing looks like an Arabian palace. But she only uses it, like, one weekend a year. . . . You know what? Let's sneak in and go skinny-dipping in her pool."

"What?"

"Come on, she isn't there now. And the caretaker lives far down the slope."

They skirted the shore to the base of the cliff. A cement dock stood out in the water with a stone bathhouse shaped like a desert tent. Two hundred yards farther out, reef surf hissed and tumbled, looking like rows of cotton in the light of a waning half-moon. The tiny blue lights were bulbs embedded into the steps that climbed up the cliff face.

The main grounds had a long stretch of perfectly groomed lawn bordered with bougainvillea, hibiscus, and white-petal oleander. There were statues and small fountains scattered among cement lawn chairs. A large, free-form pool curved around an open patio that looked out over the sea. The edge of the pool had been built so the water seemed to roll right off into space. Its tiling was exquisite, forming arabesque patterns that gleamed like jewels in the moonlight.

The main house had damascene screens and alabaster domes and spires. The patio itself was floored with white marble and had an oval mirror pool in the center, and there were delicately slender pilasters carved with silver-plated spiderweb filigree. The furniture was crystal-topped tables and, oddly, common wicker chaise longues and chairs with embroidered pillows.

They went swimming naked, the water like melted silk, like air, and Beth wrapped her legs around him and they kissed hungrily and then went up onto the patio and began to make love on one of the chaise longues, Beth already aroused to roughness, whimpering and insistent and groaning obscenities.

Their foreplay was short, both wanting it badly. Parnell quickly mounted her and lunged furiously into her body, felt her nipples hard as little thumbs against his chest, her nails clawing his back. On and on until his loins began to tremble as orgasm rushed at him. He let it come, heard himself moaning as if he were lifting great weights. There was a sense of white sunlight behind his lids. Then the ecstasy was receding away and he heard his voice cursing, the sound like a sob, as a powerful surge of guilt exploded in him. He roughly disengaged himself and slid off the chaise longue.

"What's the matter?" Beth hissed. "God, don't stop!"

He walked to the pool's edge and sat down, his legs

dangling in the water. His erection was already flaccid. The distant surf murmured beyond the cliff edge and the moonlight made blue-white rings on the pool's surface, the air thick with the perfume of gardenias and mock orange.

After a while, Beth came and quietly sat beside him. He glanced at her. "I'm sorry," he said and felt cold sober. She didn't say anything, instead slowly twirled her feet, making the moon circles merge and sunder apart to reform in segmented matrices.

"Jesus, I'm really sorry, Beth," he repeated.

"You remembered someone, didn't you?"

"Yes."

"Tell me?"

"No."

"Please?"

He did, slowly. About Annabelle Sinclair and about England and France and about finding her dead body in a stinking cell in a stinking stable in western Germany where Nazi guards had blown one side of her head off. Beth listened, her legs slowly stopping their twirling. The night became still and remote. When he finished, neither said anything for a long time.

Finally, she pushed her arm through his, tenderly kissed his cheek, and stood up. "We'd better go, John. It's probably near one. We can pick up your gear and then I'll drive you over to DeRussy. . . ."

The sound of an aircraft abruptly punched through his thoughts, coming in low, its engines powering back. He glanced out toward the channel. The wing and landing lights of a seaplane were out there against the darkness over the ocean, appearing motionless. Then they grew very bright and a moment later, the aircraft flashed in silhouette against the fort's lights and touched down, water hurling off its hull chines, the big engine rumble dropping off instantly.

A moment later, a jeep pulled up beside the team and the driver called out, "Time to load up, Lieutenant."

Sgt. Wyatt Bird was saying, "I tell ya, Hoss, that ole gal has a jelly roll'll make your nuts shoot through your asshole." He and Sgt. Sol Kaamanui were comparing Honolulu prostitutes and their specialties.

"What, at the Golden Pagoda? The one with a tattoo of a snake on her tit?"

"No, this 'un ain't got no tattoo. She's over to the Silver Slipper."

"Naw, I'm talking about Jo-Ann at the Pagoda. Blond, little plump, got eyes on her like a Chinaman?"

"Oh, yeah, I know that one," Bird said, sitting sideways on the steel seat, his back to the window showing all that ocean down there far below the gull wing of the PBM Mariner 3R flying boat. "But she all's gettin' a mite long in the fang, ain't she? I used to do her over to the old White House back in '40. Had red hair then, always used to shave her pussy."

"She don't no more," Sol said. "But, damn, she can *work* it. . . . Me, I don't like bare pussy. Feels like you screwin' your palm."

They'd been in the air for nearly four hours now, the deep-bodied Mariner part of the Naval Air Transport Service, her twin heavy-duty Scott-Allison engines roaring steadily, not missing a beat. There were a dozen metal seats and about three tons of cargo under netting aft the radar/radio compartment, the air at twelve thousand feet nippy. The other men were still asleep.

For six days Blue Team had hit the bars and brothels in downtown Honolulu, first coming in by taxi from Schofield Barracks where they'd been processed and given all their overseas shots after arriving from Europe, riding in the humid Hawaiian afternoon with the January Kona Wind blowing heavy moisture in from the south. And pulling up

in town across from the army YMCA and making a quick
stop for that first cold one at the old Black Cat Café.

Afterward, strolling down through the seedy honky-
tonks and massage parlors and photo shops and upstairs
dance halls along Hotel and Beretania and River Streets
with shit-kicking music pouring out into the street and
the air rife with the stink of greasy hot dogs and cheap-
meat hamburgers and sour sweat coming off the parade
of soldiers and sailors and marines that streamed endlessly, aimlessly, drunkenly along the sidewalks.

Inevitably homing to the whorehouses with their color-
names like Paradise Blue and the Red Robin, which always
seemed located up two flights of stairs and through doors
with little viewing holes like speakeasies and inside the
door pay cages eternally overseen by bored old Chinese
women and dilapidated jukeboxes full of "San Antonio
Rose" and "Pistol-Packin' Mama" and the bull pens where
the whores worked the cheap lays, rotating around a four-
stall booth, *bing-bang-bong* and you were gone. Those who
had sufficient money could rent a private screwing room
for thirty minutes: old and musty places with wainscoted
walls and the medicinal odor of disinfectant and pubis
and cock buckets long since impressed into the wood.

And finally, at long last, feeling again that old, anxious, tight-groin tension rising to explosive release within
the smooth, moist-slippery warmth of female flesh that
had only been fantasized about and masturbated over
during those long days and nights between furlough.

For Bird it had been a homecoming, from his prewar
days when he was with the 25th Infantry, the old Tropical
Lightning Division stationed at Schofield. That first day
back at the barracks, he walked the main company quads,
wandered through empty dayrooms smelling of that familiar garrison odor of gun oil and leather and polished
cement. He visited the payday gambling shacks still out
there and had a few icy cold cans of 3.2 in the deserted
garden of the EM Club, the place still owned by the same

Chinese couple named Lum who immediately recognized him.

It had brought up a wash of tender sadness in him, a peculiar thing for Wyatt Bird, the stolid thirty-year man, the quintessential soldier used to shifting posts. Yet there was something indefinably rich and poignant in this particular place. Perhaps it was the remnants of his youth, perhaps the scenes of old discoveries of manhood. But more, it was the memory of old friends, squad and platoon mates all gone now, most buried in sandy graves on countless, peculiarly named islands that lay scattered across the southwestern Pacific.

Still, standing in the midafternoon quiet of Quad 3, with only the distant, sporadic rattle of rifle fire from a basic training company going through its qualifying shoots disturbing the humming stillness, he had allowed himself to remember. . . .

Corporal Weesay Laguna sat up and sleepily asked, "Where the hell we at?"

"Over the ocean," Sol answered. "Where the hell you *think* we at?"

"What, still?" Laguna said. "Jesus, how long we been flyin'?"

"Six hours."

"I gotta take a crap."

"Use your tin hat," Wyatt said.

"Bullshit. Where the hell's them crewmen?" He stood up, whistled over the steady rumble of the engines. A corporal poked his head around the door of the radar/radio compartment. Laguna pointed to his butt, hollered, "I gotta use the head. Where's it at?"

The crewman pointed to the rear of the aircraft and shouted back, "Remember she's a pneumatic unit, mack. You gotta bring up pressure before takin' a dump."

Kaamuni and Bird chuckled. "Yeah, it's a pressure crapper, Chihuahua," Wyatt said to Laguna. "Jes' be sure you blow the shit *outta* the plane, not *into* it."

"*No me jodas, pendejos,*" Weesay said sourly and stumbled off over cargo tie-down belts.

The first stop on their six-thousand-mile island-hopping journey was at Johnston Island, a thousand miles southwest of the Hawaiians, the time eleven in the morning as the big seaplane swept in low over coral reefs, the water shifting from deep blue to green and then white green as the aircraft settled down onto the surface of the main lagoon, which was enclosed by a rim of beach as white as toothpaste in the sunlight.

They refueled off an old Dutch Kazbek-class tanker that was now part of the U.S. Pacific Fleet, anchored in the roadstead. The entire ship was painted in red lead. The Mariner's chief pilot, navy Lieutenant Josh Paraguirre, went aboard the auxiliary and returned with sandwiches and two gallons of steaming coffee. They lifted off again at 1400 hours, continuing west-southwestward for the next stop, which would be Kwajalein in the Marshalls.

Through the long afternoon, the men played cards or cleaned their weapons or dozed, watching the endless expanse of ocean far below them. Around five o'clock, they passed an American submarine recharging its batteries on the surface, cutting a slowly dissipating V in the sea.

It was well after dark when they reached Kwajalein, another atoll, very large with a completely enclosed lagoon and shaped like a lopsided rectangle. The naval seaplane base was on Lib Island, which sat in the middle of the lagoon like the pupil of an eye. On the southern side of the atoll was a long military runway edged with Quonsets. Everything was blacked out except for the tiny red channel markers near the island and the far-off runway lights, which came on only when an aircraft approached for a landing.

Apparently, the Mariner had been having slight fuel line problems in its staboard engine. While a crew of motor-mechs towed the big aircraft up onto a repair ramp, Paraguirre and his men and Blue Team had dinner at the navy mess: thick T-bone steaks and Pacific lobster and skillet biscuits.

Afterward, the air crew went off to transit quarters to grab a few hours of sleep. Parnell and the others chose to bunk out on the beach. They bought beer from the EM Club, a buck a case, and went down to a stretch of beach near the maintainence hangars, sat out there on the sand that was cool and as white and fine as processed sugar, and watched the tilted half-moon slowly drop toward the western sea, listening to the rustle of surf on the outer reef and the clicking of sand crabs that scurried along the tidal line.

They took off again at four in the morning, lifting up into a slight overcast that had moved in during the night. Their next fueling stop was Truk in the Carolines, thirteen hundred miles due west. Bucking headwinds, it took them nearly six hours to arrive, flying in over two-thousand-foot-high peaks misty and covered with green-black jungle.

While their aircraft was being refueled, Corporals Smoker Wineberg and Cowboy Fountain scrounged up lunch for the team and the plane's crew from a small marine jungle-training base near the landing ramp: boxes of cold fried chicken and cans of peaches and potato salad. They also scored two bottles of torpedo juice, made from torpedo propellant filtered through loaves of bread and mixed with pineapple juice. It was nearly 190 proof and carried a helluva wallop.

Just before noon, they took off again in a heavy rain. This would be the final and longest air leg of their trip, nineteen hundred miles to the tiny island of Cabugan Chico off the southeastern coast of Leyte.

Leyte had been invaded on 20 October 1944 by the X and XIV Corps of the American Sixth Army, which was led by Major General Walter Kreuger. For two months intense combat operations had been conducted against stiff opposition by the Japanese 16th Division, part of the famous crack Fourteenth Army of General Tomoyuki Yamashita, the brutal "Tiger of Malaya" who was now overall commander of all Japanese forces in the Philippines.

By Christmas, most of the island was secured. Still, strong pockets of Japanese soldiers had fled into the mountain jungles of the north and south-central highlands and remained active. By the first of the new year, Kreuger's forces were rotated back to Australia for rest and replenishment for the coming assault on Luzon and replaced by elements of the U.S. Eighth Army commanded by Major General Robert Eichelberger.

On Cabugan Chico, an Australian Commando FTC or Forward Training Camp had been set up in early November to instruct Filipino guerilla cadres and small Allied units on the techniques of jungle warfare.

So far, they'd processed two platoons from B Company of the 6th Ranger Battalion, a scout team from the 5217th Recon Battalion, and an incursion group from MacArthur's Allied Intelligence Bureau, an organization the general had personally created because of his hatred of the OSS. Currently, a six-man cadre from the Philippine 114th Guerilla Regiment was being run through the training cycle. Now it would include Blue Team.

They picked up the radar blips of two Japanese aircraft fifteen miles west of their position and following a vector directly toward them. The radar operator, calculating from blip configuration and speed, concluded they were probably A6M2-N Mitsubishi Zero float plane fighters on an air reconnaissance of American fleet operations off Leyte Gulf. It was a little after seven in the evening, an hour from Cabugan Chico, the sky still glowing with the fading yellows and deep crimsons of sunset.

At the first blip sighting, Lieutenant Paraguirre quickly dumped altitude, got right down there on the deck, thirty feet over the ocean to make his aircraft hard to spot from above in the tricky, gradually diminishing light as he raced for darkness. Meanwhile, his gunners came scrambling astern, pulling themselves hand-over-hand along the metal overhead spine beam in the steep incline of the aircraft's deck.

This particular variant of the Mariner had originally been designed as a sub-chaser but was then switched to a service transport. It was only lightly armed with a single dorsal power-operated .50-caliber machine gun and two hand-operated .50s in beam positions. By the time they reached the ocean, the gunners had their weapons uncased and were scanning the sky above them, looking for glints.

They almost made it. Right below, the sea slowly shifted into deeper shades of blue black and then black etched with whitecaps. But then one of the enemy float planes came right at them from off the ocean, up the bucket on the port-side twin fin, the thing invisible in the radar bounce until it was there, bursting onto the screen full blown.

The dorsal gunner opened on it, his spent casings flying down hot and whirling. A few seconds later came a loud, slamming crash and the Mariner's machine gun went silent. At the same moment, a perfectly round hole appeared in the port wing beside the engine, one of the Jap wing-mounted 20mm rounds going right through it but fortunately failing to fuse off.

Now the starboard gunner started firing, then stopped as the enemy float plane flashed by and up. Far out but swinging in was the other plane, also skimming the ocean. For a tiny second its windshield reflected the vanishing glow of the sunset, flashing red. Then its weapons let loose, the cannon rounds arching as slow as Roman candles toward them and the 7.7mm nose gun throwing tracer lines. All of them missed, the pilot undershooting. In a moment, he roared right over them and was gone.

Blood dripped down the ladder to the dorsal turret. Smoker and Parnell, the closest to it, immediately scrambled up. The gunner had been hit, part of his left shoulder gone. He was wild-eyed. Through gritted teeth, he kept saying, "Oh, Jesus! Oh, Jesus!"

They got him down onto the upper deck, ripped open his flight coveralls. Blood was everywhere. The young man had light blond hair. There were chunks of his own flesh in it. He stopped talking, but his eyes were still wide open, frenzied, and his skin was pale and clammy.

Parnell and Bird got out their medical kits, hit him with a shot of morphine, and began putting compression pads onto the gaping wound. The others pulled out blankets and got him covered. By now, Cowboy had taken his place in the dorsal turret. They could hear the slipstream hissing through the shattered bubble and Fountain cursing. Then he was firing, the cracking muzzle bursts clear and powerful under the engine roar.

The dimness inside the big seaplane steadily increased as they flew straight into the deepening evening. The Japanese fighters made one more pass, then broke off the attack. A moment later, Paraguirre came back, squatted beside his wounded crewman.

The young man looked at him. His name was Corporal Robert T. Peeke. The morphine had begun working, his eye lids quivering. "You gonna be okay, Bobby," Paraguirre said and brushed the bloody hair from his forehead. "Take it easy now. You gonna be fine."

He turned, leaned close to Parnell. "You're combat vets, John," he said close to Red's ear. "How bad is it?"

"He's lost a lot of blood. Have you got any plasma aboard?"

"No."

Parnell shook his head. "Not good. He's already in shock."

"*Goddammit,*" Paraguirre said. He turned to look at the young gunner once more, then went forward again.

Sixteen minutes later, Bobby Peeke died.

* * *

Forward Training Camp Hannon lay just inland of a think mangrove swamp that rimmed a lagoon on the north side of Cabugan Chico. The big Mariner had come in a little before eight o'clock, homing to an intermittent frequency signal from the FTC and setting down on the surface of the lagoon with only the glow of the already risen half-moon.

There were no lights visible anywhere, everything merely black silhouettes, even the great mountainous bulk of southern Leyte, which rose up off the dark sea five miles to the west. The lagoon was choppy with a stiff northern breeze, but Paraguirre brought the aircraft in perfectly by the shimmer of moonlight off the water.

An ANZAC sergeant in a large rubber surf-runner met them, the Mariner bobbing with her engines in idle, filling the night with the smell of hot metal and cylinder oil. Blue Team hurriedly loaded their gear into the rubber boat, a small Evinrude outboard on a wooden bracket at its stern.

Paraguirre watched, squatting in the cargo doorway. Parnell was the last man off. He paused a moment to shake the pilot's hand. "Thanks for the lift, Josh. Sorry about your crewman."

Paraguirre nodded. "Yeah. He's the first one I ever lost." He straightened up. "Well, good luck to you boys."

"Thanks," Parnell said and jumped into the boat.

Before they reached the mangroves, the big, gull-winged seaplane, running without lights, lifted off into the moonlight and soon her engine sound faded off into the night's silence.

Australian Special Service Force Major William "Bush" Hannon, head training officer of the FTC whose name was also the code reference for the camp, looked like a Melbourne waterfront thug, big-shouldered and thick-legged with a broad, rough-hewn face, standing in the moon shadows in front of his jungle hut dressed in a dirty khaki shirt, jungle shorts called "stubbies," and a crumpled Aussie campaign hat brimmed up on the left side atop his head. A cigarette dangled from his mouth.

Parnell snapped to attention, saluted. "U.S. Army Lieutenant John Parnell and his team reporting for duty, sir."

Hannon returned the salute. "Welcome to the bleedin' jungle, Lieutenant," he barked without withdrawing his cigarette, his accent heavy Digger. He jerked his head toward his hut. "Come on inside," he said, then turned to the sergeant who had brought them in and ordered, "Tommy, show the Yanks where they can stow their kit."

His hut was made of bamboo with mud-and-grass caulking in the walls, the roof covered with bundles of nipa grass. It was built off the ground on three-foot four-by-fours with little pools of oil at each base to keep the ants out. Where the moonlight hit the oil, it shone like metal.

The single room reeked of mosquito repellant and the crotch-odor of mud-and-sweat-impregnated clothing. British weapons and jungle packs hung from the walls. There was a bamboo table and two bamboo chairs, all held together with knotted strands of vine. A kerosene storm lantern and a British Hallicraft SCT-2000 transceiver were on the table. In the rear of the structure was a cot with a tentlike mosquito net draped over it.

Hannon indicated for Parnell to sit and lowered himself into his own chair. He chain-lit another cigarette and tossed his pack across the table to Red, who extracted one and fired it up with his Zippo.

The Aussie major leaned back and studied him. Two large, pale beetles banged and fluttered around the lamp. In its disturbed glow, his eyes were the gray color molten steel turns when tempered in oil. "I understand you gents're fresh from the Ardennes," he said.

"Yes, sir," Parnell answered. From the jungle came the sudden cries of a clan of monkeys, the sounds like those of women in distress.

"Quite a fight, that," Hannon said. "Bloody Huns nearly pulled it through, aye?"

"It was very close."

The major continued appraising Parnell. Finally, he said, "Are you and your mates up to this business? So soon after that?"

"Yes, sir," Parnell snapped.

Hannon nodded. "Good." He stood up, retrieved a bottle of Victoria gin from one of his jungle packs, came back, and sat down again. He took a long pull of the liquor, then handed it across the bamboo table to Red. He drank. It was hot but smooth.

"Well," the captain said, "I think we best introduce you gents to the bush straightaway."

"Very good, sir."

"I just received a signal from KK-2." KK-2 was the code name for ASSF's northern headquarters located at Kola Kola on Fergussen Island in the D'Etre Castenauix group off the northeast tip of New Guinea. "They're sending up a shipment of signals gear and ammo for guerilla units on Samar. I'll be taking it in myself. You can come along. Shouldn't be more than a few days instructing the *mangs*. That's Tagalog nick for guerillas. It'll give you blokes a look at their operation." He glanced at his watch. It was 8:31. "A PT'll be here at 2230. Bring only your weapons and spare water."

Parnell rose. "Yes, sir."

"If you're hungry, Tommy'll roust som'ing from the mess hut. And, oh, the dunny's the last hut in line."

"Thank you, sir." He braced and left.

The monkey clan had quieted, the moonlight casting deep shadows and the air thick with humidity. Parnell moved along between the silent huts. From the lagoon suddenly drifted the cry of a hornbill, its repeated *callao, callao* sounding melancholy in the night.

Chapter Two

On the other side of the world the Battle of the Bulge still raged. It would take another week before the Germans were driven back to their original positions from which the massive Ardennes counteroffensive had been launched.

Although the complete fall of Nazi Germany was now only a matter of time, there was still a lot of bloody fighting left, both in Italy and Germany. The real end wouldn't come until 3:30 in the afternoon of 30 April when Adolph Hitler would poison Eva Braun and then put a single bullet into his temple in his bunker in Berlin.

In the Pacific and Southeast Asia, the end of war with Japan was far from over. Although the Allies had pushed the Imperial forces back toward the Japanese homeland, the Nips still had a lot of fight in them. Now they had turned desperate.

The surprise attack on Pearl Harbor on 7 December 1941 had been carried out brilliantly. Instantly consolidating their advantage and control of the seas, the Japanese swept through the old British and Dutch colonial territories in the East Indies like a typhoon: from Vietnam to the borders of India on the continent; across the major islands of the Indonesian Passthrough; into Hong Kong,

Taiwan, and the Philippines and eastern New Guinea, the doorway to Australia.

In the Central and Western Pacific, the Japanese Empire already possessed dominion over many of the remote archipelagoes and island chains that had been mandated to them after World War I. All had been fortified into impregnable fleet and air bases so that, by the early months of 1942, they controlled a land and oceanic territory more vast than all of Russia and Europe combined.

The Allied forces of Americans and British had been knocked to the canvas and were damned near unconscious. Desperately, they attempted to regroup. It would not prove easy. From the start, the Pacific Theater was fought under a strong disadvantage. Early on, Roosevelt and Churchill had agreed that the European Theater would be given top priority in men and material, and the Pacific Area would simply have to get along with what was left over.

To get such a vast area under sensible control, the Combined Chiefs of Staff decided to divide the theater into separate command sectors. The Brits and Aussies would conduct operations within the western Indonesian Pass-through and on the continent. Meanwhile, the Americans would handle the Western and Central Pacific.

The U.S. command was then divided again. General Douglas MacArthur was given control of the Western Pacific, which included New Guinea, Borneo, Malaysia, and the adjacent island groups. American and Australian ground forces, elements of both air forces along with the U.S. Seventh Fleet, were also assigned to him.

His coleader in the Central Pacific Zone was Admiral Chester Nimitz, commander of the Pacific Fleet and Pacific Ocean areas. Attached to his command was the U.S. Third Fleet, the 2nd, 3rd, and 5th Marine Assault Divisions, and the VII and XX U.S. Army Air Forces.

A fourth command sector was that of the China-Burma-India area. This was given to General Joseph

Stillwell, a longtime China hand, and his XIV Army Air Force, along with divisions from Chiang Kai-shek's Kuomintang, the Nationalist Chinese Army.

The first true Japanese defeat came on 5 June 1942 when a large assault fleet with four carriers was intercepted and defeated by an American Task Group off the island of Midway. But the first real counteroffensive against the Japanese, code-named Operation Watchtower, was the successful invasion and occupation of Guadalcanal in the Solomon Islands, which began on the morning of 7 August 1942.

Now began the long, grueling, tortuous, bloody climb up through the islands toward the Japanese homeland in a war that was utterly different from that which was and had been waged in Europe and Africa, fought in some of the deadliest environments on earth. Sultry, seething jungle so dense it literally swallowed up entire companies of troops. Cloud-draped and rain-saturated cordilleras with precipices that plunged into steaming ravines where headhunters still used bows and arrows and ate human flesh. Breathless heat-saturated morasses filled with jungle rot and dengue fever and malaria and snakes and gargantuan insects and crocodiles and leeches. Lands where typhoons were spawned.

It was also fought on tiny, remote islands with milk-white beaches and blue-green lagoons that were soon scarred by the grotesqueness of bloated bodies and the residual flotsam of amphibious assault. Through old Lever Brother copra plantations where the coconut trees grew in perfect lines, and into mosquito-infested swamps and volcanic mountains and open fields of spiky golden kunai grass where Japanese Nambu machine gunners in coconut-log emplacements laid down blistering flat trajectory fire under the searing tropical sun.

Despite all this, by the late summer of 1944, MacArthur's forces were within assaulting distance of the southern Philippines, a fifteen-hundred-mile-long archipelago of seventy-three hundred separate islands that lay on the eastern side of the South China Sea. The largest and most populated were Palawan to westward; Mindanao, Panay, Cebu, Negros, the Visayans, Leyte, and Samar in the southern half; and in the north, Mindoro and Luzon, with its capital at Manila, which was the country's governmental seat.

On 20 October 1944, an invasion fleet made up of Task Forces 77, 78, and 79 steamed into Leyte Gulf to lay in a prelanding bombardment against the island of Leyte, and then to disembark the U.S. Sixth Army's X and XXIV Corps at two points on the eastern coast.

Troopers of the 24th Infantry and 1st Cavalry Divisions landed near the northern city of Tacloban on San Pedro Bay. Meanwhile, midway down the island at Dulag, the 7th and 96th Infantry Divisions stormed ashore.

Their immediate opponent was Major General Sosaku Makino's 16th Division. But this amphibious assault proved different from those that had preceded it. The Japanese had changed their tactics against seaborne assault. Makino put up only token resistance and then quickly withdrew inland, beyond the range of the U.S. Navy's deadly big guns.

Recently, a new supreme Japanese commander of the entire Philippines had been appointed, General Tomoyuki Yamashita, commander of the Fourteenth Army and infamous as the Tiger of Malaysia and conqueror of Singapore. Determined to hold the Allies in the south, he began pouring reinforcements down into the battle zone.

Five days later, on 25 October, a ferocious naval battle erupted in the waters south and east of Leyte. This was to be the first appearance of kamikaze suicide aircraft, which were to take a staggering toll on American warships. Still, here the U.S. Fleet won a sweeping victory, neutralizing the last major threat from the Japanese Imperial Navy.

Meanwhile, the land battle for Leyte continued through November amid rapidly worsening weather. Soon, two powerful typhoons swept in off the South China Sea and badly bogged down U.S. advances and destroyed supply lines. Nevertheless, advances did continue, inexorably driving the enemy into isolated pockets of resistance in the northern and southern mountains.

In December, the key city of Ormoc on the western coast was taken. The following day, elements of the 1st Cavalry Division crossed the narrow San Juanico Strait seperating Leyte from the island of Samar, and took the Catbalogan naval base located halfway up the western coast of Samar.

Then, in the early dawn of 9 January 1945, MacArthur's forces struck again. This time, Task Forces 79, 73, and six Battle Groups from TF 78 landed the I and XIV Corps on the main island of Luzon at Lingayen Gulf. It was precisely at the same spot where Japanese troops had landed in 1942. Once more, little opposition was encountered, and the assault troops quickly consolidated their beachhead and began thrusting inland toward Manila, 120 miles to the south.

Yamashita had finally realized that Leyte and Samar were already lost. Immediately abandoning the troops on Leyte with an explicit order to "kill as many Americans as possible and sacrifice your lives for the emperor," he began shuttling the Samar troops across the San Bernardino Strait into southern Luzon so as to strengthen himself for the major battle for the Philippines, which he knew was coming.

Throughout the Japanese occupation of the islands, Samar had always been a hotbed of guerilla activity. Now, as the Japanese attempted to transit out of the country, raids on their convoys and sabotage of their stores increased dramatically. Outraged, Yamashita sent down elite suppression units called Tokubetsu Rikusentai, teams of Special Naval Landing Force marines. Their single mission, code-named Operation Mujinka, was to annihilate every guerilla and enemy sympathizer.

Most of these Nip marines had operated in Malaysia and China in the early years of the war. They were extremely brutal units who tortured suspected guerillas, mass-raped village women, and slaughtered anyone they wanted to. They were shipped to the Philippines with the definitive Fourteenth Army order: *Erase all shadows of the people in the battlefield.*

For their part, the guerilla bands, called *borobos* or *mangs*, particularly those on Samar, were a disorganized mixture of patriots, ex-soldiers, deserters from the Philippine Constabulary, bandits, local warlords, and Muslim Moros. Many of these bands actually exploited and brutalized their own people as badly as the Japanese did when villagers refused them food or women. They were also continually fighting with each other for territory.

Early efforts to coordinate these groups into a cohesive fighting force, or what the Filipinos called *bayanihan*, was a near impossibility. But eventually, as the Japanese grew more and more brutal to the natives, leaders began to emerge with whom MacArthur's intelligence could work.

The lack of weapons and ammunition had always been a major problem for the guerillas. By late 1943, occasional American PT boats managed to sneak in with equipment. Eight months later, American subs began making regular supply runs into the southern Philippines. To create a workable command-and-control system to oversee these disparate groups, MacArthur issued commissions to the more powerful leaders, making them regular field officers of the U.S. Army.

16 January
2218 hours

PT 119 from Torpedo Boat Squadron Five skimmed lightly across the surface of Letye Gulf, running on a northeasterly heading so as to clear past the northern tip

of the large Jap-held, shrimp-shaped island called
Homonhon, which sat squarely in the middle of the gulf.

The boat's captain, Lieutenant Commander Pete
Harper, held the vessel to normal cruising speed, just
under thirty knots, the PT an eighty-foot Elco, its three
Packard V-12 engines howling and the props laying out
a mile-long, phosphorescent wake.

Rain had swept in from the north at nine o'clock. Now
the sky was completely overcast, the moon a dim, curved
smear of light high in the east. But the ocean was still relatively calm, with only a slight chop that actually aided
the boat, allowing the hull to break surface tension and
lift smoothly up onto the step with only its props and rud-
ders submerged.

Major Hannon and Parnell had remained topside after
loading at Cabugan Chico. Their eight supply crates containing SC-401 transceivers and small arms ammunition
were strapped to the deck inboard the four torpedo
tubes. The rest of Blue Team and the Aussie's two radio
instructors and two translators were below decks, everyone with Mae West life jackets, the crewmen also wearing
gun belts and helmets.

Pulling his boonie hat down low against the speed-
driven rain, Parnell studied the distant dark bulk of
Leyte's southern Mahablag Mountains, twenty miles to
the west. In the north, he saw flashes of artillery looking
like distant sheet lightning. The night was heavy with the
sea odor of rain and the hot reek of engine exhaust.

Hannon tapped his leg, indicating he squat to join
him and Harper, who were hunkered down behind the
control panel. The boat's exec, Ensign Joe Meehl, had
taken the wheel. To their right was the quartermaster,
facing the stern, while up in the port and starboard turrets directly aft the control deck, two gun watches were
huddled into the shoulder harnesses of twin .50-caliber
machine guns.

Parnell settled down with his back against the chart

house hatch. Harper was explaining his course plot and
speed regime, which would take them to their rendezvous point with the guerilla pickup boat a half mile
offshore southeast of the fishing village of Balangkayan.

"I'll stay at cruise speed till we cross the gulf," he said,
having to shout to be heard over the engines. Harper
was tall and lean, his long legs cranked down in their
sun-bleached khakis, his grommetless cap lifted back on
his forehead. An experienced boat captain, he'd served
with John F. Kennedy in the Solomons and Bismarcks in
'42. "As you can see," he continued, "our wake lights up
like damned neon. But it's no problem out here in the
gulf. Not since we kicked Jap ass back in October."

Red leaned in to listen, feeling the smooth, even thrust
of the PT come up through his legs. It was warm and dry
down there below the combing, their speed sending the
rain past as it came off the windshield. Everything was dark
on the control deck save for a faint green glow that came
from the boat's compass up on the instrument panel.

"Unfortunately, once we clear past Point Ngulos at the
tip of Samar, we could run into Nip vessels anywhere
along the coast. I'll keep her down in idle then, to kill our
wake. We lay one out up there, we'll have a goddamned
Dinah flying right up it." A *Dinah* was a Mitsubishi Type 1
light bomber the Japanese used on night patrols. "Besides, I don't have depth charts for that part of the Samar
coastline. Native fishermen tell me the whole area's a
puzzlework of shelving beaches and reef fields. We hit
one of them at speed, we got a major problem."

The captain shifted his legs, his bony knees showing
through the khaki. "Aerial reports say the Japs have been
moving troops toward northern Samar and then crossing
them into Luzon. So we *could* run into some mules hugging the coastline." *Mules* referred to the sixty-foot-long,
shallow draft barges the Japanese used to ferry men and
equipment.

Hannon leaned in, shouted, "Could that be trouble in getting us ashore?"

Harper shrugged. "Depends. Even if there's more than one, we might still scoot in and out. As long as our seaway separation's wide enough. Either way though, when we do unload, I want you to make it *bloody* fast. I don't like sitting motionless with our silhouette against the sea horizon." He paused, waited a moment, then added, "Are there any other questions, Major?"

Hannon shook his head.

The lieutenant nodded and uncranked himself. He retook the wheel. Parnell rose and felt the sting of rain drops in his face just as a fan of artillery flashes lit up the darkness that was the Leyte Mountains.

Now Major Hannon was saying, "Some'hing I want to warn you about, Lef-tenant. You're about to enter jungle. It's like no place you've ever seen. It's an entity, a reality that you'd best come to terms with quick. Or she'll kark ya, and no josh about it. Once we land, you people watch me and my *mangs*. Do wot we do. Don't ask questions, just do it."

Red nodded. *Understood.*

It was now twenty minutes after midnight. They'd long since cleared Ngulos Point and were now bearing north, the boat's crew at general quarters as the PT moved a mile offshore at ten knots, only the center engine in gear, with the two wing units running but remaining in neutral, ready for any immediate power in case they had to vacate the area fast. The only engine noise was a soft burbling from the stern, Lieutenant Harper having extended his mufflers to absorb exhaust sound.

The two officers were seated in the boat's tiny wardroom with its two-man table just aft the galley, everything red under battle lights so the sailors could retain their night vision. They were drinking raisin jack, dark as ale. It was cooked up by the PT crew in the forepeak rope locker, a sweet and gently hot liquid that carried a decent buzz.

Across the companionway was the radio/radar room. The rest of the soldiers were scattered about the boat, most flaked out in companionways or on ammo lockers, two atop the three-thousand-gallon, 100-octane fuel tanks aft in the stifling-hot dayroom. The air was dense and smelled of heated engine oil and stale coffee and the musky odor of enclosed males.

Hannon took a pull of jack, his broad face a landscape of red and black shadows, and went on, "Jungle combat's almost always at very close quarters. Can't see a bloody thing, so it's difficult to keep unit cohesion. Learn to depend on your ears, even your nose, more than your eyes.

"The best weapons in jungle are Thompsons and shotguns throwin' double-ought shells. Aye, and 'ere's a tip about your weapons. Always clean them with Jap gun oil. It's made with whale oil and is a damn sight better than ours in stopping moisture jams."

"What about the guerillas?" Red asked.

"Some are bad, a damned grotty lot of bushers and thieves who'd as soon slit your throat as to look at you. Many aren't even Filipinos, but renegade Yanks and brummies from my country. Go slow with these buggers, Parnell. As for the rest of the *mangs,* they're a decent lot. Patriotic as Rugby Leaguers and damned determined fighters. You treat 'em with dignity, you don't never muck about with their *amor propio,* and the little blokes'll bloody well die for you."

"*Armor propio?*"

"Aye, that's their sense of self-honor. It's also called *utang na loob.* Ya see, Filipinos are a very proud people, easily offended." He snorted. "Sometimes damned stiff-backed, actually. Particularly if they think they're obligated to you."

Major Bush Hannon knew jungles and the ways of jungle people about as well as any white man could. He didn't particularly relish this environment, nor had he gone native as some old-time whites had done. But he respected the land and its natives, and would not tolerate rudeness or the slightest insult directed toward them from the men under him.

The son of an Australian Anglican minister, he'd spent much of his boyhood at mission stations in New Guinea and eastern Borneo. At nineteen, he took off for Tasmania and bull-bucked timber crews in the dense mahogany forests around Great Lake, north of Bridgewater. In 1939, he joined the army, took officer training, and then attended the Australian/New Zealand Commando Academy at Conungra in western Australia.

He was assigned to the Australian Intelligence Field Force. It was dangerous work, penetrating the Japanese-held areas of New Guinea and the Solomons to bring in equipment and code systems to the local coast watchers. By 1944, he'd earned his majority and was sent into the Sulu Archipelago and the southern Philippines to set up secret forward training camps to train friendly guerilla bands.

The boat's radioman suddenly popped his head through the doorway. "Excuse me, Major. I've got Alamo on the wire." *Alamo* was Hannon's contact man with the main guerilla bands that operated in the Sulat River district of Samar. He was an AFS corporal named Dutchie McLish who was scheduled to rendezvous with them.

In the radio room, the operator flicked on his speaker and handed the mike to Hannon. He keyed: "Alamo, this is Dragoon One. Go ahead."

"Dragoon One, mule train sighted half mile our position. Three—" A burst of static blew the rest of the message away. Alamo was using an ancient Bureau of Posts radio, Hannon explained, coil controlled and with a tendency to drift off frequency.

He waited a few more seconds for McLish to adjust up, the static fading, then keyed once more: "Say again, Alamo."

"Repeat, mule train half mile my position. Three bearing

north. Wake ripples indicate possible picket boat also bearing north. Is kiss-and-run still in effect? Over."

"Stand by, Alamo," Hannon said to the operator. "Get the captain down here."

A few seconds later, Harper came into the room, his helmet dripping rainwater. For a moment, he and Hannon discussed the situation. Meanwhile, Alamo, getting anxious, kept coming through, requesting specific instructions, his transmission spiky with static again.

Harper turned to look at the small radar screen, which was mounted beside the radio console. He studied it a moment, its rotating line of light leaving a glowing wash behind it, which slowly vanished. "You getting any ghosts at all?" he asked the operator.

"Nothing yet, Captain."

"How far are we from the rendezvous point?" Hannon asked.

"Fifty-one minutes," Harper said. He lowered his head down, thinking. Finally, he glanced up. "If we're lucky, that barge train's already past it. As I said, if there are more of the buggers, we'll go for a dart in. But I think it'd be smart to move the contact time up about thirty minutes so we don't have to drift and wait."

"What about that picket boat?"

"It hasn't come up on scope yet. That means *if* it's out there, it's at least ten miles from us. That gives us a fair cushion."

"Good enough," Hannon said. He keyed: "Alamo, kiss-and-run is affirmative. Move time up thirty. An' be damned certain you're bang on. Dragoon One, over and out."

Forty minutes later, a target bogey popped onto the PT's radar screen, vague and misty at first, then more solid, fifteen hundred yards out, a Japanese barge hugging the shoreline so probing radar pulses would be diffused against the nearby jungle background.

* * *

Parnell and Hannon were back topside, both men braced against the fore end of the chart house, their Thompson submachine guns at their sides. Earlier, when the radioman informed Harper of the enemy sighting, the captain had come right back, no hesitation, saying they were going to fight the boat.

The two army officers had grabbed their weapons and headed for the chart room ladder. The rest of the team slipped up through hatchways to reach the deck, nobody wanting to go into a fight inside a wooden box.

When Harper saw them emerging, his only comment was a sharp order: "Everybody stay the hell out of the way."

They were still moving at idle as he and the exec glassed the shoreline with their high-power, light-collecting binoculars. The rain had eased off some. But then it suddenly swept back in a rush, a warm rain that peppered the control space and gun turrets, the gunners up there jacking back their bolts with that sharp, distinctive crack of metal locking in.

The familiar sound brought adrenaline into Parnell's blood, the copper taste in the mouth as his heart triggered up into that steady pound of alert calm. *Combat coming.* The boat eased slowly along, the hiss of the rain nearly drowning out the clear rumble of its engines and the soft popping rush of the prop wash, the mufflers now retracted.

Red craned his neck to look over the cockpit combing. Up on the bow he could faintly see the forward gunner and his ammo handler loading their double .50-caliber stand-up gun. He turned, looked aft, over the top of the chart room. There was another weapon mounted near the stern, a 20mm cannon, its gunner traversing the barrel back and forth, testing his arc.

"*There* it is," Meehl called out quietly. "Two-eight-zero degrees, relative. About fifteen hundred yards."

Harper swung his glasses around until he picked it up. He stared a moment, then barked an order without lowering the binoculars: "Stand by for port strafing run."

The exec repeated the order, then lifted slightly
higher to pass it on to the forward gun position. The
quartermaster slipped from his station on the starboard
side of the control space and ducked aft to notify the
20mm gunner. In a moment, he was back.

Harper was swinging the wheel now. Parnell felt the
boat turn slowly to port, going easily. Crossing forty degrees, it gradually straightened out and settled onto a
new heading. The rain increased, huge drops that
pounded onto the deck, fuming, creating a little green
halo around the ship's compass.

They continued forward slowly for about three hundred yards. Then Harper leaned down and hit his engine
button. There was a tiny delay as the chief engineer engaged the wing engines. Then all three Packards roared
up into full life. For a brief second, the boat trembled,
and then its stern dropped down sharply as the props
began grabbing water. A huge, phosphorescent rooster
tail erupted off the stern and the PT surged ahead as the
roaring of the engines climbed higher and higher until
it was a banshee's howl.

With his back shoved against the chart house bulkhead by the pull of inertia, legs lifting and lowering to
absorb the pound now coming up off the deck, Parnell
felt the boat begin to tilt forward as the hull lifted up
into the planing stage, high on the step, its chines hurling whitewater far out to the sides. Astern, the rooster
tail dropped away until it was only a wide, dark line of
turbulent ocean trailing them. Within thirty seconds, the
PT had gone from ten knots to forty-three.

They were eating up distance rapidly now. Parnell
watched as the hulk of Samar emerged out of the rain-
gloomy darkness. He smelled the fecund denseness of
jungle, a green, wet sourness. And suddenly there was the
Japanese barge, off the coast about eight hundred yards, a
long, low darker dark. A light flashed at its center, another.

Abruptly the night was filled with tracer rounds,

odd-looking, green and orange missiles sailing out toward them almost leisurely but all going high. Then the sound of the guns came, a hard, spaced chattering.

Harper raised his right arm and almost instantly brought it down again, and the PT's turret and bow .50s opened up with long bursts that created a horrendous explosiveness. Spent shells flew as their tracers slashed straight hot lines across the darkness.

Now the boat snapped into a sharp starboard turn, Harper whirling the wheel. Parnell and Hannon were flung against the base of the port turret, but quickly recovered. As the PT came out of its turn, they were now running parallel to the enemy barge, which appeared suddenly from off the port quarter, right out there less than seventy-five yards away, low in the water, black hulled and streaked with salt and rust.

The PT's starboard turret gun stopped firing, unable to traverse to the opposite side. Now the stern 20mm gunner immediately began shooting, his weapon going *whop, whop, whop.* Parnell saw the cannon shells rocketing out, balls of white fire, and the .50s tearing into the barge, making sharp flashes as their hot tracer ends detached and were thrown off in all directions. A cannon shell hit, creating an intense sunburst of light.

The Japanese returning fire lowered and began homing to the boat. Bullets snickered past. One struck the base of the port turret, screamed away. Others slammed into the chart house, the combing, throwing wood shards and sawdust.

Both Parnell and Hannon cut loose with their Thompsons, the noise lost in the deeper blasts of the heavier guns. The barge flashed by. Immediately, the bow gun fell silent, but the others continued hammering away. Parnell glanced up at the port gunner, saw the barrels of his twin .50s glowing red, tiny ghost-blue flames flickering around the ammo belts as its heat ignited the bullet oil.

They ran on for a few seconds longer. Then Harper

juked slightly to the left and swung hard to starboard in
a tight turn, coming around onto a reciprocal heading
for a second strafing run.

Before they reached it, the vessel blew sky-high inside
a dome of orange and yellow that lifted upward like a
rising balloon. Smoking chunks of debris and human
bodies, grotesquely disjointed as broken dolls, hurtled
through the air. From the afterdeck, Japanese troops
began frantically diving off into the water. The explosion
lit up the ocean for hundreds of yards around, made the
lines of rain and the choppy surface look metallic.

Harper swung a sharp turn to port and they went roaring seaward to escape the brilliance of the burning barge
that starkly silhouetted them. Both the amidships and
stern guns continued working the remnants of the barge
and laying in strings of geysers among the escaping troops.

Parnell watched, feeling a sense of revulsion creep into
his throat. *Shooting men in the water?* Then it occurred to
him that they were not sailors from their sinking ship, but
ground troops. When he turned, he saw Major Hannon
watching him narrowly.

Finally, the Aussie leaned forward, shouted close into
his ear, "Find that a bit distasteful, aye?" He snorted
mirthlessly. "'At's som'hing else you best learn quick, Lef-
tenant. These ain't Wehrmach troops you're fightin' now.
These are savage little brutes. Kill the bastards whenever
and however you can, whether they be upright or lyin'
down. Or else, by God, they'll bloody well kill *you.*"

They had a difficult time locating Alamo and his men
aboard their twin-hulled *banda*. Harper kept traversing
back and forth across the rendezvous point, getting
more impatient by the minute.

Finally, the radioman called up Alamo's contact, the
rebounding pulses weak coming off the double wood
and bamboo canoes and fabric sail. The captain edged

the PT in as close as he could to a line of reef. Eight minutes later, the *banda* glided in beside them.

Corporal McLish crawled aboard, all apologies for being late. Japanese patrols had been moving through the Sulat River delta, he said, and they—

Hannon sharply cut him off: "No time for chitchat. Let's get this gear loaded and clear off."

With everybody pitching in, they manhandled the heavy equipment crates down onto the center platform of the long sailboat. Before they completed the task, the radioman again called up: "I've got twin bogies, Captain."

Harper reached over the cockpit combing for his mike, shouted into it, "Status?"

"Bearing zero-four-seven, making steady twenty knots at six thousand yards in tandem. I figure they're D-class destroyers, sir."

Harper swung around. "All right, let's move it!" he shouted to the loaders.

They got the last crate aboard the sailboat, and Blue Team and Hannon's men jumped across. The Aussie major was the last to leave the PT. After a quick handshake with the captain and a thank-you for the ride, he jumped across, too.

The Packards came up slowly, water churning up from off the stern until it was a hundred yards off. Then Harper put the throttle to the wall and the boat roared off. It was soon swallowed up by the rain and the night. Slowly the scream of its engines faded off.

By reading the dim white patches of surf that broke along the edges of a main channel, the *banda*'s helmsman expertly got them through the outer reef and into smoother water. By the time they reached the beach, Japanese searchlights had appeared offshore about two miles, flashing on in bursts, sweeping, then disappearing.

They formed carrying teams for the gear crates and moved up into the jungle.

Chapter Three

The air was heavy with the smell of rain and the fragrance of gardenias the night the Japanese tortured Don Teodoro Zaquino de Veloso.

They had come in the darkest part of the night to his hacienda outside the town of Paco, pounding on doors, breaking glass, and entering through windows. Servants ran to tell the don. By then he and his family were awake, scurrying, hushed and frightened, peering down long stairways to see flashlights and mud-splattered, green-uniformed Japanese marines lunging throughout the Casa de la Madrugada, the House of the Dawn, in which Velosos had lived since the coming of the Spaniards.

Now the don hung naked and upside down from the branch of a *lanigpa* tree that grew in his courtyard, its bark shining pale as old ivory in the rain. The Japanese had beaten him with their fists and short canes of rattan. His face was swollen, his mouth purple, and his torso and thighs, all creamy beige save for his sunburned hands and face, were laced with blue-black lines from the cane.

The leader of the Japanese raider team was a Naval Landing Force senior lieutenant named Yasio Sacabe. He paced back and forth while two of his men continued the beating. He was slightly taller than most of his kind, with hunched-forward shoulders and a moon face smooth as softened tallow.

The rain pinged off his cork helmet. Now and then, the light from his flashlight would reflect off his black, mud-smeared cavalry boots and the scabbard and hilt of his Type 94 *shin-gunto* sword with its brown-and-blue tassel marking him as a combat field officer.

"*Matte yo,*" he suddenly ordered. The two marines stepped back. Sacabe moved forward and squatted down in front of Don Veloso, his head tilted slightly, like a man looking up into a pipe. He put the flashlight beam directly onto the landowner's bloated and bruised features. "Where are this American guerilla?" he barked in heavily accented English.

Veloso's body swung slightly like a metronome winding down. From inside the house came Nip curses and the heavy crash of furniture as Sacabe's men searched through it, going from room to room.

"I know . . . nothing," the don croaked mushily, also in English.

Sacabe cuffed him hard across the temple with his flashlight. It made a hollow sound in the courtyard. He rose and waved for his men to continue.

Now they used their belt knives, slicing the don's flesh with dozens of shallow, painful cuts that bled profusely. The blood dripped down onto the flagstones, some in tiny beaded strings. With the knife tips, the two marines drew ovals around his nipples, then struck lower, puncturing his testicles.

The don groaned, his teeth clenched tightly as if he were lifting stupendous weights. His skin quivered like a terrified horse's. The rain slowed, yet large drops still plunged down through the tree branches with a soft, wet, whispering sound.

A woman shrieked from inside the house, high and piercing, a wailing that echoed throughout the building and out into the night air. It dissolved down into a hysterical murmuring, as if the woman were praying. Another female voice screamed, this one carrying a more youthful pitch to it. It was cut off abruptly.

Veloso weakly lifted his head, swiveled about, trying to see the Japanese officer. "*Madre de Dios*," he cried out. "Please . . . I beg you . . . do not harm my family." His twisting splashed excrement. He had lost control of his bowels, the mess oozing from the cleft of his buttocks to trail down the ravine of his spine.

Sacabe ignored his pleadings. He continued to prowl about as the two marines returned to wounding Veloso with their knives. No further sounds came from the house.

Sacabe suddenly snapped another order. Once more he squatted before the don. "*I ya na yatsu!*" he shouted impatiently. "You wanting your women to die?"

"Please . . . know nothing . . . I swear to . . . saints." The tiny trails of blood on his body glistened in the light from Sacabe's hand torch. Again he was struck in the face.

The Japanese officer cursed and said something to the two marines. Both hurried away, wiping the blades of their knives on their canvas leggings. Sacabe rose and strolled about the courtyard, pausing a moment to pluck a gardenia blossom. He lifted it to his nose. Its petals were as white and smooth as spilled milk.

One of the marines returned carrying a three-liter canister. A moment later, the other appeared with a torch made of rolled gunny sacking and engine oil. Its flame hissed and popped, expelling a smelly black smoke and throwing dancing shadows against the courtyard walls.

A third marine came, shoving two naked women ahead of him with the tip of his bayonet. One was young, little more than an adolescent, the other an adult. The women had long black hair and moved oddly, pressing against each other and painfully shuffling forward, trying to cover their breasts and pubic areas. Both had been anally raped. When they saw the don, both gasped and began sobbing wildly.

The Japanese officer jerked his head. The marine with the canister immediately doused Veloso with the fluid it contained. Gasoline. Teodoro jerked away from it. As it poured down his body and over his face, he began to cough and gag.

The marine hurried to the women and began soaking them down, too. They bent over as if from blows. The sharp acetate stink of the gasoline fumed up into the wet air. The women's hair, drenched, hung down over their eyes, the fuel sluicing off their backs and dripping from their breasts and elbows.

Sacabe moved quickly to the don, who was still choking and thrashing helplessly. He grabbed a handful of Teodoro's hair, roughly jerked his head. "Now you speak?"

From deep within his swollen sockets, the don's eyes darted toward the women. One was his fourteen-year-old daughter, Nonita, the other his wife, Dona Enday. He screamed, "Yes . . . yes . . . I will tell you."

"Who is the American guerilla?"

"Dil-*lon.*" An expulsion of air.

"Where he is?"

". . . ran away."

"Where?"

"Jose de Buon . . . to . . . other guerillistas."

"Where he goes afterward?"

"Dolores . . . perhaps San Luis. He is . . . come to inform . . . all the guerillistas."

"Of what?"

"He carries papers." He stopped, began to gag again. He began to vomit.

Sacabe drew back as the vomit splattered onto his boots. "*Yada, hetakuso!*" He hit Teodoro twice in the temple with his light. "What he is carrying?" he roared.

"*Amerikano* plans," Veloso blurted. "The liberation . . . Luzon."

"What? What?"

"American . . . battle plans . . ."

The Japanese officer looked up at the marine with the bayonet, returned to Veloso. "Why he brings this to the guerillas?" The don didn't respond. Instead, he kept blinking his eyes rapidly and swallowing. "*Why?*" Sacabe growled.

"To gather all . . . to go Luzon."

"Ah!"

"Please, please . . . do not . . . hurt us more." The don began to pray, like a child in a dark room.

Sacabe released him and rose. He waved his hand, a dismissal gesture, then walked back into the house.

When the torch hit the gasoline-soaked body of Don Valoso, there was a *whomping* burst of blue light that instantly engulfed him. He let out a piercing scream of pain. Like responding chords, the women screamed, too, their shrieking forming a shrill, agonized chorus.

The don flailed wildly about. The flames hissed as his arms and legs slashed through the air. The rope holding his feet caught fire in a blue line and the cloying stench of burning flesh rose from the oily smoke that bubbled off Veloso's body.

Shielding his face from the flames, the Japanese marine turned and hurled the torch at the two women. It turned over in the air once, like a thrown knife, and then struck the younger female on the neck. Both women were swallowed by another eruption of blue flame.

They ran, blindly, their screams so sharp and high they seemed on the very edge of hearing. One slammed into a wall and fell back onto the ground, fully aflame, thrashing, leaving streaks of burnt flesh on the flagstones. The other disappeared through an archway into the house. Her screams echoed as the flames from her body cast flickering tones of orange light onto the walls and windows as she fled.

Weesay Laguna was having a hellish time, he and Cowboy Fountain carrying the last crate in the supply column as it moved through the jungle, the two of them grunting and panting and cursing, soaking wet in calf-deep mud, constantly stumbling over dead tree trunks and roots and rocks slippery as oiled glass.

Their radio and ammo box was slung on shoulder poles made of bamboo secured with vines. Despite that, the terrain made them heavy and ungainly to handle. Slipping and sliding, they lost a yard for every two covered, always trying to keep in contact with Wineberg and one of Alamo's *mangs* who were hauling the next crate in line.

All around them was the jungle, enclosing them like the darkness itself. Huge trees drenched in lianas and fern, massive, buttressed banyans, stands of bamboo in perfectly aligned walls with stalks the size of 75mm howitzer barrels, an impenetrable, steamy maelstrom of vegetation.

Here and there coils of peculiar light glowed where phosphorescent strangler vines shown like dim neon tubes in the darkness. From the jungle fumed a rotting, fungal, *green* odor. The rain seemed never to cease, the air dense-hot and greasy feeling. Leeches slipped from leaves to cling to their hands and faces, ants swarmed up their boots, their bites like tiny match-points of pain.

"*Chinga!*" Weesay hissed loudly. *Por el amor de Dios! What kind of fucking place is this?* It seemed to actually seethe. That gave him the creepy feeling that just beyond the undergrowth something monstrous and lethal lurked. He stumbled and fell again, his right boot shooting out from under him. He went down hard, the corner of the radio crate slamming into his chest. Fountain went down, too, the metal box sounding loud as it hit rocks.

"Jesus, man," Cowboy bawled. "You like to broke my goddamn shoulder."

"Shit!" Laguna groaned. He pushed the crate off and got up.

"Take it easy, for Chris' sake," Cowboy said.

"What you think I doin', *pandejo?* God *damn* it!"

Smoker's voice lashed at them from the dark ahead. "Keep it quiet back there."

"Hey, Wineberg," Cowboy shouted. "Take a bite outta *this.*"

"Fuck you," Smoker growled back.

They went on, the Americans getting testier and more disgusted. The trail began to climb gradually. Small waterfalls whispered all around them now, blurring the perpetual noises of the jungle: the endless drip of rain, a sharp buzz of cicadas, the drone, like a thin chord on an organ, of the clouds of mosquitoes that swarmed thickly around them. Now and then, night birds shattered the half stillness with sharp cries or long, sorrowful moans.

Suddenly, a troop of monkeys crashed past, their shrieks sounding like a banzai charge, the animals invisible up among the violently thrashing branches. They moved off, still making a racket.

Now Smoker called back, "Hold it, hold it."

Laguna and Fountain stopped and thankfully eased their crate to the ground. A moment later, Major Hannon, Parnell, and two *mangs*, one the point scout, came hustling back along the column, the Aussie officer snapping an order to each pair of carriers, "Turn around. We're heading back."

As Parnell approached, Cowboy groaned, "Why in hell we *back*-trackin', Lieutenant?"

"It's them monkeys," Red answered. "The Filipinos won't continue on this trail. They say it's bad luck to use one once monkeys have crossed it."

"Holy shit," Laguna hissed.

"Oh, Lord," Cowboy said. "So where we headed *now*?"

"To an alternate trail. We passed it about twenty minutes back."

"Why din't we take that sumbitch *then*?"

"We needed to reach a bridge across the Sulat River. Now we use this trail, we're gonna have to ford the damned river." He moved off.

"That's bad?"

"That's *damned* bad."

Going in the other direction now placed Weesay and Cowboy at the front of the column, one of the *mangs* staying just ahead to guide them, the column point man farther out. Although the guide moved slowly to let them stay up with him, the two Americans had a tough time keeping contact. Twice they lost complete sight of him, had to continue blindly on until they found the stolid little Filipino silently squatting in the trail, patiently chewing on a reed.

All the *mangs* went about barefooted, said it kept them from getting trench foot, and also let them feel out a trail in pitch-darkness with their toes. They were small, dark men, mostly bare-chested with short trousers made of gunnysacking and bandannas wrapped tightly around their heads like pirates. They carried long bolo knives in canvas sheaths and had an assortment of old rifles and bandoleers of homemade bullets. Several also had rolls of quarter-inch greased hemp rope slung over their shoulders.

When they reached the new trail, the guide turned them due north. Soon, the land began to flatten out again. Occasionally they would cross through grassy breaks in the jungle called *kaingins,* the night humming with even more insects come for the open air. A half hour later, they detected the low, growling roar of crocodiles from the river.

The fording point was at a spot where the river narrowed to about sixty yards in width. In Tagalog it was named *Kumot anong pina-kulong tubig,* which meant *blanket leave boiling water.*

It had been formed a long time ago when a plate from the river bottom lifted upward, creating a nearly dry path across the water during the dry season, the small crevices and seams in it allowing the river to sluice through. But in the wet season, as now, the river ran high, running a two-foot sheet of water across the upthrust shelf. And directly beyond it was a hundred yards of bad rapids hissing and tumbling through shelves and among scattered rock.

They reached it just as dawn began seeping through the overcast. Near the edge of the jungle, they passed into banana groves, the trees carrying great masses of fruit that hung in green layers like chili clusters. The air here was actually black with mosquitoes and the odor from the banana trunks was like crushed watermelons.

Beyond the groves, they entered a field of *kunai* grass, eight-foot-tall blades with razor-sharp edges. As they moved through it, they spooked swarms of locusts, which lifted off the ground and went fluttering and clashing through the stalks.

The grassy area didn't reach all the way to the river's edge. Instead, there was a stretch of flood area, a strip of mud scattered with broken branches and stumps and the white skeletons of fish.

The point man whistled for a halt and everyone went to ground while he surveyed the river and the opposite bank for enemy signs. Hannon crawled up and lay beside him, glassing the jungle on the other bank.

The river was the color of liquefied milk chocolate. Beyond the rapids, several sandbars extended out into the water. At least a dozen large crocodiles lay on the bars, fifteen-footers, a dark black brown.

Suddenly, as if sensing the nearness of humans, they burst into motion and wildly dashed for the water and went plunging in. The abrupt activity frightened a white egret delicately pacing the bank up beyond the ford. It surged up into the air and then came gliding past them, holding close to the surface, its whiteness almost phosphorescent in the thin gray light.

Satisfied, Hannon snapped an order in Tagalog to the point man, who rose through the grass and went sprinting across the mudflat. For a moment, he disappeared beyond the top of the bank, then reappeared, going into the water and crossing the ford. The river fumed about his legs. But in less than a minute, he had reached the opposite bank and quickly vanished into the tall grass beyond the muddy flood strip.

Again, Hannon waited. The dawn light was thickening and a breeze had started from downriver. It smelled like ocean and made the tall grass shift and rustle. A new squall of rain suddenly swept toward them, its front approaching mistily and the huge drops making dimples in the water on an advancing line. Quickly it began hissing through the leaves and making pits in the mudflats.

Taking advantage of the now lowered visibility because of the rain, Hannon leaped up and broke from the grass, Parnell and McLish right behind him. "Move, move!" he bellowed to the other men. The bearers quickly reshouldered their crates and took off after him, trotting clumsily under their loads.

The first two *mangs* to reach the riverbank slid down to the water and immediately entered, feeling their way along the flat stone, their heads down, the crate they were carrying swaying unsteadily.

When they were halfway across, Hannon waved to Wineberg and Kaamanui, Sol having switched with the *mang* who had been with Smoker earlier. "Now you two," the major shouted. "Come on, let's go, let's go."

The two Americans started across. The water was cold and went down into their boots. They could still hear Hannon shouting instructions at them: "Make bloody sure you don't let that crate get away from you. If the current knocks you down, stay the hell out of the deep water. Got that? Crocs always bunch at crossings like this one."

Crocs always bunch at crossings? Oh, yeah, Smoker thought as he gingerly planted one foot after the other on the oil-slippery rock face. It was covered with long strands of black moss like women's hair. The current was very strong, the river's mass having to funnel itself into the shallow strip over the rock plate.

Abruptly, he began hearing other voices calling, "Look out!" "*Magingat kayo!*" Wineberg's mind went, *What? What?* He snapped his head around in time to see part of a tree coming straight at him in the current, twisting and tumbling across the rock plate. Before he could react, it rammed into him and knocked him off his feet.

For a moment, he was tangled among skeletal branches. His shoulder hit stone, jarring him. He heard the metal crate crash against rock and felt the strap of his Thompson twisting tightly against his throat as the current flung him onto his stomach. He went shooting over the edge of the rock plate and down into the rapids.

Plunging into a pool, he went completely under, the tree branches clawing at him. Then they were sucked away. He opened his eyes. The water was like thin brown soup. His boots felt bottom, rocky, hard as cement. Bracing his legs, he shoved upward and broke through the surface. Brown foam was all around him as he slammed and slid into hidden rocks and finally dropped down into a wide whirl pocket that swung him once and then flung him away.

He lifted his head, trying to see. Less than fifty yards beyond, the rapids thinned out, the river leveling but still filled with curls and circles of turbulence, streaked with foam that floated and twirled like puffs of dirty cotton. Just beyond were the sandbars.

Crocs bunch in crossings . . . Oh, Christ!

Adrenaline blew through his blood and he began to thrash wildly, trying desperately to stop his momentum. An image flashed: huge crocodiles rocketing up at him from black depths. He renewed his efforts, clawing for a handhold among the rocks. The water was too swift.

He could faintly hear voices yelling over the hiss of the river. Then came the sharp, staccato rapping of Thompsons. The rounds made popping sizzles as they crossed close over his head, the gunners laying bullets into the deeper water to scare off the crocodiles.

Thirty yards . . . twenty-five . . . twenty . . .

He collided with a large rock, smacking hard into his back. He twisted, tried to cling to it. The surface was black and shiny, smooth as marble. The current sucked at him. He felt his terror turn to sudden, blinding rage. Cursing the rock, the river, the jungle, he forced his hands to hold on to the bald stone, absolutely *refusing* to let it go. He looked up, saw another, smaller branch coming, and ducked his head. It slid over his shoulder and went whipping away.

Something hit him in the neck. *Another branch?* A moment later, it hit him again, this time in the forehead. He saw a thin black thing cross before his eyes. *Snake!* No, it was the loop end of a rope. It came again, this time settling around his head, against his shoulders.

Releasing one hand, he grabbed for it, missed, grabbed again, finally got it, and quickly twisted a double loop around his wrist. For a moment, he trembled against the rock, not allowing himself to let it go. At last, he did. He was instantly swept out in a wide, swinging, tumbling half circle, bouncing hard over rocks, the rope going taut and leaping from the water, dripping. He felt it pulling at him. Then he became aware that there were no more rocks under his legs. He snapped his head around, looked downriver.

Oh, God, he was in the deep water.

A new boiling explosion of adrenaline hit him and he actually began *climbing* the line, hand over hand, his legs thrashing under the surface but without thrust, his boots too heavy. His terror created a *sensation* of reality, huge teeth grabbing him.

The rope got him back to the foot of the rapids. He went slithering among the rocks, kept going, pulling and being pulled, his body bending and caroming off immovable objects. The sky and grass and river tumbled and swung at odd angles around him.

Then hands were grabbing for him and Sol's big, grinning brown face was suddenly there, looming into his vision. He was bodily lifted, pulled from the water, his clothing making a sucking sound. He looked glassily, saw Kaamanui's huge legs moving down there, carrying him over the muddy bank.

Using a strung line, the rest of the column quickly crossed without incident. Besides pulling Smoker out, Sol had also flung their crate far enough toward the opposite bank. The two *mangs* who had crossed ahead of them were able to retrieve it and haul it to safety. On later examination, it would be found that none of the radio gear had been damaged at all.

As soon as the last man had crossed, Hannon again got the column moving fast, vacating the area lest patrolling Japs had heard their gunfire and might even now be converging on them. Crossing the peripheral field of *kunai* grass, the column double-timed it away from the river and once more reentered the dense, humid, airless jungle.

Colonel Dutch Morgan stood six feet five and weighed 250 pounds. Puffing on a thin black cigar, he stood before the window of his *nipa* hut and silently studied the newly arrived radio and ammunition crates sitting on the ground below.

It was brightly sunny now, past noon, the underbrush and open patches of mud steaming in the heat and the leaves of the banana trees looking like bayonet steel in the brilliant light. The hut stank of chicken manure from the fighting cocks kept in cages under it. Its floor was made of bamboo strips, spaced for ventilation. It was littered with jungle gear and ammo boxes and empty bottles of Japanese sake. A sand stove sat in the middle of the single room, a rusty coffee kettle hanging from a metal tripod over the coals.

Squatted beside Morgan was a slender, extremely dark young Filipino in a loincloth. His name was Rafeal, a Bagobo tribesman from the mountains of Mindanao, Morgan's chief lieutenant. He methodically chewed on a beetle nut, but every now and then he'd break into a broad grin for no apparent reason, showing his blood-red gums and teeth.

Hannon and Parnell were seated at a carved wooden table, the Aussie major boiling with impatience. In the stifling humidity, large blue flies droned about. Overhead, a sleek green gecko suddenly darted along one of the bamboo beams, snatched a fly out of the air with its long orange tongue, then retreated to cover.

Hannon shifted slightly. He closed his eyes, gathering himself, reopened them. They held a hard, opaque sheen in their brown depths. "I don't have all bloody day, Morgan," he snapped, openly ignoring the guerilla leader's new rank. "I want your answer."

Ignoring him, Morgan simply continued looking out the window. He was dressed in a dirty Australian battle smock with cotton trousers and black Converse tennis shoes. The clothing was spotted with sweat stains and dried mud.

"Goddammit, man," Hannon growled.

"You'll have my answer when I'm bloody well ready to give it you," Morgan said without turning around. "And when you address me, you call me either sir or colonel."

Hannon's face flamed. Rafael grinned.

The supply column had reached the guerillas' headquarters just before noon, a cluster of *nipa* huts high on stilts at the edge of a *kaingin* in the upland forests of the Sohoton Range north of the Sulat.

Coming in, they were challenged by two *mang* sentries, appearing suddenly on the trail ahead of the main party. They were mere boys, carrying rifles fashioned from lengths of pipe and firing nails, using powder recovered from Japanese sea mines and then mixed with wood dust.

They apparently recognized Alamo and immediately approached him. But Hannon stepped forward and spoke to them in Tagalog, the two boys nodding and grinning. They agreed to take them into the camp. A hundred yards from it, one of the sentries made the sound of a *bojong* bird, similar to a barking dog. The guerillas used it to identify each other in dense cover.

The call was immediately answered. Now the two guides veered off the trail and led the column through a field with numerous homemade booby traps, hidden bamboo stakes called *suyocs* lining off on both sides of their pathway. They went by more sentries, up in the trees, who sullenly watched them pass beneath. Many were armed with teak crossbows and bamboo arrows, which they had dipped in snake venom.

After a long, deliberate moment, Dutch Morgan turned around. He had gross features, a broad nose and thick-skinned cheeks, and his eyes beneath their heavy black eyebrows seemed dead, devoid of human expression. He silently watched Hannon.

Born in Nova Scotia, Morgan had first shipped to the Far East on tramp steamers in the early thirties. In Zamboanga, he killed a man in a barroom fight, jumped ship, and took up piracy, captaining a stolen copra schooner running slave girls out of New Guinea and contraband gold from the southern Philippines across the Sulu Sea to Chinese merchants in Malaysia.

Captured by the Japanese in northern Samar, he was

imprisoned at Catarman, but managed to escape after two years of solitary confinement. He quickly created a bandit gang that robbed and murdered both Japanese and Filipinos, becoming a scourge all along the eastern side of the island. He also married two Samar women, sisters named Opron and Ameliana, with whom he would eventually have four children, all girls.

Like all the other Philippine islands, Samar had many such bandit gangs. Morgan soon dominated those in the southern part of the island. The only other bandit leader capable of challenging him was a half-Portugese *mestizo* named Sam Goode who operated in the northern Capotoah Mountains.

After the arrival of the Japanese, all these robber warlords had quickly realized they had just been presented a great opportunity for booty and the sudden expansion of their own territories. Immediately, savage battles erupted between the bandit factions that raged for two years. Gradually, the weakest were eliminated and the survivors joined the victors.

The final confrontation between Morgan and Goode came in the small mountain town of Buta. During the fierce clash, Morgan used relatives of Goode's men as shields and won the battle since the Portugese's men refused to fire on their kin. For two weeks, Dutch carried Sam Goode's head around on the hood of his stolen Lever Brothers 1937 Ford station wagon to show everyone who the big boss now was.

When MacArthur's AIB agents arrived on Samar in early 1944 to develop the guerillas into an offensive force against the Japanese under Allied command, Morgan was the only power on the island. He was eventually given the rank of colonel, and war equipment began arriving for him and his men.

"Who now controls the south of Luzon?" Morgan asked abruptly.

"Kangleon."

The guerilla leader grunted and a tiny, cold smile flicked across his mouth. "The old one still, eh? Who else agrees to do this?"

"Fertig in Mindanao and Volkman from Leyte." These were other powerful Philippine guerilla chiefs.

Before leaving his training base, Hannon had received orders to convince Morgan to transfer his guerillas across the San Bernardino Strait to aid Colonel Kangleon in sabotage and harassment operations against the Japanese of southern Luzon.

"What do *I* get?" he asked.

Hannon jerked his head toward the boxes outside. "More of that. All you can use."

"And if I say no?"

"All Allied aid stops immediately." Hannon appraised him narrowly. The guerilla boss stared back. Finally, the major went on, "Think about this, Morgan. When the war's over, the chiefs from Leyte and Luzon, even Mindanao, will come sniffin' at your territ'ry. Make no mistake about that. Only *they'll* have top-line weapons and the backing of the Americans. With that, they'll bloody well walk right over your Canuk arse."

Morgan's thick face went flat. "You're an insolent son of a bitch, ain't you, Hannon?"

Now it was the Aussie major who smiled. Tight, steel cold. "If it were up to me, mate, I'd cut your focking throat right here an' now an' be done wi' ya. Unfortunately, it *ain't* up to me. . . . So, what the hell's your answer . . . Colonel?"

Morgan relaxed. He knew Hannon was right, the lousy bastard. He finally nodded. "All right, I'll transfer my men. Now get those radios set up and hand over my goddamned ammunition." He turned, ducked out the doorway and down the house ladder. Rafael sprang to his feet and followed him.

Parnell snorted. "That old boy's nothing to write home about, is he?"

"Ach, the man's a bloody brute," Hannon scoffed bitterly. "Unfortunately, in war we sometimes have to commerce with the devil, don't we?" He inhaled, blew it out. "You and your men best get some rest. We'll begin instructing these guerillistas on bloody radio procedure in the morning."

"Right, sir," Parnell said.

Blue Team spent the stifling afternoon cleaning their weapons with Jap gun oil and burning jungle leeches fat as black worms off each other with cigarettes, all of them looking sickly and Oriental-colored, the antimalarial Atabrine tablets they were taking daily turning their skin and eyes yellow.

They huddled inside one of the open, canvas-covered supply sheds, which held Morgan's stores that had not yet been buried. This one was filled with Japanese booty: bags of rice, wooden boxes of canned fish, barrels of machine oil, and a single carton of Kotex sanitary napkins the guerillas used for wound pads.

Dutch Morgan had supply caches scattered all over the island, everything buried on upslopes to keep them from ground and flood water. Often he'd place them near one of his ordnance manufacturing camps, *karayom botikas* or needle shops, where explosives and weapons were made by hand.

At midafternoon two old native women brought the Blue Team troopers food: carabao beef jerky and roasted corn and a sweet mush called *kalibo* made from bananas and coconut milk. The women looked like shriveled monkeys in their faded plaid *patadiong* dresses. Silently they served the men and then crept away, all the while smoking little cigars that they flipped into their toothless mouths between puffs.

By midafternoon, it began to rain again, the drops drumming loudly on the canvas cover. Beneath, everyone tried to sleep. But the mosquitoes and the ungodly heat and humidity only allowed them to doze restlessly.

It was dark when Parnell felt himself being shaken awake. He'd been drifting along in that half sleep where dreams readily incorporate the sounds and smells of the surroundings. Something about surfing off Malibu, smelling the ocean, the sour stench of garbage. Instantly, he became alert, grabbing for his weapon.

"Easy, mate," Hannon said. His flashlight cast shadows and made the rain coming off the canvas glisten like tinsel on a Christmas tree. "Get your lads ready. We'll be moving out in fifteen."

"Yes, sir." Red came to one knee. His mouth felt thick, his face puffy and damp. He scooped up some rainwater, splashed it over his eyes and cheeks. Beside him, Wyatt was already waking the others.

"What's up, sir?" he asked Hannon.

"A runner just come in. Says there's a Yank AIB agent out there with half the focking Jap army after him. Name's Dillon. He was holed up with a planter near Paco when they got hit by a Jap marine raiding party. Apparently, some damned *makapili* betrayed them."

"A what?"

"A *makapili*'s a traitorous Filipino, a collaborator. In any case, Dillon and a female servant managed to get away. But before they did, they overheard the planter identify him and tell the Jap officer he was carrying important papers. So now it's *our* bloody job to find him. And do it damned quickly."

"How do we start? Are you able to contact him by radio?"

"No, he's moving fast and light. According to the runner, he got to a small guerilla camp near Hinicaan. But he didn't stay, took off alone. But di'nt tell anybody where he intended to go. I figure the poor bastard's runnin' scared, mistrusting everybody now. I think he might be heading for the coast, maybe looking to link up with Johnny-One-Eye Maganoy. That's a minor guerilla chieftain who operates south of the Dolores River." Hannon turned his head, spat, came back. "Another shit rotter, 'at one. Bloody as Morgan."

"What're our chances of finding him before the Nips do? I suspect that's a helluva lot of jungle out there."

"Aye, that it is. But we'll make a few contacts, keep our ears to the bamboo telegraph. News spreads faster than a goddamned radio in the bush. If we can somehow isolate the general area he's in, we can set up a search grid. An' hope to Christ the Japs don't."

Now Hannon looked at him hard, his face tight, the flash making deep shadow hollows where his eyes were. "Either way, we *have* to find him, Parnell. This bloody Dillon bloke's carryin' the entire plan for the invasion of Luzon."

Chapter Four

General MacArthur had officially declared Leyte secure on 25 December 1944. Still, there would be extensive fighting on the island for months to come. Then, on 9 January 1945, 200,000 American troops landed at Lingayen Bay, located on the western coast of Luzon Island a hundred miles north of Manila.

A first they encountered minor opposition. But two weeks later, forward units of the American Sixth Army began running into stiffening enemy resistance as they moved south toward Manila. This opposition comprised a succession of quick, stalling strikes, most of which were launched at night. Called *Reimei Kogeki*, these night-mounted offensives were a favored tactic of the Japanese military.

At the same time, another prime aspect of Nip battle doctrine had been completely changed. For decades, Japanese generals had always followed the concept of total offensive action in which they committed the full weight of their armies against the initial contact zone with the enemy.

The big guns of the U.S. Pacific Fleet had forced alterations to this doctrine. Following the new precepts, General Yamashita had held the bulk of his Fourteenth Army deep inland in defensive fortifications called *bogyo chikujo*, far beyond the effective range of U.S. naval gunships.

He was still holding off any truly offensive action, choosing instead to fight these hit-and-flee attacks designed to slow up the American advance toward the Philippine capital. His orders from the Imperial General Staff were very precise on that point. They were also, in essence, suicidal.

Tokyo expected Yamashita to sacrifice himself and his army so as to garner time. The longer he could pin down the Americans, the stronger the fortifications and force buildup would be in the homeland and on those as yet uninvaded island chains that stretched south and southeast of Japan.

Meanwhile, MacArthur was growing ever more anxious about the fate of the thousands of American, European, and native civilians imprisoned in the Japanese stockades at Manila's Santo Tomas University and the ancient buildings of old Bilibid Prison.

As a result, he harangued General Kreuger, commander of Sixth Army, to speed up his advance. But Krueger was in a tenuous position, lacking adequate engineering equipment, particularly the Bailey bridges, which were needed to cross the numerous rivers of Luzon. He also feared advancing too far beyond his supply lines and thus become vulnerable to a Japanese encirclement.

Nevertheless, MacArthur's concerns were justified. The Japanese had treated the American civilians in Manila well enough in the beginning of their occupation. But they had turned more and more brutal the closer the Allies got to the islands. Now many of the prisoners were right on the brink of starvation and death. Every day, dozens died of malnutrition, rampant disease, or savage abuse. It was obvious to any intelligence analyst that these people would certainly be massacred if not freed swiftly enough.

Already, many more U.S. troops were staging for a second and then a third invasion of Luzon. The first, code-named Operation MIKE VII, was scheduled for 29 January. Elements of the U.S. XI Corps would land at San Narciso and San Antonio, ninety-three miles south of Lingayen Gulf.

Some of the invading troops would immediately drive northeast to link with Kreuger's XIV Corps and his 1st Armored Division and then race for Manila. The remainder would seal off the heavily jungled Bataan Peninsula to prevent escaping Japanese troops from creating a bastion, in the same way as General Wainwright's forces had in 1942.

The second landing, code-named MIKE VI, was set for 31 January, at Nasugbu, below the entrance to Manila Bay. Included in this assault force would be troopers of the 11th Airborne Division. They would eventually become the first American soldiers to enter the capital city and engage in the vicious house-to-house fighting that would ensue.

Securing the great port of Manila was absolutely necessary so that the massive amounts of supplies and reinforcements needed by the Americans could pour in. Yamashita's supplies, on the other hand, steadily dwindled. Nothing could get through from the home islands since the U.S. Navy now completely controlled the sea and air corridors into the Philippines. Even now, many Japanese fighting units were themselves near starvation. In fact, some had already resorted to the cannibalization of their own dead.

No matter, Yamashita was a realist. He knew he and his Fourteenth Army were destined for complete annihilation. He accepted that and fully intended to fight to the very last man to gain greater glory and safety for home and emperor. But that intention, of course, did not include him.

He had other, more personal plans.

Still, in war there's a truism that the army with the best intelligence almost always wins. If, by some twist of fate,

Yamashita were able to come into possession of Allied intelligence that could tell him precisely where, when, and in what strength the Americans would strike, he could once again recapture the initiative and quite possibly, despite the seeming certainty of an Allied victory, still drive them back into the sea.

18 January 1945

Lieutenant Jeff Dillon was moving fast, despite dodging Jap patrols, hiding in rice paddies, and avoiding barrios. He knew the bamboo telegraph, that mysterious spread of information, had by now informed the populace of the Veloso murders and of his frantic flight. So he must be very cautious, fifth columnists and *makapili* could be anywhere, waiting to betray him again.

He'd been hunted by the Japanese before, after his escape from Lawa-an and during his secret insertions into Cebu, Mindanao, and finally Samar for MacArthur's AIB. But this time the search was extremely concentrated. After the don's confession, the Japs now knew who he was, generally where he was going, and what he carried. He was a fox just barely keeping ahead of the hounds.

Dillon bore no hatred for the weakness of Don Veloso. They'd been friends for nearly fifteen years. When the Japs first came, they'd been extremely respectful of the aristocratic Philippine landowners, most of whom were descendents of the Spanish. They even accepted them into their society. The Japs needed the products of their vast plantations, and they also wanted these lords of the manor to be examples of cooperation for the native populace.

But the arrogance and cruelty of the new occupiers soon changed that. Some of the landowners turned to aiding the guerillas. Still, the Japanese refrained from turning on them. Until the Allies began appearing on the near horizon. Then their tolerance disappeared.

Now *anyone* suspected of involvement with the guerillas was arrested, tortured, and killed.

Although Dillon had seen examples of Japanese barbarity, the means of death for Don and Dona Veloso and their daughter had stunned his humanness and lingered in his consciousness like a suddenly appearing childhood trauma. He wondered how long he himself could have withstood the pain and horrible fear for his family that those Jap marines had inflicted on Teodoro. It was a question he hoped he'd never have to answer.

He shifted his weight slightly, firmed up his balance in the narrow *caba-caba*, a small dugout canoe he'd managed to steal from the riverbank, and continued pulling himself by gripping the walkway planks four feet above him as he moved deeper into the *tubig bayan*.

This was a water town constructed on pilings and coconut stumps built out into the river. This particular town, San Tago, was on the Dolores River two miles from the coast: sixty *nipa* huts packed together like a gigantic raft with narrow passageways snaking among the structures. Surrounding the town were networks of bamboo fishing traps and a wide perimeter made of oiled coconut trunks to keep out crocodiles.

It was silent now save for the steady pounding of the rain on the rickety boards and the bamboo walls of the huts. Few lights showed except for the occasional torch encased in tin containers, which marked the intersections of the main walkways. Their light beamed down through spaces between the boards, giving the water a dancing sheen and making the eyes of crabs on the uprights gleam like chips of emerald in the dark recess.

He reached another intersection, the third one he'd come to. He paused, unsure. Pilings faded off into the darkness all around him like tree trunks in a night forest. José Laya had told him the hut he wanted was three intersections from the upriver side and ten pilings toward the north bank.

He finally eased the dugout to the left and began following a winding, side walkway, counting pilings. The canoe kept slipping sideways in the current. Reaching the tenth one, he tied the *caba-caba*'s painter line to it and stood listening. He finally reached up and felt along the flooring of the hut he was under. There was a privy hole, beside it a wooden ladder with a small bamboo trapdoor at the top.

He swore. What if this were the wrong hut? Appearing out of nowhere, he would frighten whoever was up there, likely cause a noisy commotion. Still, he had no choice. Using the butt of his fist, he gently banged on the bamboo door. Silence came back. Only the click of the crabs and the soft whisper of the current curving around the pilings.

He knocked again. There was a thud in the hut, someone moving. Soft light abruptly showed through the chinks in the floor. Then the trapdoor opened and a shadowy figure, etched by candlelight, peered down.

"Who is there?" a woman's voice asked nervously in Tagalog.

"*Tao po, ginang Laya,*" he called up softly in the same language. "It is I, the *Amerikano* Dillon."

The woman was silent, staring down. Then she said, "You go away."

"Wait! Your husband has sent me."

"No, you go away."

"I am to meet a priest here."

"There no priest."

"He will come soon, *ginang Laya.*"

"He is no here now."

"*Pakisoyu, ginang Laya,* I tell you true."

The woman considered that for a long moment. "You wait," she said finally and closed the trapdoor.

He waited. The dugout kept knocking gently against the piling, and a wet coldness began seeping off the river. Many minutes passed. An hour. The night seemed endless. He checked his watch. It said 11:23.

He lay down in the canoe, an inch of water in the bottom. Some sort of winged insect dropped from the overhead, fluttered frantically against his arms and face, then flew off. He closed his eyes and tried to sleep. He couldn't. Like a ranging hawk, his mind kept circling back to the vision of the death of Don Zaquino de Veloso. . . .

After contacting the small guerilla band at Hinicaan, Dillon had set out alone, going southeast, headed for the Dolores River. He knew a fisherman who lived in San Tago, his name Jose Laya. He had once saved the man's life by killing a drunken Jap officer about to behead him. Now he needed Laya to take him to San Luis where another friend, a French Catholic priest named Father Nicholas Dobbenier, could get him a sea boat to head south in.

He reached the river just before sundown. Fishermen from San Tago were already out, a small fleet of *caba-cabas* with patchwork triangular sails, each sail individually colored, and larger, double-hulled *barotos* with paddlers pulling long-handled *naya* paddles. They were headed to the coast to fish the huge mullet schools that fed among the sandbars of the river's delta.

He watched them move slowly past, looking for Laya's *caba-caba*, its distinctive sail made of blue and white stripes. There. He stood up and waved, and the dugout heeled over and came skimming toward him. It slid up onto a mudflat. A boy of about fourteen was with Laya.

The fisherman got out and came up the bank to meet him. He was a muscular man with an odd white eye. He nodded. "*Ginoong Dil-lon.*"

"Hello, Jose."

Laya's white eye jittered as if it were under a strain. "You are very dangerous now, sor."

"I must go with you to the coast. To meet Father Dobbenier."

"No. You are too dangerous, sor. And I can not trust all the fishermens."

Dillon studied him through narrowed eyes. "Then will you at least take him a message?"

Laya nodded. "*Oo, Ginoong Dil-lon.*"

"Tell him to meet me tonight at your hut in the *tubig bayan.*"

Laya looked away, saw the other fishermen watching, looking over their shoulders. He came back. "I cannot danger my family, sor."

"I *need* for you to do this, Jose." He paused, staring directly into the other man's eyes. "You owe me," he finally said quietly. This last was the strongest thing he *could* have said, a trump card. To a Filipino, a debt owed was a debt of honor, his *utang na loob*, a commitment of *loob*, or soul. It *must* be repaid, even at the cost of his own life.

Laya's face went hard, his jaw muscles jumping. He lowered his head and said softly, "*Oo, Ginoong Dil-lon.* It will be as it must be."

"*Salamat*, my friend."

Dillon was forty-two years old, a dead ringer for the actor James Stewart. An Oregonian, he had come to the Philippines nineteen years before, first to hunt for gold on Luzon, then as superintendent of a Dole pineapple plantation on Samar's Matarinao Bay. When the Japanese came, they immediately imprisoned him and his wife, a pretty Filipina named Kerima, in the old pirate stockade built in the swamps of Lawa-an in 1884.

Kerima died of consumption in less than a year. Soon afterward, Dillon and another American, a mining engineer named Rodell, escaped. For the next eight months, they survived in the hills, always working southward.

They finally reached Mindanao in June of 1943 and traveled down the spine of the island to Talub where they stole a seagoing *banda.* Setting out with three T'boli tribesmen as crew, they spent the next four months on a harrowing voyage of over twelve hundred miles, crossing the Celebes and Molucca Seas to the Indonesian island of Buru. There they met a New Zealand coast watcher and were eventually picked up by an Australian Navy sub and taken to Darwin, Australia.

At the time, MacArthur's Allied Intelligence Bureau was desperately seeking men familiar with the Philippines to return to the islands to organize, coordinate, and supply guerilla groups in preparation for the coming invasions. Both men readily volunteered. They were put through a two-month cycle at a forward training base in the Solomons, given the rank of lieutenant in the U.S. Army, and assigned as permanent agents in the AIB. . . .

Dillon sat up abruptly. He had heard a low, rhythmic drone like surges of wind. He listened. There, again, the thing fading. Finally, he relaxed. It was the fishing fleet returning, the men singing to synchronize their paddle strokes. Lights began coming on in the *tubig bayan*, feet pounded on the walkways. He checked his watch. It was now 2:18 in the morning.

Now he had less than four hours to reach the coast.

He watched the fleet come into view up the center of the river, their prow torches, called *gembungs*, looking like orange balls of light skating past on the water's surface. He heard the whip and luff of their sails as they tacked around to approach the village landings with the current. Soon there were the busy noises of unloading, the thud of fish boxes, and the happy calling between the fishermen, glad to be home.

Someone was moving in Laya's hut again. Shoes, voices, one a man's. The trapdoor opened and a large figure came partially down the ladder holding a small hurricane lantern. "Dil-lon?" It was Father Dobbenier.

"Here, *Padre.*"

The priest held up the light, grinning. "Ah, *mon ami. Bon,* you are safe. Come, come."

The lantern revealed a tiny hut filled with fishing nets and spearheads, sleeping rugs on the floor, the air thick with the smell of wet *nipa* grass, and female body odor. The woman held a baby asleep in her arms, studying the two men apprehensively. She wore a colorful *baro*, like a sarong, and her hair was long and jet-black.

"Thank you for coming, Father," Dillon said.

"Yes, of course." The priest was heavy-shouldered, the dark cloth of his soaked hassock tight against muscle. He was about fifty and had a face of bulbs: cheeks, nose, eyebrows, all rounded like soft dough and reddened as if from the night cold. His teeth were yellow in the lantern light.

"Did you arrange for a boat?" Dillon asked.

"*Oui.*" The priest shook his head sadly. "This time the Japanese look everywhere for you, *mon ami*. They are most angry."

"Where's the boat, Father?"

"Near San Luis, a good strong *banda*. I also have for you a man who will take you south. Lauro Bulosan, a teacher at our mission school. He will be there awaiting you."

"Where's this school?"

"Three kilometers south of San Luis." He studied Dillon narrowly. "You carry important data, *non*? Something that will help end the occupation?"

"I *had* it. But I had to destroy it. Now its contents are only in my head."

"Ah, yes, of course."

Dobbenier turned, whispered gently to the woman in Tagalog. "*Ano ang pangalan ninyo, mama?*"

The woman answered shyly, "Teresa, Father."

"Don't be frightened, Teresa. This man will soon be gone." He turned back to Dillon. "Come, you must leave quickly. Your presence here creates a terrible danger for these people."

As if to prove his point, there were sudden shouts and then a gunshot. The crack of it echoed for a moment but was quickly swallowed by the jungle. Both men stiffened, lifting their heads to listen. The woman drew back in terror.

Dillon hissed through his teeth, "Japs!"

"*Mère de Dieu!*" the priest whispered. "You must go!"

Dillon headed for the door, but Dobbenier grabbed his arm. "What are you going to do?"

"Go into the river."

"*Non!* They'll see you. If they do, these people will be massacred." He frowned, thinking. Now they could hear the Japanese soldiers clearly, smashing into huts, bellowing. Women screamed. People began jumping into the river and swimming for the bank.

Dobbenier said, "Your best chance is to hide in your boat until you can sneak past the village."

Dillon nodded.

Murmuring, "*Mere de Dieu*" again, the priest squatted down and yanked up the trapdoor. He glanced up at Dillon. "God go with you, *mon ami*. And may he forgive you for coming here. Hurry, hurry." There was more gunfire, five rounds in rapid succession.

Dillon dropped into his *caba-caba*, the little thing unstable with his sudden weight. Above him, the trapdoor immediately slammed down. He untied the line and let the current move him downriver, the dugout bumping into pilings and passing through shafts of light that flashed, then disappeared. Boots thundered on the walkways over his head.

He could see a sudden, sharp increase of light ahead. Then fiery debris began falling through the walkway slits and into the river. The Japanese had set fire to some of the huts. The breeze made whirls of smoke that shifted, spreading out into the main part of the river.

Suddenly, a larger section of the *tubig bayan* crashed down into the water amid an explosion of sparks. Fiery debris scattered everywhere. A billow of white smoke came fuming toward him under the remaining huts. It was thick and smelled of fire and the stench of wet charcoal. It rolled over him, flakes of fire and ash stinging his skin.

He began blindly paddling toward the river side of the village. Almost immediately, he slammed into one of the pilings, but ricocheted off. His eyes burned. On he went.

Soon he was past the edge, out into the network of fish traps, the slender platforms of bamboo and net lines. More gunshots rang out behind him.

He continued paddling wildly. A thick pall of smoke lay across the entire river now. His heart pounded and his paddle sweeps were deep, the little dugout jumping ahead each time. He struck something hard, the little *caba-caba* snapping to the side. He had to grab its gunwale to keep from falling out. It was the crocodile barrier. In the dense smoke, the tops of its coconut trunks appeared like a line of partially submerged barrels.

He swung the dugout around until he was able to pull himself up onto two of the coconut stumps. Straining to keep his balance, he worked the canoe over the top, slid it into the deeper water, and then climbed aboard and lay down.

The current, faster here, quickly pulled him farther out into the river. He lay very still, not daring to even lift his head. The dugout turned slowly in the current and collided with smoking bits of debris. Then the rain started again, hissing into the river.

Gradually the dugout drew farther and farther away from San Tago, which was now in full conflagration. The flames leaped high, willowing like sprites in the smoke and rain, creating a flickering sheet of orange onto the river and the edge of the fringing jungle. The scene reminded him of a scene from an old monochrome woodcut of wild Africa he'd seen as a boy.

Dillon closed his eyes, held them tight. A single, distant scream came, piercing as a knife blade, hollow sounding. It made him tremble. He felt a surge of nausea shatter through his intestines. *Guilt, guilt.* He looked up into the dark sky and felt like weeping.

Wyatt Bird had taken an immediate liking to Frankie Trota, the little Filipino point scout. He stood all of five feet two, his body tight as a taut wire and brown as a betel nut. He had a round face, a flat nose that had obviously been broken several times, and a pencil mustache, dapper as a Southside gigolo's. He moved through the jungle like a cat, soundless, quick, Wyatt having a time staying up with him.

It was nearly dawn now, light coming down wet and gray, the rain gone for a while. Parnell had sent Bird up to work point with Trota in order to learn a few things about jungle movement. Ordinarily, the scout went unarmed, but Frankie now carried a U.S. M1A1 carbine, a bandoleer of spare clips slung across his chest, and a bolo in a wooden scabbard on his back, the handle up. He'd pounded brass studs into the butt of the gun, made it look like an old Cherokee long rifle. He also had a twirling stick on a leather thong hanging from his belt. Major Hannon and the rest of Blue Team with twenty-five of Morgan's *mangs* were a hundred yards behind them.

Last night, they'd crossed the eastern slopes of the Sohotons, then had gradually worked their way northeast toward the coast. Now they were a mile inland of the small port town of Borongan, paralleling the shoreline. It was comparatively easy moving now through banana groves and old upland coconut plantations, the air chilly with the smell of open ocean.

Frankie moved in a sprint-and-halt fashion, always staying in cover. Sometimes he'd pause for several long minutes to scan, listen, and smell the air before making another dash. So far, he and Wyatt had not exchanged a single word.

Yet Frankie would occasionally point something out to him, making sign language to explain it. A hand to his mouth and then a finger wag meant never eat that plant; a nod up toward the coconut tree clusters and the rapid pulling of his forefinger indicated Jap snipers often hid up there. His little black eyes continually asked, *You understand?*

By full daylight they were once more into monsoon jungle, moving through knife-blade-narrow ravines with deep rain pools and slender waterfalls behind which small black bats hung upside down in tiny fern grottoes. A morning chorus of tree frogs sounded like a section of trombones, and the wet-chilly air was perfumed by ginger lilies, which formed a green mat on the stream banks.

Frankie continued silently demonstrating things, showing how to find water in a bamboo stalk or where to dig for edible Ti-leaf roots. He gave Wyatt the juice from a jungle garlic head to keep away the mosquitoes, made him listen for the faint rustle of a moving snake, and then pointed out its quick flash of green and gold striping.

An hour later, in a drizzling rain, Trota abruptly stopped and stood sniffing the air. After a moment, he moved ahead swiftly until they came to a break in the jungle covered with tall *cogon* grass. Pausing at the edge of the trees, he pointed toward the east. Wyatt looked, saw wisps of gray-brown smoke rising over the top of the jungle.

Trota then said his first word to Wyatt: "*Hapones.*" Japs. He quickly slipped his twirling stick from his belt and swung it around twice with his left hand. Once it got going rapidly, he stopped it, smacking the end into the palm of his other hand. This created an odd sound, like a tamped-down chime. He did this three times, then replaced the stick in his belt, and he and Wyatt moved soundlessly forward, crossed through the grass, and reentered the jungle, the ground gradually rising now.

Soon they reached a ridge. It was very narrow, scarcely a foot wide at the top. A chilly breeze slipped up from the other side and there were patches of grass and jungle scrub contorted by the wind. Below them stretched a valley, about a half mile wide. Most of the slopes on both sides were shingled with rice paddies, their free-form shelves filled with water that reflected the overcast sky like dark mirrors.

In the middle of the valley was a small hill thickly

covered with teak and eucalyptus trees. At the foot of the hill, surrounding it, was a rift completely filled with banana trees, their big green leaves hiding the contours of the ravine.

At the base of the hill was a small barrio built on a ribbon of flat ground fronting the wooded hill. Below it, the land fell away again into more thick banana groves. The village itself was simply a double line of houses strung along a narrow dirt road. They were made of stone and round *nipa* roofs and looked like beehives.

At one end of the village was a small church. It was burning, the roof timbers already fallen in, the source of the smoke they'd spotted. Dead bodies lay in the road outside. Some were headless. Moving in the street and among the houses were Japanese soldiers in khaki-brown uniforms.

Frankie lightly touched Wyatt's arm, held up his hand for him to wait, then turned and disappeared back into the jungle.

Now Hannon glassed the village silently, his hands cupped over the lenses so they wouldn't reflect light. His broad, thuggish face was stone hard. After a moment, still without comment, he handed the glasses to Parnell.

Apparently, there had been a funeral going on in the village when the Japs struck. There was a dark wooden coffin in the graveyard beside the church, black ribbons on top formed into a cross, the thing tipped over. Most of the dead bodies were in the street in front of the churchyard, clustered together as if they had been struck down while waiting in a line, all dressed in black trousers and white shirts, Filipino mourning clothes.

Now the headless corpses looked grotesquely unfinished crumpled there on the ground under the gray skies. Some of the chopped-off heads lay several feet away, probably kicked there by the Jap soldiers. Parnell couldn't believe they could have flown that far by themselves. Pigs rooted about the bodies. Nearby at the edge of the road two dead children lay side by side, little ones, like dolls tossed out of a speeding car.

His stomach tightened and a sour taste came up into his mouth. He'd never seen this kind of slaughter before. Dead bodies certainly, the Krauts murdering villagers in Europe. But this somehow was different, seeming medieval in its barbarity, severed heads, sword killings.

He slid the binoculars to the right, over the tops of round roofs, people moving in and out of his vision. He stopped. There was a Japanese soldier stretched out on the ground beside a hut, his tropical trousers shoved down around his dirty leggings, his bare ass showing while most of his upper body was hidden by the eaves of a hut. He was lying between two dark, naked legs, the guy humping up and down, screwing.

A second soldier moved into view from under the eave, his tropical uniform with the red cloth insignia of the infantry on the collar. He had a thick-breech Type 96 light machine gun strapped across his back. It resembled a British Bren. He was tightly holding on to one of the woman's ankles, the leg trying to kick. He was grinning, watching as his companion raped his female victim.

Parnell couldn't take the glasses away. A minute passed, another. At last, the first soldier finished his business, rose. His partially erect penis was clearly visible, dangling as he urinated on the woman's legs, both limbs unmoving now. He slowly buttoned up, saying something. Then he pulled his sidearm from its holster and shot the woman, twice. The muzzle blasts drifted up the slope sounding like tiny firecrackers. The two soldiers walked away.

Red lowered the binoculars to find Hannon staring at him with an icy *I told you, Lieutenant* look in his eyes.

"So what now, Major?" he asked quietly, stiffly.

"I think we'll bloody well give ourselves the pleasure of killin' the bastards," Hannon answered, his eyes mahogany dark, yet with a steady glint in their centers. "Exact a bit of an eye for an eye ourselves, aye?"

"I fully agree, sir."

"Good."

For the next three minutes, the major laid out their attack plan. It was to be a standard quick raid procedure, their force split into three segments: a special task group to take out the enemy scouts and perimeter; the main action group to initiate the heaviest fire into the killing zone; and the security group to cover the approach and withdrawal.

"We'll use the *mang* bowmen to open," Hannon said to Parnell. "Most of our guns remain in the MAG. I want *your* men there to direct fire since they're combat savvy. You take the rest of the guns and set up security."

He paused to glass the target area for a full minute, finally turned back to Red. "The only defiladed approach is on the upside of the village hill. We'll work our way down between the paddy ridges, then cross through the woods at the top and set up a firing line in the grove below it. Exit's through the lower grove.

"Afterward, continue heading northeast. Here." He handed Red a small compass with a flip top. "Hold on zero-two-zero. We'll stay with our group till we're at least a mile out. There's a good chance other Nip patrols're in the area, so plan your approach and withdrawal accordingly."

"Yes, sir."

"Warn your men, Parnell, this'll be close-in fighting. When you lay in the initial volley, go heavy and sweep it. Once the Nips react, they'll charge straight for the center of the firing line. An' they'll scream. Ignore it or it'll rattle the bollocks off ya. If they breach the line, don't continue heavy bursts but pick out individual targets or you'll be shootin' each other. They'll come at you out of the brush quick as a gnat's blink, bayonets first. So keep your blades handy and be positioned to parry and counterthrust."

The Aussie looked straight into his eyes, said quietly, "Kill every one of 'em, Parnell. No quarter. *Nobody* left alive. That's an order. You understand?"

"Yes, sir," Red answered quietly.

"Orright, mate, let's get to it."

For one of the rare times in Sol Kaamanui's life, he was unsure of himself, the big Samoan feeling tightnesses inside his body, his throat, his voice when he was placing the *mangs* assigned to him along a line upside the road that curved around before entering the tiny barrio.

Now he lay hidden beneath a thick wall of banana leaves and *kunai* grass, the road at a level with his eyes, and watched the Japanese soldiers moving through the village. Little squatty fuckers in dirty, water-soaked uniforms tearing hell out of the huts, throwing things through glassless windows. Most were armed with their standard but cheaplooking Model 38 6.5mm bolt-action rifles.

But here and there were squad leaders with the more lethal Model 96 6.5mm light machine guns with the quarter-moon clips on top, wooden carrying handles, and the distinctive accordian-sheathed barrel-cooling jackets.

He studied the Japanese. He had seen a lot of Orientals, mostly in Chinatown in San Francisco, a raucous, squabbling people who spoke right into your face and who all looked as if they were Tong knife men. But these slant-eyed little shits didn't look all that dangerous in their ill-fitting, cartoon uniforms.

Still, he felt his heart banging. He breathed in, settled himself. The first time he went into combat, way back there in Morocco, he'd been steel-steady, filled with the soldier's solid belief that bad things would happen to someone else. Then he saw the randomness of death and realized it could happen to *anybody*.

But soon, however, he'd developed that stolidness of a combat soldier, relished the cold confidence it gave him. Until he was hit in Italy at the foot of Monte Cassino, the exact details of the thing still elusive in his mind, only the remembrance of the pain afterward and the sobering realization that his big, powerful body had been torn asunder and that death had come very close.

During his recuperation in France, he'd wondered about this moment when he'd first return to the line and look again into the face of an enemy who was trying like hell to kill him. He couldn't deny his nervousness. It made him feel shamed suddenly. Thinking about that, he got a little angry and then he got a whole lot angry.

A crack of thunder came, *boom!*, the sound rolling down one of the valleys like the rumble of a battery of 155s somewhere beyond the ridgeline. The drizzle had increased. Mosquitoes droned about his face, irritated his eyelids. He caught a tiny movement on a nearby leaf, watched as a foot-long cenetipede crossed it, its armored segments a pale green and brown, legs scurrying in wavering unison. It dropped from the leaf into the grass and disappeared.

Suddenly, soundlessly, Wyatt was beside him. "You set up, bud?" he whispered. His boonie hat was low on his forehead, dripping water, mosquitoes like tiny, trembling sticks on his neck.

Sol nodded. "Yeah."

He and his guerillas were on the right flank of the firing line, two of his men armed with Jap rifles, the other two with a U.S. carbine and a Colt .45., their bolos jammed into the ground at their sides, easy at hand.

Earlier, while forming up on the other side of the hill, Wyatt had paused at each one of Blue Team's men assigned a group of guerillas to relay Major Hannon's instructions. When he spoke to the *mangs*, little Frankie interpreted: wait on the Americans to open fire; go for the machine-gunners first, then the officers and non-coms; if you get overrun, fall back into the woods and form another firing line there.

Bird checked his watch. "We got four minutes," he said. "Them boys with bows and arrows're movin' into position now." He snorted. "Bows and fuckin' arrows yet." He glanced right where Kaamanui's four *mangs* were hidden, invisible. He came back, knocked his fist lightly against Sol's shoulder. "Keep the little buggers firin', Hoss. An' lay her in heavy."

"Right."

Wyatt slipped away.

Kaamanui's fingers felt restless on the trigger guard of his Thompson. To move his hands, he rechecked his belt knife, then his boot knife, sliding it in and out twice. Abruptly from across the road, twenty yards away, two Japanese soldiers appeared carrying bags of rice over their shoulders. They wore canvas-covered pot helmets with chin straps and the infantry star stamped on the front.

Besides his rifle slung across his back, one soldier had a small 50mm knee mortar hung from his web harness along with two four-round mortar pouches. The weapon was about eighteen inches long, simply a barrel on a T-shaped ground brace.

Kaamanui heard the faint *thwrrrrp* of a bowstring, the shooter somewhere twenty feet to his left. He saw a movement in the air and then an arrow's fletching suddenly appeared in the lead soldier's throat, the shaft completely through his neck. The man dropped his rice bag and grabbed for the shaft, reeled backward, and went down. He struggled to his knees. Blood erupted from his mouth, a perfectly round bubble of deep scarlet that lengthened like a thick string as he vomited blood.

The other soldier went to ground, discarding his own rice bag. He frantically began pulling his rifle around, finally got it into firing position just as another *thwrppp* sent a second arrow into his left eye. He screamed, rolled, trying to wrench it out. He went on screaming.

Sol saw the other Japs suddenly appear, coming between huts into the road and running toward the grove in their bowlegged gait, weapons coming down, bolts jamming back and forward, the men already forming into attack squads. To their right and left three machine-gunners had already thrown themselves to the ground to set up a covering firebase.

A *buntaicho,* or section leader, came up bellowing, deploying his men with wild arm movements, his sword dangling and the soldiers executing well as they formed up, some into flanking positions on either side with the bulk of the soldiers, mostly riflemen, bunching together into a phalanx that would be their point of penetration into the enemy's position.

The low-toned rapping of a Thompson opened up to Sol's left. Then he was firing, too, canting his weapon to send his rounds across one of the machine gun positions. He saw them hurl mud geysers. The full volley of the other guns was going strong now, the tinny cracks from the recovered Jap rifles, carbines, and handguns, the deeper, throaty banging of Thompsons. The banana leaves trembled and the sharp smell of cordite drifted in the rain.

Sol emptied his clip, clicked it out, and jammed in a fresh one, doing this looking out at the Japs. He saw that nearly half had gone down, dropping with that sudden, leaden-appearing fall to the earth. But the remainder were firing now. Scattered bullets whipped through the leaves.

He opened again, this time taking a different machine gun position nearer the village under fire. And in that precise movement, amid the so familiar sounds of modern warfare and the old, stark stench of gun smoke, he felt, *felt* his blood coursing through him and that old crazy, wild, numb, yet unexplainably joyous sensation of engaging in mortal combat and the knowledge of his own firepower, the reality of his own strength. It came sweeping back over him.

A machine gun suddenly lashed into the grove from some unseen source, tracers red as splinters of lightning crossing the road. They exploded through the leaves. He heard the unmistakable baseball-in-a-rug-sounding impact of someone getting hit. He dropped into the grass for an instant. The machine gun stopped, started again, traversing to his left. He lifted up, saw Jap soldiers coming on, howling, a shrill, insane screaming.

He fired, felt the weapon jumping in his hand lightly, felt the heat coming off the barrel, wisps of hot smoke blowing back into his face. Something crashed through the foliage directly ahead of him and the long, dirty blade of a bayonet, blood-grooved, appeared and then a Jap, small khaki-brown uniform etched with rain and blood, wild-eyed, lunging at him, screaming.

Instinctively, he parried the blade, felt it slice harmlessly through his sleeve. He spun around, bringing up the muzzle of the Thompson, and slammed it into the Jap's jaw. The man was knocked off his feet. Following him down, Sol drew his boot knife and slashed it straight across his throat. Blood burst out, drenching the front of his battle tunic, hot and gummy.

There was another crash of leaves. He turned. The Japanese *buntaicho* he'd seen earlier was lunging at him, his sword already swinging downward. Kaamanui rolled to his left. The blade sliced by two inches from his face. It neatly and completely severed the left arm of the soldier with the slit throat.

Before the squad leader could reset, Sol gave him a full burst, six rounds that tore into the Jap's chest. The impacts hurled him back through the leaf cover out of sight. Kaamanui came to one knee. All around him the shadowy grove was filled with the fuming tatter of the rain, the hard guttural, panting growls of fighting men, sudden explosions of gunfire, the almost delicate metallic clash of blades.

He parted the leaves. Two soldiers were running low across the road. He cut them down with the last of his rounds. Quickly reloading, he swung to the right, squatted, listening. He could smell the dead Jap nearby, an odor like vinegar and slaughterhouse blood and sweat.

Abruptly, there was a sudden, heavy silence. Only the rain and the mad surge of his blood and a scattered, harsh breathing like animals in a dark den. He parted the leaves to his right. One of his *mangs* was dead, bullet holes across his naked chest, little puckers of flesh that weren't bleeding. Beyond was a Jap soldier who had been decapitated. Another of the guerillas was rifling through his clothing. The severed head lay in the bloodstained grass with its face upward, the eyes open beneath the rim of the pot helmet.

"Blue Team, rally on me," Wyatt's voice called. "On me. Now."

Their casualties were small, two dead guerillas, three wounded. All of Blue Team had come through unscathed except for cuts and bruises, the men moving in that restlessness of still-fuming-but-stopped energy, hot-eyed.

Major Hannon came up the road in his stubbies and his cocked jungle hat, bellowing, "*Magdalahan m'la armas, mangs.*" To the Yanks: "Grab their weapons, mates. Withdraw through the lower grove. Move it, move it!"

Parnell and his security team of guerillas had come up onto the road now and he was setting out his flankers to cover their departure. Three of the *mang* bowmen scurried among the fallen Japanese, killing the wounded with their bolos. The Americans watched over their shoulders, starting down the slope.

Fifteen minutes later, all three guerilla sections had faded back into the jungle.

Chapter Five

Lieutenant Yasio Sacabe entered the *ianjo* with his samurai swagger, walking on the balls of his feet with a bounce and pelvic twist to his thick body. He paused a moment to survey the line of ordinary soldiers queued in front of a group of ten, hastily built wooden cubicles that were spaced along the left wall of the cavernous room.

Each cubicle, barely four feet wide, had a filthy curtain across its front. Within each one was a *karayuki-san*, or comfort woman, who sexually serviced the garrison's soldiers. Spotting him, the line of men braced to attention.

This enormous room had once been a storage area for newly harvested rice, the building itself a mill in the coastal town of Delores. Now it was headquarters for the 33rd Engineer Regiment of the 102nd or *Sendai* Division. On its grounds were the regimental personnel tents, material and ordnance sheds and corrals for the regiment's two hundred work and caisson horses.

Sacabe continued on through the room and into another large, domed space. The walls here had a dirty patina of rice powder and there were tall drifts of dried husks in corners. The only light came dimly through two rows of clerestory windows, their glass panes opaque with dirt.

Filling part of the space were huge roller stones set

into networks of pulleys and timbered beams. Beyond
them were several conveyors with suspended rollers of
leather that polished the grain once it had been milled.
Along the opposite wall were large metal tanks that had
once held glucose solution and talc. Now everything was
grimy, chinks filled with cobwebs, and the air was dank
and had a thick, sweet-sour odor of mold and sugar.

Beyond the main milling room were stairs that led to
a second floor where the mill's offices had been. Now
some of the rooms were occupied by the regimental
signal, medical, intendance, and supply sections. The
last two rooms had three more wooden cubicles, which
were the officers' *ianjos*.

One stall was now occupied. Sacabe could hear the
rhythmic thudding of the bedsprings as he passed. The
curtain was open in the next cubicle. A young Filipina
sat on her bed, staring at the floor. She was naked and
had short hair and a large bruise on her neck.

The only things in the cubicle beside the bed were an
ammunition box made into a bed stand, a wooden pail
with washcloths, and a leather loop that hung over the
bed. It was connected to a rope that went over a small
pulley, which was then snugged to a nail in the wall.

The third cubicle's curtain was also pulled open.
Sacabe stepped in and drew it closed. A teenaged Philippine girl, perhaps fourteen, was lying on the bed. Also
naked, she sat up abruptly when he entered. She was
quite lovely, with black, almond eyes and black hair, her
developing breasts barely larger than lemons. Her pubic
hair was a mere shadow below the curve of her belly, like
a man's three-day stubble. Her name was Rose.

The Japanese captain had been with her before. Although shared by all the regimental officers as well as
those visiting from other units, she was the regimental
colonel's favorite, young enough not to be menstruating
and thus free of the possibility of impregnation.

Without a word, Sacabe moved to the bed, sat down,

and quickly pulled off his high black leather boots. He stood and unbuckled his *shin-gunto* sword and sidearm, placed them on the floor, then removed his olive-green tunic, gray undershirt, and *fundoshi* underwear. He never took his eyes off the girl. Rose did not return his gaze, but instead lay back down and looked fixedly at the ceiling.

He could feel his arousal rising, like a building urgency to urinate. Only this was an ache that was less a pain than a hunger. He continued letting his eyes play across the girl's body. Her color was a creamy biege, the skin childish-smooth.

It reminded him momentarily of the *fan fan musume* of Tokyo, in the cabarets called *pinko saron* along the Ginza and the Shinjuku when he was attending Nihon University preparing for the law. Or the better places in Ikebukuro with its narrow alleyways filled with judo schools and craftsmen shops called *unagi-no-nedoko* and the *itoko*, the blind women soothsayers who had predicted he would one day rise in great glory, and the *turuko* baths with their delicate *kokeshi bainshunfu*, the prostitutes with faces like toy dolls who were lascivious and could do wondrous things with their hands and mouths and vaginas.

He had used comfort women in China and in the Dutch East Indies, some even white, Dutch women who had been unable to escape before the Japanese arrived. But none could compare with those of his homeland. Thinking this now, he felt a sweep of aching nostalgia for it lift through him.

Still, these Filipinas *were* pretty and well formed. Most had been virgins, kidnapped from their barrio homes by special military squads nicknamed *arabu jins*, which meant *Arabs*. All were between the ages of twelve and twenty. Set up in quarters within military compounds and constantly guarded, each girl serviced forty to fifty soldiers daily. The officers always obtained the select ones, and if a girl became pregnant, she was beheaded.

Fully naked now save for his socks, Sacabe reached down and placed the leather strap around the girl's right ankle. He hoisted on it until her leg was nearly vertical, then cinched it in tightly. She made no sound or movement while he did this. Now he moved to the side of the bed, his erection full and bobbing. Roughly, he grabbed her hair and brought her head up until she took his member into his mouth.

He closed his eyes, heard himself moan softly, murmur an obscenity. Still, it was never completely satisfying with such a young one, her mouth too small to give him full entrance. Yet his belly trembled ecstatically as he felt the girl flutter her tongue over him. Heat and pressure began bunching in his groin. He opened his eyes and abruptly slapped her on the side of the head, withdrawing himself.

"*Langis*," he barked in Tagalog. "*Langis*."

Obediently, Rose hurriedly fetched a bottle from her wooden bed stand. It contained a thick cooking oil. She uncorked it, coated her hands, then Sacabe's penis. Again he closed his eyes, felt her fingers moving back and forth with rapturous little electrical shocks.

Suddenly in a wild rush, he pushed her back onto the bed and entered her, the bottle of oil spilling onto the sheet. The girl lay absolutely still, her own eyes locked down. Yet they moved beneath their lids, as if she were watching some terrible dreamscape crossing through her vision.

Grunting, the Japanese officer lunged back and forth in a violent, thrusting rhythm, the narrowness of the girl's vagina giving him exquisite sensations. Quickly, he felt himself beginning to rise inwardly, as if with fuming, heated waves that billowed up out of his groin, his belly, his chest.

On the very edge of orgasm, he abruptly withdrew from the girl's vagina. Even in his scorching excitement, the thought of implanting *his* sperm, that of a Japanese

officer, into the birth places of this *kokujin musume*, this worthless piece of brown trash, was abhorrent. Moving in the same rhythm, he lifted the line looped to her leg. This fully exposed her anal area.

Nearly whimpering with the onset of climax, he rammed himself into her anus, shoving mightily against the utter tight resistance of it until he was fully inside her, Rose now arching her shoulders off the bed, her lovely, oval face contorted, crying out in pain as he came.

Afterward, she cleaned him with a washcloth, Sacabe disinterestedly aloof again, staring off as if considering great things while she administered to him. There were several smears of blood on the sheet. He said nothing to her when he left.

Twenty-two minutes later, a runner from regimental headquarters came to inform him that the white guerilla Dillon had been seen near San Luis.

Little Frankie Trota talked away, sitting with Bird, Kaamanui, and Cowboy Fountain, the Filipino telling about when he was the boxing champion of Southeast Asia, featherweight division, his words spiced with jazzy Americanisms, his p's and f's interchanged like most Filipinos when they speak English.

"I took heem out in t'ree," Frankie said proudly. "Purs roun' I set heem up, second I dance, man. In the t'urd, I clock the cat."

"This was a Jap?" Wyatt said.

"No, no, Chinese, from Hong Kong. Was in—" He closed his eyes, trying to remember. "T'urdy t'ree, maybe pour."

"How long were you champion, Frankie?" Cowboy asked. He liked the small dark man with a face like a beat-up monkey. He'd been close to him during the firefight, saw him go at it like a whirlwind, no fear, standing

right up there with bullets whipping past him, laying it
in with his carbine like Geronimo.

"Two year." He shrugged nonchalantly. "Den I get
whip, man. In L.A. Goddamn Mexican, Gonzalez. He
got one funch like one plashlight."

The men were taking a break, munching on dog meat
jerky and roasted jungle snails like peanuts, the rest of
the guerillas and Blue Team men strung out along the
edge of jungle just below a high ridgeline. The rain had
stopped but there was fog at this level. It came drifting
in through the trees, wet and chilly. To the east the land
sloped sharply downward, covered mostly with *kunai*
grass and small patches of peppercorn vines on sticks
shaped like Irish crosses and a few rice shelves, nobody
working anything now. . . .

Major Hannon had sent two *mangs* down into a small,
nearby mountain village to check out the word on the
bamboo telegraph, maybe pick up something concerning
Dillon. They were disguised as *carigodores*, professional
bearers, and would tell the villagers they were looking
for work.

Thus far, Hannon had kept his small guerilla force away
from the barrios. Now that the Nips were withdrawing
from Samar, he knew fifth columnists and treasonous
makapili would be desperate to go along, knowing there
would be deadly reprisals once the Allies came. And they'd
be willing to turn in *anyone* to better their chances of
evacuation.

The men had seen Jap barges on the move off the
coast, and twice Hannon had glassed small coastal towns
where he saw evidence of recent killings, houses burned
to the ground and still smoldering. The Nips had even
destroyed many fishing boats. Some of the wrecks were
still afire on the beach while others were only dark shadows out in the shallows.

He cursed and turned to Parnell. "The bloody bhas-
tards're layin' waste out there," he said. "There must be

patrols everywhere. Best warn your men to be bloody alert, Lef-tenant. We could be jumped any time. . . ."

"I eben pight in New Yok," Frankie said now. "Madison Square Garden, man. Cooba guy, I forget his name."

"You win?" Wyatt asked.

"Oh, sure." Frankie took a drag on his slender Japanese cigarette, let the smoke ease out his nostrils. "I also pight in Seattle and Reno, Nev-ada," he said, putting the emphasis on the first syllable of Nevada. He grinned suddenly. His teeth were surprisingly even and white. "Man, I like dem showgirls Reno. Almos' fock me to death, babee. They t'ink I am jockey." He shook his head, remembering.

"One of your buddies said you're a bandleader," Kaamanui said. "That true?"

"Oh, yah. Jes' like my fadder, he was beeg bandleader. All the swing songs, chu know? When little kid time, he teach me how to play the *trumpeta*."

"The what?" Bird said.

"The *trumpeta*. The horn, man, chu know, like Harry James?" He shrugged. "But when I done foxing, my lip no good no more. So I play drums, jes' like Gene Krupa, man. Then I get my own band. *Padinhari-Umuntayon*. We play Tacloban, Cebu City, eben Manila, man."

"What kinda music you play?" Sol said. "Shit-kickin', swing, what?"

"Oh, swing, man. Sure, all dat kine Benny Goodman songs, Tommy Dorsey, the Duke, all them guys. I tell you true, man."

He fell silent, remembering. There was only the soft soughing of the breeze whispering through the trees, the gentle rustle of underbrush. Now and again the call of a jungle bird came, the sound accentuating the silence.

Wyatt said, "Here come them boys we sent down."

They all watched as the two guerillas approached quickly up the slope through the *kunai* grass, disappearing and then reappearing down there in the fog. They reached the edge of the jungle and moved along it to where Hannon and Parnell were sitting.

Pretty soon, Parnell came through the underbrush. "Okay, let's go," he ordered. Everybody immediately got to their feet. "Dillon's been spotted," he went on. "Wyatt, you and Frankie on point again. Sol, set up for drag."

Within minutes, they were on the move again.

He was close enough to the two Japanese soldiers to smell them: pickled *daicon* like vinegar, a fishy, muddy stench from their clothing, both odors mixing with the sour scent of the *tuba* they were drinking, a native beer made from coconut palm sap, very strong. They had it in thick, three-foot-long cuts of bamboo called *kahon-tubas*, which they tilted high up to drink from.

They were seated near a makeshift ferry across a wide stream, swollen from the rain, its water like liquid mud, hissing and foaming along the banks. The air above it swarmed with clouds of tiny gnats through which small blue bee-eaters darted and swooped, feeding.

The ferry itself consisted of a fifty-gallon metal barrel strung on a double cable, the ends of which were anchored to two huge *nara* trees with pulleys. The barrel itself had a cover to keep rain and jungle insects out, and someone had painted a crude star on it in yellow paint.

He studied the soldiers closely. Both appeared intoxicated. They were dressed in tropical work shirts with the red squares of the infantry on their left breasts. Their leggings were tattered and their *tabi* jungle shoes badly worn. Their Type 98 Arisaka rifles with bayonets attached rested against the base of the *nara* tree. . . .

Dillon had reached the mouth of the Delores just before dawn, holding his *caba-caba* close to the south bank, shoving through overhanging jungle vines. Here the river fanned out into a network of sandbars and deep channels edged on both sides by mangrove swamps. The water along the shore was stained brown by the river and far out were lines of surf over coral shelves. The overcast had thinned and the ocean itself lay green gray to the eastern horizon.

No fishing boats were out. The area looked deserted, remote. Then he caught sight of a Japanese patrol about a quarter mile down the beach, brown figures coming along the edge of the water. A few moments later, a second patrol appeared to the north.

He quickly slipped into the mangroves, paddling along natural channels formed by the dense trees. They grew above the water, their roots making tangled masses underneath. The water was higher than usual from rain flood and sour-smelling, filled with rotting vegetation and the floating gray-white islands of bird guano. Each time he dipped his paddle, schools of tiny fingerling mullet and transparent shrimp exploded from the water, scattering in a rush.

The trees were alive with the caws and screams of gray heron and hornbill and marsh egret flocks lifting off their nests, others soaring in great, raucous circles over the trees before heading out to their feeding grounds in the coastal shallows. Occasionally, he heard the grumbling roar of a bull crocodile, the echoing slam of its tail. Once a slender golden-banded marsh python glided across his bow, leaving a spreading V in the water, its head held up like a miniature Loch Ness monster.

It was nearly 7:30 when he finally reached the edge of the mangroves. There were small rice paddies here and tiny vegetable gardens of *camote* yams, *opo* cucumbers, and *kangkong*, a slimy cabbage. Here and there were thick stands of eucalyptus trees. A half mile away was San Luis, brick and mud buildings on the edge of the ocean, *nipa* and *bahay kubo* huts and *barong-barongs*, driftwood and tin shanties, spread in clusters along the beach and also farther back among banana groves and small cornfields.

Numerous Japanese troops were visible, many riding

bicycles on the white coral roads. But he noticed few natives. And the livestock that usually roamed free in the towns were missing. Even *carabaos,* the water buffalos used in the fields and rice paddies, were all gone, everything undoubtedly slaughtered by the Japanese for food.

Dillon sank the *caba-caba* and stealthily moved into the eucalyptus, heading south, the ground brushy and filled with pieces of papery white bark that had peeled off the trees. The sharp, medicinal smell of the eucalyptus brought a memory to him: the scent of blue gum groves near his home in Lac Courts, Wisconsin, where he'd hunted squirrels as a boy. The sudden, pure clarity of the memory wrenched his heart.

Then it was gone in a rush of adrenaline as he realized there were people among the trees. He froze. Gradually he recognized them in the dimness: woodcutters, six of them, three men in ragged *barong-tagalog* shirts and three women in tattered saronglike *tapis* of *pisa* cloth, all carrying gunny-sack bundles of wood on their backs with straps wound around their foreheads for support.

The Filipinos stared silently at him, no one moving. He nodded and called out, *"Magandang umaga po." Good morning.* They didn't answer. The women looked frightened, the men expressionless. Everybody continued staring.

A full minute passed. Finally, Dillon decided he had to do something. He touched the holster of his sidearm, a Browning Hi-Power 9mm, and said in Tagalog, "You must tell no one of me. If you do, I will return and kill you." The woodcutters remained absolutely motionless. He moved away, watching them over his shoulder.

It took him forty minutes to traverse the lowland, darting between eucalyptus stands, before he reentered the jungle. Now it was easier moving, this stretch of jungle true tropical forest, part of the Delores watershed.

Unlike monsoon forest, here the trees were massive, many towering nearly two hundred feet high. Halfway up was a dense canopy of hanging vines, lianas, orchids, and air plants, which blocked out much of the sunlight and cast the floor of the forest into a perpetual twilight.

The floor itself was relatively clear of underbrush save for a thick, mushy carpet of leaves, grotesquely shaped fungi, some stinking like rotted meat, and the moldering remnants of fallen trees now completely blanketed in moss. In occasional openings where the sunlight managed to penetrate, *coogan* grass and thorny rattan palms and stands of bamboo grew, the bamboo appearing like green pipes all standing in upright rows in a dimly lit construction warehouse.

Soon after, he stumbled onto the two Japanese soldiers. . . .

Now he lowered himself onto his haunches and tried to figure out what to do. He *had* to get across this stream so he could continue on south to the mission school. He didn't think working his way up or down the stream to find another ferry would do any good; they'd *all* be guarded.

He felt a sudden, chilling sensation creep up his back, like ants crawling. He swung around and stared back into the dimness from which he'd come, suddenly, horribly, alert to something back there: Japs even now tracking him, drawing closer? He knew those woodcutters had recognized him. Could they have been *makawili*? Or just plain natives more afraid of the Japanese than him?

Goddammit!

Suddenly, one of the soldiers jumped to his feet and began shouting loudly at his companion. "*Nani ittenda teme?*" he roared and shoved out his chin pugnaciously. "*Kenka utten noka? Huh? Huh?*"

Dillon stiffened. The other soldier spat into the stream, ignoring the shouts. But he seemed very angry in that dark, sullen way of drunks. Finally, he glanced up and rapidly growled, "*Sore wa do demo. Omae wa dare da? Baka ka. Zakennayo!*"

The first soldier swore, then knocked the other's *kahontuba* from his hand, the thing tumbling away and into the stream. The second soldier got up and the two men began fighting, cursing viciously and throwing wild, clumsy punches.

For a moment, Dillon was taken aback. Then his mind screamed at him: *Now! Do it now!*

Without further conscious thought, he was moving, fast, light, covering the twenty yards to the two Japs, who were now down, rolling on the ground, entangled. They rolled into their rifle stocks, knocked them over, then went the other way, toward the stream. One was getting the better of the other and pummeled him in the face. Both had lost their field caps and sun curtains. Their heads were shaved with only a shadowy imprint of hair visible.

As Dillon bounded silently forward, he drew his pistol cross-handed, already with a chambered round, then his boot knife, this in his right hand. He loomed over the two men. They were completely unaware of him. Dropping onto one knee on the back of the man on top, he rammed his knife into the man's upper right jaw, in under the bone junction, felt the blade ricochet off bone, then go in swiftly. He hauled backward, pulling the blade up and into the brain, then out.

The soldier went totally limp. The other shifted his head to peer over his companion's shoulder. His slanted eyes, one bloody, shot open. Desperately, cursing, he tried to extricate himself.

Adding his own weight to the corpse, Dillon shoved the Hi-Power deeply into the first soldier's liver, pushing the muzzle down deep into flesh, and fired, *bam . . . bam . . . bam,* the reports muffled by the dead man's body to little more than the sounds three full paint cans would make falling onto a cement floor.

The soldier on the bottom jerked upward as each round went through his companion and into his own body, murmuring terrified, meaningless phrases. Then he opened his mouth to shout fully, but Dillon put the blade of his knife into the man's left eye, the socket erupting blood. He twisted the knife upward again, into the brain pan. The soldier gagged and puked up a ball of bloody mucus and went still.

Hurriedly, the American rolled the two dead bodies into the stream. They quickly spun out into the main current. He threw their rifles after them, buried their caps, then covered the bloodstains on the ground with mud.

As he crossed in the barrel ferry a few moments later, he saw something big suddenly explode up through the surface of the stream, caught a fleeting glimpse of the broad head and muzzle of a crocodile, its sharply ridged bosses merging into thick, horny plates the color of charcoal dust smeared on clay. It took one of the Japanese bodies, the impact making an arm flail upward for an instant before both disappeared in a whirlpool of turbulence.

He continued south.

The Japanese patrol, twenty men, was on horseback, the animals with mouth ropes, headstalls and bridle reins of oiled hemp so they'd move without sound, and saddles of gunnysacking and hemp stirrups. Two carried wooden cross-racks for a pair of Model 92 7.7mm machine guns and their tripod mounts and ammo boxes. The machine guns were exact copies of the British Lewis gun.

Trota and Bird, still working point, had spotted them passing through a small, sunlit break in the forest. Frankie signaled with his sounding stick that he'd made an enemy contact, the little ringing hum of it floating back through the trees.

They were now no longer in the monsoon forests of the upper mountains, but in true tropical jungle. The trees here were gigantic and there was a thick canopy sixty or seventy feet up, absorbing the meager daylight. The ground was much more open, yet it was still shadowy and existed in an even deeper silence that evoked the feeling of majesty, as if all the animals had been hushed and the column of fighting men traversed through a vast, abandoned cathedral.

Major Hannon and Parnell were waiting as the two men came sprinting back to the main column, Wyatt's boots and Frankie's bare feet making soft, cushiony sounds in the leafy mulch.

"How far and how many?" Hannon snapped to Trota.

"Two hundert meter, sor," he answered. "Twenty men on horses, two machine guns."

The Aussie turned to Parnell. "Goddammit, they're already too close for us to set out ambush details." He frowned, puzzled. "I don't get this. Nips don't usually patrol horse-mounted in this kind of terrain. This bunch must be huntin'?"

"We could use those animals," Parnell said.

"Aye, that we could. Orright, ever'body take cover." To the *mangs* nearby, he called out in a low voice, "*Magkubli kayo! Agad, agad!*" When he returned to Red, he added, "They'll come in single file, Lieutenant, always do in jungle. Even this kind. Let the front men pass until we've got the entire column enfiladed. Key off my burst and go for the machine-gunners first. But try an' keep from wounding the animals."

Red nodded. Silently, he and the others melted off into the green dimness beside the trail, some to the right, the rest to the left.

Everybody was hidden now, crouched down behind fallen trees or lying in grass or pressed deeply inside the root hollows of massive tree trunks. The area had again sunk into its eternal silence, only the very faint, feathering murmur of rain filtering down through the levels of vegetation. Faint shafts of gray light pierced through the upper story, and mites and flying insects made tiny whirlygigs in their beams.

By habit, Cowboy eased open the slide of his Thompson a half inch, checking to see that it had a round chambered, then eased it soundlessly back and clicked off the safety. He was kneeling behind a great mound of moss that had grown completely over a fallen *nara* tree. The moss was soft as cotton and smelled like peppermint, which cut a sweet streak across the heavier, dead-stink smell from grotesquely shaped mushrooms that grew up through the mat of leaves under him.

Laguna was kneeling close by while Kaamanui and Smoker were thirty yards to their right, hidden among tree trunks. Parnell and Bird had taken up positions far to the left and across the trail. The silence was abruptly shattered by a distant chorus of ground apes, probably spooked by the approaching patrol. Their screams were eerie, sounding like primitive women wailing in grief.

"*Je-sus Cristo*," Weesay murmured. "Fuckin' noises give me the chills, *meng*."

"What the hell *is* that?" Cowboy asked.

"I dunno."

Cowboy started to say something but stopped and leaned forward to listen tensely. He'd caught the sound of something approaching. After a few seconds, he identified it, the hooves of a single horse moving over mushy ground.

More seconds ticked past. Then the Jap patrol's point rider emerged out of the dimness, at first just a dark movement, but then a whole horse and a man, the soldier in dirty khaki and pot helmet, his rifle held upright on his left thigh, his eyes scanning the ground ahead of him.

Fountain studied him. Little prick looked like a clown up on that mount. He lowered his eyes to the animal: bay-colored, a deep reddish brown, no more than fifteen hands tall but with a deep chest and broad, muscular hindquarters. He would have said it looked like a cross between an Asiatic pony and a field animal, obviously being used now as a caisson puller. It came forward steadily, tossing its head.

The point man passed, no jingling of harness, only the pulpous ooze from under his mount's hooves. He disappeared back into the gloom and everything was silent again. Laguna moved a few feet away, widening the space between them so as to lessen the chance of both being wounded in a single burst.

They waited. Bugs crawled and probed their flesh. The distant sound of a blowing horse came. Three minutes slipped by, four. Then figures appeared, coming on steadily, horsemen in single file, the animals all bays and chestnuts. They passed, one at a time.

The Japanese soldiers looked worn and dog-hungry in their collarless tropical battle shirts, their helmets webbed and carrying the five-point yellow star of the Imperial Army. Each carried a light, patrol-sized knapsack. First were two *nitto-hei*, or privates, then the patrol commander, a warrant officer called a *jun-i*. He was armed with a Type 14 pistol in a canvas holster and a *shin-gunto* sword, which he had laid across his thighs.

Next came three two-man grenade teams, the grenadiers with Type 91 grenade launchers attached to their Arisakas, their loaders weighted down with five-round grenade pouches on their waist belts and harness straps. The two packhorses with the machine guns and tripods followed, and then came the three-man gunner teams. The last five soldiers in the file were riflemen and a *gun-so*, or sergeant, who carried a Type 92 light machine gun.

Cowboy peered through brush and twigs at the patrol, less than a hundred feet from him. They looked so small and comic, not like some of the *Whermacht* troops he'd faced. But then he cautioned himself: *Slow up, boy, don't underestimate these little bastards.* And in that moment he experienced that old copper penny taste of approaching combat suddenly in his mouth.

Hannon's first burst blew through the silence like a crack of lightning. It immediately drew with it a volley of muzzle blasts. Cowboy opened up, felt his Thompson bucking lightly as he laid out a spray burst toward one of the machine-gun teams. He stopped, heard Weesay's weapon going.

He had seen his rounds hit two men. They were knocked off their mounts. One of the horses was also hit in the head. It reared, screaming, spraying blood, and fell backward onto the ground, kicking wildly. One of the wounded Japs was already up, scooting to the downed animal. He began fumbling with the harness on the machine-gun rack.

For several seconds after the barrage opened, the Japanese didn't start counterfire. They were too busy trying to remain in their saddles, the horses panicked, bolting in all directions. But they quickly brought them under control. Then, as if by silent command, the soldiers swung their mounts off both sides of the trail and began a wild charge directly into the ambush gunfire, their own weapons coming to bear, the men standing up in their stirrups and firing like raiding Cossacks.

Cowboy opened up again just as the cracking blow of a grenade launcher went off, immediately followed by another. Then the twin explosions shocked the air, sucking pressure from around Cowboy's head. He heard shrapnel go cutting through branches.

A horseman was very close now, charging, a blur coming right at him, the animal's nostrils flared wide, its chest muscles rippling under the brown skin. It crashed into the rotted trunk, hurling chunks of moss everywhere. Caught in the tangle, it thrashed, lifting onto its hind feet.

He fired at the rider, missed him but hit the horse in the chest, four black holes stitched into its brown hair. The animal pitched to the side, shrieking. The rider was thrown off and came tumbling down nearly on top of Fountain.

Cowboy swung the muzzle of his Thompson at his face, heard it strike the man's helmet, the crack of metal-against-metal. The Jap lunged up at him with a belt knife. To the side, the horse was trying to regain its feet. Blood pumped out of its chest in four red-black streams. Cowboy parried the knife thrust with the butt of his weapon, then swung the muzzle in under the soldier's neck and fired. His burst tore up through the man's face and then blew out the top of his helmet. The Thompson clicked on empty.

Scattered gunshots and the yells and grunts of small engagements sounded from all over. Another grenade went off. Then the Jap machine gun began firing, making a slow, sharp, almost tinny rapping, which echoed off. The whole area was now sunk in a cordite-stinking smokiness, floating in the still air in differing densities. The whirlygigging mites and insects twisted and turned as if in slightly clay-muddied water.

Cowboy swung around, ramming in a fresh clip just as two more mounted soldiers hove past him on the left. A spray of bullets zipped close by. He charged his weapon and fired, behind the riders. Across the trail, other Japs had also overridden the opposite line of guerillas and were now wheeling their horses around to come charging back, shifting their weapons.

He heard Weesay firing at the two. Both were turning around, their animals heeled over. Laguna's second burst knocked one man off his horse, somersaulting into deep grass. Cowboy fixed his muzzle sight on the other rider and fired. The Jap flew into the air.

The horse still came on, its reins and stirrups flapping wildly. He leaped up, waving his arms, grabbing for them, finally got a hold. He felt the animal's massive momentum pull him off his feet as it thundered past, hooves hammering in the leaves, its eyes like eggs in its head. It dragged him over the mossy tree trunk and down the other side before he could get his feet planted enough to turn the animal.

The firing slowed and finally stopped and the silence

returned with a sudden, rushing sensation of vacuum. Through it came the high-pitched screams of wounded horses, human moans, and curses in three languages.

The horse had jacked itself backward at the end of the reins. In so doing, it stumbled into the slanted ridges of a thick tree root and nearly fell down. But that stopped its flight. It remained still for a moment, quivering, then shot out one hind foot sideways, stood snorting.

Cowboy walked it down slowly, talking softly to it: "Hey, hey, you knot-headed sumbitch. Come awn, now, easy, easy."

Major Hannon started hollering, "Get the horses! Goddammit, get the bloody horses! *Patigilin ang kabayos!*"

Cowboy got his hand on the terrified animal, felt its muscles shaking as if electricity were coursing through its veins. It snorted again, stomped. "Easy, baby," he cooed, moving closer to its left side. "Yeah. *There* y'all go." With a single leap, he was on the animal's back. It reared slightly and broke into a run, the strength of it coming up through his legs.

Dead or wounded Japanese soldiers and at least five of their horses lay along the trail and on the upper side of it, his own animal responding to the pressure of his knees, changing gaits like a leaper and clearing over them. One soldier lay on a mossy mound like a tended grave, his back carved wide open, spine bones and ribs showing clearly. Fountain rocketed past Hannon just then, the Aussie waving him on and shouting, "Go get 'em, Yank."

He rounded up four horses, the animals still frightened and jumpy yet responding to this rider who talked to them in easy words, clucking softly. From back in the killing zone, pistol shots rang out. By the time he got his little herd back to it, all the Jap bodies had been stripped of their weapons and the wounded killed. Even the horses had been shot, Parnell and his men prowling among the corpses looking grim.

The horse with one of the 92 MGs had gotten away. But they had the other gun, along with its ammo boxes and the warrant officer's big Type 96 automatic rifle, all the Arisaka rifles and grenade pouches, some of the *mangs* wearing two and three weapons slung over their shoulders.

They had lost three more guerillas. They carried them to hollows in a single teak trunk and covered them with moss. Then Major Hannon set out the men, his force down to twenty-eight with four wounded now, the point men ahead and the rest moving on the flanks, just on the edge of visibility. Battle smoke still drifted and the sticky, slaughterhouse smell of death was already coagulating in the silent air as they moved off.

Chapter Six

Father Nicholas Dobbenier had seen too much of death over the last seventy-two hours. He could bear it no more and had retreated to the small San Luis church. It stood on a low hill, a *buhangan* stone building coated with a layer of clay cement. Its upper walls were whitewashed, the lower stained a dark brown. The entrance had a rusted steel storm door and the roof was formed of corrugated tin strips painted in red lead.

Inside it was empty and still and smelled of incense and candle wax, wilted flowers, and rain. Foot-wide teak beams ran across the ceiling. The red Eucharist candle on the altar made the room shimmer, etching objects in crimson. There were only a dozen long, rough-wooden pews.

Now his parishioners were burying their dead.

Dobbenier had been in the Philippines for thirty years. He loved the *pinoy* and *indios*, the poor lowland Filipinos of Samar, as if they were his own children. But so many had been killed by the Japanese. Now the others were turning away from his teachings, believing the Lord Christ had failed them.

Instead, they were reverting to their ancient beliefs, to the nature gods called *Bathalas,* and to the *anitos* and *asuangs,* jungle demons who had to be appeased before salvation could come. At that very moment, he could hear the eerie music and the constant jangling of dancers' bells as the villagers went through rituals far older than Christianity.

Just before twilight, he had even watched two sacrificial *carabaos* fight to the death in a rice paddy nearby, driven on by spearmen so that the victor's blood could be used to anoint the newly dead.

He moved to the altar and knelt. There was no crucifix above it, instead the statue of *Santo Nino,* a copy of the image of the Christ child brought by Magellan in 1521. It stood above the small, brass sepulcher with its tiny beatific smile and purple robes now bloodied by the candle flame. Weeping, the priest begged forgiveness for his helplessness and his failure.

"Father Dobbenier," a man said.

The priest whirled around, startled. *"Hein!"*

A husky white man in jungle shorts and an Aussie boonie hat stepped from the shadows. "Don't be frightened, Father," he said softly. A second man appeared, this one tall and dressed in battle gear.

The priest wiped away his tears, so startled and embarrassed he automatically spoke in French: *"Qui etes-vous? Qu 'est-ce qui se passe?"*

"I'm Major Hannon of the Australian Army," the first man answered in English. He turned slightly to the other. "This is Lef-tenant Parnell of the U.S. Army. We're looking for Dillon."

"Ah, mon Dieu!"

"Where is Dillon, Father?"

Earlier, Frankie Trota had snuck into a group of *barong-barongs* to pick up information. Several people told him the American named Dillon had been helped by Father Dobbenier, who was now hiding in the San Luis church.

"I believe he is in this vicinity," the priest answered quietly. He rose. "I sent him here."

"Why?"

"I arranged a boat for him. And *un piloter* to take him south."

"Did you see him yourself?"

"*Oui*. At San Tago. It is a—"

Hannon cut him off: "I know where and what it is. What happened?"

"We were at San Tago when the *Japonaise* came. He left in a small canoe to come here."

"Did they capture him?"

"*Non*. I am fairly certain."

"What else did he say?"

"Only that he had knowledge of very important things."

"He actually had papers on him?"

"*Non*. He said he had memorized their contents and then destroyed them."

Hannon frowned. "You're absolutely certain he said that?"

"*Oui*."

The major glanced at Parnell. "Well, we've got that, at least."

The priest shook his head despairingly. The heavy shoulders, the thick roundness of his face ordinarily lent him an aura of solid permanency, endurance. But the sorrow now deep in his eyes destroyed that impression.

He said, "These *Japonaise* killed many at San Tago. Destroyed the entire *tubig bayan*. They also caught and executed another guerilla leader and most of his men near Delores."

"Who? Johnny-One-Eye Maganoy?"

"Yes."

"Bloody hell."

"They are like insane beasts in their search for Dil-lon. Blood-drenched. I am told now they even kill their own wounded, those from the Leyte fighting. They administer them corrosive sublimate in their water so they will not be a burden to them." He shook his large head. "I do not understand such savagery."

The Aussie stared at him silently, then said, "How do we find Dillon?"

"I told him to go to the mission school. The *piloter* is there."

"Where is this school?"

"In the jungle about three kilometers from here." He turned, pointed toward the southwest, turned back.

The front door of the church was suddenly struck violently, the sound blowing through the small stone building. Hannon and Parnell leaped back into the shadows. There was another bang and the door was flung open.

A Japanese marine officer and three soldiers came bursting in. The pressure wave created by the opening door crossed the room and made the red Eucharist candle flame twist for a moment before straightening.

Hannon and Parnell lay up on separate ceiling beams and furtively watched as the Japanese marines took the priest away, three men remaining to hastily search the little church, their flashlights probing behind the altar, into the tiny sacristy, and two quick sweeps across the ceiling before leaving.

They waited several minutes before moving or speaking. From outside, they could hear Japanese talk, which soon faded off into the more distant ululations and rhythmic tinkling of bells from the town. At last, they swung down and crept to the front door.

There were torches up the coral road, clots of people, dancers. Small bits of red paper fluttered in the air, protection against the intrusion of evil spirits. Now and then Japanese soldiers wandered into the light, watched the proceedings for a moment, then passed on. The sky was dark and it had begun to rain again, a light, feathery rain.

The Aussie cursed softly. "We'll have to go like the clappers now, mate," he said. "Those Nip marines'll work over that poor cleric for sure. He looks a sturdy one, but they'll soon enough break 'im."

The major left first, going low and fast, across the small graveyard with its freshly covered graves, the turned earth smelling rich and fecund with little rain pools that had already formed where the ground had settled. Thirty seconds later, Parnell followed.

They linked up with Trota and Bird, who had remained in a banana grove at the edge of town. Alert for patrols, they crossed along the berms of rice paddies, moving in bounding bursts, leapfrogging each other. Soon, they linked up with the rest of the guerilla force and turned to the southwest, moving fast to get to that mission school before the Japanese.

Lauro Bulosan had a clubfoot and wore a single tall shoe that kept tangling in vines and brush, the man obviously not used to fugitive flight. He was tall for a Filipino with studied, dark eyes and long, slender fingers, a pianist's hands. He spoke very precise English and appeared unafraid.

Dillon had arrived at the mission school just after dark, the place without lights, a large *bahai kubo* on coconut stumps with bamboo walls and *nipa* palm roof. It stood in a clearing in the forest at the end of a coral road and the ground around it was a sea of mud and rain pools. Children's playthings were partially submerged in the water: an old tire, a broken swing, a sandbox now filled with rainwater. On the road there was a crude wooden sign that read ANG PAARALAN NG PUSO SAGRADO: *Sacred Heart School.*

He studied the layout for a full half hour before approaching the hut, creeping forward through the rain. There was a terrible stench in the air now, of rot, of death. He slid beneath the building. The ground was covered with six inches of water. He listened. Silence. At last, he tapped on the floor and called softly, "Bulosan."

The answer in English was immediate. "Yes, sir, I am here. . . ."

Now they reached beach jungle, Chinese pines, and eucalyptus trees. As they neared the coast, the stench in the air began to thin out. Bulosan had explained its source, a small Japanese aid station a half mile from the school.

He had helped build it, the Japs commandeering villagers to clear the area and construct two large huts. It was not really an aid station, he said, more a death house. Wounded Japanese soldiers from the fighting on Leyte were simply left there to die, without food, care, or medicine.

They were deposited in concentric circles inside the huts. Those closest to death were in the middle, the others farther out. Within days, the dead began to decay, their corpses swollen with gas and black as shiny coal. Those still alive who could not drag themselves away would soon be covered with white worms. It made them appear like pale mannequins, which continually seethed, the worms sounding like the rustling of reeds as they fed.

They reached the beach. The sky above the ocean was overcast, but the moon beyond gave the clouds a faint glow. There was a brisk wind that smelled of distance and rain, and far out along the horizon tiny lights blinked, then disappeared like ghostly flashes.

Bulosan had hidden his *banda* deep under brush and flotsam that had been heaved high up on the beach by the tide. The boat was twenty feet long, made of a single teak log with bamboo outriggers extending from both sides. It had a high, curving prow and stern. The mast, sail, and spars were wrapped in banana leaves and tucked into the boat, which was filled with rainwater.

He had also packed some *carabao* jerky and two bottles of water, a torch with a gunnysack head, a two-gallon can of kerosene, and a throw net wound into a ball. The food had been ruined by the rainwater. The torch would be used if a Jap beach patrol spotted them, making them seem like night fishermen.

Bulosan suddenly stopped pulling away brush to listen. A moment later, he whispered harshly, "Someone is coming, sir."

Dillon went still. The only sounds he could hear was the wind passing through the trees and the clatter of coconut palms. Then came the bark of a dog, which was instantly joined by other dogs, a concerted howling.

"It's a Japanese patrol," the Filipino croaked. "Hurry, hide the boat again."

Dillon felt the fear leap at him like a jungle cat, to grip his heart, constrict his throat. He had an uncontrollable urge to run, back into the cover of the forest. Instead, he forced himself to help Bulosan replace the brush and driftwood back onto the slender boat. Japanese voices now drifted in, the dogs whining and huffing with excitement as the patrol drew closer, coming from the south.

He reached out and roughly took hold of Bulosan's arm. "We have to get away, for God's sake," he whispered. "Back into jungle. Those dogs will find us."

"It is too late, sir," Bulosan said.

"Goddammit!"

The Filipino bent over the boat, reached under the brush, and brought out the can of kerosene. He spun off the cap. "Quickly, sir," he said, "cover yourself with the liquid. It will hide your body smell."

Dillon obeyed, forming a cup with his hands, then dousing his chest and clothing, the raw caustic odor of the kerosene fuming up to burn his eyes. He rubbed his arms, the liquid suddenly cold in the air, then splashed some on his boots.

The Japanese were very close now. As silently as possible, they crawled down under the brush and lay still, Dillon pressing his body tightly against the *banda's* stern. His heart thudded wildly, as if it would imprint its contours into the wood. He tried to silence his breathing, shuddering with effort.

Dear God.

Long seconds went past. A harsh snuffling and the pound of paws on the rain-packed sand sounded suddenly close. There was a loud disturbance of brush and he saw the dark shadow of a dog dash by only yards away. It thrashed about as if casting for scent, sniffing and blowing air through its nostrils. Another joined it, then a third.

He closed his eyes.

The animals continued lunging here and there, crisscrossing each other. On the beach, the Jap soldiers cursed and whistled and came up into the tree line, so near that Dillon caught the sweat-dirty stench of their uniforms on the wind.

But the dogs didn't approach the boat. Instead, they kept circling it, running beyond and then cutting back. They finally moved farther off toward the beach. The soldiers followed, still whistling, their boots thumping in the sand and their equipment jingling as they chased after the animals.

He and Bulosan lay very still, not exchanging words. The voices faded. Still they remained silent. Four minutes. Five. Suddenly, a woman's scream cut through the wind and with it the ferocious growling and shrieking of the dogs. The animals had found someone and were attacking her. There was a shot, another. Once more the woman screamed, or perhaps she was another, the voices indistinguishable. A man bellowed. A third shot echoed.

Dillon put his forehead down on the sand. He felt the horrible surge of guilt again. More people were dying, innocents, because of him. Gradually his mind settled. Still, he felt hot, his body tight. Time rolled over on itself. It might have been a moment or a half hour. Eventually there was the soft rustle of brush and hands shook his shoulder.

"Come, sir," Bulosan whispered close beside his ear. "We must go now, quickly."

They went.

The walls of the San Luis *bulwagan*, or saloon, were covered with mildew and rainwater streaks that had bled from the sandstone. The serving bar was made of planks placed on wooden barrels. Behind it were three shelves containing ceramic jars and long, slender bottles of coconut palm liquor. There were no tables, only benches against the walls, and the room had the sour odor of stale *tuba* and vomit.

Father Dobbenier sat on one of the benches. The Japanese had stripped off his clerical gown. His cotton undershirt was soaked with sweat and blood. They had beaten him with truncheons, and blood now ran from his nose and dripped off his broad, bruised chin.

Captain Sacabe smoked and walked about during the beatings. His boots squeaked and each time he turned, the metal fist strap of his sword pinged softly against the guard plate. He asked only three words in his garbled English: "Where is Dil-lon?" The priest had remained silent, his head down, the muscles of his neck and arms distended.

Now the officer waved off his marines. He asked his single question again. Still no answer. Impatiently, he shoved the lighted end of his cigarette into the priest's left eye, his arm moving quick as a snake. Dubbenier twisted his head and moaned deep in his throat. The stench of burned skin drifted up.

Sacabe turned and strode to the door. Parked in front of the *bulwagan* was a two-man Model 95 scout car, tiny as a Fiat with a canvas top and twin spare tires on the back. Behind it were three box-shaped Model 97 Nissan four-by-two cab-over-engine trucks. Seated in the coverless backs was a platoon of Japanese marines, the men idly watching the funeral rituals going on up the street.

He barked orders to them, and several men dismounted and, carrying two Model 99 7.7mm light machine guns and a case of extra clips, hurried into the saloon. They quickly set up the weapons, one in the doorway, the other at a window. The slam of the receiver bolts sounded loud in the stone room.

Sacabe walked back to Dobbenier. "I ask again, Frenchman. Where is Dil-lon?"

The priest had been staring at the machine-gunners, his expression shocked. Now his eyes swung to the Japanese officer, the burned one draining. "*Non, non, Capitaine,*" he cried. "You can not *do* this thing!"

"Where is Dil-*on*?"

"*Pitie! Mon Deux, pitie!*"

Sacabe cursed loudly and whirled around. He said something to the marine gunners. They leaned forward, aiming. A block away, the street was filled with milling people, lights, music.

"Stop!" Dobbenier blurted. "I will tell you. May dear God forgive my soul, I will tell you."

The officer held up his hand. The gunners eased back on their haunches, turned to watch. Sacabe swung back to the priest. "So?"

"The mission school," Dobbenier said. "He is at the mission school." He began to weep, his face contorted with agony, his large head shaking back and forth, and his eyes clamped shut as if he were hiding. Slowly he slid to his knees and began to pray in Latin: *"Dominus vobiscum et cum Spiritu tuo—"*

Sacabe drew his sidearm and shot him through the top of the head.

The guerilla force heard the screams and gunfire and the howling of the dogs. At the moment, they were at the mission school, the damp air drenched with the cloying stench of death.

It had been difficult reaching the site after leaving San Luis. Small Japanese units were all over the place, forcing them to move in jungle cover instead of using the roads, bringing the horses along. When they finally got there, they left the animals deeper in the jungle, on the mountain side, then set up a perimeter to check out the school building. It took several minutes to secure the area, make sure no Japs would ambush them coming in.

Hannon and Parnell entered the *bahai kubo.* It consisted of a single large room filled with little cushions and badly worn books scattered around the floor. There were two blackboards on one wall and the place smelled of wet *nipa* palms and chalk and the dusty odor of unwashed children. There was no sign of Dillon.

They listened to the distant growls and screams of the dogs until they slowly faded back into the rainy silence. Finally, Hannon said stiffly, "Those be tracker dogs. Obviously, they've found game."

Parnell grunted, agreeing to the obvious.

"Well, it won't take the brumbies long to sniff *us* out," Hannon said, studying the rainwater dripping off the roof. Abruptly, he turned and brusquely said, "Orright, Parnell, set up an ambush firebase here. If the Nips come down that road in force, hold off your fire until you can be certain of wiping out all the buggers quick. If it's only a small patrol, kill 'em with your knives.

"I'm taking four men and heading for the beach. It could have been Dillon those dogs just took. Or he may already be gone to sea. There's even a chance he didn't get *here* yet. Whatever the circumstance, we've got to find out if the Nips have him *alive.*"

"He could be *anywhere* along this coast."

"This was where the priest told him to come. If he *did* make it here and linked with this Bulosan, I'd expect they'd go straight for the coast. When I get there, I'll send out a couple of *mangs* to nose about a bit among the *pinoy.* They might pick up something on the teacher."

"What if the Japs *have* taken Dillon?"

Hannon looked at him from under the brim of his cocked hat. "Then I suppose we'll jus' bloody well have to go get him *back,* won't we?" he snapped. The sentence was not framed as a question.

He knelt down and withdrew a field map from his shirt pocket, spread it on the floor, checked his watch, and then put his flashlight onto the map. "It's twenty hundred now. If we're successful and find the bloke, we'll come back here. Give us two hours. If I want you to wait longer, I'll send a runner.

"Once I return, we'll split forces and withdraw to the southwest. That way's the closest jungle cover." He studied the map a moment longer, then placed the tip of one thick forefinger onto one of the mountain towns about four miles away. "We can rendezvous here, at Milinao. From there it's over the main range to link up with Yank units near Maqueda Bay."

"All right, sir."

"If I get into a firefight, you come up fast in support."

"What about recognition signals?"

Hannon shrugged. "*You* give it a go, use some'ing your chaps'll know."

"In Normandy we used small metal clickers. How about click-click for challenge and green for countersign?"

"Click-click an' green she is," Hannon said. He lifted his eyes and stared hard at Parnell. "One other thing, Leftenant. We will not, I repeat will *not*, withdraw from the area until we either *have* Dillon or are certain he's dead. Is that perfectly clear?"

Either have *Dillon or are certain he's dead*. Of course, Red thought. The XOX addenda: *if extraction of mission object impossible, kill him!* He nodded. "Perfectly clear, sir."

The Aussie flicked off the light, stood. "I'll leave Trota with you. He's the best scout we have, so pay attention to wot he says." He folded the map and replaced it into his shirt pocket. "I'll use two of your men. If we get into a stosh, I'll need their Thompsons."

"I'd prefer to go with you myself, Major."

Hannon shook his head. "No, we can't leave our cobbers without an officer."

"Every man in my team is capable of maintaining unity of command," Parnell said tersely. "Any time and under any conditions."

The Aussie looked at him in the dark. He chortled. "Well, now, dun't 'at sound all bloody confident?"

"I know my men . . . sir."

Hannon laughed again. "Well, you're *all* still bleedin' babes in the woods here, when you come down to it." He shrugged. "But wot the hell, why not? Orright, get your other man and your orders given. We'll head out in five."

Before they could start moving the boat, they had to empty it of the rainwater, using their hands, making cups, not able to simply turn the *banda* over because of the outriggers. Both men moved with anxious speed, aware of time slipping inexorably away.

They finally got it light enough. With one on each side of the hull, they began shoving it down the sloping beach, their feet digging into the packed sand. The beach here was about a hundred yards wide and etched with long, meandering rain-runoff streaks. At the edge of the water, the shore was indented by patches of rock and coral exposed in the low tide.

They kept at it, inching the heavy boat along, both men panting from its weight. Every few feet, Bulosan would dart back and brush out the tracks of the hull and the outrigger floats with a palm branch. It began to rain, sweeping in from the sea, the drops thundering on the sand.

Black plovers and shearwaters skittered ahead of them, squeaking, darting to and from the water as they hunted sand bugs pulled to the surface by the wavelets. The surf was small, little whitecapped lines that hissed as they came in and then slid up the incline of the beach. The wind fluttered the men's clothing. It was full of the salty tang of the sea.

Far down the beach, a torch suddenly appeared. Dillon cursed. They had a mere thirty more yards to reach the shallows. Bulosan squinted at the approaching light, the torch flame dancing and whipping in the wind.

"Can you see who it is?" Dillon asked tensely. "Japs?"

"I do not think so, sir." The Filipino held his fists to his eyes and looked through the tiny slits formed between his thumbs and forefingers to magnify the distant image of the torch carrier. After a moment, he said, "It is single *pinoy*, sir, walking high up on the beach."

Dillon considered that a moment. "When he gets closer, go up and meet him. Distract him, tell him you're going fishing."

"Yes, sir."

They watched the man draw closer. He came with his head down as if he were studying the ground. Soon, they could see him plainly, wearing a white sweatshirt and heavy, ankle-length trousers.

Bulosan made a snoring sound and swore: "*Sumpain!*

It is Romulo Pineda, the butcher man. Many suspect he is *makapili*."

A collaborator. Shit.

Pineda stopped abruptly, spotting the remnants of the hull's tracks. He turned and looked directly at them. After a moment, he started down the slope.

"Go, now," Dillon said softly. He lay down so the boat would hide him. "Bring him down here."

Bulosan rose and walked toward the approaching Pineda. They met halfway down the beach, greeting each other, then talking. Dillon listened to the exchange, catching a few words. Pineda was surprised to see the teacher here.

"You are fisherman now?" he said, laughing, Bulosan shrugging, saying the children no longer came to the mission school. A pity, Pineda said. Bulosan asked that he should come down and help him launch the *banda*; it would be such a fine gesture of friendship. Pineda refused, saying he was late for his cousin's funeral. He walked away and Bulosan came back to the boat.

"You fool," Dillon growled. "Why didn't you get him back here? We should have killed the son of a bitch."

Bulosan shook his head. "I am certain he did not see you, sir."

"Damn it, *damn it!*" Dillon hissed with frustration. "All right, then let's just get out."

Ten minutes later, the *banda* slid into the shallows.

As senior noncom, Bird had taken overall command of the guerilla force after the two officers left, Frankie Trota acting as his liaison with the *mangs*. The two men worked as a team, the little ex-boxer advising and instructing, Bird issuing the orders.

Although he was badly hampered by the lack of communications and was, in truth, leading a force that was inferior in firepower and strength to the Japanese, he managed to get adequate ambush positions set out along the inland side of the clearing according to standard U.S. Army strike-and-flee procedures.

As his firebase, he placed Fountain and Laguna with the Jap 7.7mm machine gun in the center of the perimeter, dug in just at the edge of the trees. This gave them a clear, sixty-degree field of fire that covered the entry road, the entire clearing, and the school. Strung out on their right flank in fire-support positions were Kaamanui and his *mangs* while Trota and the others were on their left.

After double-checking the line and issuing instructions to hold fire until Fountain opened with the Jap machine gun and to home to its tracers once he got started, Wyatt and Frankie returned to the two Blue Teamers. Bird squatted beside the weapon. "You boys figure out how to shoot this *Nambu* sumbitch yet?" he asked.

"Yeah, we got 'er," Cowboy said. "But I gotta tell you, Sarge, this is one real piece of *shit.*"

"Frankie says she'll cast eight hundred rounds a minute."

Laguna snorted derisively. "But I bet she gonna jam quick. Some of the components are made out of wood, for Chris' sake, fuckin' *wood.*"

Wyatt surveyed the road, white out there in the darkness. "Okay, here's the fire order," he said. "Don't open on anything comin' into that kill zone until we got the bastards by the short hairs. In case they spot us, bust 'em quick with sweeping fire."

Fountain said, "Ya know, they hear our Thompsons, ever' Jap in the whole goddamn area'll come a-runnin'."

Bird nodded. "That's right. So, soon's we take 'em out, we form up and head for the coast. Keep your *mangs* moving in normal covering withdrawal. Trota and his boys go first, then you, and finally Sol on security drag."

Cowboy shifted his hips, brushing mosquitoes from

before his face. He turned to Trota. "Hey, Frankie, your buddies say the rice-heads like to fight at night. Is 'at true?"

"Oh, yeah," Frankie answered. "Especially in bery beeg assault. Purse 'chu can hear *trumpetas* jus' before they are coming. Then one heavy folley gunpire and they coming straight at you. But all quick they *stop* shooting and coming with hand-to-hand. They like the bayonet."

"Do they call in artillery?" Wyatt asked.

"Sometimes, but no here. On Samar now is no more beeg guns. All gone Luzon."

"Good," Laguna said.

Wyatt said, "How do they deploy for attack?"

Frankie looked at him. "What means defloy?"

"How do they spread out when they come on?"

"Oh, sure. Purst they splitting up." He held up three extended fingers. "T'ree units. The one, he come straight at you. Shoot, shoot all his guns. Then he stop. The other units go both sides. Chu know, make like *carabao* horns?"

"They try to flank us."

"Yeah, yeah." Trota bobbed his head in agreement. Then he spread out his arms, indicating a sweeping movement. "You hear more *trompetas* and everybody comin' and comin' and then pretty quick *bang!* they all aroun' you. I tell you true, *meng*, chu no can let them come aroun' or you gonna be dead."

Bird grunted. They let a tiny moment of silence drift about. Then Wyatt looked over at Trota. "Yo'all better get back to your men, Frankie."

"Okay," Trota said. He rose and moved off, soundlessly disappearing into the jungle.

They settled in. Rain came suddenly, heavy drops hammering down through the leaves. It seemed to almost instantly wash away the foulness in the air, replacing it with the wet, rotting spoor of the jungle floor that rose like a plasma.

They huddled miserably there in the night, not bothering to talk. Around them the leaves and tree limbs and thick trunks became indistinct in the rain's fume. A bird called suddenly from farther back in the forest, the call like the popping of someone's palms. Down under the drumming and drip of the runoff, they could hear things slithering, crawling, skittering through the drenched brush.

Abruptly, the rain stopped. Now the air felt cool and slowly the foul stench returned, yet it now had a wet, fecund density to it. Wyatt looked out at the clearing. Cloud shadows suddenly began shifting across the roof of the school, across the ground around it. Then, in a single burst, moonlight flooded down out of the sky, the clouds opening completely for a few moments, then closing again only to reopen once more. He could actually see stars beyond the blue-white gloss of the just-past-full moon.

Once more he scanned the clearing, the rainwater pools now shining like free-form mirrors. Beyond, the edge of the jungle formed a solid black wall with only the tips of the trees catching the moonlight, and here and there where a coconut tree protruded above the others, its fronds glistened like big, phosphorescent feathers.

Wyatt's head suddenly snapped around. "Y'all hear that?" he snapped quietly.

"I di'n't hear nothin'," Weesay said. "What, you mean that bird?"

"No. Listen."

They leaned forward, turning their heads back and forth like antennas. Finally, very faintly, came the steady sound of engines, rising out of the night, then fading only to return stronger.

"Get ready, boys," Bird said. "Somebody's comin'."

Parnell knew combat was very close, somewhere out there in the darkness. He felt its presence, a gut feeling from combat instincts coming up. A knowing, a certainty.

He, Hannon, Smoker, and two *mangs* had reached the coastal forest now: stands of eucalyptus and small pinelike trees separated by sand clearings. The brisk sea wind passed through the branches and made pieces of peeling eucalyptus bark slap noisily. The ground was spongy from the rain, a thick cover of pine needles and bark brush. The moonlight came down cleanly, everything washed in blue white and shadow. It was like moving through a graveyard of tall monuments on a clear fall night.

They soon caught glimpses of the ocean. The moonlight flickered on the wavelets like hot spikes. Hannon called a halt beside a pine tree that smelled of cloves. He put his hand out, pressing down on the air, indicating they wait. Then, darting from tree to tree, he moved out to the edge of the beach and went to ground.

Beside Parnell, Smoker quietly slipped off his two Jap grenade pouches and laid them and the Arisaka rifle with its grenade launcher attached onto the sand. The two guerillas also had Japanese rifles and their bolos. They waited. The breeze made their wet clothing chill up.

Hannon returned, squatted next to Parnell. "I glassed the area but di'n't see a bloody thing. Damned coral heads out there all look like boats." He turned to the *mangs* and launched into rapid Tagalog. The two men listened, nodded, then rose and sprinted away, one to the south, the other to the north.

He returned to Parnell. "We'll check out the beach for signs a boat was recently dragged out. It's a long gamble but worth a shot. I'll take the south." He pointed to Smoker. "You, head north. Go out about three hundred meters. But stay in the bleedin' shadows. In this ruddy moonlight, you'll stand out like a fockin' pub sign."

"Yes, sir," Smoker said.

"Off wi' ya, then." Wineberg rose and moved away, bent low going through the dappled moonlight.

"You stay here, Lef-tenant," Hannon said. He reached

around to unclip his binocular case from his belt and handed it to him. "Keep glassing the area." Then he, too, was gone.

Parnell moved to the edge of the beach. Sand crabs skittered about, looking like big, black spiders. He lay down and took out the binoculars. Through the lens the moonlit ocean was as bright as a tabletop under a spotlight. It was so bright, in fact, it distorted the edges of the reef heads, made it difficult to judge whether they were exposed rocks, drifting flotsam, or a low-gunwaled boat.

He scanned twice, starting in the north and working down, then going back up again. Now he swept the beach itself, looking for moon shadows on imprints in the sand, which might indicate that a heavy boat had been moved there. The heavy rain had leached out the lighter top sand of the beach, exposing larger rocks and slivers of volcanic obsidian that sparkled like tiny jewels.

He found nothing.

Shivering in his wet clothing, he recased the binoculars. Damn, he hungered for a cigarette. He squinted out at the shimmering ocean and felt a wash of irritation. He was edgy, which was not his normal reaction to approaching battle. Usually, he went quiet inside, adjusting his mind and body and focus in preparation for the death and the killing.

Something was eating at him, had been for a while now. Ever since their ambush of that mountain village. What? Hell, it didn't take a lot of thinking to figure out. It was Hannon and his goddamned ragtag guerilla army. The whole thing made Red feel uncomfortable, antsy.

He didn't like turning over the leadership of his men to a strange, foreign officer who had merged them with what was essentially an untrained rabble, instead of letting them work *in cooperation* with the guerillas.

Guerillas? Shit, what an exaggeration. Fighters with bows and fucking arrows and handmade bullets and noise sticks instead of radios? And going at it without any coordinated or rehearsed plan of combat? No, that kind of inexperience created weak links in a fighting unit that put *everybody's* ass on the line.

Besides, *he* was Blue Team leader. These were *his* men, recon men who constituted the only recognized, independently operating unit in the whole goddamned United States Army. That's how they'd started and that's how they'd survived over two and a half years of war.

He sighed disgustedly. Damn, maybe he was placing too much of an ego spin on it. No, bullshit! His men were like kin to him, the only ones in the whole world he completely trusted in a fight. Now he was relinquishing their fate and his own to a man, good jungle fighter that he was, who didn't really *know* them.

With an effort, he refocused his mind back onto the ocean. The moon sent a dazzling track of light across its surface. Beyond its nearly round, white face, the brighter stars shone like tiny chips of ice. A fetching image, that, he thought. The South Pacific . . . Paradise. He chuckled. So far, it had turned out to be only a shit hole.

He breathed in, out.

The explosive crackle of a firefight erupted suddenly, cleaving through the night's silence. Distant, in the direction from which they'd come. First the chatter of a Jap 7.7, then the lower growl of Thompsons, the distance isolating each round *bam-bam-bam,* making the bursts sound dull and hammered and vaguely lethal. There was the double blow of a Jap grenade, then another.

Here we go.

Two minutes before, Wyatt had watched the small caravan of trucks filled with Japanese troops in dark uniforms and led by a tiny officer's car come up the coral road, their engines rattling, the sounds bouncing off the walls of jungle trees.

They stopped a hundred yards from the mission school and an officer got out and stood looking at the dark building. Then he walked back to the first truck and said something, his voice a sharp growling. A half dozen soldiers immediately dismounted, formed a spaced line, and advanced on the school. Their boots disturbed the rain pools, shattering them like stepped-on glass.

Bird cut his eyes back to the trucks. The soldiers were standing, their helmets and rifle muzzles glinting in the moonlight. He counted heads: forty, a total of forty-six plus the officer overall. More than twice his meager force. He felt a dryness in his mouth, the old, familiar prelude to a fight. He pressed his lips against his teeth, then ran his tongue over them, feeling the muscles of his body quieting, almost gently relaxing like an unclenching fist, readying, expectant.

A few feet away, Cowboy was hunkered down behind the Jap machine gun. A single shaft of moonlight like a blue-white flashlight beam came down through the leaves and imprinted a bright, round coin onto his shoulder.

The Jap soldiers reached the hut. Without pausing, they leaped up the steps and crashed through the door. The slam of it echoed through the clearing. In a moment, one soldier came out again. He whistled.

The officer barked more orders and the rest of the soldiers began to dismount. The officer turned and, strutting, started across the clearing. The haft of his sword caught moonlight, sparking like an electrical short each time his right hip swiveled as he walked.

Now, Wyatt thought.

He tapped Cowboy's shoulder, saw his own pale hand in the moonbeam for a second. "Hit 'em!" he cried in a harsh whisper.

The first sweep of the machine gun took out eight Jap

soldiers, other rounds slamming into the sides of the trucks, blowing tires. Tracers sketched sharp, hot, green lines across the clearing, some ricocheting in ninety-degree angles, going straight up. The soldiers who had already dismounted dropped to the ground and began returning fire. So did the ones in the school hut, their muzzle flashes like bursts of firecrackers, the reports crackling tinnily.

Bird was already firing his Thompson. As Cowboy finished his initial traverse, he stopped shooting. Smoke drifted off the hot barrel of the machine gun as Weesay leaned over it to pop out the empty quarter-moon-shaped clip and ram in another. By now, the entire guerilla line was firing. Inside their volley was the quick, light rap of Sol with the Jap Type 96 auto and the smaller *ping, ping* of Trota's carbine.

Wyatt's trigger went dead on an empty clip. He knelt, his head down, to reload. He heard the heavier crack of a grenade launcher. An instant later something thick crashed through the foliage and exploded somewhere behind him and to the right. He felt its concussion wave sweep past, making his ears hurt. A foam of smoke was sucked with it and he heard shrapnel slicing through the leaves.

A second grenade came hurtling across the clearing, this one angled to his left. It blew the eight-foot-wide trunk of a teak tree apart, sending slivers of bark and wood whirling overhead like knife blades.

"Move position!" Bird bellowed. "They're bracketing your gun."

Laguna and Fountain were already in motion, rolling to the left, crunching through underbrush. Wyatt charged his weapon and opened again, covering them. A few seconds later, he heard Cowboy banging away once more. He darted several yards to his right, fired another full burst, stopped to reload.

This time the crack of a grenade launcher came from

near him, one of Sol's men firing an Arisaka rifle. The missile went slashing across the clearing, crashed through the door of the hut, and exploded in a smoky, orange flash that sent up a coiling rush of smoke, debris, and water. The droplets sailing through the air looked like diamonds in the moonlight.

He lifted his head, peered through foliage. Ten Jap soldiers were coming right at his section, rushing where the machine gun position had been, firing and slamming their bolts back and forth in reload as they ran in that bowlegged monkey run, their bayonets forward, long black blades.

He threw a burst at them, the leaves in front of him whipping. Two men went down. Fountain opened up. His rounds swept the rest like a scythe, men dropping only feet from the edge of the jungle. The bullets continued slashing into them, made their uniforms flutter with the impacts.

Thick smoke swirled, stinking of cordite. Bird lifted higher, quick-scanned the clearing. There! He saw shadows running along the left edge of the trees. They moved like angry dwarfs, bobbing from side to side. He fired at them, hollering, "On the left. They're going for our flank." There was a pause and then Cowboy opened fire again, the green tracers hurtling across the clearing, knocking Japs off their feet.

The enemy's counterfire had diminished drastically, now only scattered shots coming, the muzzle flashes winking in the moon glow. The school hut had been set afire by Sol's grenade. Flames flicked through the window and sparks began lifting off the *nipa* roof, whirling and twisting upward like swarming fireflies.

Finally, all firing stopped. In the aftermath stillness, the crackling of the hut fire sounded like loud radio static. There was a single shot from the jungle's edge, another. Wyatt moved to his left until he reached the machine gun position. He squatted beside Laguna. The barrel of the weapon was so hot rainwater drops from the leaves sizzled and turned to steam when they hit it.

"Watch the perimeters," he snapped. "You see leaves movin', give 'em a burst."

"I think the bastards're reforming behind that hut," Weesay said.

"How many down?"

"Maybe half."

He started to move away, thinking: *Some of them musta broke and run.* He felt vaguely disappointed. Suddenly, guerillas began bursting from the edge of the clearing, yelling, hoarse, animal shouts, charging ahead into the open and waving their bolo knives. Weak, scattered counterfire came from the jungle on the other side and from two positions around the clearing. One *mang* tumbled over, sat up, and fell over again.

Three Jap soldiers were crouched beside the burning hut. They fired. Two then turned and ran off. The third man frantically tried to reload his weapon, but a guerilla was already on him. The Jap parried his thrust and the two men squared off, circling. The Jap jammed his bayonet at the guerilla, arms stiff, missed, and backed off. At that moment, another *mang* struck him with a bolo from behind. The blow completely decapitated the soldier. His head, with its helmet still on, rolled off into a rain pool.

Once more the firing stopped and the *mangs* prowled about the clearing, killing the wounded. Kaamanui abruptly pushed through the foliage like a dark bear emerging, his Thompson cocked in the crook of his huge right arm. Wyatt turned and looked at him. A moment later, Trota appeared, too.

"Gawddammit, Sol," Bird said. "Ya'll shouldn't've let those crazy bastards charge out there like that."

"They was gone before I realized it," Sol said.

Frankie said, "When my boys get mad they no can stop. Gotta cut, *meng*."

"How many we lose?"

"Two of mine," Sol said.

"Frankie?"

"Two."

"Get the rest back under cover. Them Nips're likely to come boilin' back any minute."

Frankie shook his head. "No, the *Hapones* gone deep. They gonna come, but maybe not till t'urdy minutes."

"You sure?"

"Yeah."

"Did anybody nail that officer?"

"I don't think so," Sol said. "The prick's lucky he di'n't get his fat ass blown off, struttin' around like he was."

"I seen he had a radioman," Wyatt said. "You can bet your ass he's right now callin' for reinforcements."

Sol nodded calmly. "So, I say we track 'em out and bang the little shits again," he said.

"I agree," Bird said. He put his hand on Trota's shoulder. "Frankie, we're gonna chase 'em down. I want your best tracker on point. We'll have to overtake them before they get to the coast."

Trota frowned. "What you sayin', *meng*? *I* am best tracker."

Bird grinned. "Okay, Ace. Let's get 'er rollin'."

The quickly formed up, Frankie already out front a hundred yards, the rest in staggered column reentering the jungle on the eastern side of the clearing, the men doubletiming it. Crossing past the hissing flames of the hut fire, their flickering, elongated shadows had been thrown onto the trees, looking like a dark company of primeval hunters following quarry.

Smoker was about a 150 yards from Parnell when he heard the firefight back at the mission school. He recognized the heavy rap of Thompsons, Blue Team and the guerillas engaging.

He paused for a moment to listen. As always when he was

moving through enemy country, all his senses were tuned to a fine edge. He'd always liked that ringing feeling. It gave him a tremendous sense of being fully alive. Now he relished the chill of the wind on his clothing, deeply inhaled the sweet smell of cloves off the trees, luxuriated in the intense blue-white brightness of the moonlight.

He moved ahead again, darting from shadow to shadow. The small pines looked like dark, spindly Christmas trees. They reminded him of those he'd seen in Salvation Army missions back in the States, raggedy little things without lights and odd, crudely cut tin stars for decoration, set up in dirty-walled corners in those shabby, Christmas Eve dining halls that always stank of garbage and candle smoke.

He stopped, listening intently. Was that an engine? He slipped to the edge of the tree line and looked out. Reef surf grumbled wetly in the distance. The engine sound came again on a gust of wind. It was turning over at high speed.

Then he picked up another, softer sound: the metallic jingle and clatter of equipment, the muffled pound of boots. He leaned out beyond the trees and looked up the beach. There was movement up there but he couldn't quite make out exactly what it was.

The engine sound rose, nearing. Under it now came the pop and slam of a boat's hull. He squinted, looking northeast, and finally caught sight of a moving strip of white water out beyond the far reef line. A bow wave. It was a patrol boat.

A brilliant shaft of yellow light suddenly appeared from the vessel. For a moment, it swung high, a hollow tube hazy with salt mist, then lowered and began traversing back and forth, searching.

Smoker looked back up the beach. *Goddamn.* His blood bolted in his chest. There, running on the hard-packed sand near the water's edge, was a company of Japanese soldiers. He turned and darted away, headed for Parnell.

* * *

Senior Lieutenant Yasio Sacabe could not contain his rage at being ambushed by filthy *hafu* firing Japanese guns. Unforgivable. In the first volley, he had hit the ground like a rock, got his uniform all muddy. He crawled to one of the trucks and sat behind a tire that was warm from the coral road and began screaming out orders.

A marine darted close by him. He violently cuffed the man, cursed him, out of pure frustration. These men weren't responding to his commands quickly enough. *Kuso, garakuta!* Very poor quality soldiers, most newly assigned from duty as guards at *turyo-shuyojo*, prisoner-of-war camps, on Luzon. They were like *jiji*, fucking old men, slow to react. Not like his young and courageous *Teishin-dan* Raiders from the China and Malaysian days.

He came to his feet and strode out beyond the truck, defying the bullets that streaked across the clearing. The vehicle's radiator suddenly blew off steam as a round struck it. He looked to his left, toward the school, his men lying out there in pools of rainwater. A haiku image: turmoil and moon. He turned the other way, men now moving, hunched over, running, shooting. *Tsui ni*, at last. They were cut down like blades of grain.

A grenade exploded in the school hut. A fraction of a second later a piece of bamboo speared itself into the side of the truck fender a few feet from Sacabe. Turning about, he caught sight of his radio operator, a *heicho*, or lance corporal. He lay beside the command car, his small, two-watt Model 97/T-3B portable walkie-talkie-type transceiver in a canvas pack on his chest. Cowering beside him was his battery man, a young, boyish-looking *nitohei*, or private.

Sacabe strode over to them and viciously kicked the corporal's leg. The man was dead, blood all over his face. He grabbed the private's helmet strap and jerked him upright so he could shout an order directly into his face. The young man quickly took off his back battery pack, plugged its twin power cables into the walkie-talkie transceiver, and pulled out its short dipole antenna.

The officer took the phonelike radio mike, keyed: "*K T san-mittsu Denshin, onshitsu hitotsu-no.*" A spray of bullets hurled a line of mud eruptions nearby. He ignored them, continued repeating his call sign and that of the the 33rd Engineer's intelligence section radio unit located in San Luis.

A blast of static blew through the small speaker; then the *tokushu musentai's* operator came back with receipt of signal. Sacabe gave him his location and ordered immediate reinforcements. The operator instructed him to hold.

He waited. Ten seconds, fifteen. The radio crackled and sputtered, losing its setting. Like all Japanese radio gear, it had no frequency amplification, merely simple Hartley oscillator circuits that did not possess frequency stability. Twice he had to regain the proper setting.

An intelligence night-duty officer abruptly came on: "Greenhouse 3, repeat your location, *suru.*"

Sacabe keyed: "Mission school south your position, *suru.*"

"Be advised fugitive enemy agent found east you. Break off engagement and proceed to coast, *suru.*"

Dil-lon!

He keyed. "Acknowledge message. Greenhouse 3 terminating transmission." He tossed the mike aside and began bellowing orders.

Sacabe could feel his blood boiling in his veins. Ancient ancestors, samurai come to plunge him on. He had felt these exquisite forces in the past, in other engagements, and they had infused him with a killing power born of his Japaneseness. A sense of pure glory like a fiery red spirit in his soul.

Using the fire's billowing clouds, which had begun to blot out portions of the clearing, he managed to assemble his remaining men inside the trees at the opposite edge. There were twenty troopers. He called for his non-coms. One appeared from the flickering orange shadows, a *gunso*, or senior sergeant. Sacabe quickly issued his up-dated orders.

A point man was sent out and the rest of the force quickly formed up into a double line, the officer in the lead. Literally running, even those who had been wounded, they quickly disappeared deeper into the forest, going for the coast.

The moment Dillon heard the patrol boat coming, he knew it was over. They were trapped! For a moment, he just sat there on the narrow *banda* seat and stared off in the direction of the engine sound.

They had already worked their way about three hundred yards off the beach, moving through narrow reef channels in the low tide, following shallow sand bottoms that gleamed palely through the water. Small surf hissed and tumbled on both sides of the boat as they paddled.

Bulosan had told him he intended to set the mast and sail as soon as they crossed through the main channel and were into deep water, out where the wind would be free of the tricky turbulences created by the land mass. Now it no longer mattered.

He heard the firing from somewhere inland come cutting through the wind. For a moment, it sent a surge of hope through him. Could guerillas be nearby, come to rescue him? No. It was simply the Japanese killing more people in their search for him. That desperate, bone-chilling sense of isolation and helpless guilt returned to his mind. It was then that the patrol boat's searchlight flicked on and began its sweeps.

At the stern, Bulosan froze in place, his paddle abruptly poised, looking like a startled gandola man with his pole.

The two looked at each other in the moonlight. Then the Filipino broke into frantic action, leaning way to the left and pulling heavily with the paddle head, trying to swing the stern of the boat around.

"Turn, sir, turn!" he cried. "We must go back!"

Dillon roused himself and began paddling desperately. The *banda* came around sluggishly, then straightened and leaped ahead. A layer of black reef appeared just beyond the bow. Dillon called a warning. Busolan got the bow turned enough to slide past it, but the left outrigger float crashed into the rock. Bamboo struts splintered and part of the float tore loose, dragging.

They continued on lopsidedly. Above the churning rustle of the surf, they suddenly heard a voice shouting in Japanese. Two searchlights came on from up the beach. The beams crossed each other like sword blades, then swung out to the reef and came sweeping toward the *banda.*

My God, my God.

The lights found them, the little boat suddenly lit up like a stage. The brightness cast their shadows and those of the bow and stern out across the water. Dillon felt his body go tundra cold. He dropped to the bottom and lay pressed flat, his heart racing crazily. Forward of him, Busolan yelled something. A prayer? A curse? Then he was gone, over the side.

A machine gun opened from the beach. Green tracers went slamming overhead, shattering the air with loud cracks. They struck the ocean a hundred yards beyond, heaving up chunks of reef and tall white geysers in the surf.

Panic overwhelmed Dillon's mind. He panted with terror. *Dear Jesus in heaven, they'll torture me!* His days and nights of constant fear, the soul-searing fatigue, the fleeing like a hunted, wounded animal suddenly overwhelmed him. He began to sob without sound, his body convulsing as if caught in an uncontrolled spasm of vomiting. Near his head, the searchlight beams played across the low gunwales. He lifted his head. Another burst of bullets went slashing past.

He dropped down. The water in the bottom submerged his cheek, rising and falling as the *banda* rolled gently in the wave surge. The water danced with reflected light. He stared at it. He smelled its fishy odor, watched the sheen of its surface folding back and forth on itself. He touched it, felt its softness, the warm liquidity of it, suddenly so comforting, enfolding.

Like a womb . . . Water and flesh . . . Life and death . . .

He sensed his panic begin to dissolve. He knew what he had to do. Once his decision was made, it brought a strengthening calmness. And from its depths was evoked a slow, poignant mental montage of faces and voices from his past, the sudden remembrance of those deep, rich colors and sounds and smells of his life brought forth now, right here in this moment, and recalled with the purity and intensity of a man experiencing them for the *first* and the *last* time.

Slowly, like fading sunlight, they vanished. He took out his pistol and checked its safety, feeling the solid, *real* weight of the weapon in his hand. For a moment, he continued lying there, letting the strange calmness engulf him, quieting his heart.

At last, he stood up, turned to look directly into the lights, which were closer now, twin circles of yellow white, jiggling with motion. He had to squint against the glare. Beyond it, he saw faces and arms moving, shiny in the water. Swimmers approaching. He lifted his arm and fired, the gun jumping in his hand. The spent casing sailed away through the light, shining.

One round. He fired again. *Two.* And again. *Three.*

Don't lose count, he gently cautioned himself.

* * *

Major Hannon came pounding through the moon shadows and slid in beside Parnell on his knees, panting heavily. "Glasses," he growled. "The bloody glasses."

Parnell handed them over. He had been watching intently, swinging the binoculars from the man in the boat to the approaching Jap troopers to the patrol boat, all the time knowing, sure as hell, that that white man out there was Dillon. And the poor son of a bitch was about to be had.

That thought created an immense anger in him for a moment. It had been so goddamned close. So, what now? *We'll just bloody well go get him.* Not likely, he knew, not with only a handful of men. Was it over now? *No, not quite yet.*

He turned and looked at Wineberg, saw he was looking back at him. He knew, too. Smoker had returned forty seconds before the Aussie major, giving the click-click password and getting the countersign, coming in to quietly inform him, "We jes' got ourselves a big problem, Lieutenant."

Suddenly, he heard the low, solid report of a Hi-Power 9mm. Again and then again. His head swung around. In the convergence of the searchlights, he saw the man in the boat firing, methodically pulling off his shots as if he were merely at a Saturday afternoon firing range knocking over targets.

Red made a sound in his throat, a surprised realization. Dillon was deliberately exposing himself. He *wanted* the Japs to kill him.

But the Nip soldiers had stopped firing completely by now. More men were plunging into the water, their weapons and harnesses left back on the shore, others wading through the shallows or leaping from coral head to coral head. Outside the reef, the patrol boat had hove to and its light was now hunting for a clear channel to enter.

Hannon lowered his binoculars, sucked spit through his

teeth, sighing heavily. "It's him, orright," he said. "It's bleedin' Dillon. They've got him."

"He's deliberately trying to draw fire," Parnell said.

"Aye. But they won't kill him. Not yet, anyway."

Parnell turned to look up the beach again. Several Japanese soldiers were very close to the *banda* now, which drifted about two hundred yards off the beach. He saw Dillon fire into the group. One man jerked in the water, the impact of the round making an audible wet, slapping sound.

Hannon said, "Gimme your Thompson."

"What?"

"Your goddamn Thompson, give it here."

Parnell handed it to him. The Aussie checked it, then rose on one knee. He rested the weapon's butt into his shoulder, aimed, and fired a burst. A line of geysers erupted among the soldiers swimming near the boat. Dillon's head came up, the Jap soldiers turning to look, their faces white in the lights.

Before Hannon's burst had gone out, Parnell was already moving, lunging for the Arisaka rifle that Smoker had rested nearby on the grenade pouches. In a loud whisper, he said to Wineberg, "Get set to lay in cover fire."

Hannon cursed and took aim again, raising the barrel of the Thompson. A heavy volley of fire came from the shoreline, the snapping patter of rifle reports and the quick chatter of a machine gun. Bullets slashed through the trees, cracking branches. Red felt the slugs sizzle by so close above him he could feel the heat of their passage. Around him, small spouts were thrown up out of the sandy ground.

He saw Hannon get hit, his body flung backward and to the ground with his thick legs twisted under him. The Aussie gasped, a hard, grunting intake, and then there was a gurgling sound. He crawled over to him. Blood oozed up through the major's shirt. It made a tiny, fizzy sound, his lungs punctured, collapsing.

Parnell put his palm over the wounds, felt the blood hot as fresh urine, glistening blackly in the smoky moonlight. As the first Jap volley slowed, from somewhere close on the left, Smoker opened up.

"Kill 'im!" Hannon croaked. His eyes quivered violently, rolling back, then forward again. He gasped twice more, trying desperately to grab air. "Chroist . . . don' let . . . take 'im." He went into a violent spasm, his back arching, his twisted legs shaking violently. Blood squirted out of him. Then he fell back, gasped again, and stopped moving.

Parnell grabbed the barrel of the Thompson and pulled it free of Hannon's body, the metal still hot. Its butt and receiver had been blown apart. He cursed, twisted, and crawled back to the rifle and grenade pouches.

Working with precise speed, his mind coolly blotting out the sounds coming from the beach, he opened a pouch and took out a grenade. It was nine inches long, a hollow-charge AP fragmentation projectile shaped like a pipe with a cone head and a narrower, rifled stern. He pulled the safety pin, then jammed the grenade into the rifle's receiver cup and locked it in.

Coming to one knee, he ejected the bullet already in the rifle's chamber and bent close to check the slug head on the next one coming up, to make certain it was a grenade round with its slug-head made of wood. It was. He rammed it home, lifted the rifle, and sighted down through the muzzle's attachment ring to the rifle's sight.

Smoker had momentarily stopped firing. Now he opened up again, from another position. A fresh volley of counterfire came blowing back through the trees.

The three prongs of the sight bracketed Dillon's frame far out there. He was looking toward the beach, perfectly still, his arms down. *Waiting.* Parnell lifted the sights above him. Earlier, Hannon had told him the on-target range of a Jap Model 100 cup launcher was a hundred yards. He quickly estimated his trajectory line and fired.

The grenade rocketed away, trailing a thin line of smoke, its fuze making a tiny white dot on the stern. It arched upward, reached apex, and started down. It struck Dillon full in the chest, the tremendous weight and force of it throwing him clear out of the *banda*. A fume of blood exploded from his chest as he somersaulted through the air, then disappeared beyond the boat. A millisecond later, the grenade blew up, throwing up a tall geyser of water and reef and parts of Dillon and the outrigger and boat hull.

Parnell didn't stop to look further. He felt nothing. There wasn't time for emotion or morality. He rammed in a second grenade, jacked up another round, and fired at the Jap soldiers coming up the slope of the beach. Then rapidly a third and a fourth. His ears rang from the hard discharges of the launching rounds' propellants.

Smoker suddenly emerged out of the shadows, running close to the ground. Red waved him on. "Go! Go!" Wineberg dashed by.

He fired off another grenade. Out in the water, soldiers were frantically trying to return to the shore and their weapons. The others kept up a rolling volley, bullets making a near constant rushing sound in the trees. Then it slowed a little, picked up only to slow again.

Parnell shot one more grenade, twisted to grab up the grenade pouches, and broke into a sprint, going inland full out, his legs reaching and pulling through the dappled, smoky moonlight.

Blue Team and the *mangs* caught up to the moving Jap force a half mile from the coast, emerging from regular jungle into the stands of eucalyptus and pine trees. Firing had suddenly exploded out on the shoreline, sounding very close.

On point, Trota had trailed the last man in the enemy

column, drawing closer to him. He was very thin, puffing from the run, his head down and his rifle at high port. As they passed through a dense patch of moon shadow, Trota spurted ahead, leaped onto the soldier's back, and sank his belt knife deep into his neck. The Jap stumbled and went down, Frankie still on him, stabbing him repeatedly. The soldier died without making a sound. Afterward, Trota sat on the corpse and waited until the rest of the trailing force came up.

Moving side by side through the moonlight, Bird and Kaamanui discussed the best way to attack the Jap column, Sol saying, "They're strung out like goddamned heifers goin' to barn. If we got enough room, we could take 'em one at a time."

Wyatt considered, shook his head. "Too close to them sons a' bitches on the beach. An' there's too goddamned much light to get close in. We'll hit 'em all at once, one team up the bunghole, two on the flanks."

"Okay," Sol said.

They hurriedly maneuvered in a fan formation, Wyatt and Kaamanui pointing out men and signaling silent orders until the group was adequately split into three six-man teams. Sol and Weesay led the flankers out, sprinting away on the soft ground. Bird, now carrying the Jap 7.7, and his team continued straight ahead, their target the rear of the column.

They quickly closed with the Jap troopers.

Wyatt's first burst killed the last four in the column. The others wheeled about, dropped to the ground, and began firing back. When the two flanker teams opened up, it seemed to momentarily confuse the Nips and their counterfire tapered off.

Then, lunging to his feet, the Jap officer starting running among his men, bellowing orders. Half the enemy soldiers rose with him and quickly withdrew toward the shore. One took a bullet and tumbled away. Those still remaining shifted around, setting up a small defensive firebase, all the time jabbering back and forth to each other.

Holding the Jap machine gun by its carrying handle and trigger grip, Bird poured a fresh stream of rounds into the firebase, using a concentrated fire pattern. The machine gun bucked and bounced in recoil and heat came pouring off its barrel. Gun smoke drifted through the blue-white light, making small, transient moonbows. His clip went empty. He popped it out, rammed in another, and opened again.

Now all three teams charged right at the dwindled Jap defensive position, going in with bolos and handguns. Two of the Japs tried to run. They were shot down. It took just forty-two seconds to secure the position.

The firing from the coast came in waves now, wild volleys, then silences. Now and then a grenade went off, the hard, tight explosiveness of it riding to them on the sea wind. Wyatt listened to the bursts, thinking, *Those're frag grenades.*

He blinked slowly, feeling his body thrumming with adrenaline. Still listening, he caught now the clear, low rap of a Thompson. He waited. Only one? Somewhere out there, either the lieutenant, Smoker, or the Aussie major was pinned down. Maybe all three, some wounded.

He broke into a run, waving his arms and calling out, "Keep going for the beach! Maintain the formation."

They raced on.

Parnell and Wineberg were eating up ground, leapfrogging and covering each other every twenty yards with Japanese bullets zinging past. Suddenly, a crashing volley came from *inland*, close enough for them to recognize Blue Team weapons working.

Parnell paused, then hissed, "Hold." He moved up to Smoker, who was down on one knee, his crazy, combat grin white in the moonlight. "Wyatt's engaging and coming this way," Red said. "We're in between lines."

Wineberg jerked his head toward the new firefight. "Let's jes' bust through that one, catch the sumbitches between *us*."

"Too risky. We'd be shooting at each other." He scanned the surrounding forest, looking for a place to go to ground. Too much light. Lots of shadows but the floor was too flat, held no decent cover. He lifted his eyes. *Yeah, good.*

"Up," he said. "Into the trees."

It was a bitch shinnying up the eucalyptus Parnell chose, the bark smooth and peeling, a soft gray color in the moonlight. The Jap rifle, without a strap, was too cumbersome. He dumped it. Soon his hands were sticky with gum resin, smelling like camphor. The tree itself was about seventy feet high. He reached a thick branch cluster, the leaves narrow as double knife blades, and pressed himself tightly against the narrow trunk.

A full minute passed. He heard the soft thudding of boots on the forest floor. Shadows appeared, coming in from the inland side of the forest, men running in a double column. He tried to count them. Eight? Ten?

He caught the glint of an officer's saber, then the duller sheen from his jungle cork hat. He watched the squad cross directly under him, the men running wordlessly but panting. The firing from Blue Team had stopped now.

Then a new, lighter volley of Japanese fire rolled through the trees. The passing Japanese officer and his men hit the ground. They lay very still on the bright ground until the firing tapered off. The officer gave a command. Two men rose and ran on toward the beach. A moment later, the officer and the rest of the men got up and moved after them.

As the sound of their boots faded, Parnell and Smoker dropped back to the forest floor and went on, going straight out now, no leapfrogging, Red trying to mentally estimate how far away the sounds of Bird's weapons had been. A half mile? Closer? Every now and then, they'd hold up to listen.

In one of the pauses, they picked up the single slam of

a rifle bolt, its metallic crack sharp and piercing through the stillness under the trees, all Japanese firing gone now. They dropped down, crab-crawled to a thicket of pine trees, and went motionless.

A figure emerged from the shadows, short, running in that bowlegged, monkey fashion of the Nips. They let him pass thirty yards to their left. Then came the muffled sound of boots and naked feet slapping in the leaves and pine needles, approaching. A few moments later, three men appeared, moving fast.

As one darted through a bright patch of moonlight, Parnell recognized the silhouette of his battle blouse, sleeves rolled, boonie hat on his head. *American.* He immediately called softly, "Click, click."

The man dropped to the ground.

Red called again, "Click, goddamn *click.*"

The countersign returned, "Green, green."

It was Weesay, the stocky Mexican coming in, saying, "God *damn,* Lieutenant. We thought you all was dead."

"Where's Wyatt?"

"Comin' up."

Parnell gave a whistle: *Blue Team converge on me.* Again. More men fused out of the shadows, quickly gathered around them. Their weapons held the smell of warm metal, cordite.

Bird said, "We di'n't think ya'll was gonna make it, Lieutenant. The major gone?"

"Yeah. Dillon, too. Blue Team intact?"

"Yes, sir. Lost five Filipino boys, though."

"There's at least a company of rice-heads right on our tail. Where's Trota?"

"On point," Wyatt said.

"Damn it."

At that moment, Frankie came sprinting back. He stopped short, seeing the group of men, then quickly came over. He didn't notice Parnell. "Wy-att," he said, "flenty *Japones* comin' this way, *meng.*"

Parnell said, "Trota, I want you to scatter your guerillas. Tell them to lose themselves in the villages. We'll move faster without them."

The little Filipino's head snapped around. "What, the lieutenant back?"

"Yes, it's me. Do you understand?"

"Yes, sor."

"You stay with us."

"Sure, sor."

Trota relayed Parnell's instructions to the *mangs* standing nearby. The men listened, then instantly shouldered their weapons and departed, moving off in a direction parallel to the coast.

"Okay," Red said, "let's get the fuck outta here."

Frankie first took them to the south, angling away from the incoming Japanese troops, the team moving in bounding overwatch-extraction formation, Trota and Bird on point, Parnell, Kaamanui, and Cowboy in the center, Weesay and Smoker on drag. When they reached monsoon jungle again, they broke formation and traveled in column.

They passed through the Japanese aid station compound, Frankie saying that the other *Japones* would not set foot in this place. The air was so thick with foulness the men moved with their heads down, trying not to breathe too deeply lest the evil stench of it infest their lungs.

The station huts looked like the large spires of Siamese temples in the moonlight. The Japanese wounded moved within, silhouetted against the opposite wash of light, peering out like half creatures, crawling, dragging themselves to watch as these night strangers traversed their malodorous grounds. They made neither sound nor protest.

Beyond the station, Trota turned them northwest so they would cross near the mission school to retrieve their horses. Japanese voices came from the school clearing as they crept soundlessly past it.

The horses were quietly munching vegetation when they came near, then lifted their heads as they became aware of the humans' approach, snorting and moving restlessly against their hackamores.

The men doubled up on three of the animals, Frankie mounting one alone as the forward scout. Now they headed due west, moving steadily and as rapidly as the thickening jungle permitted. The moonlight was gone beneath, absorbed by the upper layers of the trees. They had to close up tightly, following the dark hindquarters of the animal ahead. The rains returned.

In the higher foothills they left the horses and continued on foot, hour after hour of belly-sickening climbs up steep precipices, slipping and sliding in ravines thundering with the rush of swollen streams. Daylight came and went and came again. They eventually reached the main cordillera of the Sohoton Range, foggy, windswept needle ridges where they had to inch along with their legs straddling the crests.

Beyond them, they finally descended into the rice shelves of the western highlands. Spread out before them was western Samar. They could see American screening corvettes and Liberty and Victory ships anchored off the shores of Carigara Bay, having run the narrow San Juanico Strait between Samar and northern Leyte.

Late that afternoon, they made contact with a probing patrol from 2nd Battalion, 24th Infantry Division just east of the Calbayog-Catbalogan Highway.

Chapter Seven

The drive to Manila City by General Kreuger's Sixth Army had stalled by late January, its forward elements reaching only as far as the town of San Fernando, thirty miles north of the capital on Manila Highway 3.

MacArthur continued growing more anxious about the POW situation. He felt Kreuger had shown insufficient initiative in the advance, particularly with his XIV Corps, commanded by the extremely popular Major General O.W. Griswold. But Kreuger had a good reason for the slowness of his thrust. Although Yamashita's forces had not attacked his front in division strength, they continually destroyed bridges and roadways ahead of it. Badly short of engineers and construction equipment to repair the damage quickly, Kreuger and his field commanders had no alternative but to move slowly.

Then the Mike VII landings at Zambales Province on 29 January brought him fresh reinforcements and new bridging equipment. Thus rearmed, he immediately issued new, specific battle orders to his field commanders that they were to commence an aggressive advance at dawn of 1 February, scheduled to put them across the Pampanga River within two days.

He directed I Corps to take Nueva Ecija, an important

road and rail center on his left flank. XI Corps, which had just landed at Zambales, would merge with XIV Corps at Dinalupion on the flank of the Bataan Peninsula and together execute a concerted push for the northern shore of Manila Bay. His 1st Cavalry Division, coordinating with the 44th Tank Battalion and Marine Corps fighters flying air-support fire missions, would form the spearhead of the new dash for Manila City.

Meanwhile, changes that would result in tragic consequences had already occurred within the capital. General Yamashita had never intended to defend Manila. In fact in mid-January, he'd set up his new headquarters in the old mountain resort town of Baguio and had begun withdrawing the bulk of his troops, leaving only a small defense force in the capital to maintain order, protect his supply shipments, and carry out demolitions of bridges and roads before the Americans arrived.

Unfortunately, things wouldn't work out his way. As his army left, the Japanese Navy moved into their evacuated areas. Earlier in December, senior admirals of the Japanese Southwest Area Fleet Command had decided to reinforce their defenses in Manila Harbor and within the city itself. To accomplish this task, they assigned Rear Admiral Sanji Iwabachi and his 31st Special Naval Base Force, which comprised a sixteen-thousand-man contingent of Imperial Marines. He was ordered to hold the city to the last man.

As in most navies, the officers of the Imperial Fleet had always considered themselves far superior to those of the Imperial Army. They were arrogant, even contemptuous of their counterpart military force. The army felt the same way about them. Because of this bitter rivalry, neither service branch ever fully cooperated with the other to create a solid unity of command during field campaigns.

So, when the navy marines came into Manila, word of their moves would not reach General Yamashita, despite the fact that he was the supreme commander of the entire

Philippine campaign, until the morning of 15 February. Outraged at this insult, he would immediately invoke his full authority and order the withdrawal of *all* forces from the capital. But by then it would be too late.

The first American troopers to enter the city would be elements of the 11th Airborne and the First Cavalry Divisions at 1835 hours of 3 February 1945. Quickly securing Santo Tomas University, Malacanan Palace, and the notorious Bilibid Prison, they would liberate over ten thousand civilian POWs, the very ones who had been MacArthur's greatest concern.

Still, it would take an entire month of vicious house-to-house and hand-to-hand fighting before Iwabachi's marines were totally wiped out. The battle would leave the city, which many had viewed as the most beautiful in the Orient, in ruins worse than those of Cologne, Hamburg, or London.

Although the Manila prisoners were now safe, numerous other internment camps with both civilian and military personnel still existed all over Luzon. At some, the slaughtering had already begun. Every day prisoners were being machine-gunned or forced into trenches that were then drenched with high-octane gasoline and ignited. Others were beheaded or beaten to death with stones. Some, out of sheer savagery, were blinded by acid, then released into the jungle to wander until they died.

One of these prison encampments was in a gold mine compound high in the eastern mountains of the Cordillera Central near the town of Magsaysay in northern Luzon. Before the war, it had been owned by an Australian company named Tallangatta Consolidated Goldfields, which had several mines in operation on Luzon, Mindoro, and Mindanao. This site was designated Lode Pit number 4.

The Philippines are rich in minerals: zinc, copper, silver, aluminum, gold, both placer and deep-vein deposits. In prewar years, more gold had been taken from sites all through the islands than the total extracted in California during the gold rush of 1849.

For a full year after the Japanese invaded, LP-4 had continued operations, its chief supervisor, a geological engineer named Tyrus Halperan, who optimistically believed the Allies would quickly dislodge the Jap troops. In his warehouse, he had eight million dollars in gold concentrate, part of which had been on hand when the war started.

One evening in early December, he was told that Japanese troops had been spotted in Magsaysay. He immediately disbanded his workforce and, totally alone, disposed of the gold so it wouldn't fall into enemy hands. Before he himself could flee, however, they overran the compound and took him prisoner.

Finding papers that indicated who he was, they forced him to restart digging operations. To do so, they supplied him with prisoners from the notorious Camp O'Donnel and Cabanatuan internment stockades to work the mine's quartz drifts and processing sheds.

From recent air-recon photos, many of these prisoners were still alive. How many? Nobody knew for sure. But whatever their number, these were the ones Blue Team had been brought to the Philippines to liberate.

Forward Training Camp Hannon
Cabogan Chico, Leyte
4 February 1945

They were talking about cities, Wineberg, Fountain, and Laguna in their *nipa* hut, the time nearly midnight.

All day they'd been out on jungle exercises. Now, before a few hours of sleep, they were cleaning weapons, checking each other for leeches, and burning off typhus ticks from their skin with lit cigarettes, all three in jungle scivvies, their bodies combat-lean and yellowed from their daily pills of the new anti-malarial drug Chloroquine.

Lieutenant Parnell, Bird, Kaamanui, and Frankie Trota were over at the camp's headquarters, meeting with the new training officer, Hannon's replacement, another Aussie major named Kepner who had come in by PT boat an hour earlier.

Completing the cleaning of his Thompson, Cowboy flipped the weapon around and laid it on his bunk, saying, "San Antone ain't too bad. Pretty classy, in fact. I went out there once to pick up some stock horses." He shook his head, chuckling. "Got my ass whupped, though."

"Yeah?" Weesay said. "How was 'at? Chu put the slippery noodle to somebody's *puta*?"

"Hell, I was jes' *flirtin'* with the little lady. But, *damn*, these three Texas bush-poppers like to got all agitated. They jumped me in an alley an' one sumbitch hit me with a bottle. I finally woke up in the Bexar County Jailhouse 'thout any of my gear. They even impounded my *horses*, for God's sake. Never *did* see them mounts again."

A tiny rabble of flying beetles thudded and clacked against the smoke-stained glass of a pair of kerosene lamps. The single room was scattered with muddy gear and stank of stale sweat and the incenselike odor from coils of mosquito punks, which seeped smoke from three chewing tobacco cans.

Despite their light, aimless conversation, the men had about them a deep-worn look, in their moves, their eyes, like football players at halftime in a losing game. Even Smoker, with his usual energy and aura of potential violence, seemed subdued.

"Hell," he said now quietly, "y'all ain't tasted real Texas hospitality till you been on a Lubbock County chain gang in August."

"Lubbock?" Cowboy said. "I had me a cousin lived in Odessa once."

Wineberg snorted. "First time I seen that goddamned

country down 'ere, I shoulda knowed it wan't no place to get drunked up in and rowdy. All them fuckin' West Texas towns got more *churches* than saloons."

"Yeah, I remember that," Cowboy agreed. "All of a sudden, you come onto these clusters of steeples jes' settin' out there on the flatland."

"That was the las' time I was *in* Texas," Smoker said. "An' I ain't got no inkling to go back."

After their linkup with American forces, Blue Team and Frankie Trota had undergone a complete debriefing by intelligence officers of the 37th Division at their regimental headquarters in the seaside town of San Fabian at the base of the Lingayen Gulf.

Afterward, Parnell had requested that Trota be allowed to remain with him and his men, possibly to accompany them during their coming operation somewhere in northern Luzon. The little Filipino's jungle savvy would be a valuable asset, he had pointed out.

The intelligence officers knew nothing of Blue Team's mission, didn't really give a shit about it. But they did agree that whatever it was, Trota would indeed be useful. In order to cut through the normal boondoggle of paperwork, however, they had to dip and dodge a bit. They first inducted Frankie into the U.S. Army right on the spot, even gave him the rank of corporal and officially entered him in the unit P&P roster for B Company, Second Battalion, 37th Infantry Division, detached for special duty.

Soon after, the entire team was issued new jungle camo battle clothing, underwear, utility kits, and boots. Then they just sat around for three days, waiting for orders to arrive or to get transportation back to Cabogan Chico.

On the third day, Parnell heard that Camp Hannon had been ordered moved to a new site in the mountains of Florida Blanca, north of the Bataan Peninsula, and renamed ATC Kepner for Hannon's replacement. This jolted him. Now the team had *no* place to return to, which meant no place to be dispatched *from*.

Another two days passed with still no orders forthcoming. Red hounded the division's intelligence officers but got nothing. At last, thoroughly disgusted, he decided to return to Cabogan Chico on his own. If he were actually there, he figured, maybe he could get a better look at just what the hell was going on. That night, he easily wangled a ride for him and the team aboard a PBY making one of the last milk runs to the tiny island.

There were only four instructors still there, completing closure of the camp after shipping off the last of the Filipino guerillas who had been in the training cycle. The head cadre was a hard-drinking, eye-patch-wearing Australian Army color sergeant from New Zealand named Dumbarton.

Once more, they were forced to wait for new orders. Restless and watching his men lose their edge, Parnell decided to utilize the time by having Dumbarton and his crew run them through training exercises, to improve on the jungle skills they'd already been introduced to in the field.

For the next nine days they worked at learning the finer points of fighting the Japs in monsoon country. Things like using jungle camouflage so they could effectively disappear. How to cross irrigation ditches, keeping the water at chest level so it would slow down enemy bullets.

They learned the proper way to walk in the jungle, like a cat, and how to interpret the land's endless silences. The cadres showed them the new "Commando Shuffle," a six-cut knife attack for a face-on opponent, which could kill and gut him in three seconds. They were taught how to traverse through dense cover, using listening-stops every few feet and leapfrogging one man at a time.

More, they were told how to squad-attack a small enemy camp through its unguarded latrine area, to set up double night camps, one false and rigged with wired grenades to warn of enemy infiltration. They were prohibited from using soap before an exercise mission, or allowed to

smoke cigarettes in the field, instead using cuts of stran-
gling fig root, which merely smelled like jungle hibiscus
blossoms and wouldn't give away their position. Finally,
Dumbarton quickly illustrated the proper way to slow-
hammer the muzzle of a shotgun into an oval shape so
its charge of buckshot would cut a more deadly horizontal pattern . . .

Weesay said, "I say L.A.'s the best city in the States. No
question, *meng*."

"Bullshit," Cowboy disagreed.

"What chu mean bullshit? You think anything in New
Mexico is better?"

"*Everything* in New Mexico's better, Chico. L.A. ain't
nothin' but movie stars and assholes."

"Ain't them the same things?" Smoker said.

"Shit," Weesay said. "So what chu got in New Mexico?
Fuckin' lizards and snakes."

"Naw," Smoker said, "ya'll is *both* wrong. The *best* city in
America? New-*aul*-inns, man, the Big Easy."

"Oh?" Laguna snorted. "Why? Because it got all that
good Cajun pussy?"

"Hell yes," Smoker said.

Everyone's head lifted abruptly as they caught the
sound of approaching boots. The hut's ladder shook and
a moment later Parnell ducked through the low doorway.
"Saddle up, gentlemen," he said. "Orders finally come in.
Bring only personal weapons. We'll be getting refitted at
our jump-off point up near Tacloban."

An hour later, after a short closing ceremony consisting
of the placing of a simple hibiscus wreath on the doorway
of the now empty hut used by Major Hannon and salutes
all around, Parnell, his team, now including Corporal
Frankie Trota, along with Major Kepner and his four
cademen, were headed across Leyte Gulf in the PT that
had brought the Aussie officer out.

* * *

Now Red paused a moment before the door of the small Quonset hut to check the hand-painted sign over the door. It read NAVAL INTELLIGENCE LIAISON, SERVICE FORCE SEVENTH FLEET. The building sat at the end of runway 2L of the Cataisan Point Airfield a mile east of Tacloban, Leyte.

He went in. The room was heady with cigarette smoke. Two yeoman clerks were on the right, two radio operators on the left. From one radio came bursts of intership traffic. From the other issued the voice of Frank Sinatra singing "Sunday, Monday or Always."

The duty officer, a naval lieutenant commander, and a civilian sat at a desk at the back. The commander glanced up at Parnell. He was neat in summer tans and had the lean, cool face of a Monaco prince, a vaguely condescending smile. He waved Red over.

Parnell braced. "Lieutenant John Parnell, reporting as ordered, sir."

"At ease, Lieutenant," the commander said. The nameplate on his desk said LT. COMMANDER R. PENNYCOOK. "I've been expecting you. Grab a chair."

Parnell sat down beside the civilian, a chunky man who looked to be in his late fifties. He wore the engineer's khaki shirt and trousers, the bottoms of the pants stuffed into knee-high construction boots. He was smoking a pipe. His hat, which resembled a sugar-stiffened army campaign hat, was cocked on one knee.

Pennycook smiled. "Seems we've kept you waiting a bit, haven't we, Lieutenant?"

"Yes, sir."

The commander chuckled, rubbed one forefinger across the edge of his right eye. "Well, if the truth be known, somebody lost your mission data."

So what else is new? Red thought. He said nothing.

Pennycook nodded toward the civilian. "Meet Bill Farnsworth. People call him Captain."

Parnell turned. He and Farnsworth shook hands. The man's grip was powerful, his palm callused. Farnsworth said, "So you're the bloody bother boys, eh?" He had a brusque tone and an English accent.

Bother boys? Parnell smiled. "How do I answer that?"

"No need to, Lef-tenant," Farnsworth snapped. "I know all about you and your Blue Team. Rather impressive summary, I must say."

Red studied the man. He had a chisel-shaped face, a large nose, and short hair, which was brown but streaked with gray and parted a little to the left of middle. His eyebrows held the tenure of his face, thick at the peak of the nose, then thinning out as if sculpted so as to be quick to show displeasure. His narrow mouth reinforced that aspect.

"Mr. Farnsworth will be going in with you," Pennycook said. "He's to act as your radio relay. And as your escape valve. *If* that should become necessary, of course."

Red frowned. "Exactly what does *that* mean, sir?"

Before answering, the commander opened a drawer, withdrew a small manila envelope and several form sheets. He slid them across the desk to Parnell. "These are your sealed orders and equipment requisition chits." He sat back, crossed his arms. "Look, Lieutenant, I know nothing about your mission except what I've just told you. I *do* know Farnsworth here is an old Asia hand and knows the Philippines about as well as anyone could. He's also a master boat builder and marine propulsion mechanic. Before the war, he operated a boatyard at Divilican Bay on the east coast of Luzon. That will be your insertion point."

Farnsworth puffed on his pipe, his brown eyes watching the commander flatly. Parnell nodded. "Where do we get refitted?" he asked.

"You'll draw gear from naval ordnance."

"*Naval* ordnance? How come?"

Pennycook shrugged. "I don't know that either. But I certainly don't intend to ask. Your TMS carries big gun clearances, *very* big gun. Actually, MacArthur himself."

Parnell glanced at the envelope. It bore a red diagonal

line and was stamped CLASSIFIED: LEVEL Z. He nodded. "How and when do we leave?"

"By Black Cat at 1930 hours, this night."

"Black Cat?"

"That's a PBY flying boat used for night patrols. After you and your men pick up your gear, you're to come back here and remain until a truck comes for you. We don't want you seen. No need broadcasting that a covert op's in progress." He tilted his head, his eyes shifting from Parnell to Farnsworth and back. "So, do we have any further questions?"

"No, sir," Parnell said. Farnsworth shook his head.

Pennycook eased forward, gave his sleek, cool smile, and extended his hand. "I wish you gentlemen bon voyage and complete success."

Both men rose, took his hand.

Leaving the Quonset, Farnsworth said, "Bloody stuffy little squint that one, ain't he?"

The chief petty officer studied the requisition chits, lifted his eyes and a single brow at Bird, and asked, "What the fuck is *this*?"

"Jes' what it says, Mac," Wyatt answered quietly.

"Dog-faces drawing navy gear?"

Bird's eyes held a gelid stare. "'At's right. An' I suggest ya'll get *to* it."

The CPO, with his wattled neck and booze-veined cheeks, started to say something. He thought better of it, said instead, "I gotta check this shit out." He lumbered off to a bank of four wall telephones.

The naval supply warehouse was in a newly built structure that stood beside the base's Naval Port Control building. It still held its new wood smell, shelves half-completed and unopened crates of equipment all over the cement slab floor. Three sailors in detail dungarees went sluggishly about their work, eyeing the five Blue Teamers and Trota.

The chief returned, frowning. "Well," he said to Wyatt, "I guess you got the juice, fella. Shore Command says you get whatever the hell you want." He shrugged. "So you get Gy-reen gear."

It took them over two hours to collect their weapons and field equipment, the sailors having to search through un-opened crates to find things: brand-new Thompsons along with Winchester twelve-guage Defender pump shotguns firing double-ought buck loads, spare ammo for all the weapons, two boxes of M2A1Ms, the marine version of standard fragmentation grenades, demo kits containing kilo blocks of plastique explosive, fuses, and detonation gear, medical packs, flashlights, insect repellant, extra socks, rations. Anything and everything they could think of and carry. For Parnell, Bird chose an SCR-LF-180, a light field radio with spare batteries.

"Where all're you boys headed?" the CPO probed. "You sure as hell're gonna be loaded for bear."

"Yeah," Bird said, "ain't we?"

Before they finished, Parnell and Farnsworth showed up. Wyatt had already set aside the lieutenant's equipment. Farnsworth drew a larger transceiver, a Marine SCR-MC300, which included a portable hand-crank generator. He also got a Browning 9mm Hi-Power pistol with holster and an M1A1 .30-caliber carbine and spare ammo for both.

When they left, Parnell signing the chits, the chief grinned, saying, "Wherever you all *are* going, Lieutenant, I wish you good hunting."

"Thanks," Red said.

2014 hours

Parnell and Farnsworth were sitting on piled cargo net-ting astern the afterport blister window of the Catalina

PBY5A seaplane, the night outside full of moonlight and the roar from the aircraft's twin Consolidated-Allison Seahorse engines: a solid, vibrating background.

The aircraft, completely painted black, had lifted off the Cataisan Point boat channel twenty minutes late, the pilot, an ensign named Balfour, saying their radome, the tear-shaped radar unit set above the cockpit, had been losing its calibration. They finally got it operating properly, cranked up the engines, and slipped into the channel.

The rest of the men were asleep on their gear bags, the night air chilly at eight thousand feet. Through the blister glass, Red could see the dark shape of the trailing edge of the port wing, the entire span sitting high on a pylon mount. Beneath it, the whirling prop of the port engine was visible, creating a shimmering wraith in the moonlight. Far below, the ocean spread out under a faint, hazy glow.

Red leaned closer to the boat master. "You awake?"

From under the lowered brim of his hat, Farnsworth said, "Aye."

"What's this about an escape valve that swabbie intell officer mentioned?" he asked, having to talk louder than usual to be heard over the engines.

Earlier, Parnell had gone over the Mission Task Summary, code-named Operation Purgatory, with the entire team. In addition to the specific operational goal, it also included field maps, air-recon photos of their target, watch radio frequencies, codes, and emergency signals.

After arriving on the Luzon coast, they were to proceed as rapidly as possible to the target, an isolated mining compound located exactly 4.8 miles due west of the town of Magsaysay. It now housed civilian prisoners taken in the early days of the war. No specific number was given. On the air photos, all the larger structures and main features of the enclosure had been outlined in oil pencil and identified.

Using explosives and a blitz attack, Blue Team would neutralize the Japanese guards, which were estimated to be no more than a platoon, and free the prisoners. If successful, Parnell would send a code signal to Farnsworth, using the simple Tagalog phrase *chubasco asul*, which meant *squall blue*. It was also the code name for the overall operation.

The British boat master would then pass it on to Sixth Army headquarters. Immediately a hundred-man extraction team composed of 11th Airborne troopers and code-named Fandango Force would be dispatched to make a drop at a point three miles due east of the prisoner compound in the Fuyo National Preserve, on the western slope of the Sierra Madres, a coastal range that ran from Point Escarpada at the northeast tip of Luzon down to the Polillo Strait, which was directly east of Manila.

Once assembled on the ground, they'd head directly to the prison camp, relieve Blue Team, and prepare the prisoners for travel. Using carrying harnesses for the wounded and those too weak to walk, the combined force would then retreat from the mountains by the quickest route to the southern shore of Divilican Bay, thirty miles downslope. There they would await evacuation by submarine.

The men discussed the MTS parameters, Cowboy asking right off, "Why ain't us and them troopers hittin' the target at the same time?"

Parnell shook his head. "That drop could set off too many alarms. The Japs'd slaughter those POWs before we could get near 'em. It's our job to make sure they're secure till the Airborne gets on-site."

"That means we gotta kick ass pretty damn quick, huh?" Laguna said.

"That's the whole idea, Chihuahua," Wyatt said.

Parnell laid out his general movement-and-attack parameters and then marked off schedule points on his main field map, first consulting with Frankie about the kind of country they'd be passing through and what sort of speed they might expect to make. Trota told him it was high jungle, less dense than that which they'd encountered in

Samar. In fact, many of the upper ridges were beyond tree line, only rolling hills of grass and sedge. Still, there would be rough slopes to negotiate. . . .

Now Farnsworth pushed back his hat and sat up. "I'm to cover your arses in case there's a cock-up with the Fandango," he answered matter-of-factly.

"That means you've been briefed on *my* mission task?"

"Quite so."

Parnell considered. "Okay, let's assume things *do* screw up, how are *you* gonna get us out?"

"Check your map. You'll see that a southern branch of the Cagayan River extends all the way from beyond Magsaysay down to Divilican Bay. It's also navigable for shallow-draft vessels as far as San Pablo above Magsaysay."

"So we'll come out by boat?"

"Only if something goes wrong with the para drop. Movement on the river is very risky. But if it's necessary, we'll have to accept that risk."

"What kind of boat will it be?"

"A shallow-draft riverboat."

"You mean like a paddle-wheeler?"

"A *side*-wheeler, actually."

Parnell chortled. "How in hell're you gonna come up with one of *those?*"

"She's already there. In the thirty feet of water I sank her in four years ago."

Red glanced at the man's moon-dappled profile, shocked. "You're saying we'll have to *refloat* the son of a bitch before we head inland?"

"Not we, Lef-tenant, *me.*"

"How can you do that alone?"

Now it was Farnsworth who chuckled dryly. "Look, Parnell, I've lived twenty years on that section of Luzon coast. I know every inch of it and damned near every able-bodied Filipino who lives on it. I'll have an experienced salvage crew at work within six bleedin' hours after we land."

Red grunted. He thought a moment, asked, "What

about the engine? And the fuel? With that much time in water, I figure all you'll find is rust and corroded tanks."

"She's *steam* driven, river water's our fuel. But, again, you just leave all that ruddy business to me."

Red shook his head and sighed. "I don't like this. You know? How come there's nothing in my MTS about this river contingency plan? I was told we'd be coming out with the paratrooper team."

"And as *I've* told you," Farnsworth snapped testily, "that isn't your concern. Not yet, anyway. Not until you need my services."

"In other words, when *we*, not the Airborne, have to bring out those POWs, right?"

"Quite so."

Of course. "So who decides when that becomes necessary?"

"Sixth Army, old man. They tell me, I tell you."

Parnell stared at him. He was irritated. At that moment, he didn't like this arrogant, snippy Limey. "What code references refer to that situation?"

"The phrase *Red Amazon* will indicate you are to immediately evacuate the prisoners to the Cagayan River."

"*Where* exactly on the river?"

"That depends on its height. With these storm conditions, I'd undoubtedly be able to go well past Magsaysay. But then I'd have to pass Ilagan twice. I wouldn't like to come down the second time with a full load of prisoners." He shrugged. "But I fear we won't have much of a choice." He fell silent for a moment, then asked, "How fast d'you think you'll be able to make the river at all?"

"How can I know that? I don't have any idea what condition these POWs will be in."

"Understood, Lef-tenant," the Brit said, nodding. "But understand *this*. Regardless of how slow any of those poor blokes are, you'd best keep them at the double, all the way down. The sooner you get them on water, the better chance you'll have of staying ahead of Jap patrols."

"Point taken," Parnell said, nodding.

"I've chosen three possible rendezvous points," Farnsworth continued. He withdrew a sheet of paper and handed it over. "They're all north of Ilagan. The code references are *Circus, Fair,* and *Carnival.* Their coordinates are on that sheet."

One of the aircraft's crewmen came aft, stepping over bodies and equipment. He had earphones down around his neck. He paused beside Parnell, leaned to talk to the Brit. "Excuse me, Mr. Farnsworth," he said. "The captain would like to speak with you, sir." The Englishman rose and followed him forward.

Parnell looked out the blister window. The steady, gentle vibrations of the aircraft, the still blue-white beauty of the moonlight, prompted reflective thoughts. He didn't relish the loose ends of this particular mission: its *estimates* of enemy force, its *assumptions,* its furtive, inexact, in-and-out timetable.

In covert action, he knew, you always functioned in emergency mode, fielding the unexpected and reacting instantly. But at least your initial MTS was solid enough with intelligence reports to afford you a decent chance of pulling it off. But here? There was just too goddamned much float to *this* fucking boat.

He chuckled sardonically at the irony of the phrase. Then, sighing, he shifted his mind, felt the sudden urge for a cigarette. He easily submerged it. And as he did so, it occurred to him that such *immediate* self-denial was one of the most annoying aspects of combat.

You were always wanting something you couldn't have. War conditions quickly taught you to mentally dismiss such desires. But when they were composed of the simplest, basic things, that's when it pissed you off the most. Things like rest and food, a moment of comfort, the sweetness of female flesh. Just a cold bottle of beer, for Christ's sake.

Combat was like poverty. It frustrated desire and forced you to mentally disregard its bad effects right in their tracks, before they soured inside. After a while, you got so good at doing that, you could deny yourself the human impulses to dream or even remember. The *what* and *where* that had once been you, the past, *your* past, the *back there* part of your life. And the longer you stayed over *here*, the more that part of you dwindled and faded, until, if you managed to glimpse it at all, you found it strange and no longer quite your own.

He turned and looked out at the bright splendor of the night again, felt his weariness, felt a touch of poignant sadness. With it came the flashing image of Dillon standing in his *banda* waiting to die. *Damn!* It was a jarring thing to kill one of your own.

But then this, too, Parnell forced out of his mind, refocusing instead on the sky beyond the blister's glass, so alive with light, the tissue of it a cool, pale blue softness, like the feel of silk dipped into warm water. *Enjoy the moment, John,* he told himself. *Quickly and deeply, before it vanishes.* That was something *else* combat taught you.

By the time Farnsworth returned, he was sound asleep.

It took them eight hours to reach their insertion point on the coast of Luzon, just below the bottom curve of Divilican Bay. Balfour had to divert from his original flight path when his radar picked up the blip of a Japanese patrol plane, the configuration of a Type 2-2EF twin-engine night patrol bomber code-named Nick. It was skirting the eastern coast at five thousand feet.

He swung seaward, continued out for a hundred miles, then curved back, just to be certain he was beyond the range of the Nips' aerial radar. Allied intelligence claimed the Japanese were now using more effective sets, patterned after the German's excellent Funkgerat/Wassermann WF-5000 signal units.

At 0343 hours, the Black Cat came in low, just over the ocean on a direct imaginary line that extended seaward from a small upthrust island that lay a quarter mile from the shore. The moon had dropped below the high cordillera, but the sky was still full of light. It reflected down onto the sea, made it dark but still easy to read.

The pilot set the aircraft down as gently as if he were landing on a lake, despite a fair chop beyond the windward side of the island, the breeze now coming from offshore. The landing run put them less than a hundred yards from the low cliffs of the small island, a quarter mile in length and completely jungle-covered save for the bare, sea-carved cliffs to seaward.

The plane's crewmen had already opened both blister ports. The moment the Catalina eased to a stop and settled into the water, they tossed out the team's two rubber rafts, four-man units, all black, and inflated by a pressure tank that popped them up tightly in a matter of seconds. Now they bobbed and scraped along the side of the fuselage, each on a double line that held it close while the men offloaded the gear. The night air was chilly, heavy with the smell of eucalyptus and wet rock.

Finally, the team dropped down into the rafts, their footing immediately unstable as their weight bowed the bottom. Parnell, Farnsworth, Smoker, and Bird were in one, Sol, Weesay, Cowboy, and Trota in the other. They gave the high sign to the crewmen, who released the lines and closed the blisters. The whole thing had taken less than four minutes.

Balfour waited until the rafts were safely away from the plane, then eased on the throttle to his big twin radials. They roared loudly and the Catalina's fuselage dropped astern, skidding slightly as he brought it around, facing away from the small island. For a moment, it pitched up and down in the chop. Then the full power came on, winding up, the props hurling back spray as the seaplane began its takeoff run, downwind this time. It finally lifted off, streams of water trailing from its fuselage, and headed straight out to sea.

With the rafts in tandem, the men paddled close in to

the small island, angling slightly to clear its southern headland. The soft sibilance and occasional mild crash of surf sounded along the base of the cliff, mixed with the echoing cries from nesting cormorants and gulls.

Just as they were passing beyond the headland and before starting in toward the main shoreline, there was a quick orange flash far out at sea. Just there and gone. In total silence. But they were able to spot tiny fragments of fiery debris falling through the darker strip that lay along the horizon. In seconds, they too vanished.

The men looked at each other. It was obvious an aircraft had just been blown out of the sky. What aircraft? Their Black Cat? Nobody said anything. The men wordlessly turned away, took up their paddles again, and headed for the mainland.

The beach was open and wide, without a paralleling reef, the sandy slope disfigured by long tailings of seaweed. Higher up were thick growths of eucalyptus and pines and heavy clusters of sea spurge.

They unloaded gear and dragged the rafts to the top of the beach. Quickly deflating both, they rolled them up and hid them deep in the spurge along with Farnsworth's radio equipment. For a few moments, Parnell huddled with him while the Brit pointed out the best routes to the prisoners' compound, and also reviewed their radio procedures and frequencies. At last, they shook hands and bade each other good luck.

At 0426, Parnell and his men left Farnsworth alone and headed off into the trees, everybody harnessed and weighted down with equipment, deployed out in normal overwatch formation with Frankie and Bird ahead on point.

Chapter Eight

Eugene Mallory had trained himself to come awake precisely ten minutes before the bell, so that he could pluck the maggots off his ankle. No matter how exhausted he was, his mind would override his body and hurl him into consciousness.

He sat up. The light through the barracks window was a thin gray white, without substance. The long prison barracks with its rough-sawn walls and stacks of bamboo sleeping platforms was shivery cold, a six-thousand-foot dawn cold. But the crispness did somewhat dampen the perpetual stench of dysentery excrement that lifted off the floor and the sour, rotting odor of decaying and diseased flesh.

Mallory withdrew a glass jar from under his straw mattress. It had contained guava jelly once, a long time ago. Squinting in the dimness, he delicately began picking off the maggots that clustered like opaque white bubbles on a large jungle ulcer that had erupted on his right ankle, the wound deep enough to show the edge of bone. He could feel warmth coming from the larvae, energy from their digestion of his dead tissue.

He placed each maggot into the jar, thick white bodies soft as warm wax. They made no sound now, yet always in the stillness of the night he could hear their tiny rustling like leaves in a gentle night breeze. When he had them all in the bottle, he capped it, holes in the top, and bound the festering lesion, using the same filthy strip of shirt material he used each day, the cloth stained and sticky with pus.

The bell tolled. Tinny, clanging.

All around him, figures lifted up like corpses struggling to become upright. All wore tattered remnants of clothing, some only loincloths called *fundoshi* by the Japanese. Hacking coughs, gushy farts, groans sounded. No one spoke. But many looked about with their dulled eyes, scanning the sleeping shelves to see if anyone had died during the night. If so, they would have to drag the corpse to the front. Later, a burial detail would cart it to the boiling ovens to be incinerated.

A Japanese guard entered, pounding the butt of his rifle on the wooden floor. His uniform was filthy, his body nearly as emaciated as theirs. They formed into a ragged line and shuffled out of the building.

Standing in front of the barracks, they waited, shivering in the cold. A scar-faced *gocho*, or corporal, took roll. Fog slithered and coiled along the ground, the ground itself thick with mud. Heavy dew droplets dripped from the eaves of the barracks, from the barbed-wire fences nearby.

The roll was taken twice. Then the prisoners returned to the building and two soldiers brought in a fire-blackened kettle and a small canvas bag, placed them near the door, and went away. It was their morning food.

The prisoners were fed twice a day. Now the men huddled around the kettle with their wooden bowls, dipping them into the contents, a thin rice gruel called *lugao*. It was infested with worms and weevils. Each man also took a small pebble of rock salt from the bag. They were fed this mush twice a day, without variation.

Mallory took his bowl back to his sleeping shelf. The *lugao* made his gums and mouth hurt. Scurvy had loosened his teeth and sent constant surges of pain through his bones and muscles. Many of the men also had beriberi and dysentery and could not finish their meager food, the stuff instantly setting off terrible cramps. Some tried to rush outside to shit in the barracks yard. Others simply let their bowels explode onto the floor or in their straw beds. No one seemed to care.

When Mallory first came to the prison, he'd weighed 190 pounds. Now he was down to 131. Soon after arriving, he'd been befriended by one of the inmate leaders, a man named Halperan who had been the mine supervisor before the war. He taught him many of the little ways to lessen the deadly effects of such starvation rations and the diseases that constantly hounded them.

For instance, he told him that charcoal dust mixed with the rice gruel helped to control the deadly diarrhea that came from dysentery. He showed him how to fashion a bitter tea from wild grass that would replace some of the vitamin B that was totally absent in the polished rice used in the *lugao*.

Halperan taught him how to find and smuggle back wild camotes, berries, starfruit, or kasava root whenever he was sent out on the wood detail. These fruits and vegetables were then added to the meat from the dead black-and-white cloud rats that infested the buildings or the bodies of diseased jungle lizards, giving necessary protein and vitamin C to hold off the scurvy. He had also helped him make a poultice from butterfly orchids that could help seal deep-cut wounds.

Unfortunately, the prison's Japanese commander, a *tai-i*, or captain, named Yoshimoto, thin as a Hong Kong gambler with a pencil mustache and sudden bursts of brutal rage, had recently cracked down. The Japanese themselves were beginning to starve as their own supplies dwindled. Every other day, details went out into the jungle to hunt mountain lizards and birds to offset their own diet. The prisoners' rations were cut 40 percent and the wood details were always searched when they returned from the jungle. Since then, Mallory's scurvy had quickly returned.

There were now only forty-nine prisoners working Lode Pit number 4, far down from the normal workforce of 150. In the past, whenever too many prisoners died or were murdered, replacements had been shipped up from other prisons in northern Luzon. That had stopped almost a year ago.

Many of the replacements had been American soldiers taken in Bataan and Corregidor. Now all of these were dead, every one of them caught trying to escape. They'd been beheaded in front of the barracks and their bodies hung on the wire as examples for the others. The corpses bloated in the sun until they burst open. But their remains weren't taken down and burned until Yoshimoto could no longer stand the stench.

Mallory's friend, Halperan, had also been killed, six months before when he had the rashness to plead with Yoshimoto not to cut the prisoners' food any further. The Japanese captain exploded and shot him three times in the groin. The wounded man was then thrown out into the yard. No one was allowed to help him. It took him four hours to bleed to death.

The prisoners silently reformed outside the building. Roll was again taken and then a Japanese section leader began assigning details, walking up and down the ragged lines, whipping a short, bamboo baton across each man's shoulders to indicate where he would work for the day.

On this day, Mallory was assigned to the boiling ovens. That was good duty, warm duty on such a cold day. He and the other two men on the detail were marched off, guarded by a *nitohei*, a particularly slovenly private who was known to occasionally take pleasure in urinating on his

POWs. He would also often doze in the sun, murmuring Japanese incantations.

The mining compound covered two acres, most of it on a gentle slope with jungle all around and an inner ring of double barbed-wire fencing. Two machine-gun posts were on timber towers, one uphill, the other at the bottom of the stockade.

The main prison office was located in one of the four original barracks buildings, the guard contingent in another. The third building was a warehouse containing meager food supplies, barrels of diesel fuel for the mine's operating engines, and large rolls of filter cloth. In addition, there were four twenty-five-foot-high water tanks with their network of flues that brought water down from crystal-clear lava pools higher up the slope, to feed the various processing sheds.

The main pithead was near the upper fence. Beside it was the hoist house with its huge single-stage drum running steel wire that raised and lowered the skip cages. It was called a horse whim and was turned by two mules in harness. Other mules were hitched to big-wheeled gandola carts that hauled the extracted ore down the slope to the small, steam-powered stamping mill. Tailings surrounded the pit collar.

Mallory hated working underground, being highly claustrophobic. The mine itself was shallow, no more than three hundred feet down, two levels of crosscuts and drifts reinforced with timbered square sets. Yet it was always very hot underground, the men double-jacking the stope face with eight-pound hammers and drilling blast holes to blow dikes and fissures away from the main vein. They constantly had to force themselves beyond their exhaustion to avoid the Japanese bayonets.

Before the war, the Tallangatta Consolidated Goldfields' miners, Ingorot tribesmen, had used good American dynamite, high-velocity Du Pont Hi-Cap sticks. But the Nips had a limited supply of TNT. Instead, they used a slurry made from ammonium nitrate and fuel oil, which was fired by a single 225-gram booster stick of dynamite. It produced only half the sundering power of the TNT and created a thick, gummy explosive dust that filled the lungs. But it packed well and could be used in water.

Mallory and the other men assigned to the boilers began shoveling out the previous day's ash and loading fresh firewood into the heating chambers beneath the boiling vats. The sun was just now breaking above the eastern horizon. The fog thickened, drifting through the trees.

There were two boiler ovens. This comprised the third stage of the six stages through which the raw rock was processed. First, it was crushed in a stamping mill. The resulting fine gravel was then filtered through great sheets of *kinorus* cloth made from cotton and banana leaf fiber, and then conveyed to an agitation tank containing sodium cyanide. After several hours of churning to speed up the chemical reaction, the remaining solution contained gold cyanide and sodium cyanoaurite. This thick fluid was next pumped to the boiling ovens to be deoxygenated.

When this was completed, it was sent on to another tank in which it was combined with zinc dust, and then pumped to a still larger tank that contained internal steel racks submerged in diluted sulfuric acid. Slowly a precipitate of a gold and silver alloy would form on the tank racks.

When this residue was scraped off and dried to a fine powder, it was bagged for storage and transport. This was the gold concentrate. In the old days, the bags would have been transported to Manila to complete the final stage of processing, running the concentrate through a series of flax baths to leach out the silver so that the pure gold could be melted and poured into ingots for assay.

Exhaustion quickly took Mallory and his two workmates, constantly feeding more wood to the roaring fire chambers, heat pouring back over them smelling like ozone. One of the men was a skeletal New Yorker named Galliazzo, a teacher in Olangapo before the war. Mallory watched him. He was very close to insanity, his skin a leprous color. Occasionally, Galliazzo would weep silently, then abruptly become furtive, his eyes darting, hissing softly to himself, "Don't talk in here. You must not talk in here."

The sun inched its way into a cloudless sky. The men worked on, desperately holding themselves together so as not to falter. If one fell, the dozing *nitohei* would instantly leap to his feet and beat him with the butt of his rifle until they stood again.

Baguio, Luzon

Lieutenant Sacabe had been waiting since 6:00 that morning, sitting stiffly upright in his slightly soiled dark green tropical combat uniform, his draped field cap sitting precisely on one thick knee. He was in an anteroom of the Intelligence Department of General Yamashita's staff headquarters. The building had once been the nineteenth-century residence of the Spanish governor general of the Philippines.

Two days before, the lieutenant had been summoned to the Operations Section of Admiral Iwabachi's headquarters in Manila's Intramuros Section and informed that he had been ordered to go to Baguio immediately. The order had come directly from the 2nd Bureau of the Imperial General Staff in Tokyo, the Intelligence/Special Operations arm of the IGS.

Although Sacabe was a naval officer, as a member of the Special Landing Force, he was under the ultimate direction of 2nd Bureau. Apparently some special operation was in the works and he had been specifically chosen. Now, waiting to be told what it was, he felt deep pride.

His mission to capture the American guerilla, Dillon, had been a horrible failure. Under ordinary circumstances, he would have been stripped of his rank, possibly even ordered to commit *seppuku,* ritual suicide. But at that time Admiral Iwabachi had been desperately trying to increase his marine force in Manila. Sacabe was therefore ordered to the capital the moment he returned to Luzon from Samar.

Manila was almost completely surrounded by American units now, and fierce engagements were erupting all along its perimeter. It had been a close thing for him getting out of the city. Yet he managed to escape on the Pasig River and make his way to San Jose where he caught a ride with a convoy heading north on the Cabanatuan Highway. He had reached Baguio the night before.

It was now midmorning, the room flooded with bright winter sunshine. The building overlooked a broad, well-groomed garden of lily ponds and fountains nestled in fern-covered grottoes. Soldiers in gardener coveralls worked among the shrubbery and two staff officers sat smoking on a cement bench shaped like a Roman Forum chair.

Abruptly, a junior lieutenant came to summon him. He was led past a bank of telephone operators to a double door at the end of a paneled hall. Sacabe knocked softly. A gruff voice bade him enter.

The room had a high ceiling with light gray walls, dark blue drapes, and sculptured, gold-leaf molding. The drapes were faded and the gold leaf was tarnished and flaking. A large mahogany desk stood in the precise center of the space, behind which sat a stout, completely bald major general, or *shosho,* dressed in a brown field tunic and a white cotton open-neck shirt with the collar flaps worn over the tunic's lapels. His name was Kenichi Nagai.

Sacabe quick-stepped in and snapped to rigid attention before the desk, exactly the two meters from it as prescribed by military code, his cap sharply tucked under his left arm. "Honorable General, Honorable Officer," he intoned curtly, "I am First Lieutenant Sacabe Yasio, who has been ordered to report to you."

Nagai looked at him from beneath hairless brows. He had tiny, tight eyes, their narrowness accentuating something dark and vile in the depths. His Type 94 *shin-gunto* sword lay on the desktop. It bore the two fist straps of a senior staff officer and was encased in a beautifully scrolled leather scabbard.

Without preamble, he growled, "You will immediately take a *hara-guntai* to a site near the town of Magsaysay." A *hara-guntai* was a small, quick-strike unit usually composed of a section of forty-five men. "Beyond it is a mining compound, which is also a *furyu-shuyojo*. On your maps it is designated as Site Z. You will also have papers that will instruct the camp commander that your authority supersedes his."

Sacabe remained absolutely motionless, his eyes neutral and sighting straight ahead. The sound of engines drifted drowsily in through the window on a soft, cool breeze that made the drapes tremble.

Baguio had once been the summer capital of the Philippines, all the politicians and old-family Spanish planters and rich American military officers using it as a retreat from the debilitating heat and humidity of Manila. A lovely town in the Benguet Hills 130 miles northeast of Manila, it nestled among mountain pines with wide, paved avenues and summer homes and Cardoba-style villas built long before the Yanks came. Now it was headquarters for General Yamashita's 152,000-man Shobu Group, antiaircraft gun emplacements and quad tents all over, and the entrances to underground tunnels that ran under the beautiful avenues.

"There are several hundred kilos of gold concentrate stored in the compound," the general went on. "These you will transport to the town of Tabuk where you will relinquish its custody to a Kempei-tai intelligence officer." The Kempei-tai was the Japanese Secret Police.

Sacabe waited.

When Yamashita first took command of the Fourteenth

Area Army in the Philippines, he had quickly set a secret plan into motion. Only three other persons knew of its existence: General Nagai, his intelligence chief; Colonel Shimboi Kurisaka, a dear personal friend since school days; and Count Hajime Ishii, commander in chief of the Southern Army and member of the Imperial General Staff.

All four men were realists and realized Japan was doomed. Working in concert, they had slowly and quietly begun gathering gold and silver ingots and mineral concentrate from the numerous mines throughout the Philippines, intending to use it for buying their freedom once the empire went down completely.

They followed a workable plan to isolate the gold. First they would send a small unit of soldiers to the individual mines to take possession of any stored precious metal concentrate. It would be quickly loaded aboard no more than three trucks, disguised in rice bags. The senior officer of the recovery unit would then dispose of all witnesses. This included the Japanese prison guards, the inmates, and finally his *own* soldiers! All except his two senior noncoms who would assist him in the slaughter.

The precious cargo would then be driven to one of eleven designated secret bunkers or tunnels that had already been prepared by prison and native labor. There, it would be turned over to a Secret Police intelligence officer. The Filipino laborers and prisoner workmen who had built the gold's hiding place would then be murdered and their bodies sealed inside along with the metal.

Afterward, the members of the entire Kempei-tai intelligence unit and the remaining soldiers who had picked up and delivered the gold would all be sent into areas of the fiercest fighting. General Yamashita and his coconspirators wanted absolutely no loose ends, no living witnesses.

By mid-February 1945, they had managed to gather and hide large gold and silver caches, both bullion and concentrate, throughout the country. Some postwar estimates would fix the value of these hidden treasures at over five hundred million dollars. . . .

Now General Nagai paused to appraise this lieutenant once more, his oval face registering disdain. "I personally have little faith in you naval dogs," he snapped. "But apparently IGS considers you particularly adept at your duties."

"Thank you, Honorable General," Sacabe said.

In response, the senior officer snorted derisively.

Yet the IGS report was correct, Sacabe *was* good at his job. From the very beginning, the perfect example of Bushido, the Way of the Samurai, a fanatical warrior who followed the orders of a superior without hesitation, who would kill or die in joy for his emperor and his country.

In college, he'd been a leading member of the Patriotic Student Alliance, a far right-wing organization that upheld the theory of Japan's destiny and its Greater East Asia Co-Prosperity Sphere. Quickly noticed by important people, particularly those in the navy's Military Affairs Section of IGS, he was soon inducted into service and sent through naval officer's school, graduating with excellent exam marks.

In the summer of 1941, he was ordered to China to fight the Communist Eighth Route Army. Spiked with patriotic fervor, he performed his combat duties with outstanding bravery. He was promoted to the command of a roving force of naval marines who acted as counterinsurgents and assassins, brutally killing and destroying under the doctrine of "Three All": *Burn All, Sieze All, Kill All.*

He was next sent to Indonesia and Malaya for similar duty. By now, slaughter had become a pleasant second nature to him: *chi no kiyoki,* of the pure blood. After all, he was Japanese, the recipient by birthright of supreme racial superiority, bearer of his god-emperor's power to crush all lesser mortals.

To prove he truly possessed such governance over other races, he and his fellow officers would often inflict unspeakable cruelties on captured prisoners, even made a sport of it. For example, they'd behead people simply to see which one of them had the sharpest sword or the strongest arm. They'd castrate a man and bet on how long it would take him to die. Or they'd toss a baby into the air to find who could skewer its tiny body with a bayonet precisely in the belly button.

Such savagery had started as merely their sanctified right. But now it had become a sweet addiction.

Colonel Nagai said, "You will use only two of your senior noncoms to transport the concentrate. The prisoners and the remainder of your men will be disposed of before you leave the facility. Use whatever method you find suitable. But be absolutely certain no one is left alive. Is that understood?"

He was to murder his own men. The thought entered Sacabe's mind, left it. It did not cause disquiet. "Yes, Honorable General," he barked.

"*Fully* understood?"

"Yes, Honorable General."

"Very well." Nagai shoved an envelope across the desk. "These are your orders and clearances. I do not expect contact from you until your mission is completed. However, if it is absolutely necessary to do so, transmit using your code name *Toro*." It meant stone lantern. "If *anyone* questions your authority, show them these orders. They carry the seal of General Yamashita himself."

Sacabe felt an intense, almost unbearable sensation of utter joy spread across his chest. Yet his face remained impassive.

"Your men are already entrained. Do not fail this mission, Lieutenant." The general snapped his right hand in the air, as if brushing away a fly. "Now get out."

"Yes, Honorable Officer," Sacabe exclaimed. He braced even stiffer for a count of two, then spun around and quick-stepped out of the office, closing the door silently behind him.

* * *

In truth, Lieutenant Sacabe had been one of the very few Japanese to escape from Manila before it was completely surrounded by American forces pushing in from both the north and south.

Upcountry, Sixth Army commander Kreuger's XI and XIV Corps had already sealed off the Bataan Peninsula and taken positions along a broad front to block any Japanese attempt to extricate their troops to the north. Now the main American thrust toward Manila Bay was ready.

On 3 February, MacArthur ordered him to seize the island of Corregidor, which sat squarely at the entrance of Manila Bay, and also Mariveles, located at the very tip of the Bataan Peninsula across a tiny strait from Corregidor. These assaults would be carried out on 16 February. Yet it would take nearly two weeks of serious fighting before both sites were actually secured.

Meanwhile, the troopers of Major General J.M. Swing's 11th Airborne Division continued driving toward Manila from the south. They soon took a key Japanese position at Tagaytay Ridge, which lay between the capital and the huge Lake Laguna de Bay, which lay inland.

By 4 February, they had reached the Paranaque River, crossed it under intense fire, and ran head-on into the heavy bunkers and pillboxes of the Japanese Genko Defensive Line. This heavily defendable line was anchored by Fort McKinley with its big emplaced barrage guns in the east, Nichols Airfield to the southwest, and to the Lunetta, the capital's famous waterfront boulevard to the west, now covered with bunkers, MG positions, and two-man foxholes.

The paratroopers, aided by the artillery batteries of XIV Corps, which were now within range of southern enemy positions, hammered at the Genko Line, clearing bunkers one at a time with rifle, grenades, and flamethrowers. However, it wouldn't be totally penetrated until 17 February. On the following day, forward units of Swing's troopers would link with elements of Kreuger's 37th Infantry Division east of Marikina and thereby complete the encirclement of Manila Bay.

Now would begin the bloody destruction of the capital city itself as American forces combined to annihilate Admiral Iwabachi and his sixteen thousand sailors and marines in vicious house-to-house fighting. Meanwhile, within the city, the Japanese would systematically slaughter over a hundred thousand Filipino citizens, out of sheer savagery.

Farnsworth had understated his ability to gather a salvage crew in six hours. Actually, it took him only four, old friends coming out of the woodwork as soon as they knew he was there, the news traveling fast on the bamboo telegraph.

They hugged him and kissed his hand as if he were a saviour. He told them what he intended to do and why. They immediately volunteered to help, leaving duties, crops, and families to go with him.

Farnsworth quickly noticed changes in the usually happy brown faces of his friends, a coldness in the eyes now where once there had been a carefreeness. These men had endured unspeakable atrocities at the hands of the Japanese. They told him of the deaths of other mutual friends, slaughtered like goats. Gone was an old innocence, now become instead a dark seething for revenge.

By late morning, he had his salvage crew picked, sixteen men. The two leadmen had worked for him at his boatyard in the old days: a journeyman machinist named Ignacio Rafareal whom he called Raffles, and a marine carpenter, Rosendo Panay. As a young boy, Panay had shipped out on square riggers that ran the copra trade to the Celebes. He had the natural knack, could lay a keelson and hull frame with an astounding sense for water flow and balance. The rest were fishermen, reef divers, and woodcutters, one an auto mechanic.

They assembled near where Farnsworth had stowed his radio and weapons. After instructing one of the men to constantly monitor the radio for calls from Sixth Army, he dispatched ten men with *carabao* carts to begin cutting forty-foot-long bamboo stalks, all at least a foot across.

These would be his lifting units to get the side-wheeler to the surface. Each would take three divers to attach it to the hull of the boat. When at least two dozen bamboo lengths were affixed, their hollow, watertight sections would exert a tremendous buoyancy that would lift the side-wheeler right off the bottom.

Farnsworth had built the boat himself. It was forty feet long with a fifteen-foot beam, a square bow, and a stern like a barge. The side-mounted paddle wheels were eight feet in diameter. The interior framing of heavy, milled teak stringers was laid longitudinally so as to create a large underdeck compartment for cargo stowage and space for the engine, the twin locomotive-type boilers, and their water tanks. The hull itself was formed of molded teak plywood with autoclave-joined decking and a small afterhouse and canopy frame. He had christened it the *Betty T*, after his deceased wife.

Before the war, he'd run it up the river to Ilagan, hauling passengers and personal cargo in and raw timber and cargo bound for the old Maconacon loading station on Divilican Bay when he came back down.

During the first tense days following the Japanese invasion and while the battles for Bataan and Corregidor still raged, American PT captains from Motor Torpedo Boat Squadron 24 had come to his yard for repairs, their boats all shot up in night enemy engagements off Luzon and Samar. His was the only medium-sized dry dock on the eastern coastline from Point St. Vicente on the northern tip of Luzon to Baler Bay, 180 miles to the south.

As the days passed, the news reaching him grew ever

more ominous. The PT officers urged him to leave, to come out with them. When the Japs come here, they told him, they'll kill you and use your boatyard to repair their own patrol vessels.

Bataan finally fell on 9 April 1942. Twenty-seven days later, Corregidor was secured by the Japanese. When word reached him, Farnsworth knew it was time to go. But first there were things to do. For three days and nights, he and his workers dismantled the boatyard, carting the expensive milling gear and tools inland where he buried them in scattered caches in the foothills.

Next, he set fire to his pier, dry dock, and working sheds. The final task was to sink the *Betty T* so the Japs could never use it in any capacity. He ran it out to a tiny rock island called Niyog-intim just off the coast, found a suitable spot on the lee side, and opened the boat's petcocks. It took eighteen minutes for it to settle gently onto a flat reef shelf under five fathoms of water.

Before sinking it, however, he had prepared it for his return. He stripped the boat of all dunnage, rope, life jackets, mess equipment, and unnecessary metal deck gear. He plugged all the steam engine's ports, flooded the boiler, and double-packed all the metal parts, shafts, bearings, rudder hangers, and plating with heavy marine gear-grease made of calcium base and rosin, enriched with lime and mineral oil to completely lock out the seawater. He even mounted strips of zinc along the flat bottom and across the paddle blades to prevent electrolytic corrosion created by the wave currents moving across the reef.

Two days later, he left aboard PT 235, skippered by a lieutenant from Nashville, Tennessee, named Claude Woodhead. A week later, they were strafed by two Japanese fighters off Baganga, Mindanao. One of the tanks of high-octane fuel was hit and exploded. The only survivors were Farnsworth and a machinist mate called R.E. Nycum, both wounded.

They managed to reach the shore where native Filipinos

rescued them. But Nycum soon died from his wounds.
When Farnsworth was able to move, the Filipinos led him
across the island to an Australian coast watcher named
Geoffrey Noel, code-named Manger, who operated in the
dense jungles of the Malita Peninsula at the southern tip
of the island on Saragani Strait. One year later, he was
picked up by a British submarine and taken to Australia
where he immediately went to work for the Allied Intelligence Bureau. . . .

It was now nearly noon. He and Raffles stood and
silently surveyed the site where his boatyard had once
been. The scorched areas and burn-scarred stonework of
the buildings were still visible beneath weeds and wind
drifts of debris from eucalyptus new growth. Off the beach,
the burned posts of his pier protruded above water, a
double line of weathered, guano-covered posts poking out
of the water.

He shook his head sadly. "Bloody shame, this," he said
sharply. "Damned bloody shame."

Raffles shrugged and gave him a toothy grin. He had a
silver tooth in the center of his mouth. It had dulled to the
color of pewter. "No matter, sor," he said cheerily. "Jew are
back, no? We will make it like *bepore.*"

Farnsworth looked at him, then slapped an arm over
the Filipino's shoulder, chortling. "By God, Raffles, we'll
bloody well just *do* that."

It was late afternoon when he donned a pair of goggles
made from bamboo and tire rubber and dove down for his
first look at the *Betty T,* two native divers with him. A sand
drift nearly covered one side of the hull up to the gunwale,
and long tendrils of seaweed trailed from it in the shifting
current. There were patches of barnacles and black mollusks shaped like tiny teepees on the planking, and small
reef fish darted and flared among the holes in the reef
shelf.

Using hand signs, he needed several dives to fully instruct his men precisely where he wanted them to place

the long lengths of bamboo so as to gain the greatest lift. Then they all returned to the shore and waited for dark.

The good weather had held all day. But as evening neared, the wet smell of rain and storm began drifting in from the south. It turned the sunset into great splashes of scarlet and orange and yellow that fumed up from beyond the mountains, coating the edges and hillocks and ravines of the clouds that had slowly been working their way north into layers of pure, fiery color.

As soon as it was dark, they returned to the salvage site, a half dozen *bandas*. The divers had to work completely without lights, struggling with the long stalks of bamboo, dragging them down against their own buoyancy and then placing and keeping them in position while they tied in blindly, by touch, the black water around them alive with the creaks and trills and boomings of the reef's night creatures. Now and then something larger would move in, drawn by the smack and pop of the *bandas'* hulls overhead, the big animals moving past, leaving little feather trails of turbulence.

When they mounted the ninth length, the *Betty T* shifted, the side opposite the sand drift scraping loudly on the reef shelf and lifting off slightly. It quickly stabilized, the deck slanted. Now they worked faster, fearful the shifting would damage the bottom. Occasionally, the boat would move again with the harsh, abrasive grumble of wood on coral.

As they tied in the sixteenth length, the entire boat suddenly lifted off the shelf and began drifting slowly toward the surface amid a cloud of sand and coral chips, the divers riding it up. It broke through the surface with a deep, sucking sound, wallowing heavily, the bamboo holding ropes squeaking.

Farnsworth and the other divers gave a little cheer, the Brit calling out in Tagalog, "Cracking good work, lads, *cracking* good."

Using two hand pumps, they began sucking the ocean

water from the hold, the *Betty T* slowly riding higher and higher and pitching in the increasing chop as the wind swept into its bow after ricocheting off the rocky face of Niyog-itim.

It was well after ten o'clock before they got the boat tied to several *barotos,* narrow, dugout canoes made of *lanigpa* or *colantas* logs with five paddlers in each. Stroking in unison with one man up on the *Betty T* softly grunting the tempo, the men towed the boat toward the mainland.

Farnsworth had chosen a small inlet near the southern curve of Divilican Bay, close to the delta of the Cagayan River, to clean and refit his boat. It was very calm inside the bay, the banks dense with jungle that hung out over the water. With the side-wheeler run down under these over-hangs, it would be hidden from anyone moving along the coast or from a patrolling Japanese aircraft.

By midnight, he and his men were hard at work aboard the *Betty T.*

Chapter Nine

0121 hours

Weesay sat beneath a huge banana leaf, trying to stay dry in his marine camo poncho. Not really dry, just *less* wet, the rain coming down as if somebody had opened floodgates up there beyond the trees. The downpour sent drops like heavy gravel into the leaf, made it bend and whip. He scowled disgustedly out at the darkness and swore an oath. He'd *never* set foot into another goddamned *hijo de puta* of a jungle for the rest of his goddamned life.

All through the early evening, the rain had hit them in sudden bursts, roaring through the trees. Within ten minutes, it would taper off and finally stop, leaving the jungle silent again until the next onslaught. Trota called these intermittent deluges *chibascos*.

Still, they at least washed the jungle air clean for a while, made it sweet and cool. In between the assaults, the night sounds returned, scattered and endless, merging slowly out of the after-rain stillness. Cockatoos shrieked, owls made their trilling little coos like mourners in a church, and the *Kalow* birds exploded into sudden wild choruses that would last fifteen seconds. Then they'd stop, all at once, and remain silent for exactly thirty minutes before they started another raucous cantata. Curious, Weesay had timed them, found they were absolutely on the dot.

The other jungle sounds came, too, the rustling of things moving stealthily through brush, among leaves, the forever close-in flitting wing-clatter of flying insects, and the wrathful, high-pitched drone of mosquitoes. Once, he heard a pack of wild boars cross to the south, the animals snorting and crashing through vegetation, their musk drifting out, smelling like a urinal in a border-town cantina.

Soon after leaving the coast, the team had passed through farmland, fields of winter corn and sugarcane, Filipino men and women working. Some saw them pass, stared in shocked surprise for a moment, then turned back to their tools lest watching Japs see their attention. Twice the team spotted small military patrols on the roads, the Nip soldiers riding bicycles with their rifles shoulder-slung.

Up on point with Bird, Frankie Trota kept them in cover as much as possible, only occasionally taking them across open ground, the men darting one at a time from one cane field to another as they worked their way ever closer to the edge of the monsoon jungle higher in the foothills.

The cane fields had thin rows of stalks, the leaves papery and beginning to turn brown. Their serrated edges nicked the men as they passed through. The few days of sunshine had dried out the ground, and now there was the constant buzzing of cicadas, and patches of large yellow ants infested the leafy mulch on the ground. Their bites burned like bee stings, and within two hours, everybody except Trota was slightly feverish from them.

They were a mile from the jungle when they stumbled across three Japanese soldiers sitting in a ditch between two cane fields. Apparently, the men had stolen some fruit and were now eating it down on the bottom, out of view of their unit's noncoms and officers.

As Trota and Wyatt came suddenly up to the edge of the ditch, the Jap's heads snapped up in shock, their half-eaten mangos and papayas stopped in midair. For a fractional, deadly, silent moment, the two sides stared at the other. Then everybody moved, lightning quick, Bird leaping down into the ditch, his belt knife flashing out, Frankie right behind him, lunging forward with a growl as he unsheathed his bolo.

Two of the Japanese soldiers turned to meet the charge, fumbling for their rifles. The third one scrambled up the opposite side. Before the first two could get squared off, Bird slammed into the first one and knocked him down hard onto his back. Quick as a snake's tongue, he slashed the soldier's left carotid, the man's eyes wide open, yellow, then his right in a backhand cut. Blood instantly pumped out of the wounds in two pulsing streams that ran down the soldier's neck.

A few feet away, Frankie swung the long blade of the bolo around in a crosscut. It struck the second soldier's left hand where he held the rifle stock. The hand was severed at the wrist. With an agonized scream, he dropped his rifle, his fingers still clasping the stock. Holding the bleeding stump of his arm tightly against his belly, he whirled around and went stumbling up the ditch side. A moment later, he dashed into the cane field where the other one had gone.

Bird and Trota took off after them.

The moment the rest of the team, still inside the opposite field, had seen the reaction of Bird and Trota, they dropped to the ground, their weapons up and eyes scanning out through the stalks. Parnell hissed. He pointed at Weesay and Smoker, signaled them to join the hunt for the fleeing Jap soldiers. He then pointed to his belt knife: *kill them with a blade.*

Both men rose. Back-slinging their Thompsons, they drew their knives and broke from cover, crossing the space between the fields hunched over. For a moment, they disappeared down into the ditch, then scrambled up the other side and slipped into the cane, slightly to the right of where Wyatt and Trota had gone in.

* * *

A few yards from the edge, Weesay stopped to listen. Somewhere directly ahead, he heard the crackle and snap of crushing stalks. The sounds stopped and a tense silence settled down through the cane, disturbed only by the soft soughing of the wind through the leaves.

With his heart racing and the drumming of adrenaline going in his temples, he slowly scanned, first to the left, then back to the right. He could just make out Wineberg's camo jacket among the stalks about twenty feet away. Smoker had also stopped. They looked at each other. Smoker made a half circle to the left in the air. Laguna nodded. They moved ahead, drawing apart.

In a few moments, Weesay came onto a blood trail. Large drops had splashed over the leaves and ground debris. They looked very bright in the shadowed light. A few yellow ants had already discovered them, and were excitedly darting about in circles and dashes.

He followed the drops cautiously, gently placing each foot down heel-to-toe, as he searched through an arc of ninety degrees, looking to catch the slightest out-of-synch movement of the cane.

Time was seamless, like the buzz of the cicadas. A full minute passed, another started. Suddenly, the wounded Japanese soldier burst through the wall of cane stalks at an angle off his left shoulder, the man coming straight at him in a thrashing rush, slamming the stalks aside, his truncated arm dangling while the other held a bayonet at arm's length. Its slender, black blade looked exceptionally long and lethal.

Instinctively, Weesay braced himself to meet the charge, his body lowered to a half crouch, his arms out and low in a knife-fighter's stance. He watched the bayonet point come on, straight at his chest. Beyond it was the Jap's contorted face beneath the brim of his field cap, its sun curtain flapping. On his collar was the red rank

bars of a *jotohei*, a superior corporal, and his ill-fitting
brown uniform and wraparound putees were worn-
looking and filthy with mud.

All this Laguna saw in a crystal-clear, flashing image.
Then he was moving, neatly deflecting the bayonet with his
own blade, feeling the weight of the charge in it, and twisting his own body away from its momentum and line of
attack. It passed just to the side of his rib cage.

The Jap soldier, seeing that his thrust had missed,
shifted his own weight so as to come around in a side cut.
Weesay, moving on pure reflex, was a half second faster.
Closing, he came under the soldier's one-armed guard,
knocked it slightly away, then slashed the left side of the
man's neck wide open with a swinging slice. Carotid blood
burst out in a spray.

Still moving with his knife hand as it finished its cut, he
immediately came right back, lower, and rammed the
blade into the Jap's upper back as he stumbled by, going
for the rear of his heart.

Throwing him off balance, the soldier's momentum
took him to the ground, Laguna going down with him, his
knife all the way in the man's back up to the hilt guard, the
wound bloodless. He felt the man's weight go off as he hit
the ground. Jerking his blade out, he rammed it in again,
then again, hearing himself grunting with effort.

The Nip never made a sound. He just went dead flat, his
head turned away, spreading wider the throat wound that
was still gushing blood. It saturated the shoulder pad of his
tunic, its edges spreading rapidly like a dark, wet fungus re-
producing at speed.

Weesay extracted the knife and sat back on his haunches.
There was blood all over his chest. Through the cloth, it felt
warm, sticky. The sound of more thrashing stalks came, scuf-
fling and grunts. He whirled, came up into fighting stance
again. There was a strangled cry and then abrupt silence. A
moment later, Bird came pushing through the cane, wiping
his knife on a leaf. Quickly dragging the Jap corpses back to

the ditch but deeper into the cane field, they left them there, covered with cane debris, and moved on.

By midafternoon, they finally reached true jungle. The rain that had been impending all day had arrived by then, sweeping in from the sea to the southeast and across the lowlands in long gray-white bands.

The team switched into single file now, the jungle growing steadily more dense the farther they got, and the ground gradually rising into foothills. Soon, they were into a deep valley. It was bordered by misty, knife-sharp ridges a thousand feet above them, which converged as they became part of the Caraballo Range of the Cordillera Central. Farther north, the Caraballo merged with the remote, deeply forested Sierra Madres that ran along the east coast.

Again, it became an agonizing, endlessly enduring labor, slogging through the nearly impenetrable, soaking-wet, mud-slick, water-rushing greenness, its gloomy, pulsing mass swallowing them up as it sucked their strength away. They stumbled over huge roots, fell when vines broke under their weight. Everything became hateful and they cursed all of it in short, panting sobs, dragging their gear bags after them like sinners weighted down with penance stones.

At nine o'clock, Parnell finally called a halt for the night. Everybody stood limply around like dark straw men hanging in effigy. He discussed the need for a dummy camp with Trota. The little Filipino shook his head, told him the *Hapones* patrols never came this deep into the forest. Instead, Red set out a two-man guard, which would be relieved every two hours. Then the rest sought out whatever shelter they could find and immediately sank into sleep.

Laguna heard a finger snap close behind him. Again. He pulled his hand from the poncho and snapped back.

A moment later, a huge shadow loomed out of the darkness. It was Kaamanui. He squatted beside him.

"I'll take her, Chihuahua," he said quietly. "Go get yourself some sack time."

At the moment, they were in between downpours. Now, after two hours of listening to jungle silences and nature noises, Sol's soft voice seemed discordant to Weesay, oddly inappropriate.

He rose. An obscenity about the rain, the jungle, the whole fucking night rose in him. He started to give it voice, stopped. He was too tired. *Fuck it*. He simply moved way, found a spot between two roots, pulled banana leaves over himself, and was sound asleep in less than a minute.

The two American Black Widow night fighters attacked the train carrying Lieutenant Sacabe and his *hara-guntai* at one minute after three in the morning, the aircraft suddenly blowing out of the darkness, totally lightless, two black shadows flashing past in the rain, the muzzle bursts from their 20mm cannons and 50mm machine guns like orange white candle flames. All their rounds went high, tore up the left side of the rail bed cut.

These were Marine P-61s from the light carrier USS *Ticonderoga* of Task Group Three, part of Admiral Bull Halsey's Third Fleet. For the past three days, TG-3 had been operating off eastern Luzon in search-and-destroy missions against the remnants of the Imperial Navy.

The aircraft were big, black, twin-engine fighters specifically designed for night combat and bombing runs. Equipped with the latest radar gear, they were conducting target-of-opportunity runs over the interior of the island.

All through the long day, Sacabe and his men had run into frustrating delays. At Baguio, there had been possible sabotage inside the town's small train terminal where a section of track was disabled by an as yet unexplained explosion. The line had to be completely repaired before any outgoing traffic could move.

Then, when they reached a point about a mile from the big junction town of Sante Fe, eight miles southeast of Yamashita's HQ, they were informed that the only rail bridge across the Agno River had been partially destroyed by Filipino guerillas two hours before. Engineer companies were hurriedly trying to get it repaired, had already jury-rigged a narrow footbridge over the river. But there would be no train or truck traffic for at least another day, perhaps two.

Fuming, terrified of another failure, Sacabe had ordered his men to use the foot span and then double-time the remaining distance into Santa Fe, carrying all their gear, weapons, and spare ammo.

Since they were essentially a mobile ground unit and lightly armed, their gear was not particularly burdensome. Each rifleman carried an Arisaka 7.7mm carbine, four grenades, extra ammo pouches, and a Nambu 8mm sidearm. Among the riflemen were at least six equipped with the cup-type grenade launchers and missile boxes.

The attack force's automatic weapons section comprised three Model 99 light machine guns, each one manned by a three-man crew: one to fire, one to load, and one to haul ammo. All the soldiers were skilled combat veterans from various other companies and battalions, most of them experiencing intense fighting in the southern islands.

The Santa Fe junction turned out to be a madhouse, with long supply convoys and troops all jammed up. Still, Sacabe's orders, bearing Yamashita's personal signature, immediately cut through red tape. By late afternoon, the senior yardmaster had supplied him with a small switching locomotive, a Wilcox-Todd steam-powered two-four-two unit, pulling a coaler and two flatcars.

Just before dusk, they left Sante Fe and headed northeast, the rail line paralleling the main Cabanatuan Highway. It was 198 kilometers to Magsaysay, all of it through mountainous terrain. Their first stop would be at the large town of Bayombong, about three hours away, to take on water. Next would be Santiago, another three hours. From there, they'd turn north, pass through the tiny mountain barrios of San Mateo, Aurora, San Manuel, Roxas, Mallig, and then on to Magsaysay.

The little switcher engine strained as it crept along the narrow, ever-climbing rail bed, which had been blasted out of sheer cliff. It didn't make good time at all and didn't reach Bayombong until nearly midnight, everybody soaking wet from the nearly constant rain. They left thirty-three minutes later and made for Santiago.

They were halfway there when the Black Widows hit them. . . .

Now the planes swung around for another run, coming in higher this time, at an angle to the rail line. The muzzle flashes from their weapons came silently, the cannon rounds and bullets shattering the air first, and then the rapid explosions of the guns as they caught up to the bullets. Both Widows went into steep pullouts and rocketed past in leader-wingman formation.

All the Japanese soldiers had dropped either to the flatcar bed or to the ground. Many had managed to open fire with their small arms. But the two aircraft were gone in less than a blink, only a flicking glimpse of their engine exhausts blowing white hot and their prop washes creating snapping curls in the explosion dust and fragmented debris that had blown into the air.

Most of the lead plane's strafing fire had struck the cut bank forty yards high. Chunks of rock and dirt and tree fragments came raining down through the true rain. But the wingman's guns stitched a line of eruptions along the rails ahead of the locomotive. One of the 20mm cannon rounds struck the little engine's boiler dead-center. The thing exploded in a ball of orange laced with pure white steam. Metal shrapnel sizzled off in all directions.

The coaler was blown into the air and over the edge of

the railroad cut. It went tumbling end-over-end down the steep slope, crashing through forest and leaving a deep scar behind it. The two flatcars were immediately derailed, the front one skidding head-on into the upper slope before being plowed into by the second. Both turned over.

Since the engine had been moving so slowly, many of the soldiers had been able to leap clear before they hit. Still, there were bodies on the tracks and wounded men stumbled about in a daze. Bellowing, Sacabe formed a search detail that began scrambling over the wreckage, pulling out more injured.

While they were at it, the American fighters came back for one final pass. Again, most of their rounds went high. As quickly as they had come, they now climbed sharply and disappeared back into the night and the rain.

There were nine dead and eighteen wounded. Sacabe immediately sent a radio message to the garrison at Bayombong notifying the military garrison there of the attack. He also ordered its radio operator to relay a message to Baguio, directly to General Nagai, assuring him that the special mission team was continuing despite its loss of men.

Cursing and lashing out with his fists, he got the walking men into a ragged formation beside the rails. There were also seven wounded men included. They set off at a quick march toward the nearest barrio, a tiny mountain hamlet named Diadi that was three kilometers away. He intended to commandeer any vehicles he could find there, then continue on to the garrison at Santiago where he would requisition trucks.

Four years of ocean water, currents, sand, and the clinging of crustaceans and mollusks had left the hull of the *Betty T* a couple hundred pounds heavier than when Fransworth had put her under.

Throughout the dark morning hours, he and his salvage

crew, sixteen Filipinos working in silence, handled the hull, scraping off barnacles and salt buildup, checking seams, doing it all in the dark while the rain periodically hammered down through the trees. Structurally, the boat was stronger and tighter than before, its long months of immersion expanding the wood to fully seal seams and joints.

By daybreak, they had cleaned up the hull enough to turn to the below spaces, to completely check out the condition of the engine and drive systems, the heart of the old boat. With meager light coming down through the four deck hatches, they found that it was in surprisingly good shape. Farnsworth had done an extremely thorough job of sealing and packing and the metal appeared to be free of corrosion.

He and Lauro Rafareal began peeling back the thick coatings of oil and grease that covered everything. First, they unsealed and pulled the plugs from all the engine portals, going slowly with each step to be sure there wasn't any internal damage. They used tool kits recovered from the boatyard, the things themselves grease-coated and shiny as new despite the time underground.

Next, they pulled the heads of the three cylinders to be sure their pistons and cylinder walls were free of condensation rust. They also unpacked the D-slide valve sleeves, cleaned the linkages, crossheads, and connecting rods, then repacked them with fresh marine grease and oil, which the Filipinos had long ago stolen from the Japanese to use as cooking fuel.

Finally, they yanked the crankshaft and flywheel housings, then the main gearbox. They couldn't believe how clean it all was. Working in reverse, they replaced everything, reoiling and regreasing the gears and bearings.

Then they ran into trouble. The packing in the main shaft bearing had leaked and partially rusted out the rollers themselves. Farnsworth cursed. The unit had to be pulled. If it was totally ruined, that would be that. Without milling equipment and acetylene gear, they'd never be able to rig a decent bearing that could take the strain from the crankshaft.

It was a hellish job extracting it, using a quickly made block and tackle with twisted-fiber ropes, the men lining up topside and pulling on the double lines that ran up through two hatchways, one man calling the cadence. At last, the bearing exploded out and went skidding across the hold deck.

Farnsworth shoved it over to a shaft of light and got right down there close, ran his fingers along the viscosity channels and rollers, then the journal head, feeling for rust. He finally turned and flashed a grin up at Rafareal. "By Christ, we're still alive, Raff. She's usable."

He assigned several men to meticulously sand off the rusted metal. It took nearly two hours. Repacking the entire bearing, they inserted it, using *narawood* blocks as buffers so the sledges wouldn't scour the seal covers. Eventually, they got them reseated, aligned, and sealed.

He knew the slight loss of metal that had been sanded from the rollers would cause some vibration. Maybe enough to lose him a couple of miles an hour from the normal cruising speed of ten. It might even create leaks in the sponson seals. But he'd simply have to watch it closely, setting the best RPM to the engine to minimize the shudder, and then periodically inject grease through the journal nipples.

A bigger problem loomed. The sponson seals in the hull through which the axle shafts ran to become the main driving shafts of the paddle wheels had swelled enough to seize up completely. They were made of New Zealand *lignum vitae*, an extremely dense wood that had been used in old sailing ships for their capstan and rudder bearings. The shafts were now locked tight.

They first tried to unwork them by heaving on the paddle wheels. But that put too much strain on the shafts, Farnsworth afraid they might warp enough to become useless. They next considered slow-heating the wood to shrink it enough to move the shafts. But without a welding torch and collar rings, that would be impossible.

Farnsworth and Raffles squatted in the now sweltering engine hold and silently considered the problem, narrow-eyeing the machinery and thinking. The Brit finally decided the only thing they could do was use boiler steam to shrink the seals.

When he told Raffles, the little Filipino frowned, sweat pouring down his narrow, brown face. "Is gonna be berry tricky dat way, sor. What we make pire in the hull? Or the seal, she get big too past, making crack." He slapped two fingers into his palm to illustrate the snap of the wood.

Farnsworth nodded. "Aye, she could do that, indeed. But we've got Cobber's Choice, mate."

Meanwhile, Panay had been working on the boilers, water tanks, and transfer lines. He'd already thoroughly cleaned off the salt deposits from the fire tubes, grate bars, and ash chamber so any stray crystals wouldn't explode, risking fire tube damage. The bricks in the refactory wall had also been checked for seam breaks, and the pressure lines blown and checked for leaks.

Another mechanic, Iliandro Nazareno, had been working topside, breaking down and cleaning the two deck donkey engines that operated the forward winch used to pull the boat off sandbars, and the main pump that transferred water from the water tanks to the boiler tubes. Both were gasoline fed, but Farnsworth intended to use alcohol distilled from *tuba*, which the natives made into a drink called *alak*.

By this time, the woodcutter crew had assembled nearly two cords of eucalyptus logs and stowed them belowdecks. In the old days, Farnsworth had used high-carbon coal as fuel. He knew these freshly cut logs would burn inefficiently and leave a film of sap distillate on the fire tubes. But it couldn't be helped. At least, eucalyptus smoke was white and easily dissipated so as not to expose them on the river as coal smoke would have done.

It was nearly noon when they fired up the boiler, Raffles and the others excited, their dark eyes shining: *finally a chance to strike back against the hated Hapones*. The eucalyptus logs burned quickly, putting a pale smoke out the stack, which then quickly dissolved in the rain.

They had run a steam line out a hatchway to release the pressure. Now it slowly climbed, the gauges flicking to life and moving upward: 90 psi/150 degrees Fahrenheit . . . 140 psi/205 F . . . 160 psi/230 F . . .

When it reached 200 psi and 245 degrees F, Farnsworth signaled Raffles, spun the steam valve, and they began putting heat to the starboard sponson bearing. The hold filled with the roaring hiss of the steam, Raffles and another man holding the nozzle three feet from the hull, their faces and upper bodies hidden in wet gunnysacks.

Four seconds of steam, then off with the valve. A count of three, then another four seconds of steam. They did that five times, then shut down and released pressure up through the stack, stabilizing the gauge.

It worked. The *lignum vitae* bearings shrank, forming a watertight seal around the shaft but still allowing it to revolve. The port-side bearing needed a double shot, the hull blackening, condensation running off the overhead and metal engine and tanks from the drifting steam. But it, too, finally locked in.

Farnsworth retrieved his radio and weapons. While a *culesa* cart was dispatched to the nearest barrio for more stolen Jap grease and oil along with eight wooden, fifteen-liter barrels of *alak*, they tested the engine, engaging the driveline just enough to turn the paddle wheels one full revolution, the push of the water shoving the *Betty T*'s bow gently against the bank.

Everything worked beautifully.

The final touch to the boat was the restructuring of the canopy. It was lengthened to cover the entire deck and a large canvas tarp was laid over it, on which were placed tree branches to camouflage the boat against Jap air surveillance or attack.

It was now dusk. The two men who had gone for the oil had also brought back food: ceramic pots of a fish stew called *sinigang* and packets of *babingka* pancakes made from rice and eggs, fried *camote* slices and fresh coconut meat and garlic-spiced *kangkong*, a cooked and diced swamp cabbage, everybody sitting cross-legged on the upper deck in the wet, deepening darkness, hungrily eating and grinning happily, greasily at each other for the success of their work.

Farnsworth kept Raffles, Panay, and Nazareno with him to crew on the run upriver. He profusely thanked the others and promised he would not leave Luzon this time. They kissed his hand, wished him to "go with the Father," and departed.

Rafareal broke out his can of homemade cigars made from wild tobacco leaves mixed with sugar and bits of lemongrass, then rolled in banana leaves and sealed with rice paste. They were strong and gave off the scent of ginger. The four men smoked, sitting under the canopy as the jungle night sounds came on.

Farnsworth took the first radio watch, the unit stashed up in the trees to prevent interference from the metal components of the side-wheeler. The three Filipinos quietly curled up and were soon asleep.

0843 hours
8 February

Blue Team found fifteen skeletons up in the high pine just beyond Magsaysay, the corpses with their clothing almost completely rotted off, their bones a dull white. They lay near a stream, now swollen and foaming with mud-thick water and storm debris. It appeared as if the men had been lined up parallel to the bank, back a hundred feet, and then shot. The back of each skull had a big, jagged hole blown through the base. Several had two.

The team trooped past without comment. To their veteran combat minds, dead bodies, skeletons, the entire panorama of death had lost its frightful power to shock. But they did notice that some of the skeletons had broken arm and leg bones and the dark bruising marks created by bayonet blades. Before the killings, the men had obviously been tortured. *That* they filed away.

They'd been on the move since before dawn, traveling the high ridges of the Fuyo National Preserve. Just before noon, they had come in sight of Magsaysay, and swung south to give it a wide berth, the place known to house at least one company of Japanese soldiers.

The *bayan*, or midsized town, was a rail terminus. It had cobbled streets lined with merchant *tindahans*, a white wooden church with a stone steeple, and a dirty, flat-roofed, brick *pamahalaan*, or government house, which was undoubtedly now headquarters for the Japanese.

The circular square in front, which had previously been used for religious fiestas and Sunday afternoon cockfights, was now filled with Japanese field equipment, including four 40mm Model 96 antiaircraft auto cannons, garrison tents, several hurriedly built outbuildings, and a stone horse corral. The native houses were made of red mud bricks with corrugated tin roofs and spread away from the town to the surrounding woods amid fields of corn and tobacco.

The mining compound lay eight miles from the town, up into high forest, which was different from the jungle of the lower slopes. Everything here was shiny, deep green. The trees were a dense mixture of silver pine and mahogany and *nara* wood, the understory covered by great banks of orchids and fern clusters and deep carpets of moss. Fog continuously slipped through the trees in distinct layers, yet always from up the slope. It gave the air a crisp, wet-heavy feel and a half-sweet fungal perfume.

The wildlife was different, too. Red-faced monkeys with unusually long tails screamed at them, while golden monkey-eating eagles, big as buzzards, drifted on the air currents close above the treetops, ranging with high-pitched squeaks as they hunted.

Acetylene-blue *tarictic* birds flashed in the gloom like sudden glimpses of a summer sky and flying lemurs glided silently through the fog, their webbed skins vibrating. There were blue-green reticulated pythons with bodies so thick a man couldn't touch his fingers around them, and three-foot-long monitor lizards that snorted and hissed as they passed their dens.

At four in the afternoon, amid a frigid downpour, they reached a ridge that overlooked the Tallangatta Consolidated Goldfields Lode Pit number 4.

Through the binoculars, the prisoners looked and moved like stick figures in tattered costume. The rain made them appear even more pathetic. Parnell could almost feel their misery coming up at him from all the way down the slope.

The separate crews for the different stages of the processing system of the mine tended their machinery and tanks, the rain steaming off hot metal, billowing, the men shoveling and guiding hoses and carrying ash with the slowed-down, mechanical movements of robots with their power supply running down.

The Jap sentries squatted a ways off, their heads covered with straw mats. He examined them closely. They all had filthy uniforms, looked emaciated, and stood their guard slovenly, without any crack or spit-and-polish.

Lying beside him, Wyatt commented, "Them POWs is in pretty bad shape, Lieutenant. They ain't gonna be goin' fast nor far."

Red grunted agreement. He slid the binoculars up the slope to the crest of a ridge that was another eight hundred feet beyond the mine compound, much of it shrouded in mist. But through breaks he could see all the way eastward to the hazy, high spines of the Sierra Madres that ran along the coast.

Swinging back down, he focused on the mine pithead. Two horses or jackasses, he couldn't tell which, in rope harnesses were going round and round the lifter drum with the same slow dejection as the crew of prisoners who were trying to get a cage up and swung over, the thing loaded with chunks of rock.

He scanned around the entire compound, studied the two guard posts, the soldiers moving around inside, the structures up on poles. Next, he checked the placement of the buildings and what they appeared to be used for. It was obvious the Japanese unit was concentrated in one of the barracks and the company building beside it. A Nip flag hung limply from a pole made from a single pine trunk. Between it and the company building was a small assembly area, now deep in mud.

Parnell's mind was already beginning to sort out the details of his assault plan, laying out potential entry points, fire zones, convergence moves. Swinging the binoculars back across the compound, he passed three huge water tanks lined out between the pithead and boilers. He stopped, came back for a better look. Something in his head went *click*.

They were made of welded sheets of steel, about thirty feet across and ten feet high, looking like truncated silos. The metal sheets had long since become coated with dense layers of rust. The tops were covered with boards and there were bamboo pipes that emptied into them from a network of flues that came through the upside of the fence from the woods. A fourth tank was located across the compound, right next to the barracks and company building.

"How much water you figure's in them tanks?" he asked Bird.

"I'd say a good bunch, Lieutenant." Wyatt smiled coldly. "Make a fair-sized flood they was to all bust open, wouldn't they?"

"Just what I was thinking."

He gave the compound one more sweep, and then he and Bird slipped back into solid cover. The rest of the men were lined along the edge of the woods. Parnell waved Kaamanui and Trota over. They came quickly, went to one knee beside him as he pulled out the recon photo pack and laid two on the wet ground. Rain droplets immediately beaded on the slick surfaces.

"There are only two guard posts," he began, pointing them out on the map. "Here on the upside, and here at the main gate. I figure there's about fifty men in the guard unit. At night, they'll undoubtedly be concentrated in the last barracks near the headquarters house. Right here. If we hit both sites simultaneously, we can bottle up most of the force."

Sol shook his head. "I gotta tell you, Lieutenant, these slope-heads got some shitty daylight security goin' here."

Red nodded. "Yeah, sloppy as hell. They aren't first-line troops, probably never were. And guarding starving prisoners has undoubtedly made the bastards *really* careless. That's in our favor." He turned to Trota. "What's the usual Jap *night* security?"

The small Filipino shrugged. "Eb'ry time is two guards on main buildings and in machining gun fosts."

"What about inside, with the prisoners?"

"Always two outside, sometimes two inside."

"How about guard dogs?"

"Sometimes, but I no see any here."

Red looked down at the primary photo, again visualizing the positions of his assault teams, their entry points and key targets. Finally, he said, "We'll go in at the two gun posts. Wyatt, you and one man take out the gate, with Sol and two men as your security. Once you're inside, Bird's team lays charges on two of those water tanks. Make sure you blow the ones that're full, I want this place flooded. Sol's team, you move to the left and set up on the prisoners' barracks." He turned back to Bird. "As soon as the charges are ready, come back down and link with Kaamanui."

The two sergeants nodded.

"Take out the two outside guards right off," Parnell went on. "Just before the tanks go, I want three men inside, right *now*, before any guards with the prisoners can start gunning people. Outside team pops a flare, then starts putting ordnance into the front of that Jap barracks. It's here, and that there's the HQ house. Keep your rounds in the forward part of the building so you don't friendly-fire me and Frankie at the back.

"We're gonna handle the upslope guard post. Then I'll place charges on the fourth tank. That's this one, near the HQ house. Twenty seconds before they trigger, we'll start fragging the Jap barracks on the backside."

He glanced around. "Remember one thing. Once those tanks blow, there's gonna be a helluva lot of water coming at you all at once, wherever the hell you are. Brace yourselves and be ready for it. I want these sons a' bitches to think they're under artillery or air attack, rattle the hell out of 'em. I figure that'll give us three, maybe four minutes before some of them start reacting. As for the prisoners, hold 'em inside the barracks until the area's secure."

Another heavier sweep of rain suddenly came pounding over them, rattling the underbrush, slamming onto their heads and shoulders. Parnell returned the recon photos to their plastic bag and tucked it into one of the pockets of his jump pants. He looked around.

"Check your weapons and demo packs," he said. "Wyatt, especially double-check those timers. One of them sons a' bitches goes off too soon, we lose surprise." Again he scanned faces. "So, is everybody clear?"

The three men nodded again.

"Okay, go get some rest. We'll move down to preassault positions at midnight."

Chapter Ten

Although the outcome of the battle for Luzon, and thus the entire Philippine campaign, was no longer in doubt, General Yamashita still possessed nearly 200,000 troops scattered throughout Luzon itself.

With him in the north was the Shobu group, 130,000 strong. In southern Luzon, there was the Shimbo group of 30,000 troops under the command of Brigadier General Iteki Yokoyama, a fierce and stubborn officer. The balance of the forces were in pockets at the tip of Bataan, around Lake Taal southwest of Manila, and in the Zambeles Mountains where the Kembu group had split into guerilla-type units northeast of the capital.

On 5 February, while bitter fighting still raged in Manila, MacArthur ordered General Kreuger to prepare his 158th Regimental Combat Team for landings at Legazpi on the Bicol Peninsula in southern Luzon. This strike would signal the beginning of mopping-up operations in the south, and would open the San Bernardino Strait route between Luzon and Samar for supply traffic. The RCT was then to link with elements of Eighth Army crossing from Samar.

Elsewhere in the Philippines, the American reconquest of the islands was now running on a full head of steam.

Schedules had already been set for landings at Mariveles at the tip of Bataan and on Corregidor, both aimed at wiping out the stubborn Japanese resistance that still lingered there and thus fully secure Manila Bay.

Batangas, the biggest port south of Manila, was also scheduled to be taken by early March. In addition, fleet and ground units were now moving to assembly areas for the first major landings on the island of Mindinao, along its Zamboanga Peninsula.

But the planners in the War Department and Southwest Pacific Area Command had gone far beyond the Philippines in their strategy protocols. Operational and logistical orders for the next two major invasions had already been put into effect.

The first was scheduled for 19 February 1945, and would be on the tiny island of Iwo Jima in the Bonin chain. The second was on the far larger island of Okinawa-Jima in the Ryukyus, this one timed for 1 April 1945. These landings would be the final stepping stones to the invasion of the Japanese Archipelago itself.

Since late January, most of the big navy transports used in the Philippine campaign had begun returning to Pacific Fleet Command, while the Liberty and Victory ships were reassigned back to the War Shipping Administration. Meanwhile, in depots throughout the Pacific, the 3rd, 4th, and 5th Marine Divisions were staging for Iwo. And the Okinawa assault forces, including the 1st, 2nd, and 6th Marine Divisions along with the 7th, 96th, 77th, and 27th Infantry Divisions of XXIV Army Corps, were now in refit and training.

But those battles lay ahead. On Luzon, Yamashita was now frantically shifting his Fourteenth Area Army divisions to create strong points throughout the mountainous interior of the island. His aim, the only rational one he *could* have at this point, was to act as a delaying force to slow down the Allied thrust toward his homeland.

Among his major northern units in the realignment were the 58th and 79th Independent Mixed Brigades, one from the north coast town of Abulug, the other from Aparri. Each comprised six thousand troops. Also moving south with them was the Second Armored Division from garrison Pamplona. From the northeastern and mideastern coast came the Tenth Division along with the 54th and 55th IMBs, both veteran outfits of the fighting on Leyte after which they had escaped through Samar.

One of his best fighting units, the 39th Raiding Brigade, under the command of Colonel Motoichi Shibasaki, a dashing, audacious onetime tank officer, had also been ordered from its mountain training base at Dinapigui at the foot of the coastal Sierra Madres.

The bulk of this force, four thousand men, had already crossed a tributary of the Cagayan River at Benito Soliven. They were to eventually link with the 79th IMB at Tuguegarao and Tabuk, then turn due south to take up defensive positions outside Baguio. Three of its forward companies had already passed beyond Ilagan on Highway 45, fifteen miles from Magsaysay.

At the same time, another elite force, this one American and composed of a hundred volunteers from the 11th Airborne Division, had already been pulled from the fighting in Manila and sent into reserve at the airfield of Agono outside the capital.

They were preparing for a special operation, a jump two hundred miles northeast of Manila in the Fuyo National Preserve located in the western highlands of the Sierra Madres. Their mission objective was the evacuation to the coast of an unspecified number of prisoners from a Japanese gold mining camp near Magsaysay. They'd already drawn gear and were simply sitting and waiting for the go-signal to arrive from a recon team already on the ground.

Frustration was mounting for Lieutenant Sacabe. He actually trembled with outrage at how badly things could go. Not smooth and in control like back in China or Malaysia.

Zakennayo! His men desperately tried to stay away from him since he was apt to suddenly strike out at anyone near him, savagely beating the man with his fists.

At Diadi, they had found only a tiny collection of typhoon houses, shed-sized structures with roofs formed of bound bundles of *nipa,* which were lapped over their peaks like the spines of a book. It was pitch-dark, no one moving about. He and his men raged among them, kicking in doors, rousting cowering Filipino families out into the rain at bayonet point, screaming in their faces and demanding a vehicle.

They finally managed to gather up six two-wheeled farm carts pulled by *carabaos.* The wooden carts stank of manure and rotted tobacco leaves and sour rice hulls, and the buffalo moved at a ponderous pace, the soldiers beating them with the butts of their rifles. Rain pounded at them, and there were small mud slides along the road that slowed them even more.

Santiago lay four miles away, beyond a high ridge. As they drew closer, however, they heard gunfire and saw a bright orange glow, with occasional flashes, coming from a large fire that silhouetted the higher peaks and made them shimmer in the rain. The undersides of the billowing smoke resembled storm clouds. When they finally cleared the ridge, they could see it was Santiago that was aflame.

When they tried to enter the town, the *carabaos* balked with fear, then bolted. Two carts were tipped over, spilling the soldiers out into the muddy road. They quickly formed up and jogged the rest of the way.

The town had been bombed by a flight of six American night fighters who laid in two-hundred-pound bombs and strafed the Japanese garrison. Most of it had been destroyed, tents gone and supply buildings turned into smoking rubble. Blackened vehicles and the smoldering bodies of soldiers and caisson horses were strewn all over. Wounded animals screamed.

Two small fuel tanks belched out great billows of black smoke, and now and then star shells and tracer rounds went off, shooting into the sky like fireworks. Fire-control teams raced about, trying to control the flames, using hand pumps and canvas lines to suck water from the rain-swollen ditches.

Parts of the town had also been hit. Several buildings along the main road were burning, and there was the thick smell of tobacco in the air from a tobacco-curing barn that was in full blaze, and the bell tower of a church that faced the main plaza had been blown away. Filipinos confusedly milled about the streets, some uselessly throwing bucketfuls of rainwater onto the fires. Each time explosions came from the garrison area, they would fall to the ground, covering their heads.

Sacabe rushed about grabbing soldiers and demanding to know where the commander of the garrison was. No one could tell him. He finally located the man in one of the small mess buildings. He was a *shosa no seisaku*, a construction major, well formed and, under normal conditions, might have been handsome. Now his face was red and puffed up with rage, his uniform smeared with blood and ash.

Seated on a wooden bench near the door was an American pilot, his hands bound behind his back. The major had been interrogating him. The pilot kept lurching forward toward the floor as if in a faint. Each time he did, a soldier beside him would grab his hair and pull him upright again.

He had been beaten severely. His face was covered with fresh blood, his cheeks and lips bruised and swollen grotesquely. His khaki-colored flight suit was torn, soaked with rain and mud and blood. He still wore his Mae West lifejacket and an empty shoulder holster. With his arms twisted behind him, a bloody elbow bone protruded through the ripped left sleeve.

Sacabe strode forward and braced at the major's side.

"*Dozo*, Honorable Major," he snapped. "I must speak with you immediately."

"Get out and fight the fires," the major shouted back.

"But, sir, I have orders signed by General Yamashita."

Without warning, the senior officer struck him across the face with the back of his hand, then glowered at him. "*Baka*, get *out*!"

Sacabe, eyes quivering, stepped back.

The major continued interrogating the American pilot, bellowing at him in Japanese. The man stared back, uncomprehending. Through swollen slits, his light blue eyes darted with fear. The Japanese officer put his face down close to his and screamed insults. Then he punched the man, first with his right, then his left fist. The American fell backward heavily and hit the floor with his head, jerking it forward.

The major barked an order. With two soldiers supporting the enemy pilot, they took him out into the garrison street. It was raining hard again. The air stank of burning wood and flesh, tobacco and cordite. The soldiers shoved him to his knees and stepped back. The American was visibly trembling. The rain made his dark hair shine in the light from the mess building and the fires.

The major drew his sword and with a single double-handed cut beheaded the pilot. Blood shot out of the severed neck, steaming in the cold. The rush made a soft hissing sound, like when a tiny droplet of oil lands onto a hot skillet. The head tumbled away into a rain pool, facedown.

Wiping his sword blade with a handkerchief, the major stomped back into the mess building. Sacabe followed, again braced. "Sir, I *must* speak with you. It is most urgent."

The senior officer turned and looked at him. He was panting with emotion. "Give me your orders," he barked.

Sacabe handed over the mission order he had received from General Nagai. The major scanned it, frowned, read

it again, slower. He finally looked up. His voice was quieter.
"Where are you going?"

"To Magsaysay, sir."

"What do you need?"

"At least two trucks, sir."

The major snorted. "There *are* no trucks."

"Then what must I do, sir?"

The senior officer's eyes looked at him, then away. He
waved his arm. "Take whatever you can find."

"Thank you, *ga-Shosa*." He braced, turned, and strode out.

He and his men combed the area for usable vehicles. All
they found still in working order were two Model 97 motorcycles with sidecars, a Model 95 four-by-four scout car
with the commanding officer's rank flag attached to the
windshield, and a decrepit 1934, diesel-powered Graham-
Bradley bus, built by an American tractor company.

Most of the bus's windows had been broken out and all
the seats removed so it could be used to haul food supplies.
The floor was coated with rice powder and there were two
cases of canned squid beside the driver's seat.

Driving the scout car with his senior *gunso*, Lieutenant
Sacabe finally led his small strike force, riding the bus and
the motorcycles, back onto Highway 45 and headed north
toward Ilagan, forty-three miles away. The time was 11:35.

0307 hours
8 February

The first signal Wyatt got that there was someone else in
there with him was the smell. A rank, dried-blood stink
that came clearly through the other odors of chemicals
and waterlogged wood and rust, all gathered down there
in the tight space between the number-two water tank and
a pump house tucked in beside it. Old metal pipes ran
across the space, some packed with gunnysacking clamped
over leakage points, and boards had been randomly

placed overhead, holding out most of the rain save for that which blew in from the sides.

He went perfectly still, all his senses notched up about a hundred percent from their normal intensity. He stared into the darkness, slid his chin slightly to the right, looked out from the side of his eyes, an old combat soldier's trick to better see objects in the darkness.

It was *pitch*-dark in there, no faint glow from anything, the narrow space funneling and magnifying the rushing hiss of the rain and the sharp ping of drops hitting the top of the pump house and overhead boards. He slid his chin the other way, peered out again. Nothing.

Jesus!

He suddenly *sensed* that something had just reared up directly in front of him, maybe three feet away. His heart leaped into a higher gear. He had been partially upright with his legs under him and his demo bag around his left shoulder. Now, moving with slow, methodical smoothness, he reached for his boot knife, slid it from its sheath between sock and canvas, held it ready in his hand.

He tried to pick out a sound, any sound to offer a hint of what and where precisely his opponent was. Over the rain, there was only a wet silence. In his head, he cursed it. In the same moment, he caught another wave of the rank odor, like the stench he remembered when field-dressing a deer, slicing its belly open to let entrails fall out.

He stared so fixedly, his eyes began to sting. He'd forgotten to blink. He blinked. There was a rustle. He caught that sound despite the rain's noise. A visualization leaped into the mind, the soldier out there coming right at him, going for his face, his chest. He braced, stiffening his entire body for the impact, absolutely motionless.

An entire minute went past, agonizingly slowly. He considered slashing out with the knife, cut the fucker in whatever body part he cold reach, slice right to left, then left to right and cut him enough to make him commit.

No, wait, wait.

Another entire minute dragged by.

Fuck this.

He slid his left hand slowly up to the lapel of his fatigue battle tunic, felt for the tiny light pinned there, turned it until it faced directly ahead, inhaled, and flicked it on, then off.

What he saw in that flash froze his soul. . . .

Earlier, neutralizing the lower guard post had been easy, the two Jap soldiers up there all scrunched down in their tropical canvas parkas, their pot helmets covered with camo netting. He and Cowboy had slit their throats, cutting right through the helmet straps. Both died soundlessly.

Leaving Sol's team to set up positions near the prisoner building, they crossed the compound, holding near the fence, and approached the water tanks from the upside of the slope. By tapping on the metal sides with their knife handles and then listening for sound rebound, they found that all three were full.

Wyatt chose to blow the top and bottom ones of the three, hoping the explosions and sudden surge of water would also knock over the middle one. He touched Cowboy's shoulder, leaned in, whispering softly, "Take number three. Lay force toward the center." He felt him move off; then he turned and headed for the one highest on the slope. . . .

In that fraction of a second of light, Bird had seen a large snake, its upper body lifted off the ground. It swayed ever so gently, its tongue flicking to read the heat signals coming off this thing that had just entered its space. The rest of the body lay alongside Wyatt's right leg.

It was about twelve feet long, as big around as a sewer line. The color of its scales was a wet-shiny brown with net-like patterns of black, the belly a creamy white. Its head was long, blunt-nosed with a shallow groove down the center. It was a reticulated mountain python.

Wyatt's brain had absorbed its entirety in that little burst of illumination. His eyes had looked for a fraction of a second into its brown-green stare, the bony ridges over it giving it a fixed lethality. And he froze.

Bird hated snakes, dreaded them with a loathing and terror out of all proportion to anything else he feared. Now the seconds decelerated until they seemed barely to move. He felt as if all the cells in his body had also slammed to a stop, save for those in his heart, in his coursing blood.

But thoughts continued shooting through his mind with supersonic speed. From somewhere, he recalled that a snake this big would not be venomous. *Shoot it, shoot it, empty your gawddamn sidearm into its fuckin' head.* No, he couldn't do that, a gunshot now would alert the whole Jap camp. *Then use your knife, slice it into tiny pieces.*

He couldn't move at all.

The snake swayed.

Visions of the creature lunging forward, taking his head in its huge jaws, coiling itself around him in the darkness made him tremble inside. Then, from deep in his memory banks, older images regurgitated into his consciousness, recollections from way back, at the zero-point and beginnings of his terror: *a wooden church-house outside Tracy's Crossing, Tennessee, the Brethren of the Valley Church, a rainy evening, people, his father, too, handling snakes, rattlers and cottonmouths and black moccasins, the things writhing in their hands and the men glassy-eyed, like his father got sometimes when he was deep-down drunk, trancelike, the people chanting and shouting praises to the Lord and passing those writhing bodies down close to his little four-year-old face, and him looking into eyes as bright and steady as agates and suddenly knowing what Evil was. . . .*

He felt the snake's tail curl over his right calf, gently, almost daintily, exploring. He could feel the unbelievable musculature pressing down through his pant leg as it moved, enclosing him. *Sweet Christ, it's gonna eat me alive!*

A surge of rage swept into him. *No!* Forcing all his mental energy into focus, he willed his hand to move, flicked on the lapel light again. The snake lifted its head slightly in the sudden beam. Its eyes sparkled, like amber seen through oil. Wyatt felt his entire skull go icy cold. He gripped his knife.

Steeling himself, his teeth clenched until they hurt, he brought his mind and body together into that coordinated tension of fight: his legs, arms, shoulders readying up. *All right, you big cocksucker, one of us is gonna die here, but it ain't gonna be me.*

Yet before he could spring forward and close with the snake, it abruptly lowered its head to the ground and began to move past him along the side of the pump house. *What? What?* He held the light on it, watched its entire body uncoil, moving. He saw now that there was a large bulge in its belly. The thing had obviously recently fed.

It crossed by his right leg, seeming oblivious of him now, the long length of it forming slight curves, the belly bulge bumping along. Slowly, just as gently, its tail slid off his calf. He couldn't take his eyes from it as the huge reptile slowly, majestically disappeared out into the rain and the darkness.

It took him two whole minutes to settle himself down enough so he could begin laying his demo charges.

For an inexplicable reason, Eugene Mallory had awakened suddenly from a dream. It was something he had not done since coming to the mining compound. Ordinarily, his exhaustion always sent him into depths where dreams didn't exist.

This one had been wonderful, himself alone in a mountain stream fishing for trout, the day bright and warm with the pleasant countering sensation of the cold water surging over his wading boots. Pines edged the banks and there were little patches of melting snow lying in blue shadows beneath the trees.

His abrupt extraction from it left him feeling a terrible restlessness. Surges of unusual energy made his emaciated body want to leap from his sleeping shelf, run through the barracks, out the door, and up into the forested hills.

He tried to calm himself. Why had he awakened? Had his mental clock gone askew? He made himself lie very still, listening to the rain drumming on the barracks roof. He did not hear the soft rustle of the maggots.

At last, he shifted his head to look down the line of bamboo sleeping shelves. Now the scattered snores, hacking coughs, and groans that had been hidden in the rain sound emerged. Odd. He had noticed this peculiar phenomenon before, the inability of his mind to register multiple sounds or smells at the same time. It was as if the sensory part of his brain had narrowed, allowing only single impulses to enter. With a surge of his heart, he wondered: *When that portal becomes too tiny, is that death?*

That reality drained down through him, made him suddenly, extremely, unbearably sad. He pushed it back. It took a great deal of effort to do so. But that had been another bit of advice Halperan had rendered to him that he had strenuously taught himself to follow: *Never allow yourself the luxury of despair.*

Because of it, Mallory had maintained his will to live, despite the horrors of his life. To despair was to *want* to die. To end his life here would have been terrible. But to *want* it to end here would have been worse: a surrendering, a cancelation of his *faith* and Catholicism, even. In essence, a denial of the existence of God.

He closed his eyes and tried to recapture the tendrils of his dream, perhaps let its warmth entice him back into sleep. But it didn't, and *that* failure almost made him cry with frustration. He desperately wanted sleep, needed it. The wash of sadness once more rose in him. He tried to push it away. *Don't despair.* But he couldn't this time.

Oh, Father, why hast thou forsaken me?

Frightened, he opened his mouth to pray. Instead, a sound issued from him, so wretched, so vivid with helpless self-pity that he began to tremble as the sound gradually became a sobbing.

It was a little touchy for Parnell to get his charges placed on the downslope tank, no sounds permitted, the thing too close to the headquarters building. He needed to rupture it on that side, create a sudden deluge so the Japanese soldiers would be moving around in knee-deep water, trying to find their weapons. If he was lucky, the sudden surge might even knock down part of the structure. It was small enough, made of wood with a porch and steps down to the assembly area.

Fortunately, the rain had continued its periodic downpours, which limited the night visibility. Still, he couldn't be sure whether the guards moved around or not. The HQ shack and everything beyond it was in deep rain-darkness, no lights showing anywhere.

Before the preassault briefing, Red had worked out the exact amount of explosive each tank would need to sunder a single plating seam, using the breaching chart normally needed for blowing reinforced concrete. Naval Ordnance had issued the team the newly developed plastique explosive called C-4, which had so far only been supplied to the Marine Corps.

It looked like beige-colored cookie dough and came packed in two-and-a-half-pound blocks. It would take at least three, with another to cover for a misfire, all four laid in a staggered line directly on a seam so as to breach it.

His hands were slightly numb from the cold as he ran his fingers along the rusty steel of the tank, feeling for a key seam. The blood from the Japanese guard in the upslope post he'd killed had quickly coagulated in the cold and gave off the faint odor of freshly cut meat in a locker. At last, he found a good, wide seam, two feet from the bottom.

One of the guards posted on the porch of the headquarters building suddenly said something to his companion, his voice softly guttural. The other man laughed. Then a metal object fell tinnily to the wood floor of the porch. One of the soldiers cursed.

Parnell had dropped to the ground at the first word, and lay tightly against the tank's cement foundation, sharp tufts of grass poking him painfully in the cheeks, his clothing mud-drenched. The guards fell silent again, but he remained motionless for a minute. Another. Finally, he cautiously returned to the seam and began setting the C-4 blocks.

Before sticking each block against the curve of the tank, he pressed a shallow indentation into it with his thumb on the side that would be against the metal. This created a small shaped charge that would increase the penetrating force of the explosive. With his face in close, he could smell the C-4, like vanilla, and the rusted, old steel stench of the tank, mixed in with the sharp sting of chlorine, the Japs using it to purify the water.

Working by feel, he next inserted an electric blasting cap into each of the explosive blocks, making certain he didn't damage the two leg wires on the top of each cap. In order to form a simple-series firing circuit, he then connected each set of leg wires to a master, waterproof Thermalite firing wire.

Next, he unraveled both leads of the wire and hooked them into a Dupont CDI-28, a capacitor discharge ignition unit about the size of two packs of cigarettes, one on the other. It was powered by a simple flashlight battery and coil booster. In "Fire" mode, it could send an electrical surge of 60 volts to the blasting caps along the circuit.

From the jungle came a sudden chorus of screeches, howler monkeys moving along the perimeter of the compound. The sound was unnerving, coming like the screams of the damned. It had made Red jump. Cursing under his breath, he blew on his hands and went back to work.

On the front of the CDI box were two timer dials and

a switch marked *Charge* and *Fire*. One dial had ten-minute gradations for a total of two hours, the other sixty-second markings. Using his lapel light, yet keeping it hidden beneath his battle jacket, Parnell checked his watch. It read 3:29.

He flipped the switch to *Charge*, held it down while he ticked off fifteen seconds by his watch, then switched it to *Fire*. Next, he quickly spun the minute dial to thirty, the second dial to 60. The unit was now charged and ready. In precisely thirty-one minutes, it would ignite his set of C-4 blocks.

Frankie Trota sat there in the rain, his back against the compound wire, and picked off bugs that occasionally skittered across his drenched trousers. He'd squish them between his thumb and forefinger, then pop them into his mouth. Round, black beetles about the size of a raindrop.

Parnell sat quietly, his legs crossed, eyes near closed, drowsy looking. He was waiting for that old precombat feeling to come, jump into his muscles, make his blood kick up like a rain-swollen stream. A tense settling, preparing. Oddly, he wasn't feeling it yet.

Jesus, he was tired. The jungle took a man's energy out of him with incredible speed. How in Christ did anybody live here and still function?

He looked up at the sky, couldn't see anything up there, yet sensed movement: rain clouds, high fog slipping up over the higher ridges and then sweeping down cross the compound, carrying with it the smell of the high forest, wet and dense as black moss.

He felt one of Trota's bugs scurry across his cheek. Reaching up, he flicked it off, and caught the faint odor of the Jap's dried blood still on his hands, down in the fingerprint indentations despite the washing of the rain.

He thought about the kill: little, scrawny Nip soldier in his hands, trying helplessly to counter Parnell's comparatively massive weight and strength. Like fighting a skinny teenager and putting the knife to him, hearing his throat rattle, feeling the shaggy clothing with bony arms inside simply folding to the floor of the guard post, down there with the other soldier, neatly beheaded by Trota's bolo.

So terribly easy.

Thinking of it now, he realized he felt nothing in particular. Neither regret nor abhorrence. Shouldn't he? Why? He'd seen what these little, scrawny bastards did to people. Still, he hadn't felt much passion *then*, either. A moment of rage, a few seconds of sickened horror. But they passed as swiftly as if he had merely observed a dead dog or a bloated jungle boar on the trail.

That brought a chill across his back. He knew it wasn't from the cold, or the night, or the coming battle. This had come from deeper inside. He started to explore it, then didn't. No time for bullshit. He ducked his head, slipped his arm under his battle jacket, and checked the time: 3:51.

He tapped Frankie on the shoulder. "Nine minutes," he whispered.

Trota nodded.

Automatically, he began rechecking his weapons. Didn't even think about it, just *did* it. The heft of his Thompson, the thick, solid weight of his Winchester *Defender* twelve-gauge as he slung it over his shoulder, butt up for a fast, swinging retrieval, the chunky, steel-feel of the M3A frag grenades. Old companions, as familiar as his own breath, his own skin.

These brought the before-combat feeling on now. Everything checked, he rose from his crossed legs and went into a squat, his eyes fixed on the back of the Jap barracks, thirty yards away. The copper-penny taste in the mouth, the rise and steady pump of his heart, his body coming into controlled expectation.

The barracks had four windows, small affairs, two up front, two in the rear. Five seconds before 4:00 A.M., he and Frankie would pitch two grenades apiece through those rear windows, him on the left, Trota on the right. He'd shown the Filipino how to cook off a grenade, heave it just before it blew. He now turned to look at Frankie, the little man all movement, squatting, too, but continually shifting his weight, anxious to get this thing started.

Now 3:55.

A fresh wave of rain came sweeping across the compound. It rattled on the barracks roofs, pinged and popped on the top of the water tank. Parnell hunkered down tighter, felt it pelting his shoulders and head like spitballs of ice.

At 3:58, he tapped Frankie again, held his fingers close to the man's face: *two minutes.*

Time went into a crawl. He glanced to the right, toward the back of the prisoners' barracks. Couldn't see anything. Back to the right, peered through the space between the Jap barracks and the HQ house toward his tank. Couldn't see that, either.

Now 3:59.

In his head, he started counting off seconds: *one-one-thousand . . . two-one-thousand . . . three-one-thousand . . .*

The rain began to abate, the front moving on up into the higher slopes, the soft roar of it like surf. He heard the runoff sluicing from the barracks roofs, his hearing now so acute he could actually pick out each, separate stream.

Twenty-two-one-thousand . . . twenty-three-one-thousand . . .

When he reached forty-one-one-thousand, he slapped his hand against Trota's arm, whispered harshly, "Now!" Leaping to his feet, he dashed down toward the back of the barracks.

The first grenade crashed through the window with a shattering of glass. He heard it hit the floor, a woody thud. By then, the second was sailing through the broken window. He dropped to the ground, heard cries of surprise, the click and hiss of the grenades' fuses, and finally the explosions, one right on top of the other. The ground shook and wooden debris and metal shrapnel went slashing over him.

Two seconds later, he was up and running, hunched over, back to the fence. He nearly fell, stumbling over a long piece of floor beam. As he reached the wire, there was the loud crack of a flare gun. The sizzling, spark-filled arc of a flare shot over the compound and burst into a brilliant white ball of light that instantly flooded the entire area into midsummer-noon brightness.

Voices, screams, then the loud, solid blast of a twelve-gauge from inside the prisoners's barracks. Now two Thompsons opened up, long bursts, their rounds thudding into the front of the Jap barracks. A pause, in it the single treble crack of a Japanese Arisaka rifle.

Oily smoke began pouring out of the windows of the barracks and seeping from the cracks between the wall boards. It merged with the thin fog to create up-currents that swirled into the phosphorous light, looking like strands of dirty orange cotton.

An even denser, darker smoke gushed from the shattered rear of the building. Both walls and the back had been blown outward by the force of the grenades. The smoke feathered along the eaves. A tongue of fire appeared, faded, reappeared, larger this time. They could faintly hear it sizzling deeper inside the wreckage.

Jap soldiers began lunging out of the front of the barracks and down onto the assembly area, the figures darting through the smoke and fog like partly naked savages. At that moment, two other Nips staggered out through what was left of the rear wall. They, too, were naked save for loincloths. One had his hair aflame and his left arm hung down, bent crazily. He stumbled and fell down the stairs. The other blindly fell on top of him. They tried to get up. Parnell put two charges of double-ought slugs into them. They flopped for a moment, then went flat, contorted.

The tank charges went off then, three distinct *baruumps*. Mud and water and twisted metal plating were hurled into the air beyond the roof of the headquarters house. The water droplets made a wash of tiny rainbows in the brilliance of the flare, flashing and instantly disappearing. As the concussion waves rolled down the slope, they imprinted ripples in the fog and smoke.

Red could hear Trota cursing in Tagalog as he repeatedly fired into the forward part of the barracks. The Thompson fire from over near the front of the prisoners' barracks was still going hot and heavy. Then two grenades went off out there. Mud flew.

Despite the racket, Parnell caught the faint sound of rushing water. He saw it suddenly burst upward in a solid wave as it plowed into the upslope side of the headquarters house. Fingers of water blew off the roof like a sea surge striking exposed reef.

The small building held for a moment, then began to come apart.

Parnell yelled at Trota, "Look out! The water!" He braced his legs and moved back until he was touching the fence wire with his back. Then, cradling his Winchester, he partially squatted, waiting for the onrush.

Chapter Eleven

Sol, Cowboy, and Weesay slammed through the rear door of the prisoner's barracks four seconds after Parnell's and Trota's grenades went off, rushing in hunched over in normal room-insertion style, their Thompsons back-slung so they could use their short-barrel Winchester Defenders, close-in weapons with incredible killing power.

Laguna was first, lunging through the shattered door frame, then dodging to his right and going to one knee, weapon traversing his quadrant. The room was filled with partial shadows: the square edges of sleeping shelves, the outlines of skeletal bodies sitting up, faces turned to him, staring. Some were bisected by the white-hot flare light that had suddenly seared through the windows and wall seams.

He shouted, "Right clear."

Cowboy came in right behind him, veering to the left. Now *he* shouted, "Left clear."

Under normal insertion situations, two grenades would have been hurled into the room before entry, the men then going in firing, each neutralizing his own quadrant. But with prisoners here, no explosive ordnance could be used. And each team member had to be absolutely certain of targets before firing.

Now Kaamanui, insertion leader, lunged through the

doorway, his huge frame bisected by light lines. His quadrant was dead ahead. He stopped, scanned, then moved forward. A Japanese soldier suddenly rose before him. He held a rifle, yet he seemed in shock, just holding it uselessly down near his groin. Sol killed him with one shotgun round, the muzzle blast like a small cannon, the Nip literally blown off his feet. "Front clear," he bellowed and charged deeper into the room, racking in another round.

It was like entering a charnel house, the air viscous with the stench of human effluvium, of rotting flesh and shit and the unmistakable putrid reek of death. Cordite fumes drifted through the sheets of brilliant light. As the flare outside descended, it made the squares cast by the window frames jiggle slightly.

Two Thompsons opened from beyond the front of the barracks. At that instant, a shadow crossed near the front door. Sol leaped into a sprint, heading toward it, his shotgun following the shadow's movement.

Behind him, Cowboy and Weesay were bellowing, "Ever'-body stay where you at," and "We're Americans. Nobody move, nobody move."

The higher-pitched crack of a Japanese rifle came inside the building and a bullet zipped past Sol's head, high. Focusing on the muzzle flash, he fired at it, slightly to the left, rammed another round into the chamber, and fired again, this time to the right. A man screamed.

The charges on the water tanks exploded. Their jolting *thrummmpps* spread out, lifting, echoing off into the forest. A second later, the barracks shook as the concussion waves swept past. In the momentary silence that followed they could hear horses screaming, then the distant hissing of water rushing over ground.

The front door banged open, letting in a great rectangle of light through which Wyatt and Smoker hurtled, immediately going to the floor.

"Two down," Sol yelled at them. "Watch it. There may be more in here."

"Brace yourselves," Bird shouted back. "Water's comin'."

When the grenades went off and the rear door of the barracks was smashed open, Eugene Mallory had gone stone stiff all over. He hadn't yet been able to return to sleep, not even the peripheries of it. His first thought was that the Japanese Kempei-tai had come to slaughter them all.

There was the thud of boots on the barrack's floor, then a man speaking English, yelling, "Right clear." A moment later, another voice in the same language: "Left clear."

Good Lord! His mind couldn't absorb the import of what was happening. *Englishmen here?* It did not seem possible. *Is this a dream? Am I hallucinating?* He did not move, lest it shatter the exquisite fantasy.

Suddenly, a brilliant light appeared somewhere in the sky outside the barracks. In his state of mind, he suspected it was the Lord arriving. *No, silly, silly.* The light came through the windows, casting brilliant squares onto the floor, and also through the spaces between the wall boards, forming delicate plates of light all the way down the long barracks.

There was a powerful blast, a shotgun going off inside, and more automatic fire from somewhere near the front of the building. A third voice called, "Front clear." The other voices were shouting again, too, telling everyone to remain where they were, that the intruders were Americans.

Dear God, it's true!

A voluminous, triple-crack explosion came, powerful, dynamite of some sort, not weak like the slurry they used in the mine. He felt the walls and his sleeping shelf shake violently. His breath caught in his chest.

More firing came from outside. Another shotgun blast sounded and the front door slammed open, more men rushing in, shouting, something about water coming. He grabbed the edge of his shelf. His mind whirled. *Salvation!*

The only coherent thought he managed to form in that moment was that he would no longer need to keep his maggots. Two breaths later, a wave of water hit the side of the building and blew streams through the cracks.

Parnell and Trota had had a difficult time staying upright when the wave hit them, swelling around the edges of the headquarters house and striking them full bore, thigh high. It was icy cold and jolted their breaths out of them for a second.

But the steepness of the slope quickly drew it off, the level dropping within a few seconds. Red glanced toward the headquarters house. Part of it had folded in on itself. He saw a lantern flame up; then it was extinguished. Small wooden objects, a stool, part of a desk, a long piece of two-by-four were vomited through a cracked-open wall. The light from the flare made the receding water shimmer like molten silver.

He saw three partially naked Japanese soldiers come splashing out from under a part of the headquarters house roof. One had a rifle. He spotted Parnell and Trota and quickly fired at them. The bullet slashed harmlessly by, making the air pop. Before the Nip could reload, Red put a shotgun blast into his chest, the distance wide-spreading the slug load.

The other soldiers tried to retreat behind part of a wall. Red pulled a grenade from his harness, yanked the pin, let it cook off for two seconds, then threw it in a shallow arc at them. It bounced off the portion of wall and immediately exploded in the air, tearing the wood to pieces. A soldier darted out and was instantly brought down by Frankie. Another tried it. Parnell blew off his right shoulder. The man ran a few feet lopsidedly, fell, jumped up, and ran another few yards and collapsed.

From somewhere in the front of the enemy barracks, he heard a single Japanese voice roaring orders. More Nip soldiers went lunging through the forward door, leaping to the assembly ground in front. Two Thompsons sent a stitching hail of bullets at them. The last two men were knocked back through the doorway.

Most of the Japs were in loinclothes, a few with fatigue blouses. All were barefooted, squatty, thin little men with skin the color of corn flour dough in the phosphorous brilliance of the flare. A short stocky officer darted about, himself wearing only a white cotton shirt and his black, calf-high leather boots. He cursed his men and swiped wildly at them with his sword. In his other hand was a pistol.

"*Magingat kayo!*" Frankie shouted, forgetting himself. "Lieutenant, Lieutenant, they gonna make banzai charge."

Both men fired at the assembling Japs, now about twenty in number. One man fell down. The others ignored him, milling like frightened sheep. The wounded soldier tried to crawl back toward the porch. The officer saw him and, screaming invective, shot at him twice. The second bullet struck him in the back of the head.

The officer whirled about. Waving his sword in the air and bellowing, he charged off down the hill. The soldiers followed him, everybody screaming. They quickly disappeared beyond the corner of the barracks.

"Get to the front!" Red yelled to Frankie. "We'll take 'em in a cross fire."

They ran along the side of the barracks, plunging through smoke and drifting embers, feeling the heat of the growing fire on one side of their bodies. The ground was mushy and slick and stank of wet ash.

From the corner of his eye, Parnell caught a quick movement to his left, twenty yards away. He swung the muzzle of his shotgun around, homed to it. As he did, he saw a small dark object tumbling toward him in the bright air, heard the distinctive sizzle of escaping fuse gas.

"Grenade!" he shouted and dove for the ground. He hit

hard, ramming his shoulder against a block of concrete foundation cement, a shot of pain jabbing down his arm. His shotgun went skittering away from him.

The grenade hit the muddy ground with a muffled *plop*, then rolled under the edge of the barracks. It exploded. Pieces of wallboard, slivers of cement and metal hurtled over Red like high-speed sleet. Mud and water blew back across his body and his ears rang, burning.

The sharp, high-pitched crack of an Arisaka rifle came from close by. A bullet thudded into the ground two feet from him, gouging out a muddy divit. Parnell twisted his head. A completely naked Japanese soldier was charging right at him, his rifle and bayonet in full thrust position.

He reached out, searching for his shotgun. The back of his hand touched the edge of the muzzle. He scooped it up, the metal warm to the touch. The Nip was almost on him, growling from his throat. Parnell spun the weapon in the air, caught it, and fired.

The tight cluster of big slugs struck the Jap in the throat. His head flopped to one side, hung there by fleshy strings. His momentum threw him into the side of the barracks. The head completely fell off. Twin jets of blood thick as a pencil pumped from the hole where the head had been as the body dropped to the ground like a bundle of discarded clothing.

From down the slope, the firefight was still going hot and heavy, the rap of Thompsons and Arisakas chorusing together, the charging Japs still screaming, but the voices thinning out. Two American M3A frag grenades exploded from that direction. Their bursts heaved smoky fountains into the air, which contained body parts, a hand, the bend of a knee, all carried upward like shapeless chunks of rock embedded in a burst of powdered shale.

The flare was less than a hundred feet above the ground now, visibly swinging slightly back and forth at the end of the chute cables. The swing made the light cast long shadows across the compound that leaped and receded and leaped forward again.

Trota groaned softly.

Parnell whirled. The Filipino was on his hands and knees. The back of his battle blouse was pockmarked with small holes that had spouted blood. Red knelt down beside him. "Easy, Frankie. How bad?"

"I'm hokay, Lieutenant. *Sheet*!' I t'ink was sand."

"What?"

"I t'ink dat grenade bust one bag of sand under the house."

"Can you walk?"

"Sure, sor, sure."

Parnell lifted the back of the little man's battle blouse. His back had dozens of tiny pits in his skin, oozing droplets of blood. Suddenly the light from the flare vanished as it came down in a pool of water. It sizzled and popped for a moment. The compound went from midday to sunset, the only light now from the burning barracks building.

As if by order, the night went silent. Gradually, smaller sounds began to creep back into hearing: the trickle of water runoff, the louder crackle and hiss of burning wood, the faraway screech of a night bird.

Partially lifting Trota, Red said to him, "Let's go."

Holding to the deeper shadows that danced beyond the edge of the firelight, they moved around the enemy barracks and approached the prisoners'. Its rear door had been knocked off its hinges and lay crookedly across the frame.

They eased up onto the small porch, inhaling a dense smell mixed with the sharp tang of cordite, which fumed through the doorway. Remaining to the side, Parnell whistled, then called the password he'd assigned before the assault: "Chess."

From inside, someone immediately called out the countersign: "Board."

They stepped over the door and into the building. Even

in the darkness, Parnell could *feel* the prisoners, dark, shapeless shadows lined off on each side. Their presence seemed to percolate off the walls, forming a heavy plasma in the air, a transmigrated emotion forever imprinted into this specific place.

Familiar. But where?

He grasped the link, a memory: he and a college buddy, Joe Gillespie, on spring break in '37, both drunk on a rainy day in Cheyenne, Wyoming, wandering into the holding pen of a slaughterhouse, for no good reason, simply because it was *there:* a place from which steers had recently been driven to the killing rooms, their screams still echoing back through the filthy shaft ways. He remembered now the same charged atmosphere in the pen, as if the animals' frenzied terror had been absorbed by the air, lingering.

Like here.

A flashlight probed his face. "You okay, Lieutenant?" It was Smoker Wineberg.

"Yeah. Frankie's been hit. Everybody in here all right?"

"No problem, Lieutenant. But them Nips, man, they come at us like they was *wantin'* to get shot up."

"That's a banzai charge."

"Fuckin' banzai assholes," Weesay said from the darkness.

"Check out Trota," Parnell said. "And stay on this door. Where's Bird?"

"Up front, Lieutenant," Laguna said.

He found Wyatt and Sol hunkered down beside the bullet-punctured door. He squatted beside them. "How's it look?"

"Ain't no sounds out yonder, Lieutenant," Bird said. He shook his head. "*Damn,* I ain't never *seen* troops throw away their goddamn lives like that."

"Yeah." He peered out through the window screen for a moment, came back. "Better put up another flare, see if anybody's still alive out there."

"Right, sir." Bird moved over to a field pack a few feet away.

When he fired the flare gun, it sent a hollow, *shooshing* bang through the building. Quickly it flooded the compound with that intense, phosphorous light. Dead Japanese soldiers lay scattered out in front of the barracks. In their near nakedness, they resembled sunbathers on a white beach. The officer lay barely ten feet from the porch.

Red scanned the corpses, pausing to closely study each one before moving on. Two had been badly mangled by the grenades. Others looked as if they had simply dropped from exhaustion and were now soundly sleeping. Nothing moved.

"What do you think?" he said, still peering out.

"Hard to tell, Lieutenant," Sol answered. "Could be others still up in them machine works. Maybe even some hidin' in the mine shaft."

Parnell nodded. He put his wrist up into a sliver of firelight to read his watch. It was 4:08. He thought a moment, then said, "We'll sit tight till first light, in about an hour. I don't like waiting with that fog thickening up fast, but we keep popping off flares, we'll have Jap patrols up here sure as hell." He sighed tiredly. "Keep a tight watch. If *anything* moves out there, nail it."

"You got it, Lieutenant," Sol said.

Parnell looked down the long reach of the barracks building, the sheets of white light partially illuminating the prisoners now, sitting up there on their bunk racks like chickens in a roost. The light separated things into segments, exaggerating the emaciated bodies, the too-large heads, the shoulder bones sticking up like coat hooks.

He walked slowly down the line, speaking loudly enough for everyone to hear: "I'm Lieutenant Parnell of the United States Army. Everybody here speak English?"

Men instantly called back, "Aye, we're most Diggers and Yanks, mate," and, "We unnerstan,' Lieutenant, jes' keep talkin'. Sounds like bloody angels' wings." One man sourly said, "Took you chaps bloody long enough to get here, di'n't it?"

Red went on: "Soon, a larger force of American paratroopers will arrive to escort you all to the coast. From there, you'll be transported by submarine to southern Samar." He had to stop then as the prisoners broke into wild cheers. Some sobbed, overcome, others murmured prayers of thanks.

He let it go on for a full minute, then put up his hand. "Hold on, now. Come on, settle down. There's a lot to do yet." Slowly the voices died away. "This camp is not yet completely secured. There may still be enemy stragglers in the compound. So, remain where you are until we're certain. Who're the leaders here?"

The men started calling out names and pointing. One man dropped from his bunk, another, then a third. Parnell told them to come forward. They shuffled out and stood in front of him.

They all looked frail and stooped. Their faces had dark hollows, eyes like black pools in their skulls. Their clothing hung in tatters, and they smelled of offal and foul dysentery breath. He asked each his name.

The first one snapped into a hunched brace. "I'm Yoeman First Terry Fagan, sir. Late of His Majesty's Merchant Service." He had an Irish lilt to the words.

The second man identified himself as Walter Pytel, an American civil engineer who had worked for Firestone Tire Company in Manila. The last was Kenneth Burmiester, a sugar technologist with the University of Hawaii who had been on a research junket when captured by the Japanese in northern Luzon.

"What's the total prisoner count?" Parnell asked.

"As of last night, forty-three, sir," Fagan barked.

"Okay, you three start getting them ready to travel. Is everybody strong enough to walk to the coast?"

"I fancy most are, sir," Fagan said. "A bit slow, they might be. But we'll bloody well *carry* the blokes wot can't."

"Good. Where do the Japs keep their supplies?"

"There are two small warehouses," Pytel spoke up. He was tall and stooped worse than the others, but his voice was low and strong. "One's up near the pithead. That's where they store the mining gear and the concentrate bags."

"The gold's in concentrate form, then?"

"Yes."

"How much?"

Pytel shrugged narrow shoulders. "Close to a million dollars, I'd say."

Parnell grunted. *A million dollars.* After a moment, he put that aside. "Where's the other one?"

"Just beyond the lower water tank. It's for food and the rest of the camp supplies."

The second flare was nearing the ground, its light coming in at a shallow angle. Red said, "We're going to wait until dawn to check out the compound. Once that's done, everybody gets chow and medicine."

"Ah, now," Fagan said, grinning, showing three missing teeth. "A blessed thought, that. But, sir, might I first have the privilege of shakin' yewr hand?" His voice quivered slightly as he spoke the request.

They shook. Fagan's hand was thin, yet Parnell felt strength there, raw and defiant. The others also shook, their gratitude so intense it embarrassed him. The flare landed, sputtered loudly, then went out.

He returned to Bird. "Where's the radio?"

"Cowboy's got it, sir."

Two minutes later, he was busy raising Farnsworth.

Iliandro Nazareno had the radio watch, Fransworth having instructed him to simply be alert for the red receive-send light on the SCR-300 transceiver. The moment it started blinking, he was to come running for him.

Now he was shaking Farnsworth's shoulder, the Brit way

down there in sleep. At last, he lifted his head, then sat up quickly, coughed, and asked, "Wot's up?"

"Captain," Nazareno said excitedly, "the radio light she go flink, flink."

"Aye." Farnsworth rose quickly. He and Iliandro scurried to the bow of the *Betty T* and jumped to the bank.

He had placed his radio under a thick tarp to keep it out of the rain, leaves and branches camouflaging the site. The antenna had been run up into one of the trees. Now he knelt beside it and lifted the edge of the canvas. The red receiving light was blinking rapidly, a little crimson dot floating in there in the darkness.

He called to Nazareno, "Start running up power, laddie." Iliandro immediately began to turn the small wheels on the hand-cranked generator.

The Brit waited a few seconds, to let the electrical energy build up, then flicked on the main power switch. Rolling static slurred from the speaker. It wasn't Sixth Army, he realized. Had to be Parnell. He swung to Blue Team's first assigned frequency and adjusted up the amplitude modulation, fine-tuning it. Static continued, this one sounding like the rush of surf over sand.

Abruptly, Parnell's voice came through the speaker. It was weak at first, but rapidly rose in strength: ". . . point. Do you copy?"

Again, Farnsworth waited several seconds, then keyed his mike button. "Spearpoint, this is Dee Kay. I'm reading you clear, go ahead. Over." He released the mike key. He had been assigned the call signature *Dee Kay*, which stood for Delta King. Parnell's was *Spearpoint*.

Red came right back, his weaker SCR-180 signal wavering a bit, "Dee Kay, message is *Chubasco asul*. I repeat, *Chubasco asul*. Do you copy?"

"Affirmative. Bloody good *show*, old boy, *bloody* good. Over."

Parnell was already gone.

Raising Sixth Army headquarters' intelligence unit

proved more difficult. He'd been assigned a priority frequency that was constantly monitored, its call signature *Magma One*. In addition, he had been given a V-sequence, a verification number to identify himself.

His radio operated on an ultrahigh-frequency wave pattern, with a 300-kilohertz channel separation. This particular propagation level had been chosen since it functioned well under storm conditions. His problem now, however, was trying to punch through the heavy traffic coming and going on the Magma One circuit.

It took him nearly twelve minutes to get lined into the loop, the operator at the intelligence section of General Kreuger's HQ finally coming back sharp and clear: "Dee Kay, this is Magma One. What is your assigned V sequence? Over."

"Magma One, V sequence is Zebra-zebra-niner-four-niner, over."

There was a pause, then, "You are cleared, Dee Kay. I have you on lock. Go ahead."

"Magma One, message relay is *chubasco asul*. I repeat, *chubasco asul*. Do you copy? Over."

"Affirmative on that, Dee Kay. Stand by."

He had to wait another five minutes, the seconds crawling past like beetles on a leaf. Around him, the jungle was beginning to come alive with dawn sounds. The air seemed denser, colder. Nazareno glanced at him. In the faint glow off the radio's lights, the beads of sweat on his dark forehead glistened mutely.

"Dee Kay, this is Magma One," suddenly blew loudly through the speaker. "Fandango is go. Advise you switch to alternate two and keep four-eight watch. Switching now for clearance check. Out on primary."

Whenever a covert agent was sent into enemy territory, he was always allotted three usable frequencies. If the primary one was compromised, he could go to the others. These were always in-between frequencies, so as to make it more difficult for mobile enemy ranging stations to triangulate a fix on him. Now Magma One had just ordered him to switch to his second emergency frequency and then constantly monitor it for further orders for the next forty-eight hours.

He started to twist the frequency dial to the number 2 emergency setting, but stopped. He'd forgotten the bloody thing. *Imbecile,* he cursed himself. Then it came to him abruptly. He eased the dial delicately onto the new setting.

Morse code immediately came back, forming a steady stream of electronic dollops of sound: *Dah-di-di-dit . . . dah-di-di-dit . . . dah-di-di-dit.* It was the letter B being repeated over and over, Magma One running a check signal for him to test his reception on the new frequency.

Farnsworth clicked his mike key three times: *reception loud and clear.*

Flicking off the main power switch, he turned and grinned broadly at Nazareno. "Well, laddie, the bloody Yanks have by God *done* it."

Dawn came so stealthily, they hardly knew it was there until the drift of fog across the compound began to take on a soft, grayish glow. Inside the barracks, the air thickened with cold, everybody sitting silently, waiting.

At first, the prisoners had talked excitedly among themselves while Fagan, Pytel, and Burmiester went among them to pass on Parnell's orders and to check out the men for their journey to the coast. Excited as little children, they had huddled in the darkness as if it were Christmas Eve night. Gradually, the conversations dwindled until there was total silence again, each man having returned to the familiar sanctuary of his own thoughts.

Parnell kept looking out at the fog and the increasing light with *his* thoughts constantly on the move, figuring possible problems and then mentally counteracting them. At 0538, he whistled Bird and Kaamanui over.

"It's time. Can't wait till full daylight. Leave two men here. We'll start here and crisscross up the slope to the pit-head." Taking one last scan outside, he saw that the fog lay on the ground waist high, hiding the dead Japanese. He added, "Use your Winchesters. A Jap patrol hears us, they might figure it's the camp soldiers hunting."

Wyatt silently rose and went back to inform the others. Sol swung his shotgun back off one huge shoulder and down under his arm. He began to slip rounds into the tubular magazine, the click and metallic snap of the loading gate sounding loud in the frigid stillness.

He asked, "Hey, Lieutenant, is it true there's over a million bucks of gold somewhere in this compound?"

"Yeah. Gold *concentrate*." Parnell racked a round into his own twelve-gauge with a loud crack and flicked on the safety.

"Concentrate? What's that, like dust?"

"Sort of."

"If we find it, are we gonna haul it out?"

"Couldn't. It'd be way too heavy. Besides, it's in chemical combination and has to be processed before it's pure bullion."

Sol snorted. "You mean we couldn't spend the son of a bitch even if we took it?"

"That's right."

Now the big Samoan chortled and shook his head. "Ain't *that* the shits? We about the richest goddamn dogfaces in the whole *Philippines*, but we still couldn't buy a friggin' beer."

Parnell chuckled. "Yeah, that's right, too."

Bird returned with Cowboy, while Smoker and Weesay stayed in the barracks to keep watch on the prisoners. Each man wore a bandoleer of shotgun shells over his shoulder, made them look like hill bandits. Outside, it was steadily getting ever brighter. The low, dark overcast of yesterday had dissipated, and thin streaks and patches of gray-yellow light were beginning to fuse across the sky.

"Everybody stay in sight," Parnell ordered. "Normal overwatch. Wyatt, you take point. Check every corpse you run on to make certain the bastard's really dead. And watch out, these sons a' bitches booby-trap themselves." He nodded at them. "All right, let's get her done."

It was like moving through a scary movie stage set, mists of dry ice drifting along the ground. But this mist was wet-cold and pervasively seeped through the soles of their jungle boots and up around their legs where the boot tops ended.

Each man stepped gingerly, putting his foot down so softly he could barely feel the gentle contact with the ground, easing along as if he moved through jungle. Parnell was in the center, Sol and Cowboy on flank, Bird up front. Everybody's legs from the thighs down were cut off by the fog layer.

They first crossed through the banzai charge, the corpses appearing as dark shadows under the mist. As they got to each body, they paused to bend down close enough to gently touch carotids, feeling for a pulse. The familiar smell of death drifted off the corpses, a cool, sticky scent like wilting flowers in a cold box. They had not been dead long enough for internal putrescence to begin.

Slowly working their way diagonally across the compound, they reached the animal corral. The wire fence around it had been trampled down in two places. There were three animals on the ground, the rest having escaped into the jungle.

Two horses were dead, their bodies already stiffened in the cold dawn air. The third animal was a large, gray mule. Its stomach had been ripped open by a jagged piece of steel plate from the water tank. It was still embedded under the animal's right foreleg. Blood lay on the ground beside the wound, a large, black, irregular-shaped smear in the fog. It was still breathing, slowly and laboriously. Its upside eye was wide open and white, and it swiveled it about in terrified rapidity.

Bird shot it in the head.

They got to the lower storage warehouse. It was constructed of lava rock bricks and a wood-and-tin roof. The men entered it as if it were occupied by enemy troops, three men rushing in, right, left, and center, shotguns covering particular quadrants.

The place was dim and sparsely stocked. Two dozen cases of canned goods stood against one wall. They brought some out. They all bore red-and-yellow labels full of Japanese writing, and contained such items as fish and rice cakes, black beef, sardines, seaweed, pickled plums, and condensed milk.

There were also boxes filled with bottles of sake, hardtack, biscuits, and strips of a black jerky. A few fifty-kilo bags of unrefined rice and soybean powder were there, the rice bags bearing the stamp of the *Southern Cross Refineries, Melbourne, Australia.*

Two large crates made of plate steel contained grenades and ammunition, along with satchels of friction-type detonators. Farther back were wooden pallets of demolition explosives: small-charge blocks of picric acid, TNT, and mixtures of toluol cheddite and ammonium perchlorate, wrapped in straw fiber. The last items were three field first-aid kits and a surgical case with nickel-plated carbon steel instruments and bulky transfusion apparatus.

They moved on, cutting back and slanting up toward the processing tanks and machinery.

Fountain flushed a Jap between the crusher plant and a big, rusty tank that stank like soured almond nuts. A conveyor track ran overhead between the two, and there were intertwining pipes hidden under the fog. Wyatt had already passed on the far side of the tank.

Cowboy spotted the man as he scooted on hands and

knees away from him. The movement gave him away since the fog, sliding over his back, had created tiny suction curlicues.

He threw two shotgun blasts at the spot. A fan of blood pellets shot up through the fog and he heard the man thrashing violently. He waited, then approached cautiously. He squatted down, peered at the Jap. He lay over a pipe. One side of his buttocks had been blown away, the second burst bisecting his head. Thick blood lay all around the body in a bright red, glinty carpet. Its heat had dissolved some of the fog above it.

From his right, Parnell suddenly hollered, "Cowboy! Jap charging, in front of you." Two shotguns banged off. But they were too far back. The short barrels of the Winchesters spread the charges of double-ought slugs too wide. Some of them slammed into the edge of the tank, made it ring dully.

Cowboy was already on the ground. He lifted his head slightly, saw another Nip soldier running toward him, perhaps twenty yards up the slope, wearing his helmet and a filthy white undershirt. He had two Model 97 fragmentation grenades in his hands, pressed tightly against his chest. He made no sound save the pound of his *tabi* shoes in the mud.

Fountain fired at him, missed, jacked in another round. The Jap reached up with both arms and knocked the heads of the grenades against his helmet. Cowboy heard the sharp, twin hisses as the grenades' percussion gases vented out, setting off the four-second detonator fuses.

The blasts of two shotguns boomed again, closer this time. For a fraction of a second, the Nip faltered. He stumbled, recovered, and came on again, but running crookedly now. He'd been hit in the left side, a jagged hole blown through his flapping undershirt. A coil of small intestine suddenly flopped through it and hung down, swinging. It looked like a huge blue blood vessel filled with black streaks like wires.

Cowboy lowered the muzzle of his twelve-gauge and fired at the man's legs. Instantly, the Nip went down, face first. He hurled himself backward, twisting, going back to ground, yelling, "Grenades!"

They went off with a double burst, a crashing *barooba-roooom*. Things hit the conveyor and the edge of the tank. The ground shook. He heard slivers of metal fly past him like bullets and the sharp, acrylic stench of cordite rolled down and over him as the echoes of the explosions quickly faded off into the woods.

His ears hurt and whistled loudly, a high-pitched sound, seeming too high to be heard. He pushed himself to his feet, felt dizzy, just as Parnell and Kaamanui came up, their torsos cleaving the fog like ships' prows. He put his head back and inhaled deeply. Above him, a naked leg, jaggedly severed at the hip, dangled from the conveyor track, dripping blood.

They found the second warehouse, also constructed of bricks and wood-and-tin roof, this one the size of the other. Its lower half was sunk into the ground. Inside were huge rolls of cloth and grease-encrusted machine parts, drums of chemical liquids, filters, machinery tools, pulleys, mining gear, tubs of ammonium nitrate like wine casks, and metal fifty-gallon drums of fuel oil.

In a smaller, secondary room with a rusted metal door they found the gold concentrate, eighteen gunnysacks of it stacked on pallets. The room smelled like foot powder. Parnell slit an opening in one of the bags with his knife and brought some of the concentrate out on the blade. It had the consistency of talcum powder and looked like glossy beach sand.

The men milled around, checking out the stack of bags, poking their fingers in, feeling it. Cowboy looked up, disappointed. "This ole shit don't look like no gold to me."

"It's not completely processed yet," Red told him. "This stuff's probably a flux of gold and silver oxides."

"How much you figure them bags is worth, Lieutenant?"

Parnell shrugged. "Depends on the percentage of gold. The prisoners claim it's worth about a million."

"A million *bucks*? U.S.?"

"Yeah."

"Holy Willy Christ!"

They encountered two more Nips up near the pithead. The men were hiding behind the cage drum and immediately opened on them with an old Model 11 light machine gun, a single five-round burst of 6.5mm lead. The bullets all went high, the men too frightened to remember to compensate for the slope.

The four Americans quickly converged on them, going to their bellies in the fog. Two shotgun rounds hit one, hurling him back and down into the pit. They heard his body hitting timbers on the way to the bottom. The other Nip leaped up and ran toward the fence. They cut him down, too.

Then, for the next thirty minutes, they scoured the rest of the compound. There were no more enemy soldiers. By now, the sky was full of sunrise light, the blue of it tinted with yellow and then deepening into denser azure to the west. Parnell waved them back to the prisoner barracks.

Going down in the new, stronger light, they came onto small pools of water below the three tanks they'd blown. They were shiny blue, as if reflecting the sky. They also noticed that patches of mud had been stained the same color, as were the soles of their jungle boots.

Parnell finally paused to scoop up a bit of the discolored mud. He smelled it, ran it between his thumb and forefinger. It felt grainy. He grunted, frowning. Wyatt came up and knelt beside him.

"What the hell *is* that, Lieutenant?" he asked. "There must have been some kind of chemical in them tanks."

"Looks like," Red said. But something else had crossed his mind.

They went on.

There were about thirty prisoners in front of the barracks, wandering around in the thinning fog, kicking and spitting on the Japanese corpses. They looked vicious and grotesque, like dark, skeletal denizens from the slums of Victorian England or mythical gnomes suddenly released into light, moving methodically through the fog in dead silence.

Smoker and Laguna were on the porch, watching. "Sorry, Lieutenant," Wineberg said as Parnell came up. "We couldn't hold them boys back, once they got a glimpse of the bodies."

Red shrugged. "I guess they got the right." The men stood silent after that, their shotguns resting on their shoulders like tired hunters.

Watching, Parnell suddenly recalled the thoughts he'd had over the killing of the scrawny post guard, and again realized how terribly *easy* it had become for him to kill people. And now to even accept their brutalization. All of it becoming only instinctive reaction, acceptance without thought or passion or injunction.

Then another, deeper question: Was there pleasure, too? A pride in possessing such efficient strength and power and the will to kill without hesitation? Of course. A survival skill learned and executed with such finely honed authority demanded pride. All right, did revenge give acquiescence to barbarism? Hell yes, an eye for a fucking eye.

Yet, in the back of his mind something tugged at his thoughts, would not go away: *When was the moment when survival had become savagery?*

He felt a moment of confusion. And sadness. Where in

Christ had morality gone, all the small things that had been inbred in him, strictures so deeply planted that they made him hesitate at the brink of inhumanness? And were they gone forever, like a blown-off arm or leg? Or, would they return someday, somewhere, like the scarred flesh of a wound to cover the holes combat had punched through his soul?

He shook his head and roughly discarded *that* wasted self-interrogation. What the hell difference did it make? Here and now? Tomorrow there would be another goddamned hill to climb, another mission to carry out. And one day, on one of those hills, he'd be killed or wounded and be out of it, and *that* would be *that.*

Fagan spotted them and now came over, limping, his straw sandals covered with dark blood. He snapped to attention at the bottom of the step. "We'll be beggin' your indulgence, sir, for our unseemly conduct." In the dawn light, his eyes were a light green, nearly white, and as stone cold as an iceberg's shadow. "But in our defense, sir, we've seen and endured a great bit of savagery from these mongrels."

Savagery. An odd repetition.

He nodded, said, "When you're through, get your people back in here for chow."

They returned to the lower warehouse for the food. While the rest of Blue Team went through the small reserve of Japanese ordnance, picking out what they could use on the trip down to Divilican Bay, Parnell and Wyatt, along with four of the stronger prisoners, carried two cases of the Japanese canned goods down to the barracks.

The men, starved for so long, rushed at the food, frantically trying to cut the tins open with slivers of metal, then gorging themselves with whatever they found inside. It was too fast. The sudden, unaccustomed richness of the food hit their shriveled stomachs like bombs.

Many quickly began to vomit everything back up, half-chewed fish cakes and beef and sardines spewing out. Others, unable to hold back sudden, horrible cramps, tried to flee outside, couldn't make it, and shit on the floor, their bowels explosively releasing.

Parnell and Bird went outside to get away from the stench. The sun had nearly reached the tops of the distant peaks of the Sierra Madres, throwing them into solid relief. Wreaths of mountain mist hung about the higher ridges and seemed to tumble down into the valleys like moving rivers, the sun tinting them into pink cotton.

Here and there the highest peaks and slanted meadows were visible. They had no forest cover, only patches of mountain grass and sedge and black castles of rock, everything looking wet-cool and morning fresh in the distance, like the Scottish Highlands.

Eugene Mallory sat in the mud and stared at the little pool of blue water. He didn't touch it, just looked. Then he lifted his eyes and studied the remnants of the center water tank where the three had sat near the processing machinery, now only shards of plating and chunks of cement foundation.

He started laughing. Slowly at first, just a chuckle, which grew to a head-shaking gaffaw, tinged with hysteria. His eyes teared up.

Parnell had been watching him, this once husky man shriveled down, sitting there looking as lonely as a waif. *Oh, yeah*, he thought. He walked up the slope and hunkered down beside Mallory.

"It was in those tanks, wasn't it?" he said. He had strongly suspected what the blue water was. Now this man's reactions proved him correct.

The prisoner wiped his eyes and looked at him. They were bloodshot, the lower lids loose like an old man's.

He inhaled deeply and let out a long sigh. "Just the middle one."

"You mixed the concentrate with potassium hydroxide to turn it into gold hydroxide, right?"

Mallory nodded. "*We* didn't do it, Halperan did. He was the mining superintendent when the Japs came. They killed him a short time back. But one night long before he died, he told me how he'd hidden it in the tank just before they got here."

Red scanned the compound, here and there other small pools of blue water glinting in the sun. He came back. "How come he got to use only the *one*? Gold hydroxide particles are heavy, they'd have sunk to the bottom. Even with the water turned blue, I don't figure the Japs would've realized what was in there."

"That particular tank's an emergency water source," Mallory said. "He knew the Japs would never have reason to use it. They probably wouldn't even look inside."

"How much did he dump in?"

"He said eight million dollars' worth, American."

Parnell's head came up. "Eight million?"

Mallory turned and looked at him with his old man's eyes. They held a sad smile. "Ironic, isn't it? All that work and suffering, and now the damned gold's going back into the ground where it came from."

"Eight million," Parnell repeated. "God *damn*."

At precisely 0751 hours, the paratroopers of Fandango Force, arriving to relieve Blue Team and move the prisoners of the Tallangatta Pit number 4, jumped into a wide, sloping mountain meadow at the western edge of the Fuyo National Preserve.

It was a good drop, no one injured, the men coming down into rain-softened terrain in deep, rich mountain grass. Quickly burying their chutes, they hustled to squad assembly points, everybody carrying light jungle packs but heavily armed with platoon weapons: BARs, Thompsons, full-auto paratrooper M1A3 carbines, and three light-weight, Browning .30-cal M2 machine guns.

Aboard two, twin-engine C-47 Skytrain cargo aircraft, the paratroopers had taken an hour and a half to fly from their boarding point outside Manila to the drop zone, the pilots first going northeast to the coast before turning north and dropping down to sixty feet off the ground for the last 180 miles, following the long, curving Cagayan River valley that lay between the ridges of the coastal Sierra Madres and the eastern peaks of the Cordillera Central.

In bright sunshine, they gained altitude again to clear the peak line of the Fuyo National Preserve, hugging it closely, barren ridgetops of grass and open rock stands, and then once more dropping down again to skim the western slope.

At first, they missed their DZ by nearly a mile. The navigator in the lead plane quickly reoriented himself and figured new vectors. Then the two planes swung in a wide half circle and headed back to the proper DZ point to begin their launch run.

This small error would prove fatal.

Unknown to the task group, they'd been spotted much earlier. Flying the Cagayan, they'd had to pass almost directly over the small *nayon* hamlet of Naguillian. Just beyond was the larger town of Ilagan through which troops of Yamashita's crack 39th Raiding Brigade had just passed.

To the Japanese observers on the ground, it was obvious what these two American cargo-carrying aircraft were doing this far in the northeast, dropping supplies to mountain guerillas. Immediately, field radios crackled, reporting the sightings.

The planes were next seen executing a wide reciprocal turn northeast of Magsaysay by Colonel Motoichi Shibasaki himself, commandant of the 39th Raiding Brigade. He immediately ordered his three lead companies, over six hundred men, to swing eastward and head directly to the area of the sighting and strike the guerilla force that was there to receive it.

Commanding Fandango Force was Captain Tony "Buzz" Barbetta, son of a West Pointer, class of 1918. He and each of his volunteers were from the 11th Airborne Division and its 187th Glider Infantry Regiment, all combat-hardened vets of the street fighting in Manila, the savage battles in upland Leyte, and, farther back, jungle drops into New Guinea.

By 0810, he and his men were on the move, headed due south toward the old gold mine. But while transiting an open slope two miles from the DZ, they ran head-on into the advance elements of the combined three-company Japanese unit from the 39th RB. An immediate, fierce firefight erupted.

Although holding a strong advantage in manpower, the Nips were surprised to find an American airborne unit this far north. Could it be the advance force of a much larger airborne attack? The news was relayed to Shibasaki, who called for defensive positions to be set up beyond Magsaysay. He then ordered the field officers of his advance companies to attack the enemy paratroopers in a classical Japanese envelopment.

At first contact, Captain Barbetta had been able to hold his position, waiting to see what he was up against. Quickly realizing it was what amounted to a full Japanese regiment with more troops already approaching from far down the slope, he shifted his men into a defensive perimeter, hoping to hold until dark so they could slip away and head for the coast.

But the Japs quickly surrounded them. Realizing he was far beyond artillery range, Barbetta immediately called for air strikes. Then, for nearly an hour of vicious fighting, his paratroopers repeatedly hurled back attacks on their flanks and rear. But they were steadily losing men, either killed or wounded. Everybody knew it was only a matter of time before their position would be completely overrun.

Where in Christ was his air support?

Unfortunately, luck had turned against Fandango Force. Because of a series of unforeseen glitches, the cover planes would not arrive in time. The first problem appeared as soon as his request reached Sixth Army headquarters. Its fighter command liaison officer immediately relayed it to USAAF's 133rd Air/Ground Fighter Squadron newly based at a field in Agano, outside Manila.

However, all the squadron's usable aircraft were already committed to operate with other Sixth Army units in the south, attacking between Legazpi and the San Berdardino Strait, as per MacArthur's 5 February order to Kreuger. It would be way too much time to order flights back for refueling and then the long deployment north to lay in cover for Fandango Force.

Frantic, the liaison officer tried to work out viable solutions. He came up with something. Raising Task Group Three's Air Operations Center aboard the USS *Ticonderoga*, which was still operating off the east coast of Luzon, he passed Barbetta's request for air cover to the Navy. Immediately complying, the AOC duty officer assigned the mission to his VMF-124 squadron of F4U-4 Corsair fighters aboard the light carrier USS *Langley*.

It was now that the second fateful glitch occurred. Two years earlier, all Corsair aircraft of the F4U type had been pulled from carrier service because of poor performance, particularly in their cockpit visibility. They were used instead only for air cover during close-in operations deployed from land bases. But then the Japanese began hitting U.S. Fleet units was kamikaze attacks. The corsairs were reinstated for carrier operations. VMF-124 had itself only arrived at Task Group Three ten days before.

A flight of four F4U-4s was dispatched to assist Fandango Force. Its marine pilots were very good, highly experienced in close-in air support action from combat missions they'd flown during the Mariana and Peleliu campaigns. But they were *not* accustomed to pinpoint target-locating following a long over-ocean flight. By the time the four Corsairs reached the Luzon coast, they had already veered ten miles from Fandango Force's position.

They eventually got themselves squared away. But it was too late. All they found when achieving Barbetta's perimeter were dead bodies. Bitterly disappointed and raging against their own miscalculations, they went after Shibasaki's 39th Raiding Brigade, which was strung out all along Highway 45 outside Magsaysay.

Buzz Barbetta's final radio message had been received at 1058, not at Sixth Army HQ, but rather at the Pasig headquarters of Major General Joseph Swing, commander of the 11th Airborne. It was a farewell.

The operators could hear the constant chatter of gunfire behind the captain's strained but calm voice: "Red Matador, this is Fandango . . . perimeter fully penetrated . . . hand-to-hand . . . no air support . . ." Static drowned him out for a few seconds, then: " . . . half force down . . . will attempt breakout to . . ."

Then he was gone completely.

Chapter Twelve

While the battle for Luzon and the bloody siege of Manila continued, the rest of the war also went on unabated around the world. The month of February would prove decisive for the Allies in the three major theaters of world conflict.

In Europe, the Germans were steadily being shoved farther and farther back toward the heart of Germany. By 9 February, American advance units would actually reach the Rhine River near Millingen. The next day, Soviet forces under Marshal Georgi Zhukov would cross the Oder. And within six days of that, the dreaded Siegfried Line would be completely breached by the U.S. Third Army.

By now, all key German cities, including Berlin, were under day and night air strikes by the USAAF and the RAF. These would culminate in the worst bombing raid of the entire war, the fiery destruction of Dresden on 13 February, in which seventy thousand civilians would be killed.

In Burma, British units, led by the Seventh Indian Division, would finally cross the great Irrawaddy River at Myangu on the twelfth. Quickly consolidating, they'd then launch immediate strikes southward toward the important Japanese supply bases of Meiktila and Kangaw, and the capital at Lashio.

But undoubtedly, the most important thing to take place in February, which would have dire consequences for the postwar world, had been the Yalta Conference at which Roosevelt, Churchill, and Stalin met in the Russian Crimea on the fourth of the month.

The Allies desperately wanted the Soviets to fully commit to the conquest of Japan; the Russians, in their turn, wanted huge after-war territorial concessions, particularly those concerning the Polish border. They also sought to obtain a greater role in the world following Hitler's downfall.

The American president was extremely ill. In fact, he had only sixty-seven more days to live before being struck down by a massive brain hemorrhage. Because of his weakened condition, the times that had been allotted for in-depth debates over key issues Churchill had considered absolutely essential were drastically cut. As a result, Stalin emerged with nearly everything he wanted, including the complete postwar isolation of Berlin within the Soviet sector.

Despite his victory, however, it would take this brutal but wily Russian leader less than thirty days to breach the Yalta agreements he'd just signed by bringing powerful Soviet pressure on King Michael of Roumania to dissolve his own government and replace it with one dominated by the Communists.

Across the world in the Pacific Theater, Tokyo was also about to suffer an Allied air strike, the first since Doolittle's historic raid in 1942. On 15 February carrier aircraft from Task Force 58 would send twenty-seven hundred sorties against the Japanese capital and the nearby city of Yokohama.

On that same day, sea- and airborne landings would take place on Corregidor against deeply entrenched Japanese forces. It would take ten days of intense and costly fighting to secure the island that had, along with Bataan, come to symbolize America's humiliating defeat in the Pacific during the first terrible days of war.

February would also see the initiation of the next major step toward Japan, the invasion of Iwo Jima. Again Task Force 58, after encountering fierce weather at sea, would begin preinvasion bombardments of the eight-square-mile barren rock on the seventeenth. Landings, to be undertaken by the Third, Fourth, and Fifth marine divisions, would follow two days later.

It turned out to be a bloody affair, and would take till 1 March for Iwo's three airfields to be taken, with another twenty-eight days for the entire island to be secured. The cost would be the lives of 6,821 U.S. Marines.

By then, busy Task Force 58 would already have departed to begin carrier strikes against the next stepping stone to Japan, Okinawa-shima in the Ryūkyūs, and its nearby shipping lanes in preparation for the landings on the island scheduled for Easter Sunday, 1 April 1945.

But for now, back in the Philippines and still-contested Luzon, Lieutenant John Parnell was about to be informed that his mission task had just taken a more deadly turn.

Wyatt, working the radio watch, took the call from Farnsworth, the little red transmission light blinking and the Brit already coming through, static and his raspy voice calling for Spearpoint through the SCR-MC-300, sounding like a man in a hollow barrel.

Bird was with half the prisoners in their barracks, the men still gathering together their pathetic little carry bundles of raggedy clothes, jars, and personal mementoes, meaningless to anybody else yet deeply treasured for having been clung to through years of imprisonment. The already completed bundles were stacked on sleeping shelves now like refugee ditty bags.

The remainder of the prisoners, the healthier ones, were out with Parnell and the rest of Blue Team, digging graves in the soggy ground to bury the Japanese dead. No one knew precisely when the Fandango Force would arrive. To leave the corpses in the open, even in the cool mountain atmosphere, would have created further health and smell problems.

In the barracks, heads now turned curiously to watch Wyatt cross the long room to the radio set that sat in its canvas backpack near the front door. Once more, the speaker blew out a clap of static and Farnsworth's voice, insistent now, repeating, "Spearpoint, this is Dee Kay. Do you bloody well read me, over?"

Bird knelt beside the radio and picked up the mike, keyed: "Dee Kay, this is Spearpoint. Go ahead."

"Spearpoint, condition is now Red Amazon. I repeat, condition Red Amazon. Do you copy, over?"

"Affirmative on that, Dee Kay. Condition is Red Amazon, over."

"Spearpoint, you are to achieve code reference Circus. I repeat code reference Circus. Over."

"I have affirmative on code reference Circus. Do you have further instructions, over?"

"Message is complete, Spearpoint. Good luck. Dee Kay, out."

Wyatt found Parnell digging, all the Mohawkers, even Trota, working with their shirts off in the crisp mountain air. Frankie's back was slightly swollen and covered with black-and-blue patches like ragged, dark coins.

Among them, the prisoners worked slowly, laboriously, like old men with aching bones. Yet many were surprisingly strong. They'd already deposited several Japanese corpses into the shallow ditch they'd dug, the legs and arms and torsos askew in that grotesque, limp posture of dead men. In the sky, the sun was bright, yet there seemed to be the faint hint of rain-smell in the downslope breeze.

Coming up the slope, Bird called out, "Lieutenant?"

Parnell looked up. His skin was stark white save for a slight tanning of his arms and face. He was a powerfully built man with muscled shoulders and a deep chest. He frowned at Wyatt, suspecting what he had come to tell him.

Earlier in the day, they'd heard the faint chatter of gunfire suddenly erupt from the northeast, in it the low, steady rap of American machine guns discernible. It eventually faded off. Had Fandango Force engaged? Or had it been a guerilla strike?

Around noon, another firefight started, the big booms of fragmentation bombs going off and the *pom-pomming* of mobile AA guns and the distant whine of big-bore aircraft engines. Using his binoculars, Parnell scanned the sky toward the northwest and watched as planes suddenly appeared above the trees far off, pulling hard climbing turns. Later, three American Corsair fighters crossed over the high ridges above the camp, heading east. One was trailing dark smoke.

Carrying his battle tunic, Parnell came down the slope to meet Bird. Wyatt, squinting in the sunlight, said, "Looks like that firefight we heard *was* Fandango, Lieutenant," he said. "Dee Kay jes' radioed." He shook his head slowly. "Them paratroopers ain't comin'."

Red grunted, his eyes tight for a moment. He turned, looked back up at the prisoners, came back. "What's the rendezvous point?"

"Circus."

The other team members had been watching, along with Fagan and Pytel. Now they all walked down, the Americans shrugging into their tunics. Parnell told them of the change in plans. He had to explain to the two prison leaders. "We have to leave right now," he said. "That paratrooper force we expected won't be coming. So, instead of going straight for the coast, we'll head for the Cagayan River."

Fagan and Pytel nodded, exchanged glances. The Irishman turned back, fixed a narrowed gaze at the lieutenant. "Might I ask some'ing, sir?" he said.

"Shoot."

"Sounds as if we might have to fight our way out a' this bit. 'At true, Lef-tenant?"

"Yes."

"Then may we arm ourselves?"

"Hell yes. Grab yourselves whatever Jap weapons and ammo you can find."

"One more thing, sir. Might we be takin' some of that concentrate with us?"

Parnell frowned. "That ain't a good idea. We're gonna be moving fast, it'll just weigh you down."

"Might I point out, sir, that it's become a kind of symbol to us? You know? A prize, you might say. A fair lot of us *died* takin' that bleedin' stuff from this ground."

Red considered that. He finally nodded. "All right. But understand, if it slows you up, it's gone."

"Ah, now, *thank* you, sir," Fagan said, flashing his wide, tooth-missing grin.

"Since we'll be taking out some food and medicine, too, select your strongest men as bearers."

"Aye, sir." The two prisoners hurried back to the others, shouting out orders.

"Well, boys," Parnell said, exhaling wearily. "This one's gonna be a bitch. We've got about seven miles to cover." He nodded toward the prisoners, now excitedly gathering around Fagan and Pytel. "With *those* poor souls. There's no telling how fast or how far they'll be able to go."

He turned to Bird. "We better set up in column, keep things tight so we can keep a close watch on 'em. You and Frankie take point. Don't get too far ahead. Sol and Smoker with me in the column. Cowboy, Weesay on drag."

Everybody nodded silently.

"If anybody makes contact, don't fire unless you have to. Withdraw back to us, quick." He fixed on Kaamanui and Wineberg. "Keep the prisoners moving as fast as they're able. Drive 'em hard, if you have to. If somebody drops, appoint people to carry him. Questions?"

"Do we blow wot's left of the Nip ordnance, sir?" Bird asked.

"Yes. With that swabbie air strike, the Nips see our smoke and flash, they'll figure it's another one. When you lay the charges, key in on those nitrate barrels. That'll sure as hell scatter concentrate all over hell. I don't want them goddamned slant-eyes laying hands on *any* of it." He looked around. "Anything else?"

There were no further questions.

He checked his watch: 2:53. "Okay," he said, "let's get it done and the fuck outta here."

Colonel Shibasaki, CO of the 39th Raiding Brigade, always wore a white silk scarf around his throat. Coupled with his shaved head and neat goatee, it gave him the roguish aspect of a fighter pilot.

At the moment, he was poring over maps in his temporary HQ located in a shabby little rock typhoon-house that had been a doctor's residence outside Magsaysay. It was within shouting distance of Highway 45 and the shattered equipment of his reserve force strewn along the road. With him was his adjutant, a *tai-i*, or captain, named Oda.

The senior officer was in a white rage. After achieving a real coup, the complete annihilation of an American paratrooper unit, his brigade reserves had then been attacked by enemy fighters. His losses were disastrous, in equipment, especially transport vehicles, and personnel. He was now trying to reorganize the brigade to hold together its peak efficiency for when he got to the defensive positions around Baguio.

A sergeant entered the small stone room that still contained empty medicine cabinets and instrument cases. He braced stiffly, then informed Shibasaki that a Naval Landing Force lieutenant was outside, demanding to speak with him.

The colonel's head jerked up. "He *demands*?"

"Yes, Colonel-*san*. He says he carries a personal letter from General Yamashita."

The two officers exchanged glances; then Shibasaki snapped, "Let him enter."

A moment later, Lieutenant Sacabe came in briskly, braced straight as a ramrod before the senior officer, and barked, "Honorable Colonel, Honorable Officer, thank you for receiving me."

The colonel studied him, open disdain in his dark eyes. "So, what is this idiocy about a letter from General Yamashita?"

"Sir, the general has assigned me a special mission for Fourteenth Army. I have his personal letter. Unfortunately, this morning I was prevented by one of your officers from fulfilling my task. Instead, he assigned me to a reserve company."

The colonel snorted a chuckle. He put up his right hand, fingers moving. "The letter." The young lieutenant withdrew it from his tunic and handed it over. Shibasaki quickly scanned it, grunted, and handed it to Captain Oda. He turned back to Sacabe. "What *is* this mission?"

"I'm sorry, sir," Sacabe answered stiffly, staring straight ahead. "I have strict orders to speak with no one about its purpose."

Oda returned the letter. Shibasaki again looked it over, then nonchalantly tossed it onto the map table. Sacabe immediately bent forward, retrieved it, then snapped back into his brace.

For a long moment, the colonel continued staring at him, his eyes small and black and cold. Finally, he flicked at the air, a dismissal. . . .

Coming north that morning, Sacabe and his men had run smack into the bulk of the 39th RB as it moved through Magsaysay, truck convoys and small armored units and infantry strung out along the highway.

He immediately sought out an officer, found a rotund, sweaty major, and requested motor transport for him and his men. The major looked at him as if he had just shit on his boot. Sacabe repeated his request, took out his Yamashita letter, and held it forward.

Instead of even looking at it, the major ordered him to merge his men with one of the brigade companies in reserve. Outraged, Sacabe protested vehemently, demanded to speak with the brigade commander personally.

In response, the major jotted something on a slip of paper, shoved it at him, and gave him exactly five seconds to comply with it or get shot on the spot. The slip of paper was a *shidai-kassen*, or Order of Battle chit. It had consigned him and his unit to First Platoon, Second Company, Third Battalion of the Brigade, which was now a quarter mile along the march line.

Once in place, the Second Company captain told him a force of American paratroopers had been sighted landing somewhere in the mountains of the Fuyo National Reserve. Also that there had been mysterious explosions in the hills during the early morning. Everyone assumed this might all be part of a major enemy airborne offensive. Colonel Shibasaki had, therefore, ordered his advance units to converge on the enemy drop zone.

Soon after, heavy firing came from the higher slopes to the east. It lasted about forty minutes, then ceased. At three minutes before noon, the entire column was attacked by four enemy fighters, Corsairs strafing with their .50-cal machine guns and 20mm cannons and skip-dropping five-hundred-pound fragmentation bombs, the thick, barrel-bellied aircraft flashing past at nearly five hundred miles an hour, big Pratt & Whitney XR-2800 Double Wasp engines roaring.

They managed to shoot down one of the attackers, the plane heeling hard over and then exploding in a great ball of orange fire in a rice paddy a mile away. Another was trailing smoke as the flight departed. But their strike had decimated sections of the brigade. At least 250 soldiers were killed, another two hundred wounded, along with the loss of a third of the vehicles.

In the confusion that followed, Second Company was assigned to act as a graves unit. For two hours, Sacabe endured this ultimate humiliation, collecting corpses, his clothing soaked with blood. Finally, beyond further self-control, he simply walked away from the detail and went striding back toward Magsaysay and Colonel Shibasaki's headquarters. . . .

Now he said, "Thank you, Honorable Colonel. May I also request at least two vehicles to transport my men. Now I only have my officer's car and two motorcycles, which—"

Shibasaki's head came up. "You possess an officer's car and a pair of motorcycles?"

"Yes, sir."

"You will leave them here."

"But, sir, I—"

"*Get out*," Shibasaki roared. Blanching, Sacabe braced, whirled, and hurried out.

At seven minutes after three, he and his shrunken *haya-guntai*, now down to only nineteen men, departed the brigade's position, everybody now riding in the dilapidated old bus.

Beyond Magsaysay, they turned off the highway onto a narrow dirt road that wound up into the foothills. A line of *kunai* grass grew densely in its center, and there were deep rain channels in the hardening mud that badly jolted the vehicle's ancient springs. Seven miles away, up there in the high country, was the object of his mission: the Tallangatta Consolidated Goldfields' Pit number 4 compound.

The *Betty T* strained, her blunt prow buffeting against the strong flood current that swept down the Cagayan River, the water forming little pressure dimples on the surface. Flood debris, parts of tree trunks, bush clusters, the bloated carcasses of animals drifted past, occasionally thudding into the metal plate across the bow. In the dusk light, the river shone golden crimson.

Farnsworth was agitated. He estimated they were making only about five knots against the current, the boat's engine pounding away, her stack belching white smoke from the raw eucalyptus logs. *Bollocks!* At this rate, it'd take them at least eight bloody hours to reach rendezvous point Circus. Well, he realized, they'd just have to add some juice to the old girl.

He whistled Nazareno off the bow watch to take the helm; then he slipped below. Heat poured out of the hatch as he swung it open. Raffles and Panay, stripped to the waist, moved about in the smoky engine hold, their flashlights making milky slashes in the darkness. The space was scattered with fire logs and stank of hot metal and the peppermint scent of eucalyptus oil.

He checked the boiler panel and the pressure and temperature gauges. Pressure was steady on 195 psi, temperature holding at 367 F. He reached over and slapped Rafareal's sweat-sleek shoulder, nodded him over. They hunkered down on the port side of the boiler. Nearby, the sound of the furnace formed a muffled roaring through the grate bar door.

He had to shout over it: "We need more headway. Kick up the pressure to 330."

The Filipino frowned, the sweat droplets rolling down his dark cheeks. "Fritty quick she gonna hit *redline*, Cap'n."

The Brit shook his head. "No, she'll hold up, all right. Inject about three thumbs of alcohol in the feed line. But watch out for that temperature. Don't let it get beyond four hundred."

"Hokay, sor."

He returned to the helm. Four minutes later, their speed climbed to eight knots.

Slowly, evening eased over them, turning the golden crimson of the river to a velvety indigo, the sky still holding a deep red like fresh blood seeping into cloth. Then it was night, coming swiftly as in all tropical lands, the richer colors of evening abruptly gone, replaced by the chiaroscuro blue-and-white light from an already-risen half-moon that sat thirty degrees above the eastern horizon.

From both banks began the eerie night noises of jungle animals. The wild screeches from challenging monkey troops. The sorrowful willowing of a nocturnal bird. The sudden, wild vicious growl and furious thrashing of a prowling hunter striking its night's game. All of it melded into a thrumming, burring, twittering, whistling sonance, audible even over the pound of the engine's pistons and the hard, rushing surge of water off the side-wheel's paddles.

Farnsworth ordered Nazareno to switch on the bow spotlight so they could see the heavy debris islands coming at them, and also to check the banks as they followed the trace of the river. A moment later, the bright beam shot out ahead, instantly creating jumping shadows in the jungle and making the river glisten and dance in a sweeping, elongated circle where it hit the surface. Brown bats the size of sparrows darted and wheeled through it.

Twenty minutes later, something hollow gently struck the starboard side of the *Betty T.* Again, a dull, wooden thump that came up clearly over the boat's own sounds. Farnsworth's head tilted, frowning. *What the hell's that . . . debris?* He started to shout to Nazareno. The thudding sound came a third time.

But it wasn't moving with the current. *Oh, Christ!*

In a rush of adrenaline, he understood what it was. His temples pounded wildly as he spun the little helm wheel hard to port and bellowed, "*Uwaks! Uwaks!*"

At the bow, he caught a glimpse of Nazareno silhouetted against the searchlight beam. Then a shadow appeared in the moonlight, lunging up over the gunwale just forward of the starboard side-wheel's sponson brace. It was a man. He dropped to the deck. Right behind him came another shadow, then two more.

Farnsworth swung the helm back sharply to starboard, felt the boat stall for a few seconds, then skid to the right. A burst of spray flew off the starboard-side wheel. Letting the helm spin free, he dove for his carbine, which was propped against the helm stand. Grabbing it, he jacked a round into the chamber, and again screamed, "*Uwaks* boarding! Come up, come up!"

The word *Uwak* meant black vulture. It was also Tagalog slang for a river pirate.

The column moved through the misty glow of an early-risen moon like monks in some sacred, medieval funeral procession, their heads down, bodies shifting with slow, sluggishly agonized motion.

They were still in high forest. On Parnell's orders, Trota had kept them up there where it was easier walking, the ground thickly moss-covered and without brush, and the huge trunks of towering trees spaced far apart, their dark solid shadows looking like the keeps of fortress castles.

The moon was still beyond the eastern Sierra Madres. But its penumbral glow was strong enough to cast faint blue-white pools of light on the forest floor, down where the density of the moss cover smoothed the edges of objects, rocks and fallen trees, and gave the landscape a gentle, elfin appearance.

They had been moving now for nearly five hours. Occasionally taking a compass bearing using the few dim lights from Magsaysay and Tumauini, Parnell had been able to estimate how much ground they had covered. Surprisingly, it was now nearly three miles.

Occasionally, he, Sol, or Smoker would pull out of line and stand beside the trail, watching the prisoners move past, checking them out, and issuing soft words of encouragement.

In the beginning, the men been charged up, hyped over their newly acquired freedom, and would call out to the

Americans happily in their croaky voices: "Aye, don't you worry, Yanks, we won't quiddit," or, "Let's sing to keep cadence, like oarsmen in college."

It had been a particularly beautiful thing for them to hear the demo charges going off back in the compound when they were forty minutes out, several separate blasts merging together into a thunderous booming crack that extended itself, echoing dully off into the distance. The men cheered, knowing that the horrible site of all their long misery had just disappeared.

But their exuberance quickly dissipated as their weakened bodies sank deeper and deeper into fatigue. They fell into a struggling silence, doggedly, blindly plodding ahead, each man keeping close behind the one ahead of him, as if their ankles were chained, as if in some strange way they might share and combine their reserves.

Now it was Parnell watching, listening to the deep, gasping wheezes from tortured lungs and the low moaning of men pushing themselves beyond their own limits. Suddenly, one of the prisoners gave out, spinning in a half circle and then falling heavily to the mossy ground.

The men behind him immediately stopped, tried to lift him. Parnell hurried over. The man was unconscious, his eyes fluttering. Red waved the others back into line, then lifted the fallen man, again feeling those protruding bones and shrunken skin through his ragged clothing, hiked him up onto his right shoulder, and headed off.

He finally called another halt. The prisoners silently dropped to the ground like puppets suddenly devoid of their string supports. The one he'd been carrying had regained consciousness and seemed strong enough to walk on his own. Parnell ordered him to remain close to him.

The spot he had chosen for the rest stop was near a large outthrust of rock. He climbed up onto it and looked out over the wide vista of the lower foothills, sloping away in open moonlight. Here and there were tiny, isolated lights from barrio fires, appearing like little droplets of backlit ice in the carpet of the land.

A moment later, Bird scrambled up beside him. He squatted, his Thompson slung across his back. "How're them boys holdin' up, Lieutenant?"

"As good as can be expected. But they're fading fast. We gotta give 'em some food and a decent rest damn soon."

Wyatt turned his head, spat, came back. "Frankie says we gonna be headin' down into shit jungle in about a hour."

Damn it, Parnell thought angrily. He knew that if these prisoners went into that kind of dense ground now, none of them would make it out. He considered the situation, mentally calculating options, times, and distances.

Quickly deciding, he said, "We'll go on for another half hour, then halt up till 0300. We can feed 'em something then and give the poor sons a' bitches a few hours of sleep."

"Right, sir," Wyatt said. He turned and climbed back down. The moonlight made the rock look like a huge granite headstone in the moon-blue colors of mourning.

Farnsworth's first two carbine rounds instantly killed a pirate, damned lucky shots, the .30-30 slugs hitting the bloody bastard smack in the forehead. He immediately swung on another shadow, fired again, two more rounds.

For centuries, pirates had roamed the coasts and rivers of the Philippines, outcasts from the barrios and *bayans,* forming into raider gangs to survive. On Luzon, particularly in the north, most were Ilocanos, members of the most destitute of the three major ethnic groups of the island.

Driven into slave camps or slaughtered by the Japanese, hordes of them had fled into the highlands where they gathered into prowling bands of young men who would often attack tiny, isolated *nayon* hamlets or travelers in the jungle or village workers, anyone they could overpower with their bolos and stolen weapons.

There were now eight aboard the *Betty T*, rushing about and bellowing wildly in *Ilicano* dialect, grabbing whatever was loose on deck. Two headed for Farnsworth just as the after hatch slammed open and Panay came charging up onto the deck, carrying a heavy pipe wrench. He waded into them.

Farnsworth opened up again, firing at moving shadows on the port side, heard the hard thud of a round go into flesh, the other ricocheting off into the night. Someone screamed, a high-pitched, hollow sound against the back-drop of the driving side-wheel paddles.

He glanced toward the bow, tried to locate Nazareno. The spotlight beam jumped crazily, then pointed straight up and out across the water, finally settling down and facing directly into Farnsworth's face, blinding him for a few seconds.

Through the light now charged a pirate, small, emaci-ated, wearing filthy sail-canvas shorties. The Brit saw the sidelight flicker of metal off the man's bolo blade and dropped to his left. The blade just missed his shoulder and slammed into the helm post, made it ring. He threw up his weapon and shot the pirate in the chest. The man was so close he fell onto Farnsworth's shoulder, his body stinking of fish and urine and mud.

Nazareno screamed, *"Lord God!"* Lunging forward, Farnsworth swung the barrel of his carbine like a scythe, felt it connect. The spotlight had now fallen to the deck and was rolling about. The beam silhouetted thin, scurry-ing legs as more *uwaks* came scampering over the side.

Bellowing curses, he drove straight ahead, shoving, firing, swinging his muzzle. Suddenly, the *Betty T* stopped dead as its bow rammed up onto the left bank. The jolt hurled him down onto the deck. A body landed on top of him.

He shoved it viciously away, started to rise. Something

smashed into his back, near the right shoulder. He felt a shock of pain hot as a furnace door spread from the impact, fuse up his neck and into his head. It created flashing lights behind his eyes. He went down again, stunned.

In a haze, he sensed things striking him. Yet he couldn't feel their impacts, as if all his senses were too busy fixing on the still throbbing pain in his shoulder. Then he was vaguely aware of being rolled over onto his back. Hands ripped at his pockets, someone tugged at his shoes.

As if from far away, he heard a hissing. *What was that? Steam line break?* His mind groggily probed the sound, seeking explanation, his seaman instincts clicking into higher focus. A chorus of shrieks abruptly broke out around him and a thick wave of intense heat rolled over his chest and stomach, exposed arms. His vision began to return, dark shapes falling into place, though still looking misty, even the now motionless searchlight beam dimmed into a shaft of orange.

Smoke? No, steam!

His full consciousness rushed back to him. He shoved himself to his feet. The whole night seemed clothed in steam, the air scorching hot. Through the surging pound of the still-running paddles and the screams, he picked out Rafareal's shadow, braced, growling curses in Tagalog. He was driving the *uwaks* from the *Betty T* with a steam hose.

The raiders surged away in a group, tumbling, falling down, rising, slipping, getting knocked down again by the force of the steam, everyone trying frantically to reach the gunwales and escape back into the river. One man's clothing burst into flame as he dashed wildly across the deck. Screeching, he leaped off the boat, the flames immediately disappearing.

Farnsworth ran for the helm pedestal and slammed the driveline into neutral. The side wheels stopped moving. He turned and made his way back to Raffles's side to help him hold the steam line. After a full minute, the Brit slipped below and turned off the hose valve.

Three *uwaks* were dead. They could hear the others still whimpering and yelling in pain as they swam away. Farnsworth grinned broadly, wildly at Rafareal and slammed his arm around the small Filipino's shoulder. "God bless your bloody Christian soul, laddie. That was *damned* quick thinking."

They searched the deck with the spotlight. All three pirates were little more than boys. Their blood made sticky smears on the plating. The third one had had his skull smashed by Panay's wrench. His face looked partially caved in and blood had run out of his ears and nose.

But Iliandro Nazareno was missing.

They heaved the corpses into the river, reconnected the steam line to the boiler leads, and backed off the bank. For the next forty-five minutes, they moved up and down the river, hunting for Nazareno. There was no sign of him.

At nine o'clock, Farnsworth finally gave it up. He swung the *Betty T* around and once more headed up the Cagayan toward rendezvous point Circus.

The mining compound was still smoldering when Sacabe and his depleted *haya guntai* arrived, the men drenched in sweat from a five-mile run, all the way going against a constant grade.

The old Graham-Bradley bus had finally broken down soon after leaving the highway, a cracked axle from hitting a deep rain rut that had bounced everybody against windows and each other.

They unloaded gear and set out on foot, running two abreast, the lieutenant raging at them to move faster. The soldiers double-timed it in grim silence, narrow-eyed at this *ketsu no ana,* this asshole of a navel officer giving them shit instead of respect for their combat experience. Still, they plodded ahead, their faces and hands sun-seared to the color of old leather, their uniforms ripped and worn out from accumulated sweat and dirt.

The long day's sun had dried the road, hardening it, forming jagged edges that made it difficult to place boots down squarely. Men kept wrenching their ankles. On both sides of the road, the jungle rose like a wall, humming with humidity and compacted heat.

Once, a pack of wild boar crossed ahead of them, the animals humpbacked, bristled, their tusks curved and a dirty yellow in the sun as they darted quickly past in that scooting way, ignoring the approaching soldiers.

Suddenly a series of muffled explosions were heard, rolling down the mountainside. A huge, black-and-white mushroom of smoke rose over the trees far up the slope. It looked oily in the sunlight.

Sacabe was so shocked he stopped running and stood staring up there with his mouth open. He knew they *had* to have come from the mining camp. Had there been an accident? Or a guerilla raid? Why? The chilling possibility hit him that resistance fighters were after the objects of his mission. He leaped forward, tongue-lashing his men to even more speed.

The remnants of the afternoon dragged past in heat and sweat and deep gasps for air. But Sacabe refused to halt for a rest. His little double column got ragged, men stumbling along.

Gradually they got up into cooler air, the jungle changing into oak and then pine forests, with evening coming on. Now they could actually see the mining camp, a great patch of bare earth among the trees, like a gigantic scab in the rich green of the high forest. The smoke from the explosion fires had long since dissipated, yet a thin, greasy pall remained over the camp. Through it big vultures drifted on air currents, now and then one breaking from the rest to drop heavily down and out of sight below the treetops.

It was dark when they at last drew to within two hundred

yards of the compound. Sacabe set his men into cover positions along its lower side, then sent two scouts in to reconnoiter.

Waiting, he constantly paced, unable to remain still, slapping his fist against his thigh. The air stank of burnt wood and explosive residue and the gamy essence of death. The thought that his mission might again end in total failure made his stomach lurch. He slapped his thigh with such force it made his muscles hurt.

The scouts returned to tell him that the compound was deserted, that many of the structures had been destroyed, and that there were corpses of Japanese soldiers all about. Many more had been thrown into a shallow, uncovered ditch, their bodies partially burned by explosion debris.

In an advance double column, with flankers ahead and at the rear, they moved up through the lower gate and into the campground. Sacabe walked slowly amid the rubble, prodding this or that with the toe of his boot. When he reached the burial ditch, he shone a flashlight down into it. The bodies were covered with a layer of fine dust and powder, some of them naked, others with only *fundoshi* underwear on. Huge black beetles like perfectly round coins crawled about on them, their shells glistening in the light.

His senior sergeant merged out of the moonlight. His name was Kasanaru. He snapped to attention. "*Chui-san*," he said softly. "I found this." He held out a shred of gunnysacking.

Sacabe took it, put his light on it. The fabric was seared and contained a sandlike residue adhering to the cloth, some of it turned ashy from explosion heat. It was gold concentrate.

He looked up. "Where did you get it?"

"In a storage building up there, sir." Kasanaru pointed up the slope.

"Show me."

The storage building had been blown completely out of the ground. Great chunks of brick and rock, shattered roof timbers, twisted parts of machinery, bits and pieces of barrels lay everywhere. The explosion pit still smoked, embers down under the debris hissing softly like boiling water.

Much of the debris was coated with the same dusty residue as the strip of sacking. Some of it had heat-imprinted into the metal parts, tempering them and forming tiny, red-orange whorls. Pools of oil and water also lay about. In the flashlight, they had the dark blue color of deep ocean.

He left the demolished storage building and slowly prowled about. Everywhere he looked, he found heavy powderings of concentrate and the same blue discoloration of the pools. He didn't even curse. He just stared and stared, half conscious of the jungle noises that sifted out of the moon-dappled darkness like mocking laughter.

Several small, shiny objects flashed in his light. He stooped, picked them up. They were spent shells carrying English makings. He heard someone approaching and swung around. One of his men hurried up and snapped to attention.

The man informed him that the tracks of a large number of people had just been found, exiting the compound and headed out into the forest. He added, "Most wore straw *zori*, *Chui-san*. But there are also the prints of American jungle boots."

"*Ah, honto?*"

"Yes, sir. There were at least fifty men."

"*Yatta!*" Sacabe snapped and, for the first time, broke into a leering, savage grin. *At least they will die.* He swung around to the sergeant, growling, "Assemble the men. Quickly."

"*Wakarima, Chui-san*," Kasanaru said, turned, and dashed off.

The lieutenant placed the two best trackers on point, instructing them to follow the retreating enemy as fast as they could, leaving strips of luminous vine to mark their trail. Since the unit would be moving so rapidly, Sacabe saw no need for a formal rear guard. Instead, he positioned his men into a rapid-pursuit formation, everybody in tight parallel flanker positions so as to coordinate in a surprise-penetration-concentrated firepower attack as soon as they caught up with the fleeing enemy.

At precisely 8:03, Sacabe's small force pulled out of the demolished mining compound and plunged into the moonlight-drenched forest, running.

Chapter Thirteen

2113 hours

The *Betty T* was showing the effects of her years under-water, things beginning to create unusual noises, boiler pops, the engine hesitating slightly in its power strokes. Farnsworth's experienced ear tracked them. They were getting worse. The boat's speed had already dropped back to five knots.

He now detected the sharp stench of overheated metal. Grimacing, he listened tensely, finally managed to pick up a faint, high-pitched, metal-on-metal chuffing that seemed to be coming from the starboard paddle wheel's hub case. He suspected what it was. Retrieving his spotlight, he flashed it on the hub, saw smoke seeping through the seals, looking in the bright white light like coils of fine mist.

He listened a moment longer to be certain, murmured a mechanic's curse, and then disengaged the driveshaft. The boat immediately lost headway as the paddle wheels stopped rotating, the prow falling off to starboard in the buffet of the current.

He allowed the boat to swing until they were nearly broadside to the flow. Then he quickly engaged the shaft and headed toward the right bank, searching for a landing point with his spotlight. He chose an area where thick tree growth hung out over the water. A few moments later, he disengaged again and eased the *Betty T* in under the trees and gently up onto the bank.

The hatch opened and Raffles climbed out. His brown body was covered with sweat and wood ash. They both leaned out over the gunwale aft the starboard paddle wheel to examine the bearing hub. Smoke still eddied from it, the cap discolored and stinking of scorched metal.

"Bearing's running loose," Farnsworth said. He hissed disgustedly. "We'll have to pull the bloody thing and shim 'er up a bit or she'll seize up, sure."

"But we no got sledge or chisel, Cap'n."

"Aye," he agreed. "We can shrink the seals with river water and work her out with screwdrivers and wood blocks. It should do adequately."

As they headed below for the necessary tools, the Brit asked Raffles about another matter, the boiler pops that had occasionally sounded up through the decking. "How bad's the salt, laddie?" he said.

The boat's long immersion had created a salt buildup inside the water feed lines, like plaque in a human artery. Heat transferred from the furnace had started partially melting the deposits, causing chunks to break off. Once these hit the superhot steam lines, they'd explode. If this continued, it could possibly rupture the furnace tubes.

Rafareal shook his head sadly. "She get mo bad, Cap'n. Bugga go bang-bang plenny now."

"Then we'll have to steam-flush the bleeding lines, too."

"Wot about the shapt, boss? She make noise, too."

"I know, but there's still some collar clearance left. We'll just take her up till she's tight as a drum."

There was a sudden series of bursts from inside the boiler furnace, sounding like Chinese firecrackers. He leaned down and flipped open the furnace door with a light-off rod. Heat poured out, the eucalyptus logs humming and sizzling with flitting blue green flames that coiled up out of the ash trap. He visually checked the overhead steam tubes. They appeared okay.

Farnsworth put Panay to flushing the lines, while he and Raffles set to work on the hub seal and shaft bearing. It wasn't easy, hanging over the side down there under the trees with bugs falling out of the branches and hordes of mosquitoes swarming up off the bank.

After a while, a snake dropped onto one of the paddles and curiously came toward them, moving with a peculiar belly lift, like a caterpillar. It was a *chrysopela* or rainbow snake, bright green and red, three feet long and slender as a gambler's cigar. Without breaking from his work stride, the Brit turned and popped it on the nose with his forefinger. It pulled back into a coil, then propelled itself down into the river.

They finally got the hub seal off, ruining three heavy-duty screwdrivers in the process, and shimmed up the bearing casing so it couldn't shudder on the end of the shaft. Its casing and the inside of the shaft housing had already been scoured, bright metal showing in the light. They repacked it with heavy grease impregnated with powdered graphite from the tool chest and resealed the hubcap.

By now, Panay had finished the water lines and reconnected the pressure-release line to the boiler intakes. Now all three turned to the main driveshaft, the men hunkered down between the line and transmission housing to pound with five-pound hammers and two-by-fours until they could inch the shaft out far enough to reach the adjusting screws and set the collar clearance. Farnsworth did the adjusting, turning down the screws to their elbow rings. Then they quickly realigned the shaft and closed everything up. Panting from the labor, the Brit sat back on his haunches and checked his watch: 10:47.

They'd lost one hour and ten minutes.

* * *

2333 hours

Smoker hunkered down in the moonlight, watching the back trail. The moon was way up now, almost overhead. *In its zenith,* Wineberg was thinking. He liked that phrase, in its zenith. It smacked of class.

Although he had never been what anybody would call classy, this ex-boxer who had spent his prewar years in cheap hotels and backwoods lockups, shuffling in mission kitchen lines or in the sweat-and-urine-and-liniment stench of shabby smoker rings, he nevertheless recognized class when he saw it. Or heard it. And to him the word *zenith* definitely had class.

The night was giving him all kinds of noise, things he had become accustomed to by now. Yet, it still wasn't easy picking out the *unusual* ones, the *dangerous* disturbances of brush or limb that warned of approaching enemy. There were too many subtle tones and whistles and screams to isolate things.

Not like back in Europe where his senses had been so keen he could differentiate between the footfall of a Kraut paratrooper's boots and that of an ordinary infantryman's, where he could actually *smell* Fritz in the air, could even pinpoint to within a hundred yards a firing .88's position solely by the echo of its muzzle blast and the slam of its recoil.

He sat atop a moss-coated dead tree in moon shadow. Insects moved about, in and out of his space, biting, crawling, winging off. The moonlight cast wonderful patterns onto the moss, gave it an odd luminescence, like Christmas glitter, and the air was alive with scents: forest dampness and rain and greenness and, now and then when the breeze shifted slightly, the stench from the bodies of the prisoners, a gamy and diseased odor.

He turned his head and looked back at them sleeping, dark humps in the moonlight on the ground, like corpses. *Poor sumbitches.* He remembered his own imprisonments, back in the States, later in Germany. As rough as they had been, it was obvious these pour souls had borne deeper, more hellish conditions, starved and murdered as a matter of course.

He heard a soft rustle and someone whispered, "Chess."

"Board."

Trota came scooting over, squatted beside him. "Chu hearin' the noises?"

Wineberg sat up. "What? From where?"

"Listen, listen."

Smoker put his head down, tuned up his hearing, probing the pale, blue-white darkness. Distant night birds, tree frogs thudding, a screech, a sound like a dying woman. After a moment, he turned back to Frankie, shrugged. "What the hell am I supposed to hear?"

"The jungle sounds, *meng*," Trota said. He pointed toward the north. "Listen."

Smoker tried again, clamping down harder, focusing all his senses into his hearing. Far off was a faint flurry of jungle sound, so far away it might have merely been the peculiar sound of nonsound. It faded. A moment later, it came again.

"See? See?" Trota said. "Like the sound, she stop?"

"Yeah. Somethin's approachin' out there."

"Right, *meng*, one puckin' *Hapones* fatrol."

Wineberg was instantly on his feet. "How far out you figure they're at? Can you tell that?"

"Maybe hap mile."

"How many?"

Trota shrugged. "I no can tell dat."

"Hang here, Frankie," he said and trotted off, quickly disappearing into the moonlight.

Somebody was shaking him, Parnell asleep but not down deep, his mind still up in the forest scanning things.

He came up, grabbing his weapon, which lay across his chest. It was Smoker.

"They's Japs trackin' us, Lieutenant," Wineberg said quietly.

Parnell came up into a squat. "How far out?"

"Frankie figures about a half mile. Can't tell how many, though."

"Get Wyatt and Sol up here. Then wake the prisoners. But keep 'em quiet. Send Fagan up, too."

"Yes, sir." Smoker moved off.

Red checked his weapons, feeling the combat calmness coming into his body, his hands. Around him, prisoners were rising, stiffly, inhabitants of dark places lifting up off the earth in the moonlight. He heared soft groans, coughs. He wondered how many of them could fight. Well, they were all about to find out.

Wyatt and Sol came up through the moonlight. "Somebody's comin' in for sure, Lieutenant," Bird said. "Y'all can hear them jungle animals kickin' up a fuss as they pass." He looked north, came back. "If them Nips ain't guard units and are jungle savvy, they'll hear *us*, too."

Parnell grunted. "Won't make much difference, Wyatt. The trail we're leaving in this mossy ground a blind man could follow. . . . Where's Fagan?"

"He's comin', sir."

The Irishman came scurrying, carrying his Jap Arisaka at port arms. "They're on us, are they, Lef-tenant?" he asked excitedly.

"Yes. How many of your men can handle weapons?"

"I dunno, sir. But ever' last one of us is willin' to give it a bloody go."

Parnell turned back to his two sergeants. He thought a moment before speaking. "Sol, you go with Fagan. Form up some of the prisoners into a rear guard and assign flanking fire zones. Keep 'em in tight." He swung around to the Irishman again. "Fagan, you make goddamned sure your men are *certain* of a target before they start shooting

people. You got that? Some of my men'll be coming
through you. I don't want them shot."

"Aye, sir."

"All right, move out." Sol and Fagan trotted off.

He returned to Bird. "Trota stays on point. We'll have to
go down into primary jungle now to make it harder for
them to track us. You take the rest of the team and set up
an ambush. Pop the bastards, withdraw, then pop 'em
again. Get us as much time as you can."

"Right, Lieutenant."

"You've got the coordinates for Circus?"

"Yes, sir."

"We'll wait at the river unless things get too hot. When
you come in, stick with Chessboard for sign and counter.
If we're not there, head downstream. You'll have to move
fast to overtake that steamboat running with the current."

Bird nodded.

"Let's do it," Red snapped. Wyatt darted away.

Parnell stood up and waited for Trota to come up. He
watched the prisoners already moving, going in grim in
silence, their heads turning to look at him, staring a
moment, then passing on like the dark refugees in old
prewar newsreels, trudging from chaos to chaos. One man
gave him the thumbs-up sign. He returned it.

0034 hours

Cowboy had positioned himself beside a moss-encased
rock. He checked his weapons, a methodical procedure:
Thompson locked and loaded with two spare clips taped
to the stock; shotgun slung; Colt 1911 .45 with a round in
the chamber; belt and boot knives in place.

He finally relaxed back against the rock, the butt of the
Thompson resting in the crook of his arm, and bloused
his trouser legs. When it came time for him to move, it was
going to be damned fast. There wouldn't be time for

clothing snags. Last, he smeared his face with moss, the stuff smelling cool and fungal, like the banks of a mountain stream.

He resettled, looked out at the back trail. Bird had set up the ambush position about two hundred yards behind the area where the prisoners had bedded down. It was on a gentle rise with clear fields of fire on the trail and a rocky abutment fifty yards beyond.

They had laid several booby traps, trip-wired grenades on the upside of the approach trail. If the enemy attempted to flank up the slope, the explosions would force them back across the trail to rock outcroppings on the opposite side. Two other grenades were forward of their ambush position, between themselves and the retreating prisoners. These would take care of the advance scouts, whom they would let pass.

Cowboy had set these two booby traps himself, placing them in the trees with their trip wires running down the trunk and across the trail. He had a helluva time concealing the wire in the moonlight, finally had to strip off a length of moss, dirt and roots together like sod, and lay it across the entire trail, tucked and blended so the wires would look merely like ripples in the ground. A mite hairy, that, draping that weighty moss onto an active trip wire.

He scanned the approach back trail again and also its upper flank. The lower ground was speckled with patches of moonlight, perfectly imprinted shadows of tree branches and the edges of rocks. The slight breeze that had been working through the trees earlier was gone now. Nothing moved out there.

He brought his gaze to a point across from his own position, Smoker and Weesay down there. They would act as withdrawal security, covering him and Wyatt as they pulled back along a prearranged line. Once he and Bird were out of the killing zone, they'd pause to wait for Laguna and Wineberg, covering each other until they were completely clear of the enemy force.

Damn! He didn't like all this light. Almost straight above him, the half-moon looked white and hot, as if it were a broken metal plate just drawn from a furnace. The main advantage of night ambush, he knew, was the ability to fire and move in darkness. Now *that* opportunity was at least partially gone. So, moving in this much moonlight, they'd damn sure have to pick and choose defiladed positions plenty fast.

Around him, the night divulged its constant murmur of life, a subdued drumming, thrumming undertone. Now a tree frog peppered through it for a few seonds, sounding like the rapid tapping of a pencil eraser against an empty desk. It finally fell silent.

He moved his hearing beyond the closer sounds, probed farther out. For the past several minutes, the flurry of night sounds that had marked the approaching Japs had fallen off. Now there was only that normal undertone which seemed to stretch away through the forest. Had the Japs halted? he wondered. Worse, had they spread out and were now coming toward them in a frontal line?

A dark figure loomed. Wyatt silently came to a crouch a few feet away, returning from checking the others. Wordlessly, he went over his own weapons, spat, and turned to look at Cowboy. His face was cast in chips of shadow and moss-smeared gleam.

Abruptly, even the normal hum of night sounds stopped. Seconds slid past. Then there was a sudden clamor of animal sounds about a hundred yards up along the approach trail: the raucous, irritated challenge of night birds, the tree frogs hammering out a warning, and the squeak of a mountain deer as it dashed through vegetation.

Here we go.

A full minute passed. The animal noises continued unabated, then abruptly ceased. Another minute. A shadow appeared on the trail, disappeared into a deeper shadow, then reappeared. It was an enemy soldier treading very stealthily, his head down, reading sign. There were branches and leaves on the back of his field pack.

A second shadow appeared several yards behind him, also wearing leafy camouflage. This one had his head up, scanning the surrounding moon-dappled ground. They came on, the leader kneeling once, feeling the ground, then sprinting ahead swiftly, his *tabi* shoes barely making a sound in the mossy cover.

Cowboy and Wyatt watched the two Japs go by them, no more than ten feet away, neither soldier saying anything. In the moonlight, they could clearly see their weapons: Type 100 submachine guns, stubby weapons with cooling jackets on their barrels, and bandolier-style pouches slung over their shoulders for spare magazines and Type 97 frag grenades. The Japanese moved with expertise, obviously jungle fighters.

These sumbitches ain't from no prison guard unit.

He looked up to see Wyatt looking at him. Then the sergeant pointed at his own Thompson and knocked the heels of his palms together, reminding Fountain to take out the Japs carrying automatic firepower first.

Cowboy nodded back.

One more minute dragged by. A night bird came sailing through the moonlight, wings silent, gliding like a night spirit. More shadows emerged into the killing zone right behind it. Two men, then three, moving tightly. *Stupid, stupid,* Cowboy thought, *bunched up like fuckin' sheep.*

They came on. Suddenly, one of Fountain's booby traps went off, the sharp detonation tearing apart the momentary stillness. A half second later, the second grenade went off. Before its echoes could fade away, Blue Team opened up, all four Thompsons laying in concentrated, fixed bands of fire. Their muzzle flashes and tracer rounds cut hot white lines in the half darkness.

It took the Japs less than a half minute to respond: first a sporadic firing, then a more concentrated fusillade as they homed to the ambushers' muzzle flashes. But by then, all four Americans had moved, Wyatt and Cowboy cutting to their right into deeper shadow and better defilade, Smoker and Weesay moving down the slope. Bullets *whanged* off rocks and clipped branches as they opened again, this time focusing on the *enemy's* muzzle flashes.

One of the approach trail grenades exploded. It made a quick orange-white burst in the moonlight. They could hear the Nip officer or lead noncom rallying his men. The soldiers began moving back across the trail and down among the rocks to reform.

Cowboy's second clip was empty. He ripped the last of the two off his stock, rammed it home, and slammed forward the bolt. Rising slightly, his back against a rock face, he jerked a grenade from his harness, the safety arm popping up and the fuse sizzling softly as he counted *one-thousand-one . . . one-thousand-two*. He heaved it, throwing back and over his head. A few feet away, Wyatt did the same.

Another grenade went off, farther down the slope this time. But it was clearly an American M3A frag, giving a deeper *boom*. Then his own went off, followed by Bird's: *boomboom*, a quick-double slam. The Nip fire died off for a moment, down to a single shot, another, then total, ringing silence.

Through it came the solid bang of metal on metal and a pair of hissings. *Jap grenades fusing up.*

Two dark objects came sailing through the moonlight. Cowboy and Wyatt dropped to the ground, both men following the direction and flight of the incoming grenades by the sizzling of their venting fuse gas. The closer one blew up on the other side of their rock, a few feet above the ground. Shrapnel slammed against the opposite rock face. The other went off down where Weesay and Smoker were.

There were the double slams of grenade launchers, cracking like shotgun blasts. These were immediately followed by the impact explosions, somewhere beyond their position and up the trail. Smoke drifted, making the moonbeams shimmer mistily as coils of thicker smoke roiled up through the light to form convoluted patterns like oil shifting on a watery surface.

Bird tapped Cowboy on the head, twice: *withdraw.* Then he gave a sharp whistle, a single, short sound, and opened up again with a final burst. From downslope came the immediate heavy pound of two Thompsons laying in cover fire. The Japs returned another fusillade.

Zigzagging, Cowboy and Wyatt sprinted back along the trail. Thirty yards out, they went to ground again, behind another rock outcropping. Bird was on the higher side. They once more started firing, cutting long bursts and then ducking as return fire chopped up the mossy ground and tree limbs around them.

Fountain's last stock clip was now empty. He reached back and grabbed another from his belt pouch. Suddenly, he heard the soft pound of feet behind him. He whirled around. Ten feet away, one of the advance scouts was charging toward him.

Jesus!

He dropped his empty Thompson and frantically clawed for his Winchester Defender, slung across his back. He nearly had it around when the Jap ran right by him, so close Cowboy could have reached out and touched the man's leg. A few strides away, the Jap leaped up onto the root base of a large *nara* tree and began climbing up the gnarled trunk.

Cowboy rose and let loose a blast from the shotgun, firing from the waist. The Nip's back exploded in a shower of blood and shattered spine. The horrendous impact of the double-ought load slammed him hard against the trunk. He slid down slowly, as if he were peeling off the tree, and fell between the roots.

Fountain ducked, retrieving his Thompson for reload. Bird was still hammering away at the trail. Several seconds later, he caught sight of the shadows of Weesay and

Smoker running past their position. They quickly disappeared into moon haze.

Something came spitting and fizzing through the air, trailing a thick bloom of smoke. *Gas!* It hit the ground and rolled, spewing more smoke. He heard Wyatt curse. For a moment, before the smoke began to spread, he saw Japs moving forward, running hunched over and firing as they came, their branch-covered packs making them look like moving bushes. He fixed on one, fired, missed.

Wyatt tapped his head again, this time on the upslope side of his skull, a single tap: *move to a new firing position upslope.* They took off at the same instant, both running very low. Behind them, the smoke had expanded into a thick cloud, its foaming, rising upper edges gleaming in the moonlight like minute crystals of salt, fuming thickly until the moon itself was blotted out.

They reached the new firing position, down among the thick roots of a Tasmanian cedar tree. They both fired a burst. The Japs answered right away, swinging their concentrated fire up the slope.

Wyatt bent closer and growled, "Hold till they've blown their wad, then go . . . now!"

Again moving together, they ran along the upside of the trail, paralleling it. Quickly, they were engulfed in smoke. It smelled powerfully of ammonia. The Jap fire started again. They dropped to the ground, waited a few seconds, then took off once more. They passed the indistinct shadows of Weesay and Smoker, both down on one knee, firing cover.

"Full withdrawal," Bird yelled. "Go! Go!"

Within minutes, moving rapidly beyond the smoke and back into the moonlight, covering the back trail, they soon reached the point where Parnell and the prisoners had veered away from the high country and headed directly down the slope toward the edge of dense typhoon jungle a half mile below.

Forming into a tight column, Wyatt out front, they turned and followed the trail downward.

The shock of the first enemy grenade had pulled Sacabe up out of his desperate rage in an eyeblink, the heavy bursting sound coming back along the trail. Then the second went off. Around him, his men were already on the ground as a double volley of enemy fire now lashed at them. Some of the soldiers quickly began crawling off the trail, clumps of leaves moving in the moonlight.

The lieutenant had been near the rear of the column, pushing his men to keep close, to move faster, maintaining movement discipline. When the grenades blew, he, too, dropped to the ground and lay there flat, his face pressed against the mossy ground that smelled like wet stones.

Quickly his men began putting out counterfire, the thin reports of Arisaka rifles, the deeper chatter of submachine guns. Firing with his own sidearm, he shouted for the column's flankers to deploy farther to the side, to envelop the enemy ambush site so they could converge on it from three sides with full firepower.

Meanwhile, in another part of his mind, he was counting enemy muzzle flashes: two to the left, two to the right. *A very small ambush force.* A grenade blew up somewhere ahead and to the left. He saw the shadow of a limp body sail through the air for a second. It looked like a paper cutout.

The upslope flank is mined.

For a moment, he hesitated. Was this an enemy feint, bait to draw his men into a concentrated position that would then be hit by a much larger force? More enemy grenades went off, two of his own. There was a pause. Then came the loud blowout of his grenadiers launching rifle grenades, the missiles exploding a half second later with a sharper, tighter sound. Bullets and shrapnel *whanged* into stones, clipped branches around him.

He lifted his head and screamed, "Lay out smoke candles. Smoke candles."

A few feet from him, a soldier came to one knee, drawing out a round canister about eight inches long and three inches wide from his pack. He immediately flipped out its small metal spike and propped it onto the ground. He lit it off with a small, match-head scratcher and the smoke missile shot away with a hissing rush.

Sacabe heard it strike the ground thirty meters out, dense smoke bursting up and out like a sudden fog, rising into the moonlight. The top of it glittered. "*Shugeki!*" he shouted wildly and leaped up. "Charge the center!"

Men came off the ground and surged ahead, everybody laying in focused fire down the center of the trail, which was now hidden in the smoke. There was scattered enemy counterfire. Sacabe ran on, his sword drawn, flailing, his pistol firing and then clicking on an empty chamber, his voice scourging his men on, desperate to overtake this small force before it could fully withdraw and set up a second ambush.

They broke through the other side of the smoke, their charge quickly petering out. The enemy had already withdrawn. All firing stopped and the night became thickly silent again, stinking of ammonia. The soldiers prowled, moving like specters through the slowly thinning mist, and the night's sounds returned, gradually, stealthily, like something surfacing out of the sea.

Sacabe sent two scouts forward to reconnoiter the trail while the rest quickly set up a small defensive perimeter. He shouted for his *gunso*, or section leader. The man hurried up, braced. His camouflage branches bobbed in the moonlight. "How many?" the lieutenant barked.

"Four dead, Honorable *Chu-i* san. Also two badly wounded."

Sacabe cursed. He was now down to only thirteen fully functional men. He turned and walked off by himself, his boots squeaking. He sat down on a rock to consider. His determination to reach and annihilate this enemy force that had deprived him of the glorious completion of his mission for General Yamashita was now a raging blaze inside his chest. His deep sense of dishonor scalded him like acid. When he caught them, he swore silently, he would make them pay dearly.

One of the scouts returned to inform him that the larger enemy column had abruptly turned to the west and was now headed down toward dense jungle. *To the west.* He frowned, and then his spirits suddenly lifted. *They're heading for the Cagayan River. Why? Someone must be meeting them there.*

That would be the perfect place to attack their rear. Hampered by so many prisoners, they would be totally vulnerable. Then he paused. How large *was* this force? Did he now have enough firepower to conquer it?

He was certain the enemy would wait in ambush for him again. To stall him, slow him up while the main force got to the river. Angrily, he realized he'd now have to follow with less speed, with greater care. He could no longer spare any more soldiers.

There was another problem: How could the enemy be held at the river long enough for him to come up? Obviously, he'd need help. He cursed at the necessity for that, but there was no other choice. He summoned his signalman, who came swiftly through the smoke and stood at rigid attention in front of him.

The only radio equipment they had were two MU-1A Type 66 squad radios, similar to American walkie-talkies, which they had found at the mining camp, the things undoubtedly used for interdetachment communications. The units were battery-powered and crystal operated in the 3,000-kilocycle band. But their range on voice mode was only two miles. Still, each had a built-in CW or Morse code key designed for use in foul mountain weather. It also extended the radio's normal signal range to over five miles.

While the signalman set up, Sacabe estimated their

position on his field map, then constructed the message in his head. The radioman handed over the key and he began sending in the open, using international Morse code and its abbreviated character sets and Q signals in *romanji* or romanized letters: HR HR . . . CQ . . . CQ . . . BK2430point3 . . . K. Translated it read: *Hear, hear . . . calling any station, calling any station . . . come back on frequency 2430.3 . . . go ahead.*

He sent it out twice, waited. Nothing. He did it again, the radioman listening on the single earpiece for a reception signal to come back. A third time. Finally, the operator's head came up. "Sir, I am receiving." He handed the officer his earpiece.

He heard, "QRZ . . . QRZ." *Who are you?*

He immediately switched to the Imperial Army's General Purpose code called *koku angoo-sho 3*. Its code base worked off a system of four-letter or four-number groups and utilizing specific cipher additive tables that each senior officer and all elite unit officers had to memorize. The Allies referred to the code as the 3366.

Translated, his message would read: *Special operation for Fourteenth Army (Rome). Code name Toro. Present position 32JN25c25/178. Prisoners from Z-10 involved. Need assistance.* The coordinates of his position were rendered in the standard JN-25 Red Code communication and map reference system used by the Imperial Navy and most elite army forces.

The answer came right back. Apparently, he had raised a small detachment of Kempei-tai, code-named Takahaqame, which meant *Steelhawk*. It had been conducting guerilla-suppression operations near the small town of Pinagsa, west of Ilagan. The operator told him to stand by while his identification was verified at Rome, or Baguio HQ.

Sacabe paced around and around, the stink of ammonia still dense in the air, desperately aware that the loss of each minute meant the enemy raiders and POWs were getting farther and farther away.

From somewhere near, one of his wounded men suddenly cried out. The lieutenant whirled toward the sound. He angrily let loose a string of invective, cursed him, and ordered him to bear his pain in silence like a samurai. The soldier instantly stopped.

Fourteen minutes later, Steelhawk came back: *TORO* . . . *QUBJ* . . . *DITP* . . . *LYOC*. *WPRG* . . . *KKKK*. *Toro* . . . *request granted* . . . *deploying immediately* . . . *what contact position ???* . . . *respond*.

He hurriedly tapped back the coordinates of the rendezvous point he had chosen on the Cagayan, just south of the town of Tumauin. He requested their estimated time of arrival. All that came back was *AR* . . . *SK*, which was Steelhawk's Morse shorthand for "end of message" and "end of work." Then the Kempei-tai radioman was gone.

Kashikan Tazuko Hirano was the leader of Steelhawk, which was a *bukentai,* or twenty-man detachment, of Kempei-tai soldiers. He was a warrant officer, a rail-thin man with a scarred horse face, simpleton Oriental eyes, and a long-standing opium habit.

Such addictions were not unusual among Kempei-tai personnel, even the officers. Like Hirano, most had developed the habit in China and Thailand. For them it was never difficult to maintain a constant flow of the drug for their own use or even for sale. Loads came in with normal army medical shipments. As for Hirano, he still had four two-kilo loaves of Red Tiger raw opium, black as road tar.

The Kempei-tai was a secret police unit of the Imperial Japanese Army, quite similar to the Nazi Gestapo. Totally independent of normal military lines of command, it functioned under the direct control of the Ministry of War. This meant it was virtually untouchable. Its men possessed tremendous influence in all phases of the war, both military and civilian, particularly in territories newly captured by the IJA.

Although it had barely six thousand members, *everybody* feared the Kempei-tai, from its lowliest *johotei,* or privates, to senior officers. All had the legal power to arrest anyone, including regular army officers up to flag rank.

The men wore their own distinctive uniform, patterned after an earlier cavalry version: khaki tunic and riding breeches, knee-high black boots, a cavalry saber, and an 8mm Nambu pistol. On their left arms, they wore a white armband that bore the red *kanji* characters for *law* and *soldier.*

Their reputation for inhuman savagery and unspeakable cruelty was legend. Their usual raiding tactic against target villages was to quick-strike it with only a handful of men, relying on shock and surprise to overwhelm any defense. Once inside, they'd begin systematically slaughtering the peasants and raping the women. The younger, prettier ones would later be carried off to become "comfort women," prostitutes for the army. Their favorite weapons were the sword, bayonet, and flaming gasoline.

In Manchuria, the Kempei-tai had operated a medical experimental "hospital" code-named Unit 731. There, thousands of Chinese prisoners were used as living guinea pigs to undergo tests in disease production, horrific vivisections, physical endurance runs for frostbite data, and deliberate woundings so that battlefield surgeons could practice on actual humans.

Now, stretched on his straw tatami in the dim light of a red-glass hurricane lantern, Hirano glanced up with half-lidded eyes as his radioman, a lance corporal named Sugimura, pushed through the flap of his tent and braced at attention.

The warrant officer had been smoking opium, his pipe a long ceramic tube bearing carved dragons and a tiny bowl containing a mixture of raw opium gum and charcoal. The air in the tent felt greasy and smelled sweet, like burnt sugar.

"*Juni-san*," the corporal barked. "Your message to Toro has been logged and transmitted." Its log time had been 0108 hours. "The men are already assembled."

"*Hai*," Hirano replied dreamily, his voice thick from the drug. He took another drag off the pipe.

For the last two months, he and his men had been roaming the country between Bayombong and Santiago hunting guerilla camps and auxiliary cells of sympathizers. In the process, they had killed over twenty-five hundred natives, many completely innocent of any guerilla connections.

The lance corporal waited a moment, then asked, "Sir, what are your orders?"

"Kimura," Hirano mumbled. "Send Kimura's squad." He closed his eyes. A dreamy smile spread his mouth open. There was dried saliva at the corners, his teeth yellowed. In his mind, he floated over a hallucinatory landscape, tiny dollop-sized green islands sitting in a sapphire sea.

"*Ei, yo mitai desu!*" he suddenly cried happily. "There is the Inland Sea down there. See it? See it?" He tilted his head, listening to magic music that was as substantial as perfume.

At last, he opened his eyes again. The vision of the Inland Sea vanished. He was drowsily surprised to discover that his radioman was still there. Bringing up his pipe for another hit, he waved his other hand lazily, murmured, "Go, go."

"*Hai, Juni-san*," the man said, and briskly withdrew.

0211 hours

It was an agony for Parnell to watch the prisoners struggling through the hot, moist density of the jungle, its sudden, humming thickness having come up out of the moonlight suddenly to quickly engulf them. They moved without speaking, only the wordless moans and panting of men now tight inside themselves, fighting their own battles against the pain and exhaustion and fear.

Yet, by God, they were doing it, he could see. Apparently, the memories of back *there* had proffered some mysterious inner strength and stamina, was now keeping them moving, falling but rising to go on, helping those fallen, plodding endlessly through the animal-noisy blackness of the jungle night.

Parnell and Kaamanui repeatedly went up and down the column making certain the men remained close to each other, cautioning them not to drink too much water from pitcher plants or water vines, passing out salt tablets from their med kits. The prisoners made a pathetic chain of human misery. Yet they were covering ground faster than Parnell had anticipated.

Most of them had long since abandoned unnecessary weight, including their bags of gold concentrate. But Fagan kept a close watch to see that they did not discard the Japanese weapons they had brought from the compound.

Periodically, he'd croak out to those carrying guns, "Jes' don't be droppin yewr weepons now, gents. Remember, this 'ere's yewr bloody chance for revenge against those slant-eyed heathens. Don't be fockin' it away."

Nevertheless, Parnell and Kaamanui, even Trota, had shouldered some of their burden, slinging Arisakas along with their shotguns and some of the rifle grenade canisters. Periodically, Frankie returned to the column from his scout position to update Red on how far away he figured the river was. Whenever he came in, he'd identify himself by sounding his whirling stick.

He was doing a superb job, taking time to lay out the trail over the easiest ground. He marked it by using strips of luminous vine. They shone brightly in the darkness, almost like the tiny lights along a movie theater aisle. At this point, he estimated they had traveled about two miles since leaving the upper forest. That left three more to go.

Earlier, when the ambush firefight started, Parnell had tried to count the enemy muzzle bursts, easily identifiable from the American weapons. It had been difficult. Yet from the overall sound, he surmised the Jap force was small. Perhaps no more than twenty or twenty-five men, minus any that Bird's team had killed or wounded.

That fact buoyed him slightly. With at least some of the prisoners armed, he felt confident they could mount a decent defense. Still, other questions gnawed at him. Were there other enemy units prowling out there *ahead* of them? Would Farnsworth be able to reach point Circus? And even if he did, now that the Japs knew who and where they were, what could they encounter going back down the river?

He fielded these what-ifs as best he could, exploring contingency options, then let them go. One of the key survival skills he'd quickly learned as a combat soldier was to be able to focus on only what confronted you in any precise instant. Battle was a constant readjustment to a constantly changing situation. Allowing yourself to become enmeshed in all the potential scenarios would overload a man's concentration, lead to a total confusion and loss of command discipline. And *that* was fatal.

He started forward again, passing dark shadows on the trail one by one, their presence mostly felt and heard rather than clearly seen. To each, he said a few words of encouragement, made a joke, putting a grin in his voice.

No one answered him.

Chapter Fourteen

Farnsworth had approached Ilagan with banked steam, down to just barely moving against the river current. Yet the *Betty T* still put out enough sound to scatter night birds from the treetops, storks from off the banks.

The town was dark, only a few scattered kerosene lanterns showing. He smelled wood smoke, stronger than mere cooking fires, the sharper scent of cut beams and burnt mud bricks mixed in with the usual odors of dried fish and hemp rope and muddy river residue.

Along the banks, trees and thick grass hung out over the river and there were narrow footpaths so hard-packed that they gleamed in the moonlight. A couple dozen floating houses were tethered together and then to trees on the west bank. Each had at least one *baroto* tied to it, and all were lightless now.

Slowly, they drew abreast of the town itself, the main wharf avenue, Bilang Bilang Street, running deeper inland, all the way to the dark square where a church steeple and the thick mushroomlike clusters of galvanized roofs shone blue-white under the descending moon. Small trails of smoke seeped into the air from the dark buildings that looked like piles of rubbish.

As they moved farther up the river, they came to another, smaller knot of floating houses. It was surrounded by a network of fish traps, only their tops now showing in the high water. Suddenly, Panay up on the bow called softly and pointed out at the houses. Someone was moving on the walkway at the end of the cluster. Then a *baroto* slipped away from it and came drifting swiftly toward them, angling across the current.

As it came closer, a single man in it stood and shouted, "*Cay-o, cay-o.*" This was the traditional Tagalog phrase used when hailing a passing vessel. As the slender canoe passed the *Betty T,* the man swung it hard over and came up astern. A line came flying over the transom. Farnsworth quickly retrieved it and tied it to a stanchion. A moment later, the canoeist clambered over the stern and dropped to the deck.

Farnsworth squinted out at him in the moonlight. Then his face broke into a wide grin. "Liko, you old sod, you," he cried happily and held out his open arms. The two men embraced, the Filipino nodding and nodding.

His name was Liko Capistrano. He had worked for Farnsworth in the old days as a ship fitter. He stepped back and looked up at Farnsworth. "Ah, chu have coming beck, Cap'n," he said. "Chu have truly coming beck." He was a sturdy little man in a loincloth with thick white hair that covered the tops of his ears. "I hear chu steaming boat, I t'ink maybe, maybe. Ah, ees so good, so good."

"How are you, my old friend?"

Liko's grin disappeared. He shook his head, then nodded toward the town. "Ees berry bad. When the *Hapone* leave, he make big mess. Burn house, kill many people."

"When?"

"Maybe one week." He turned, sliced his palm through the air toward the north. "Dat way, *Hapones* go dat way."

"They *all* bloody left?"

"*Oo*. Maybe only few *patrolyas* now. Moving, moving in the jungle. Sometimes soldier come, want food. Dey no eat long time. If we can, we kill these ones. *Bastardos!*"

"Bravo, lad, bravo. . . . And *your* family?"

Capistrano shook his head sadly and made the sign of the cross. "Many, many dead. Chu remember my Casamera?" She was Capistrano's granddaughter, only nine years old when Farnsworth had last seen her.

The Brit's face went stiff. "She's not dead."

"No, but dey takin' her away. Making her pleasure girl for the *Hapones*."

Farnsworth made a sound like a growl. "*Damn* these yellow savages. *Damn* their souls to eternity."

Both men fell silent. Then Farnsworth gently put his hand on Capistrano's shoulder. "I'm deeply sorry, Liko." They embraced again, quietly wished each other good luck, and the old Filipino slipped over the stern. A few seconds later, his *baroto* slid away from the steamboat, riding the current, and headed back toward Ilagan.

Farnsworth increased speed. Soon the *Betty T* disappeared upriver in moonlight.

Kaamanui could smell the river. He'd always been familiar with water, any water: oceans, rivers, lakes. It was in his blood, the deep Samoan gifts of his Polynesian ancestors.

The scent of it came through the amalgam of all the other jungle odors, a trace breath of coolness and moving liquid. About fifteen minutes earlier, another firefight had erupted behind them, Wyatt's team again hitting the Nips. But this one didn't last long, mostly Thompsons with only a few enemy countering shots. The sounds seemed dull and compressed and directionless, more like distant firecrackers instead of weaponry.

Sol had moved back to the end of the column and now fell in with it, Fagan and four of his armed men on drag.

Now even the spirits of *these* men had begun to lag. They were no longer alert or ready for a fight, but like the rest, merely gasping, grunting shadows that struggled ahead of him.

They were now traversing a gentle slope, the ground covered with rain trenches and shallow gullies, everything wet and slippery with thick curtains of vines. But Trota was still doing his best to lay trail through the least dense part of the jungle, more rugged terrain on either side. Unfortunately, the moon had now slid lower in the sky and the diffused glow that had earlier filtered down through the trees was almost completely gone.

Parnell's sudden whistle came drifting through the jungle like a birdcall. Kaamanui patted Fagan's shoulder, ordered him to keep a sharp eye, and picked up speed, passing the other prisoners as they trudged from one of Frankie's little vine lights to the next.

The lieutenant was hunkered down beside the trail when Sol found him. "Frankie says we're about a mile from the river," Parnell told him quietly. He paused to listen to the column of men dragging by for a moment, then turned back to Kaamanui. Even quieter, he said, "I didn't think these poor sons a' bitches could get this far, you know it?"

"Yeah, me neither, Lieutenant. I guess they got a lot more tough than we figured."

Parnell grunted agreement, then said, "When we reach the river, I want a defensive perimeter with Fagan's men on the outside and slightly upriver. If there *are* other Japs waiting for us, I figure they'll attack from there. Tell the Irishman to aim for gun flashes and assign each man a fire zone."

"Right, sir." He paused to look up at the sky, turned back. "We might still have some moonlight when we get there."

"That could be good *and* bad." Parnell considered a moment. "Wyatt should be coming in pretty quick. You drop back again and hold drag until he does. Damn it, I'm still worried about Fagan and his boys banging away at the first sound they hear."

"I'll keep 'em in line, sir. You think the Brit's here and waitin'?"

"I sure as hell hope so." Parnell rose. "As you work your way back, notify every man that we've only got a short ways to go. Give 'em a boost."

"Yes, sir," Kaamanui said and moved off.

Sacabe had outfoxed them this time. When the firing broke out, the enemy going after the two scouts up front and not waiting to ambush the main force, his men had pulled back and gone to ground, listening to muzzle bursts instead of returning focused fire.

It had worked, only one man wounded, one of the forward scouts shot in the leg. Without clear opposition, the enemy had quickly withdrawn. He had waited a good twenty minutes before ordering his men forward again, this time with only one advance scout. Now with the Kempei-tai force deploying to intercept and stall the enemy, he felt it unnecessary to rashly rush ahead and, quite possibly, into a third ambush.

Instead, he intended to go forward with extreme caution now. Even if the enemy raiders reached the river far ahead of him—even ahead of the Kempei-tai, they'd be badly slowed by malnourished prisoners, he knew, who *must* be on the verge of collapse by now. When he finally *did* make contact with the enemy force, the *gaijin* bastards would find themselves in a cross fire and their backs to the river.

He allowed himself a moment of pleasurable anticipation. It was going to be a massacre.

Wyatt lay very still, straining to sound-separate things in the night. Goddamn jungle gave you so much shit it was hard to filter things out. Still, he had already incorporated some of the little tricks Frankie had taught him about jungle movement.

The darkness was nearly complete where he was, below a small cascade of rocks, shit-slick with rain and mud. Separate sounds came off them, little hisses of water slipping through the moss, soft poppings like soap bubbles bursting, and the barely audible buzzing of a large insect periodically fluttering into the air.

Earlier, he'd hung back after the second ambush, sending the others on ahead. He wanted the next Nip scout who would soon be coming along. The ambush hadn't done much, the Jap point men moving with much more caution and ready to drop to ground at the first sign of danger. Without at least one kill, Wyatt Bird felt dissatisfied.

They hadn't placed any booby traps along the trail's side to again funnel Nips into their own flanks. There wasn't any recognizable trail through here, anyway. Once they'd left the high country with its spaced forest trees and meager underbrush they had been forced to change their ambush tactics. Now it was quick strikes and quick withdrawals, wear down the gawddamn rice-heads by taking out one or two each time.

Their first burst had dropped the lead scout. The second one, twenty yards back, put out a little counterfire, then stopped just as the wounded Nip opened up. Then he, too, stopped firing. There was the thick, ringing silence again, both sides listening for the other. But nothing came from farther back, no Japs advancing to reinforce.

Wyatt knew why. The little shits were playing it cagey now, not allowing themselves to be suckered into another clean ambush. *Okay*, he decided, *then we'll go one on one.* He shifted to the right until he reached Laguna. Signaling by touch, he instructed Weesay and the others to pull back about a hundred yards and set up a rallying point and firebase. Without a word, Laguna turned and silently moved off.

He had waited a few seconds, then moved to his original position and slightly beyond, feeling his way in the darkness. He came to a tumble of rocks that was slanted uphill. It was like a fractured wall that was wet and spongy. He eased himself back under brush beside it and waited.

Wyatt knew there'd be another scout coming along soon, picking up where the last one had gotten hit. Frankie had told him that the Japs never deviated patrol routes in jungle. "Dumb little fucks," he said silently, but moving his lips. Another trick of Trota's, talking to himself in the dark. It kept a man focused. Also, Trota told him to always keep his mouth open when he scanned, for better sound reception.

Mosquitoes now swarmed around his face, his hands, *goddammit,* like tiny pinpricks in his flesh. He shifted his head, his mouth scanning for sounds like a pickup microphone. From everywhere came the cicada-like trills of tree frogs, the drip of water, anonymous slurs and snaps and slitherings and sudden marsupial screams. *Shit,* he said in his throat, moving his lips, *fucking jungle.*

He suddenly stiffened.

He'd caught something out of the ordinary, a tiny, out-of-place sound. *There!* The rustle of brush against cloth. He listened tensely, trying to fix its source and position. It seemed to have come from his left, out maybe thirty or forty feet. He leaned forward but nothing more came to him. His fingers and palms began to tingle, old combat instincts telling him something dangerous was right out there.

He lifted his head a few inches. The darkness over and beyond the rocks seemed softer, gently diffused with remnants of moon glow. Solid blocks of shadow, darker shapes on the overall darkness, emerged. Still, nothing moved. Then he got a whiff of human odor, *Jap* odor, the fartlike stench of pickled turnip sweat, dried fish, and caked excrement.

There was a sudden hissing. *Grenade!* He heard it snapping through branches and instantly went flat to the ground, his eyes closed tightly against the coming flash. It struck the ground behind him, bounced, struck again farther back, then went off.

He was showered with moss and sundered branches. The shock wave whipped over him, made his ears ache for a second. Then they started ringing loudly. But he was already rising, coming to one knee, knowing the Nip scout would be coming right for him, firing.

The rapid *ba-ba-ba-ba-bam* of a submachine gun exploded through the receding echoes of the grenade blast. He spotted the Jap's muzzle bursts, back-blowing through his weapon's cooling jacket. Bullets cut past him. One ripped through his collar, another snapped at his sleeve above his elbow.

He opened up, traversing the Thompson from right to left across where he'd seen the gun's flashes, coolly, grimly pulling off three-round bursts, one after the other, smelling the hurl of cordite and heat coming up off the receiver. He stopped and rolled to his right, away from the rocks. He laid down his Thompson and slipped the Winchester shotgun from his back, feeling to be sure the safety was off.

The submachine gun rapped off again. Bullets skidded off the rocks where he'd been. Before the Jap's burst was complete, Bird rose and triggered off three quick rounds from the Defender, firing and racking back the pump, aiming at the Jap's muzzle flashes. He saw sparks nick off into the air, the buckshots hitting metal.

He ceased firing and listened, the powerful echoes of the shotgun's explosions riffling off. Then everything suddenly dropped into a kind of flat silence, as if the jungle had absorbed all sound like a padded room. Only the receding ringing in his ears. Through it, he began to pick out other sounds, faintly, then louder and louder. Strongest was the crunching of twigs, a thrashing of brush. Then a long, pitiful groan, like a deaf man trying to form words. He tried to fix its position with his ears. The groaning stopped.

Wyatt chortled, coldly murmuring, moving his lips, "Bingo, cocksucker."

Ten minutes later, he reached the RP, first coming onto Cowboy, who called softly, "Chess," Bird countersigning. The others merged out of the darkness. They paused for a moment as Wyatt took a quick compass fix, working off his field map. Then the four men moved off again, heading due west.

0349 hours

Munti Balagan was jerked out of sleep by the icy press of a rifle against his forehead, the slender thirteen-year-old coming up into consciousness, crying, "*Magingat kayo!*" *Watch out.*

The room was full of jabbing flashlight beams. He heard his mother sob, heard roosters and a single piglet raising a ruckus under the floor, and Japanese shouts from outside. The one holding the rifle on him suddenly jerked the muzzle upward. A pain shot through the boy's jaw from the sharp edge of the sight. He rolled away from his sleeping blanket and came to his knees.

The Kempei-tai squad had reached the river at the small fishing hamlet of Palandog, little more than a dozen *nipa* huts on stilts, with *barotos* and a few *bandas* tied to stakes beside the river. Now they were bursting into huts, rousting people, looking for fishermen who would take them down the river.

All the men and two teenaged boys were herded out to the edge of the river. A stocky Japanese sergeant shouted at them in bad Tagalog, wanting the best boatmen to transport him and his men. No one stepped forward. He waited a moment, then angrily struck the nearest Filipino with his fist. It was a thin old man, who fell down and lay still.

Again, the Jap sergeant demanded someone to sail them down the river. He threatened to start killing people if someone did not volunteer. Munti Balagan shifted his feet in terror, trembling, feeling sweat running down the crease of his spine. Why didn't someone step forward? He wanted the *Hapones* to go away from here. Even if the boat was lost, it was only a boat. But still the men refused to comply.

Suddenly, things began to happen very quickly. There was a loud *boom* and one of the men fell down. He made a peculiar sound and crawled about on the ground like a jungle spider. Another soldier came up and shot him again, this time through the back of the head. Munti could not see who it was.

Women began screaming, high-pitched, terrible cries. One came rushing from a hut toward the line of men. She was immediately struck by a rifle butt and dropped into a cross-legged position, her head hanging down on her chest. Munti recognized her clothing. It was his mother. An explosion of anguish filled his chest. He started to weep. A Japanese soldier hit him on the side of the head with his fist.

The remaining males were herded down to where the boat lines came up onto the bank, the women and children following in the moon shadows, crying and whimpering. The Japanese sergeant had gone ahead and was now standing on the bank where the painter line of a large, double-hulled *banda* was tied to a thick stump. Several soldiers began hauling in the line, the boat coming slowly toward the bank. In a moment, its twin prows slid up onto the mud.

The soldiers began loading their backpacks and weapons, including a Model 96 light machine gun. It was braced on top of the bamboo span that connected the two hulls. The sergeant turned, pointed at the first three men standing near him, and ordered them to get aboard.

One was Munti Balagan.

Parnell heard the steamboat's engine, a far-off sound coming through the jungle in muffled bursts, as if it were intermittently crossing behind thick walls. The distance broke apart the acoustics of it, made it seem as if he could hear each power thrust of its pistons, each blow of steam.

The men close behind him began to murmur. He turned and grinned in the dark at them, calling softly, "Hear that, boys? That's your ticket home." They gave a subdued, weary cheer.

He glanced at his watch: 4:17. An hour before daylight.

The drumming sound of Trota's whirling stick came, and a moment later, the little scout hustled out from among the trees and headed for Parnell. "The riber only t'ree hunnnert yards straight ahead, Lieutenant. Chu can hear da boat?"

"Yeah. What's better, there ain't no gunfire."

He whistled. Soon, Sol came forward, pushing through brush. Parnell told him, "We got a couple hundred yards to the river. I'm going ahead with Frankie. Bring 'em down fast, but don't break jungle until I whistle."

"Got it, Lieutenant."

The land was still sloped slightly, but they were already into riverine growth: thicker ground brush, stands of bamboo and scattered breaks filled with *kunai* grass and groves of coconut trees, their frond blades clicking gently in a slight northern breeze. They could smell the river very strongly now, the moist, cool scent of mud and moving water like the odor of flower petals on the verge of wilting.

They reached the edge of one of the groves and peered out at the river, a hundred yards farther on. Edging it were flat areas of sand and pools of trapped floodwater inter-spersed with thick patches of mangrove.

The farther side of the river was in heavy shadow, the moon deep in the western sky now, just barely above the dis-tant peaks of the Cordillera Central, its light coming in at a steep angle. Yet the center of the river still glistened and shimmered with light, and the near bank was brilliantly lit up, the coconut palms casting long, tufted shadows onto the sand.

They could hear the steamboat clearly now, no breaks in the steady pound of the engine and the swashing slaps of its side wheels. About a quarter mile downriver, a rising line of smoke was vaguely visible above the trees, floating back, thinning out as it climbed, yet leaving a gossamer smear in the moonlight.

Then, there it was, pushing around a slight bend in the river, water making white riffles along its blunt prow, a dark, boxy shadow moving against the current, smoke laced with sparks belching from its stack.

Parnell put his binoculars on it, saw the silhouettes of the helmsman and a man moving on the forward deck. He chuckled. "Now ain't that a goddamned pretty sight."

"Gotdamn jivvy, Lieutenant," Frankie said, his grin white in a shaft of moonlight.

Red waited a few minutes, watching the side-wheeler ap-proaching closer and closer, the sound of it now getting convoluted as the hiss of steam and slam of her pistons bounced off the banks, clashing with each other. Finally, he stepped out from among the palm trees, onto hard-packed sand, feeling it cool under his soles. Using his code mirror, he moon-flashed: S-P-E-A-R-P-O-I-N-T. The answer flashed back, a spotlight coding: D-E-E K-A-Y.

Precisely thirty-two seconds later, the steady churn and throb of the *Betty T* was overridden by the rapid, slamming crash of a Japanese light machine gun from upriver. Rounds stitched themselves across the surface a few yards ahead of the boat, kicking up geysers.

* * *

The gunfire came to Kaamanui like an automatic hand weapon going steadily: *pop, pop, pop. Shit, Nips on the river.* For a moment, he considered the possibility that the trailing force had passed them, gone onto the river. No, no, it had to be *another* Nip team.

He and the prisoner column were not far from the river now, perhaps a half mile, still moving decently, the men exhilarated somewhat at the closeness of freedom. It was also easier ground now, down out of the thicker jungle into grassy places and coconut groves where the cover was soft with frond debris.

He listened for a few seconds longer, trying to fix the enemy's gunfire position and count weapons. Then he heard a Thompson open up, another, south of the Nips' fire zone. Right off, another volley of Arisakas and the Jap MG came back.

The bastards're bunched, a small force.

He broke into a run, back toward the end of the column, the prisoners standing around not knowing what to do, shadows passing on his left as he crashed through brush. A moment later, Fagan, Pytel, and the other leader he couldn't remember the name of emerged out of the dark, coming to meet him. There were three additional armed men with them, all gasping and wheezing, dragging ass, but ready.

Fagan came up to him, croaked breathlessly, "How you . . . want to handle this . . . Sahr-gint?"

"I'm going down to the river," Sol answered in his slow, calm way. "Can you people keep up with me?"

"We'll bloody well try."

"Okay. Leave one man here to bring in the column."

"Roight." Fagan started to turn away.

"Hold it," Kaamanui said. "Whoever it is keeps a sharp eye on the back trail. But remember to fire only into your own fire zone. My teammates'll be comin' through soon, and real fast. Next, when you get to the river, remain in cover until we come find you. You got it?"

"I'll see to it, Sahr-gint," Fagan said. He turned to Pytel. "You stay." Without a word, Pytel turned and hurried away.

Sol was looking closely at one of Fagan's men. It was Eugene Mallory. He was holding one of his legs off the ground. "You, there," the big Samoan said to him. "Maybe you better stay here, too."

"Don't worry about me," Mallory wheezed. "I'll keep up."

Kaamanui shrugged. "All right, partner."

They headed out, going for the sound of the firing, Kaamanui breaking trail with his huge body.

Parnell had dropped to one knee when the enemy MG started up. He watched the bullets tear up the smooth surface of the river, shattering it like glass in the moonlight. He swung around, squinted upriver, and immediately picked up the double-hulled *banda* about three hundred yards away, its sail all blue white, the dark shape of the boat clean against the gleaming river.

He heard Farnsworth begin shooting his carbine, uselessly, far out of range, little feeble pings like a kid with a .22-caliber hunting rabbits. He tapped Trota's shoulder. They rose and headed toward the riverbank, moving at an angle yet staying in the shadows. In his mind, he was already setting up their position for counterfire.

They crossed a muddy overflow basin, the water still as a mirror. It was deep with mud and they sank down to midway up their calves, their boots making sucking sounds as they pulled free with each step. Out on the river, the Japs were still firing, full volleys now, the sounds of their bullet impacts striking the steamboat with loud metallic thuds, like pebbles striking an empty barrel.

A thought jumped at him: *One round into that steam boiler and that'll be all she wrote.*

They reached the other side of the little basin and went up onto rain-pounded sand. The *banda* was 150 yards away, skimming swiftly, riding the current. The bulge of its crescent-shaped sail popped in the breeze, ragged cloth flapping. There were Japs standing or kneeling on the center platform, firing.

He opened up immediately, the Thompson canted up slightly. At his back, Trota's weapon began banging away, too. He saw a Jap drop off the platform into the water between the hulls. He laid in another burst, then smacked Trota's shoulder. They dashed to the right among coconut trees and went to ground just as bullets came slamming back at them, cracking overhead, smacking into tree trunks with a sizzling, juicy sound. Far off, he could hear Farnsworth still pulling off single shots with his M1A1-3.

Using the coconut trunks as defilade, they opened up again.

0437 hours

Wyatt and Smoker overran the column, didn't even slow down to sign and countersign, just came crashing through brush, crossing the line of men somewhere near the middle, all these dark, hunched, slow-moving shadows in the darkness.

The moment he heard the firing from the river, Wyatt had ordered Cowboy and Weesay to take rear guard position, but to fall back toward the river rapidly. They were then less than a quarter mile from the end of the column. Then he and Wineberg took off to support the lieutenant and the others.

Now as they rushed through the column, some of the prisoners flinched away, uncertain of who they were. Soon after, they emerged into a coconut grove, the ground speckled with moonlight. They could hear the side-wheeler venting steam from somewhere downriver,

hear the bullets striking its hull. The gun flashes of the
Japanese weapons showed over the tops of the gallery
trees farther upriver, like the flickering splashes of light
from an out-of-sight movie screen.

Wyatt spotted figures moving ahead of them, crossing in
and out of shadow. One was the unmistakable bulk of Kaamanui. He whistled at him and the figures halted, Sol
whistling back. They headed for them.

"How many y'all got wi'ya?" Bird asked Kaamanui.

"Five."

"Anybody here carryin' Nip grenades?"

Sol unslung his two Arisaka rifles, handed them over,
and one of the prisoners gave Smoker a grenade canister.
Wyatt shouldered the long guns, then pointed toward the
river at a point slightly farther south of the Nip gun flashes.
"Sol, head 'em yonder an' set up a defensive line to protect
that boat. An' watch for Cowboy and Weesay comin' in."

Kaamanui and the prisoners turned and crossed back
through the edge of the coconut grove. Bird and
Wineberg sprinted on, running through the steeply
slanted shafts of moonlight, the Jap rifles clanging softly
against each other on his back.

Two minutes later, the USS *Barracuda*, code-named
Chariot for Operation Purgatory, and a fleet boat attached
to WestSubPac's Support Fleet of Vice Admiral Charles
Lockwood's Task Force 17, achieved its rendezvous watch
station fifteen hundred yards off the mouth of Divilican
Bay at a depth of thirty fathoms.

Its captain, Commander Phil Herbold, held the conn.
The OOD was his executive officer, Lieutenant Ron Gerrard. Herbold ordered his vessel to periscope depth for a
look around. The compact CIC or Combat Information
Center was hot, its air smelling of sweat and Bunker C
diesel fuel and electrical gear.

The CIC resounded with repeats of the captain's order

as the sub, blowing ballast, began a slow rise to the surface.
Soon after, the dive officer called out, "We have periscope
depth, sir."

"Up periscope." There was a soft whine and the thick
bronze shaft of the periscope slid up out of its sheath, the
captain slapping down the handles and fixing his eyes to
the viewing pads, following it up until the shaft eased to a
stop. The OOD quickly stepped to the opposite side of the
scope to call off position marks.

Through the viewer, the ocean was full of moonlight. To
the west, Herbold could see the land mass of northern
Luzon, a solid black silhouette topped with distant, moon-
etched ridges. He swung through a 180-degree arc, then
spun around and did the same to seaward. Satisfied, he
popped up the scope handles and stepped back, calling,
"Down periscope. . . . What's bottom depth and drift
conditions?"

The sailor manning the Series J-15 depth-finding unit
came right back, "Depth off the keel is one-eight-eight, sir,
with tidal drift holding one-quarter knot at zero-eight-one
degrees."

"Trim for slow descent. . . . Stand by to deploy radio
buoy." Voices cracked through the humid air. The sub
began a slight tilt as the dive officer began droning off
the sink rate and depth updates. As the buoy left its topside
encasement, the soft rustle of unreeling cable came down
through the hull.

Fully deployed, the small unit would sit three feet beneath the surface with its small antenna extended. It was
capable of both transmitting and receiving. Normally it was
only used to listen for messages, maintaining transmission
silence so enemy radio detection stations couldn't fix its
position. To break radio silence, however, was always left to
the captain's judgment.

At 110 feet, the main WFA-19C combat passive scanning sonar operator suddenly called out, "Conn, I'm
picking up faint cavitation. Bearing one-seven-niner

degrees True. Range is seven thousand yards, speed constant at one-four knots."

"Stop descent," Herbold immediately snapped. "Bring to hover and rig for silence." A few seconds later, the soft hum of machinery ceased, blowers wound down. The *Barracuda* went silent in a state of neutral bouyancy. "Quartermaster, designate target."

"Target is designated S-3, sir," came the answer.

"Sonar, profile?"

"Conn, profile is consistent with Japanese Kwaiken-class FFE vessel." The term *Kwaiken* meant *Dagger* and referred to the Japanese Navy's class of FFE escort frigate warships, smaller than destroyers and usually used with convoys or as coast patrol gunboats.

"Maintain her track."

"Maintain track, aye."

Herbold glanced at the XO. "Well, now, ain't *this* shitty timing?"

Gerrard nodded. "That it is, sir. Well, at least these little Daggers don't carry top-grade sound gear like their Sagashi boats." Japanese Sagashi-class sub chasers were known for their deadly German-built sonar equipment.

"What's her armament?"

"Standard ASW gear off a single-rack depth-charge launch, sir." Gerrard frowned, mentally drawing up the Nip gunboat's nomenclature. "A forward dual-mounted forty-seven-millimeter turret and twin 7.7 MGs amidships. I think she also carries a single thirteen-millimeter AA aftergun on the later models."

The captain grunted. "Not worth a torpedo but still capable of giving us trouble, huh?"

"I'm afraid so, sir."

"Sonar, target update?"

"Conn, TD S-3 is still maintaining constant heading and speed. Range is now sixty-five hundred yards."

"Track her out and away."

"Aye, sir."

* * *

Parnell saw Wyatt and Smoker moving on his left, dark shadows in the moonlight, but so familiar, saw the Arisakas around Bird's shoulders and Smoker lugging the grenade canister. *All right!* He waved them into position, nearer the river.

Out there in the water, the *banda* had swung its double prow toward their side of the river, its sail popping as it shifted across the breeze. The Japs kept up a steady firing at their position, and obviously intended to come straight in, homing to their muzzle flashes. Branches and tree trunks rattled and thudded around them with bullet impacts.

Red put another burst into the approaching boat. No hit. Then Frankie let loose. Still no hit. They moved to their left, skidded to ground behind two short, thick-trunked palm trees, big coconuts hanging right there within standing reach. The ground immediately around it got chopped up with incoming rounds.

Abruptly, there was the hard crack of a grenade launcher, heavy as a shotgun, and the hot sizzle as the missile rocketed through the air. *Wyatt.* The grenade exploded four feet from the sailboat's starboard hull, hurling up water.

Shit.

The Japs immediately turned their focus-of-fire toward Bird's launcher burst. Parnell and Frankie put in another round of bullets and saw one of the soldiers near the stern of the port hull suddenly throw up his hands and fall. He lay for a moment, straightened, and then in slow motion, slid backward into the river.

Bird put another grenade out there. Parnell saw the sparkly trail of it flash past and then explode in an orange-white ball of fire between the *banda*'s twin hulls. Chunks of wood and canvas patches and one body flew up in a watery upheaval that glistened like surf in the moonlight.

* * *

Munti Balagan couldn't control his terror. He was shaking all over as bullets zipped past, the *Hapones* firing and the powerful stink of cordite drifting, spent shells flying off the machine gun with its tripod legs steady on the *banda*'s bamboo platform.

He had seen one soldier pitch over into the river. Through his fear, he thought of the crocodiles, the huge *diwas* and *buhayes*, those black river spirits instantly taking the body. Then he heard one of the soldiers yelling at the man on the tiller, pointing toward the far bank. The boat swung over and headed that way, its sail momentarily collapsing, fluttering gently before catching the breeze again.

A powerful explosion came off the right side of the boat. Water sprayed all over him, smelling of burnt powder. Immediately, the *Hapones* began firing in a different direction. One more soldier got hit, slumped over, and slid off the boat.

Next, the man on the tiller got hit. He screamed and bent forward, holding his head in both hands as if he couldn't stand the noise of his own voice. Even in his terror, the posture and the sound reminded Munti of those dark-dressed, weeping women that followed a black coffin on Good Friday, their sobbing high-pitched and stark.

Another explosion came, numbed his ears. This time, the front of the boat lifted high up into the air and things went hurtling past him. He grabbed for the side of the hull as the Japanese machine-gunner came somersaulting backward and landed on him just as the boat came back, hard. It was no longer stable. Its center platform had been blown apart, the bamboo cross pieces splintered into shreds.

Hapones soldiers were in the water, thrashing, seemingly unable to swim. Munti started to push the machine-gunner off him. He was dead, very heavy. He finally got him off. Out there, the moonlit surface of the river was all choppy from the explosions and the soldiers' thrashings. It looked oily, too, flashing colors in the moonlight.

A bullet struck him in the neck. His entire upper body went numb. He gasped, felt air escaping from somewhere and, shuddering, realized it was from his throat. He tried to reach up and touch the hole but couldn't move his arms. Then he was in the water and slowly sinking, unable to swim or make his body respond at all. He went under, screaming in his head, but making absolutely no sound.

Sacabe knew he and his men were again alone in their battle against the enemy raiders, hearing the firing from the river stopping suddenly, only enemy weapons trailing off with scattered shots.

The realization shocked him. An entire Kempei-tai unit beaten? Then, how large *was* this raider force? He felt hopelessness take him. Then rage again. And finally decision. He would hurl himself and his men at the enemy, make one last, glorious banzai charge and die a samurai's death for emperor and homeland.

He looked down the line of men, twelve, watching him, waiting to be given a command, their faces etched in moonlight and shadow. There was no longer any firing at all, only the slow, steady *shush* of a steam engine that came in spurts through the trees.

He stood, shouting for everyone to stand with him. He informed them that they were about to die. Wordlessly, each man rested his weapon onto the ground and withdrew a strip of white cloth from his tunic.

All contained similar *kanji* characters for the words *taiatori* and *ohka,* which meant *suicide* and *cherry blossom.* These were called *meiyoshi* or glorious death banners and were always donned by soldiers who were about to commit themselves to a suicide charge, or a pilot preparing for a kamikaze attack.

The night became strangely still as the men picked up their weapons again, gave them one final check, and came to attention. Sacabe walked by each man, nodding, nodding. He felt a great, fierce torrent of pride. For himself, for these gallant men, for his beloved emperor who would know of their sacrifice and honor them.

But there was still one thing left to do. He ordered his radioman forward with his gear. He intended to transmit again, let any unit out there know that there were enemy on the river. He ordered the radioman to set up.

Then he walked off by himself and sat on a rock and looked through a break in the trees at the moon as it finally slipped below the far ridges and pure darkness again swallowed the jungle, leaving only the last glow of moonlight still in the sky, which made the ridges look like black cutouts against a silver backdrop.

The tranquil beauty of the scene and the moment of commitment drew into his mind a famous haiku by Bosho:

Bird song like mist
Raindrops trembling
The moon is not alone

He wept, overcome by patriotic passions.

Parnell and the others had immediately rushed the bank after the *banda* got blown apart, firing at the men in the water, throwing Thompson bursts and shotgun rounds. Farther down the river, Farnsworth had swung the sidewheeler into the eastern bank where it now sat at the edge of a mangrove, its engine thumping quietly.

Between their bursts, they could hear the roar of crocodiles out on the river, sudden explosions of water as the

animals, drawn by the noise and disturbances on the surface, plunged into the river, hunting food.

Red saw two figures drawing close to the near bank, one
swimming strongly. He fired at them, saw one roll in the
water. The other began shrieking frantically in Tagalog
and waving his arms. Red lowered his weapon, watched a
moment, then waved the others off. "Hold it, stop firing."

Trota ran down the sloping bank and went into the shallows, his body slanted against the current. The swimmer,
drawn by it, came abreast of him. He lunged for the man,
missed, tried again, and got a hold of his leg. He hauled
him back and together they worked their way back to the
bank, slipping and falling in the mud.

The swimmer's name was Teting Escano, he told
Frankie in excited Tagalog. He said the *Hapones* had come
in the night and forced him and three others, one only a
boy, to sail them down the river. They had also killed some
people in the village. Now the others that had come with
him were all dead. His voice shook with outrage and
sorrow and he turned and viciously spat toward the river
and then turned back and said the *Hapones* had been
Kempei-tai.

When Trota translated this, Parnell said, "Kempei-tai?
What's that?"

"Secret police, Lootenant." Frankie drew his fingers
across his forehead, a sign of extreme danger. "*Magingat
kayo!* These are berry bad."

"Ask him if there are any more Kempei-tai out there."

Frankie asked Escano, then turned back to the lieutenant. "Escano say he no t'ink so. These only go in small
units and are always far from each other."

Parnell waved Bird and Kaamanui over. They came, running hunched, their gear jingling. Now and then, a violent
thrashing erupted in the river, crocs taking prey. No one
even looked.

He nodded to Sol. "Get the rest of the prisoners down

to the boat and start 'em loading. Make it fast." He now turned to Bird. "Where's Fountain and Laguna?"

"They must be in by now, Lieutenant. Prob'ly down where them prisoners is at."

"Take Fagan and his men and set up a defensive line to protect that boat." He lifted slightly to look down the river, searching for dark cover. But the light had suddenly dimmed as the moon began disappearing below the high ridgeline of the Cordillera Central.

He finally pointed toward a grove of coconut trees inland from the steamboat, their high frond clusters now merging into a single darkening shadow. "Use that coconut grove east of it. Looks like there's a stretch of open ground between it and the edge of the jungle that'll give you good fire lanes. I'll talk to the Brit and then come up."

Wyatt and Sol silently rose and sprinted off.

Sacabe's signalman was sharp, the *jotohei* knowing subtle things about radios. When the lieutenant ordered him to start ranging again, putting signal out there for anybody to pick up, he knew a few little tricks to extend his signal.

He set up his Type 3 walkie-talkie in a small, open patch of sand, laying it on its side atop a mossy rock. Thus, its tapped coil-and-switch antenna was on a horizontal plane and would increase the possibility that his signal could be heard by receivers that were also aligned to that same polarization. Like those aboard a ship offshore, as an example, or even one located in a radar station.

Furthermore, he knew that since the moon had gone down beyond the mountains and left them in its shadow path, the atmosphere would have immediately dropped minutely in temperature and density. Although small, that differential would cause a slight lessening of the air's interference level. Last of all, he spun his band dial down to

2,200 kilocycles, the most favorable frequency range for propagation of a ground wave.

Finally, he began tapping out a Morse code "All Call" in the open. He stopped a moment to listen. The atmosphere was full of signal, all of it in Morse code, coming from both enemy and Japanese transmitters, everything mixed together, a jumble of high, pinging tones at different intensities and pitches and speeds.

He hissed with irritation. There was no way he'd be able to punch through all that traffic. He considered for a moment, then returned to the key and again transmitted in clear: KOKU-ANGOO-SHO 3 ... KOKU ANGOO-SHO 3 ... K. He waited a half minute, then tried again. Another half minute. Still nothing came back.

He desperately probed his mind for something else. Got it. He tapped out: QRAP ... DRTT ... CDFP ... TORO ... ROME ... KKKK. *Tokubetsu Rikusentai code name Toro ... contact Baguio ... come back.* The term *tokebetsu rikusentai* referred to the Special Naval Landing Force, which was Sacabe's original unit.

Someone had been monitoring closely. He'd barely completed his message when a strong signal came right back, using JN40 code, the Imperial Navy Operational Cipher Base. He was informed that he was being received by an IJN warship, a Kwaiken-class medium frigate designated FFE-147 that was currently operating off the coast of Luzon, just east of Divilcan Bay.

Moving among the palm trees, banging his boots into fallen coconuts, the trunks like dark pillars all around him and the fronds clicking, Parnell sensed different light coming into the darkness, dawn not far off, the colors subtly changing in tone and substance.

Meanwhile, back at the steamboat, the prisoners were boarding the *Betty T,* the boat shoved in among the mangrove trees. It had been chewed up a bit by the Jap fire, but

Farnsworth quickly assured him nothing important had been hit.

Kaamanui and the Brit's helpers had run planks lifted from the deck out over the trees' spider roots so the prisoners could reach the boat. They were totally exhausted, falling, stumbling, yet still grinning their withered smiles, *God Almighty*, unable to believe they were actually safe. But once on the deck, they slowly, painfully lowered themselves and stretched out on the night-cold boards and closed their eyes.

Parnell whistled softly and was immediately answered by another whistle from his left. He moved toward the sound and abruptly came up on Cowboy. He knelt beside him. "Any sign yet?" he asked.

"Nothin', Lieutenant. But they're out there, I can *smell* the bastards."

"How many? Were you able to make a count?"

"Yeah, no more'n a dozen now."

"Where's Wyatt?"

"Yonder, on the right."

He worked his way over to Bird, knelt beside him, and quietly studied the jungle. It made a dense black wall a hundred yards from the edge of the coconut grove. From this position, he was able to see most of the sky. It was beginning to lighten, a faint grayness seeping into the night with a nearly imperceptible fusing.

He asked Wyatt, "Do you think they'll come in on us?"

"Hard to say, Lieutenant," Bird answered. "They must know we busted that Jap poo-lice unit. An' they themselves ain't nothin' but iddy-biddy." He shrugged. "Still, these gawddamn Nips is crazy for makin' them bands-eye charges, ain't they?"

"Yeah."

"How long before them POWs is full loaded?"

"Just a few minutes." Red looked at his watch: 0452. "It'll be light pretty quick. I want to get on down the river before dawn gets here full. If they're gonna hit us, it'll be then."

He was quiet for a long moment, then, "Okay, we'll pull everybody out now and set up a firebase near the river."

They withdrew in standard bounding-overwatch fashion, leapfrogging each other as the line came slowly back through the coconut grove and across the open ground to the mangrove, the Blue Teamers moving swiftly, silently, but Fagan's men going with sluggish clumsiness.

By the time they reached the boat, the rest of the prisoners were aboard, and Farnsworth was rebuilding his steam pressure. Leaving Bird and Laguna as a security team at the edge of the mangroves, Parnell also boarded and quickly set up his own men and some of the armed prisoners in firing positions along the forward and port side of the *Betty T.*

Then he went aft to once more check with the Brit. The sky was now brightening more rapidly. "How long before we can shove off?" he asked Farnsworth.

"Any time now, Lieutenant. I suggest you get your last men aboard now."

"Okay, let her rip."

"Rip she shall, old man," Farnsworth said and started throwing levers.

The boat trembled as the side wheels began to turn heavily, chewing off mangrove branches. Red felt the deck jerk hard, once, and then they were moving, backing away from the trees. He whistled loudly, again, finger-in-mouth whistles that cut through the increasing pound of the engine.

Two bursts of Thompsons came suddenly from the edge of the mangroves. He swung around, saw their steady flashes like candle flames. He heard shouting, then saw dark shadows emerging from the coconut grove. They were firing as they came, and screaming the Japanese suicide yell.

Goddammit, here they come.

"Hit 'em!" he yelled, opening up with his Thompson himself, putting rounds across the open ground. A volley immediately erupted along the front and side of the boat, the sharply clipped cracks of Arisakas, the deeper raps of submachine guns, and the chatter from a single Japanese Type 100 machine pistol. Some of the charging shadows fell, tumbling, rising, falling again.

He caught sight of Bird and Laguna as they came plunging into the mangrove, crashing through branches and then down into the mud and spider roots. He darted to the front of the boat, it moving faster and faster now, out into the river, the current pulling at it.

"Come on, come on," he yelled to them.

The two men were having a tough time getting through the dense network of roots. The deck planks that had been laid out to form a walkway were now gone, down in the water. They clawed their way past them, grabbing branches, and finally got into waist-deep water.

"*Goddammit!*" Parnell hollered. He turned toward the stern, waving frantically. "Cut power. Cut your fucking power." Bullets pinged off the side of the boat, cut through the canopy.

The boat stalled for a moment as Farnsworth threw his drivelines into neutral. But the current continued pulling the stern farther out into the river, swinging it slightly with its bow, pointed toward the north. In the water, the two Blue Teamers were straining to reach the bow, which was rapidly moving away from them.

Red yelled out, "A line, somebody gimme a line." Panay ran forward with two coils of rope, Sol right behind him. Wordlessly, Parnell and Kaamanui quickly fashioned bowlines and tossed them out.

Shit, they can't see the ropes in the dark.

Parnell had a sharp memory flash of those crocs taking dead bodies. *Oh, Christ!* Pulling hand over hand, he quickly dragged the line back, slipped the bowline loop around his shoulder, and dove in.

The water was cool, oily-feeling as the current grabbed him. He swirled under the surface for a couple of seconds, then bobbed up again. There was Wyatt right beside him, sculling strongly, yet drifting away. From the corner of his eye, he saw Sol's big arms pulling through the water toward Weesay, the little Mexican shouting, "Ova' *here!* Ova *here!*"

"Grab hold of me," he shouted to Bird, and felt his arm come around his waist. Again came the image of shuddering bodies as the crocs hit them. He raised an arm, twirled it, shouting, "Haul in, haul in."

They skimmed through the water. Soon arms were reaching down over the side of the boat, grabbing their battle jackets, pulling them up over the gunwale. A moment later, Kaamanui and Laguna came climbing over it and sat on the deck, grinning and running water.

Farnsworth had already reengaged the drivelines. The *Betty T* straightened out and began to back farther out toward the center of the river. But it was facing the wrong way. A few scattered shots were still issuing from the bank.

The Brit let the side-wheeler continue in reverse for about seventy yards; then he threw the wheels into forward and began playing them, alternating power between the two so as to pull the bow around. The boat skidded sideways for a moment as it came broadside to the current, then straightened quickly and began picking up speed, running straight down the center of the river. Along both banks, the tops of the gallery trees were sprinkled with dawn light.

The Brit turned his helm over to Panay and came forward, squatted down beside Parnell. He looked at him. "Well, you certainly gave those bloody Nips hot, didn't you?" he said quietly. "For now, at least."

"How many prisoners were hit?"

"Two chaps dead, two wounded."

Red nodded. "How long will it be before we hit the coast?"

Farnsworth tightened his lips, made a sucking sound. "Running with this current we should make at least eighdeen knots, easy. That'll put us into Davilican Bay in about three hours . . . as long as we don't run into anything else."

"Yeah," Parnell said.

0503

General Kenichi Nagai had not had a decent night's sleep in weeks. He looked haggard, his thin, lethal eyes more stark than usual. He'd just finished his usual breakfast of fried tofu cakes and goat's milk. Tasted like shit, but it always settled his stomach after smoking six packs of cigarettes a day and drinking powerful *remon* tea to keep awake.

One of his staff clerks, a *socho,* or sergeant major, knocked at the sill of his office door and then came in quickly and snapped to attention. "Excuse me, Honorable General. Radio has just picked up another message relayed from Toro."

"*Nani?*"

"Its source is a naval ship, sir, a frigate-class on station off the east coast near Divilican Bay."

Nagai broke into a stream of invective, his face livid. He rose, ranged around the room, condemning all *Kaigun* dogs, *Kaigun* being the name for the Imperial Japanese Navy. The *socho* clerk stood with eyes riveted on the wall behind the officer's desk. At last, the general snatched the yellow radio decode sheet from his hand, returned to his chair, and sat down heavily.

He scanned the decoded message, twice. It read:

XXXX navopcb rik-sho 4
TT: 042215 OC 4//DD2605
D: IJN/FT 147
CO/ROME-chff-ID0000

Rec mes sr SNLF off des TORO . . . TT 041835 OC 4 . . .
pos: 29JN25c33/143 . . . Req
assis per ene raider/pow force (des Z site) . . . via vessel bound E coast
(Divilican) . . . ship eff alt cur to intercept.
CO Cpt. Kowara (LCK)

IJN/FT 147
Pos (see Purple) assign Z100mm/Qcode

He sat back, thoughtful, worried. He hadn't informed
Yamashita of the first message from Toro. But what had
happened to the Kempei-tai unit that had received his
initial call for assistance? More than that, the first message from the police unit had explained nothing of what
precisely had happened at Site Z. Where was its gold concentrate? Had the enemy raiders and escaping prisoners
taken it? Impossible. Still, now a damned *Kaigun* was
involved?

Imbeciles!

Nevertheless, he must not allow this situation to deteri-
orate any further. What to do? He looked up from under
his hairless brows. "Get me Major Tatsui."

"Yes, General-*san*."

Shosa Tatsui was a slender, strikingly handsome young officer. He had once been a *Kabuki* actor and moved with an
almost effeminate grace. He was Yamashita's intelligence
section's liaison officer to the Fourth Air Army, despite the
reality that only remnants of it still existed on Luzon.

He braced before the general's desk and waited. Nagai
growled, "I need at least two aircraft immediately. Prefer-
ably fighters."

"What is the mission, sir?"

"Just requisition them," Nagai snapped angrily.

Tatsui's dark, girlish eyes went soft. "General-*san*,
please allow me to point out that that will be most difficult. There are only thirty-two functioning aircraft still
on Luzon. And all are being refitted for *Kikusui* duty
and—" The term *Kikusui* was the code word for the
newly organized kamikaze program and literally meant
floating chrysanthemums.

The general's fist slammed down onto the top of
the desk. "You have an order, *Shosa*," he screamed, his

poisonous eyes going knifeblade thin. "You will carry it out *immediately*."

The handsome young major's face instantly went stiff, his soft eyes blank. "Yes, Honorable General."

"I want order verification and implementation notice from the airfield you choose within ten minutes. Do you understand me?"

"Yes, sir, most clearly, sir." Tatsui spun around and hurried out.

They buried the two dead prisoners, both shot in the head. One was Mallory. Not wanting to place them in the river because of the crocs, Farnsworth picked out a sandbar and eased the *Betty T* gently up onto it and they all trooped off and buried the corpses in a coconut grove, the dawn in solid now, the sun not risen yet, but the sky full of gray light.

The ground was easy to dig into, sandy, covered with coconut cotton and dead palm branches. They laid the two men side by side, the edges of the hole already sliding in before they could get them settled properly. As Farnsworth was captain of their vessel, it was his duty to say a few words over the grave. He gave a short prayer, paused, then added a portion of a poem from memory, his British accent and quiet voice giving it a fine-toned solemnity amid the sounds of awakening jungle:

> *Standing amazed, staring from left to right,*
> *They seek first their ancestral altars,*
> *Then the hearth long cold with rains.*
> *Where once old terrors lodged,*
> *Where now only the dead sleep in silence.*

Fourteen minutes later, again on the river and steaming at flank speed, they were attacked by a Japanese A6M Zero fighter, the aircraft coming in low from the north, following the river, the sound of its approach hidden in the steady *shushing-bang* of the engine.

The first warning came from Smoker, posted on the stern of the steamboat, hollering, "Jap fighter coming in!" Then his voice disappeared in the sundering explosion of 20mm cannon rounds and the higher pitched *zips* of 7.7mm machine-gun fire that crashed over the top of the vessel to impact in the river two hundred yards ahead.

Smoker had already opened on the plane. Then it was there, rocketing overhead, the rest of the Blue Teamers cutting loose as its prop wash hurled spiraling gusts of wind down onto the boat and made the surface of the river ripple. The aircraft was all black save for a wide white strip around its after fuselage, red balls on the wings and a rising sun symbol on the vertical stabilizer.

Parnell yelled at Farnsworth, "Get to cover!"

The Brit was already doing just that, shoving levers to reverse the side-wheels and slow the boat's speed as he swung its bow toward a thick stretch of overhanging jungle. In the sky, the Zero had gone into a sharp vertical climb. For a tiny second, it seemed to strain. Then the engine roared up full again and it rolled to the side and began a quick, arcing turn.

Parnell watched as the aircraft abruptly disappeared below the treetops, coming around, the sound of its engine vanishing. He thought: *Inexperienced pilot, damn near stalled it. Too preoccupied with firing to power up for the climb.*

He shouted to Sol and Weesay nearby, "Use the Jap grenades. Go for the prop hub." He snapped another clip from his belt pouch and reloaded the Thompson, squinting down the river, scanning, trying to estimate where the Zero might reappear. His heart raced, his mind visualizing the thing coming in again, cannon flashes and heavy-duty rounds coming straight at them.

A moment later, the steamboat plowed into a wall of jungle. Branches whipped across his face and body and a dense cloud of white stack smoke flooded through the trees, across the deck. He ducked and scooted toward the stern.

He didn't hear the Zero at all until more cannon and MG rounds came slashing in to explode in the river, heaving up cascades of water forty yards out. He felt the shock of the blasts jolting the air.

The pilot had again overshot his target. The plane streaked past amid the thundering rush of its engine as someone fired off a grenade. The missile slammed across the river and blew up among mangroves on the other bank, throwing shrapnel and torn branches back out into the water.

They waited for the Zero to make its third pass from up-river, all of Blue Team kneeling or crouched in the stern of the *Betty T*, Thompsons and three Arisakas with grenade launchers ready.

He came. Once more the pilot was high in his aim, rounds slashing through jungle off to the right of the boat, tearing up trees with sundering explosions. Their own firing drowned out by the deafening noise of impacting ordnance, Parnell and his men opened in a solid volley. Hits registered on the plane's cowling and forward edges of the port wing. Two grenades arced out and past it, exploded in the air in bursts of white smoke.

Then there was a bright flash in the Zero's cowling and dark smoke erupted from it, trailing back in whorls on both sides of the fuselage. The aircraft hurtled by. They could see the pilot, a white band around his head, black-edged goggles. The trailing smoke, tumbling, rolled down and out into the trees, stinking of scorched metal and burning oil.

The pilot tried to climb. But suddenly the aircraft rolled sharply to the right and began falling off. Its starboard wingtip slashed through treetops and then struck the water, for a second cleaving a large V in the surface. The drag of the wing threw the plane into a wild tumbling, over and over, the prop flinging out curtains of spray each time it came around, and parts flying off, some floating lazily away, and then the water erupted into a wall of white foam as the aircraft smashed fully into the river.

A second later, it exploded into a perfectly round ball of orange and white light that expanded into a boiling mushroom cloud of steam and smoke that shot up into the air, shedding burning pieces of debris that flew out and down, forming fiery rainbows.

0619 hours

The *Barracuda*'s sonar man called out, "Conn, I have cavitation. Bearing zero-one-one degrees, True, range eight thousand yards. Speed steady at one-zero knots. Profile consistent with TD S-3."

Commander Herbold immediately rigged for silence. The submarine was still in hover, drifting slowly with the outgoing tide. Earlier, they had tracked Target Designate S-3 until it moved beyond their sonar range, continuing north.

He glanced over at his XO. "So the little shit's back. But backtrailng his own patrol area and moving slowly? Something's up." He quickly stepped to a small chart table adjacent to the sonar panel, studied it a moment, then called for track update of the S-3.

"Conn, bearing zero-zero-four degrees, range seven-four-zero-zero yards, sir," Sonar answered. "Target appears to be closing the shore."

"Damn it," Herbold snapped. He returned to the conn deck, saying to Gerrard, "This son of a bitch's gonna set up off the mouth of the Cagayan. I'd bet my ass on it." He sucked air through his teeth. "Looks like Op Purgatory's cover just got blown."

"Do we take him out, sir?" the XO asked.

Herbold considered a moment, shook his head. "Not yet."

The next few minutes went sluggishly by, everybody listening for the distant churn of the approaching Japanese frigate's props, the only interruption of the silence now the sonar operator's quietly spoken TD S-3's position reports. The Japanese vessel was now four thousand yards away and still closing the shoreline of Divilican Bay.

Suddenly a distant, muted *thump* came clearly through the hull of the submarine. Everybody's head came up. *What?*

A few seconds later, Sonar came on the overhead: "Conn, double burst on the surface. Resonance indicates ship ordnance firing off. Possible gun turret ignition."

"What's impact point?"

"Bearing two-seven-three degrees, True, sir."

Herbold leaned away from the periscope shaft, frowning deeply. *Due west. The prick's firing the shore.* He thought a moment. *Is he going after the Purgatory team?* But if they were this close, why hadn't they made contact?

He reached up, grabbed an overhead mike, keyed: "Radio, this is the captain. Have you received *any* signal from team Purgatory?"

"Negative, sir."

There was a second, faint *thump*. Herbold cursed, then began shouting orders, each echoed and reechoed: "Sound General Quarters . . . Recover radio buoy . . . Engine, all ahead one third, Rudder Amidships . . . stand by for emergency surface . . . Lookouts, stand by . . . Gun crews, stand ready for immediate engage."

The submarine came alive, the klaxon for battle stations resounding metallically throughout the vessel, the whine of motors coming up into speed, the roar of blowers. Several moments later, Herbold gave the order to surface, followed immediately by the heavy rumbling rush of venting air. The deck trembled slightly, tilting, as the USS *Barracuda* headed for the surface.

* * *

The two Japanese 47mm rounds, coming in at twenty-seven hundred feet per second and carrying armor-piercing warheads, crashed into the jungle far astern of the *Betty T.* Their impacts were loud enough to punch right through the racket from the boat's engine and paddle wheels. The missiles threw up twin eruptions of sundered trees and mud.

Farnsworth immediately disengaged the drivelines, the big paddles slowly revolving to a stop. But the boat itself was still moving on the current and gently beginning to swing to starboard. The Brit waved Parnell to the wheel.

"That was Nip naval ordnance," he called out as the big American officer hurried aft. Prisoners' faces turned to look, sudden despair dragging down their gaunt features. "There's a bloody enemy ship out there homing to our smoke."

Parnell looked eastward a moment, then swung back. "Where's your radio?"

"Stowed below."

Red retrieved the SCR-MC300, hauling it up out of the stifling heat of belowdecks, Weesay carrying the crank generator. As he set up the antenna on one of the stanchions, his mind focused, trying to recall the precise code phrases and correct frequencies he'd use to raise their rendezvous submarine.

If she was out there.

He waited a moment till Laguna had cranked up enough power, then flicked on the set and spun the dial to the first designated shortwave frequency of 27.34 megacycles. He keyed, "Chariot, Purgatory One, copy?" The air was filled with tight static, sharp-pointed sounds like needle tips. Again: "Chariot, Purgatory One. Copy? Over." Still nothing.

Another twin brace of Jap rounds came in, whistling just before they exploded in the water downriver about sixty yards away. Parnell watched the geysers, thinking, *They're bracketing us.* He keyed and tried one more time, waited.

Come on, for Chris' sake, come back. Then it occurred to him that the sub might not want to break radio silence with the Jap ship in the area. *Shit!*

Suddenly, he heard the distant staccatto of .50-caliber machine guns firing off, at least three of them distinguishable. *American weapons!* Then came the hard, sharp crack of what sounded like a three-inch field gun. These were answered by a more distant rattle of weaponry, Jap ordnance this time.

Abruptly, the radio crackled a burst of static and then: "Purgatory One, Chariot. Movie pass. Repeat, movie pass, over." *Movie pass* was code for Purgatory's Clearance Set, a series of numbers and letters used to authenticate their identity.

Parnell keyed: "Chariot, movie pass is one-five-zero-Baker-Baker-Zulu, over."

Three counts later, Chariot came back, "Purgatory One, take your seat. Loge or general admission?" The sub's operator was now asking him for his current position.

"Chariot, stand by," Red answered. He hurriedly took out his tactical map and located his estimated positon on the river, a half mile from the coast. He keyed: "Chariot, loge is Dog Sector three-eight-niner cross zero-four-four, over."

"Purgatory, stand by."

Out there in the ocean, the firing was still going hot and heavy, MGs banging away and the bigger pieces exchanging rounds, the American gun crew working very rapidly.

Farnsworth came over: "Our bloody submarine, aye?"

"Yeah."

"While she keeps the Nips occupied, let's make a bleeding run for the bay."

"Hold it a minute."

The radio blared again: "Purgatory, roll film. MRSQ." MRSQ stood for "maintain radio silence."

"Roger that. Purgatory One out." Red keyed off, turned, and grinned at Farnsworth. "Let's go."

Through his high-powered binoculars, the smoke from the steamboat looked to Herbold like a train out there in the trees, coming on with a full head of steam. Standing at his bridge conning station atop the sub's sail, he watched the smoke for a long moment, then swung his glasses far to the right, slowly, studying things, checking for anything moving. Then to the left, all the way to the gradual rise of foothills southward. No sign of movement.

He swung all the way around and glassed the fleeing Nip frigate, out about three miles already and hauling ass, no longer zigzagging. The gun crew of the *Barracuda* had easily bested the Jap sailors, blowing one hole into the vessel's amidships and another two forward that had silenced her main gun turret. He'd given chase for about a half mile, then turned back, his mission task far more important with the Purgatory One unit now approaching the bay with all-out speed.

Down on the forward deck, the gunners were securing, replacing unused shells back into the powder gurney, which was still thrust up through the foredeck hatch. Periodically, his two spotters called out environment status reports as well as that of the rapidly receding Japanese frigate.

He returned to the steamboat's smoke trail. "Keep her coming, gentlemen," he murmured to himself. "Haul that barge, lift that fucking bale."

The *Barracuda* was now hove to only a mile from shore, well within range of land guns. He didn't like sitting on the surface like a goddamned wounded duck. That Jap frigate could easily have called in an air strike or even artillery.

He spotted the *Betty T* at the same moment his port spotter called out, "Bridge, visual on small craft emerging from the bay." And there it was, this boxy vessel suddenly breaking out of the jungle and pushing into the small wavelets that spread across the mouth of the Cagayan River.

Herbold leaned forward and punched the surface panel intercom button. "Conn, Bridge, ease her in, Ron. Purgatory One's visual."

"Aye-aye, Captain. Commencing approach." The sail deck trembled faintly as the submarine began to move forward slowly.

Herbold lifted his glasses again. The steamboat had crested past the small shore break off the river's mouth and was easing into a slight starboard turn to follow the channel out into deeper water.

"Sir," the starboard spotter suddenly shouted excitedly, "the enemy frigate's executing a 180."

Herbold quickly swung around and fixed his glasses on the horizon, scanned, lowering, picked up the small picket boat completing its turn, coming out of its heel, straightening, then picking up speed, water hurling off its bow.

Her leaned over the conn panel and shouted down, "Gun crew, stand ready for action," then punched the intercom. "Conn, Bridge, the Nip's coming back, head-on. Set up for bow-on intercept."

"Aye-aye Skipper." The *Barracuda* heeled slightly and began coming around to starboard.

Everybody aboard the *Betty T* started shouting, pointing: "The bloody Nips comin' back!" "Oh, shit!" "Watch out, here comes the Jap again!"

Several seconds later, they saw flashes from the frigate's forward gun turret and watched the rounds coming their way, balls of bright light in a shallow arc. They exploded seventy yards to starboard, the steamboat now deep in a main channel between the reef and going swiftly on the outgoing tidal current, the water green-turning-to-blue. The concussion surged through the water, made the boat rock slightly.

Now the sub opened with her deck gun, banging rounds out, heat shimmering into the air as the breech was slammed open, the empty casings rolling out across the deck. As the Jap vessel drew closer, the sub's machine guns opened up, their rounds going in arcs, tracers floating like Roman candles.

Parnell glanced back at Farnsworth, the Brit's face grim, bouncing slightly, an unconscious translation of his body's energy down to his engine, which he had wound up to red-line, white smoke pouring from the stack.

Another brace of shells came in. Red had just turned forward again, everybody lying flat on the deck, when he saw them. *Oh, sweet Christ!* These were coming right down their throat. He shouted a warning, heard both shells strike the water in a *whomping* collision followed immediately by a violent explosion, both going off at once.

He felt the deck heave upward. The horizon, partially blotted out by the explosion geysers, disappeared completely and he was looking at only sky, pastel and deep as eternity. Men tumbled against him, yelling, thrashing. He gripped his Thompson, instinct, the final salvation.

Then the boat turned completely over, the forward portion of it coming apart, decking, plating, stanchions sundering apart with wild metallic screeches. He went down into beautiful green water, sunbeams dancing like filmy curtains all around him. Dark objects dropped through the surface, their contours hazy: men, planking, chunks of metal.

Suddenly, as if a switch had been thrown, most of the light disappeared save for the brilliant glow off the sandy bottom forty feet below him. He looked up. A massive shadow hung above him, the deck side of the steamboat. There was the wild hiss of escaping steam.

The boiler!

Kicking fiercely, he moved out from under the boat. A man appeared nearby, floundering. He grabbed his clothing and swam on. Another. He took hold of him, too. He started up and soon broke through the surface, into brilliant sunlight again.

The haggard, withered faces of the two prisoners he'd brought up looked sickly white in the light, both gasping and gagging. "Strip off your clothes," he yelled at them. "So it won't weigh you down." He peered closely at them. "Can you swim?"

"Yes," one man croaked. "We'll be okay."

"Get as far from the boat as you can. That boiler could go when the water hits it." Both men stared dumbly for a moment, then quickly began dog-paddling away.

Parnell swam back toward the boat, went past the edge of its stern. The copper bottom was a deep green, laced with streamers of seaweed and a few barnacles like black pustules, the paddle wheels looking odd upside down but still revolving sluggishly.

Heads and shoulders were popping up all around him. He took a deep breath to oxygenate his blood, let it out, took another, and dove down to search for others. The shadowy shape of a man was silhouetted against the bright sandy bottom twenty feet below him. He went down to it. It was a prisoner, already drowned.

The water around him began to get foggy with smoky steam bubbles. It felt heated, slick, and filled with the creaking of cross braces and the sucking rush of water as the steamboat settled deeper.

He returned to the surface. He could still hear the sub firing, the thunder of the muzzle bursts closer now. Tracers cutting white-hot lines through the air. There was a distant explosion, first a loud crack, then a more muffled blow like a drilling charge going off underground. A moment later, a cloud of dense black smoke boiled up into the sunlight to seaward.

They nailed the Jap ship.

Prisoners floated all around him, yelling to each other and clinging to bits of debris, planks, and strips of decking, a single large wooden box covered with oil. The steamboat was deeper in the water now and great bubbles of steam erupted through its shattered forward deck and along the gunwale's seams, hissing and casting spray into the air.

He quickly spotted his men, first Bird, then Laguna and Cowboy. Beyond them Sol was moving off, lying on his back and kicking his legs, his arms around the shoulders of two prisoners, pulling them along in his wake. Wineberg abruptly broke the surface, surging through and sucking in air. He had another prisoner by the collar.

Where the hell's Farnsworth?

He began waving his arms and yelling, "Get the hell away from the boat. Her boiler could blow." Everybody began stroking off. He finally caught sight of the Brit, still wearing his hat.

The high-pitched whine of a small motor and the flat, popping sound of a rubber bottom came. *A raft.* Everybody started waving and shouting. Soon, a wide, black rubber raft with a small outboard on the stern came skimming in, lunging and bouncing. The sound of another motor came and a second raft appeared, swinging to a stop.

Quickly the sailors on both boats began hauling in men.

Parnell turned and looked back at the steamboat. The outgoing tide had carried it about a hundred yards from him. Now only the flat bottom and paddle wheels were visible. Then in a final heave it went under completely. A few seconds later, there was an explosion from under the water. He felt the shock of it riffle past him as a dome of water lifted above the surface, churning for a moment before receding.

He turned and swam toward one of the rafts. Beyond it, a thousand yards out, was the sleek gray bow and sail of the USS *Barracuda* coming to meet them.

TETSU NO BOFU
(TYPHOON OF STEEL)

Chapter Fifteen

By March 1945, the momentum of the war in Europe was decisively on the side of the Allies. Although the month would see fierce German counteroffensives both on the eastern and western fronts, the outcome was no longer in any doubt. Germany and Hitlerism were doomed.

Major enemy cities were now falling like dominoes to Allied thrusts: Trier, Roermond, and Dusseldorf on the Rhine by 2 March; Cologne, Remagan, Bonn, and Erpel on the ninth; on 20 March, Mainz, Saarbrücken, and Kaiserslautern surrendered, as well as Gdynia and Danzig in the east.

On the same day in the Burma campaign, Mandalay fell to the 19th Indian Division after a horrific, pitched battle with starving but fanatical Japanese jungle units. The final drive southward toward Rangoon also began, and in the northern border country, the Chinese First Army captured the key mountain town of Lashio.

In the Pacific Theater, the battle for the Philippines still raged, although Manila had finally been declared secure on 7 March. But continued stiff Japanese resistance was being encountered in northern Luzon, as well as on the islands of Mindanao and Negros. As for the smaller, isolated pockets of ragged Japanese troops in the other sectors of the islands, these were being left to Filipino guerilla groups to finish off.

On Iwo Jima, U.S. Marines were still locked in fierce combat with the deeply dug in soldiers of the Japanese 109th Infantry Division, commanded by Lieutenant General Tadamichi Kuribayashi. The island would not be totally secured until 26 March after a final enemy suicide attack would be annihilated. By then, only two hundred Japanese soldiers out of the original twenty thousand would still be alive.

The final step in the Allies' push toward the Japanese homeland was already under way, the conquest of the Ryūkyū Islands Group, a chain of 161 islands stretching across the South China Sea from the tip of Kyūshū in the Japanese Archipelago to Formosa.

Control of these islands was absolutely essential for staging areas and air and fleet jump-off points in the coming invasion of Japan, which was already scheduled for early November 1945. The centerpiece and capital of the Ryūkyūs was the island of Okinawa-Shima.

The overall attack on the Ryūkyūs was code-named Operation Bunkhouse, while the specific invasion of Okinawa was referred to as Operation Iceberg. The landings were to commence at 0830 hours on 1 April 1945, coded H-hour of L-day. However, smaller landings by units of the U.S. 77th Division and the 420th Field Artillery Group would be made on several of Okinawa's outlying islands a week earlier so as to establish fleet refueling, rearming, and repair bases for the main invasion.

Chosen to carry out the Iceberg mission task was the newly created Joint Expeditionary Force or Task Force 51, under Admiral Raymond Spruance. This would be the largest and most powerful invasion force ever mounted in the Pacific Theater. It was also the first truly joint operation, combining units from the American Army, Navy, Marine Corps, and Air Force, as well as those of British

Carrier Force, TF 57. All would be under Spruance's single command.

Appointed as his two senior commanders were Admiral Richard Turner, in charge of all amphibious operations of the Third and Fifth Fleets, and Lieutenant General Simon Bolivar Buckner Jr., commanding Tenth Army, which included the army's XXIV Corps and the marines' III Amphibious Corps.

Air operations against Okinawa had begun as early as 29 September 1944 when it was bombed by B-29s out of Saipan. It was again hit on 10 October by carrier aircraft sent to neutralize its airfields for the coming invasion of Leyte. Then in January and early March of 1945, the island was repeatedly struck by air strikes from the Fast Carrier Force, now designated TF 58.

American submarine operations had also been intense throughout the Ryukyus. Nearly 95 percent of all supply shipments from Japan had been intercepted and sunk. Throughout early March, there were more B-29 raids, which decimated the island, including its capital of Naha City and the adjoining harbor and port. Also turned to rubble was the famous Shouri Castle with its ancient treasures of Okinawan and Japanese history.

On 11 March, Joint Expeditionary Force fleet and ground assault units began their preinvasion staging at numerous sites throughout the Western and Central Pacific, including Espiritu Santo, Guadalcanal, the Russells, Saipan, Guam, Eniwetok, New Caldonia, and Leyte. Eventually, over 1,300 ships and 163,000 ground troops would be involved in Iceberg.

On the opposing side, the commanders of the Japanese forces were two of the Imperial Army's best: the cool and methodical Lieutenant General Mitsuru Ushijima, who was CinC of the 32nd Area Army, and his chief of staff, the heavy-drinking, hotheaded Major General Isamu Cho. While he was serving in China in the fall of 1937, it was this officer who had been responsible for the slaughter of 300,000 Chinese during the Rape of Nanking.

The total military contingent on Okinawa included 116,000 IJA soldiers, plus 5,000 Okinawan conscripts including 1,500 youths of the Iron and Blood Society, and 12,000 Korean laborers who would be pressed into combat when needed. Only a month earlier, Ushijima had lost his crack ninth Division. Imperial General Headquarters, fearful the Allies would strike at Taiwan, had ordered it there.

He was furious, yet it all really didn't matter. Ushijima had no illusions about the purpose and cost of defending Okinawa. For those who would fight there, their mission was simple: kill as many Americans as possible, and stall the enemy long enough to allow the homeland forces to prepare for the inevitable and final invasion of Japan. No one was expected to survive on the island.

Like all the banzai and kamikaze suicide attacks launched throughout the latter part of the war, this commitment to death by Ushijima and his 32nd Area Army was pure Bushido, the moral code that demanded that a Japanese warrior happily and deliberately sacrifice his life for emperor and country.

The rocky, mountainous terrain of the island was ideal for just such suicidal and in-depth defense. Thousands of pillboxes, bunkers, weapon emplacements, and fighting positions had already been dug, many utilizing terrain features with excellent overlapping fields of fire. Supplies and munitions were protected in deep dugouts and caves connected by over sixty miles of tunnel systems.

Also assisting the Japanese commander in destroying Allied naval units were nearly two thousand kamikaze aircraft, including newly designed Baka suicide bombers from the 341st and 721st Air Groups, which were slated to strike the invaders from bases in southern Kyushu and from small, isolated fields on Okinawa and its outlying islands.

In addition to aircraft, suicide boats were also to be

hurled at the enemy. These were Q or *Renraku* boats, eighteen-foot plywood speedboats ironically powered by eighty-five-horsepower Chevrolet engines. Each would carry a six-hundred-pound explosive charge in its bow, as well as two 264-pound depth charges mounted on either side, all of it powerful enough to sink even an enemy cruiser when the Q boat was driven into its side.

Scattered throughout Okinawa's outlying islands were several Sea Raider units, code-named *Akatsuki* or Dawn Fighters. Company-sized, these outfits each possessed forty to fifty Q boats hidden in caves or highly camouflaged shelters with maintenance personnel and boat pilots, all volunteers, sixteen-year-olds in their first year of officer training.

20 March 1945 (L-13)
Saipan, Mariana Islands

Weesay Laguna was stretched out prone on warm sand, his rifle snugged in against his padded shoulder in perfect sniper shooting form, his firing hand gripping only the stock and trigger of the weapon so he wouldn't disturb its balance, his body relaxed and comfortable with weight evenly distributed to support both muscle and bone. The rifle's muzzle rested on a small sandbag for steadiness.

The weapon was a .30-caliber M1903-S Springfield, this model utilizing a slightly heavier barrel to protect it against heat warpage. Mounted above the receiver was a Weaver 12X SS100 telescopic sight with light-absorbing optics for use in near-dark conditions.

With it a sniper marksman could put a full five-round clip into an eight-inch grouping at six hundred yards. The bullets used had 185-grain lead-antimony slugs with gliding metal jackets to tear the insides of a human body to shreds.

Fountain lay beside him, glassing his target with a range

scope, the target four wooden paddles set on five-foot poles placed in a line 550 yards away. In between were gently undulating sand dunes topped by patches of sea grass and, farther in, stands of *keawe* trees, which resembled scrub oak. The dunes were totally scarred by amphibious vehicle tracks and most of the trees had been torn apart by explosives.

It was early dusk, the sun already gone beyond the ocean horizon. Yet the sky was still filled with red and orange and indigo light, which made the sea look ink-black. The four paddles had been painted white. Now they shone out there like big cue balls suspended in air.

He fired. The loud crack of the weapon spooked the beach plovers and sand runners that had been hunting along the surf line. The birds flurried and squeaked for a few moments, then resettled as Laguna jacked out the empty casing and rammed in another round. He fired again, and still again until his five-round clip was empty.

Glancing at Fountain, he asked, "So?"

Cowboy shook his head. "Only two hits, Chico. Both high and to the right."

Weesay hissed. "Fuckin' light's for shit, *meng.*"

"That's the name of the game, baby." Cowboy eased away from the scope and rose to his knees, swinging his own Springfield off his shoulder. "Now move over an' let a real shootist show you how it's done."

"Bullshit," Laguna scoffed.

For the last eight days, they and the rest of Blue Team, including Lieutenant Parnell, had been undergoing sniper training with a special assault team from the 1st Marine Division of the III Marine Amphibious Corps, part of Iceberg's Northern Landing Force. It had been refitting for a month on Saipan and was now into final staging for Okinawa.

Their instructor was a leathery, broad-shouldered corporal, a veteran of Tarawa and Peleliu. His name was Barney Oldfield, so his buddies naturally called him "Racer." He possessed a Georgia twang, a vocabulary consisting of a mixture of marine slang and profanity, and a healthy disdain for all GIs.

Yet he knew his business and had taught them well, all the finer points of sniper combat. Like how and where to set up a firing position, and the proper formulas to precisely sight in a rifle for the ambient temperature, pressure, humidity, and wind conditions. He also taught them advanced methods of Pacific island camouflage and concealment, the tips that helped a shooter lessen wobble and muzzle circle, and how to *mentally* aim and shoot. He even had each man constantly carry his piece, even at mess and during sleep, so as to develop a complete relationship with the gun.

It had frankly been humiliating for the Mohawkers to work with marines, the fucking jarheads always making barking noises at them, and Oldfield calling them "doggies" and "lads." Not the lieutenant or noncoms, of course. But, Jesus, what the hell was this shit? *Them* teaching *us* about combat? How to shoot a gun?

Fountain began quick-firing, pulling off all five rounds: *bam . . . bam . . . bam . . . bam . . . bam.* Then he turned and winked at Laguna in the fading light. "Six-inch group, right?"

Weesay didn't answer, still peering through the scope.

"Well?"

"Yeah, right, right, six fuckin' inches," Weesay finally blurted, turned, and spat disgustedly.

Corporal Oldfield came jogging over from his watch position on another dune. His light green combat dungarees, even this late in the day, were still pressed and sharply creased. "Pretty goddamned good, doggie," he said to Cowboy. "Y'all mus' be from Georgia."

"New Mexico."

"New *Mexico?* Well, fuck a duck." He turned to Weesay. "Now *y'all* shoot like a fuckin' pussy, Lag-*oona.* You jes' ain't squarin' away your breathin', man."

Weesay swung around. "Chu call me pussy?"

"Yeah, I called y'all pussy," the marine said. "Y'all fire that weapon like you got a cunt between your legs."

Weesay twisted and lunged to his feet, his boot stiletto already clearing its sheath by the time he was fully up. "I gonna kill you, *cabron!*" he hissed.

Oldfield snapped around to face him, squaring off, his arms spread. "Then come awn ahead, doggie."

Cowboy leaped up and grabbed Laguna's collar, yanking him back. "Easy now, easy," he said soothingly and flung his arms around Weesay's shoulders. "Come on, Chico, let it go." After a moment, Laguna relaxed but continued glaring at the corporal.

Oldfield also relaxed, then gave them both a grin. "Damn, you boys is on the edge, ain't y'all?" he said.

Now no longer under blackout watch, the staging of the 1st Marine Division created a city of light and sound in the night, acres of men and equipment spreading away from the edge of Saipan's Tanapag Harbor.

Everywhere was movement, activity, endless lines of tanks, amphibious combat vehicles, and cargo trucks hauling weapons, ammunition, explosives, food, and medical supplies for the division's Transport Groups Baker and Charlie, their waiting AKAs, LCTs, LCIs, LCVPs, and LVTs lined along the harbor wharf and adjoining beach.

Out in the roadstead were more ships of Task Groups 53.3 and 53.6 of Rear Admiral L.F. Reifsnider's Northern Attack Force TF 53: escort and screening destroyers, oilers, maintenance vessels, minesweepers, support and pontoon ships. And far beyond the ships, silhouetting their up-structures, were the lights of U.S. bomber airfields located on the smaller island of Tinian across the Saipan Channel.

In three days, with full troop units aboard, they would head to sea to rendezvous with other elements of the NAF deep in the Philippine Sea, then steam due north to Okinawa.

Parnell waited a moment, then slipped his gray navy jeep through a column of trucks and pulled up in front of a Quonset hut bearing a red-and-gold sign that read:

INTELLIGENCE SECTION
FIRST MARINE DIVISION
WESTPACCOMM
TANAPAG, SAIPAN

Inside, it was a beehive of activity, several marine clerks and radio operators working intently, all snappy in tropical tans with the distinctive three creases down the backs of their shirts. He waited beside the door a moment, then stepped over to a sergeant major seated in front of a paneled door.

"Sergeant?" he said.

The man's head came up. He was deeply tanned and had a thick scar across his forehead. "Yes, sir?"

"Lieutenant John Parnell to see Colonel Stapp as ordered."

"Aye-aye, sir." The sergeant rose, moved to the paneled door, knocked softly, and stepped in. He was back in a few seconds. "You may go in, sir."

Marine Colonel Claude Stapp stood nearly six feet five. His brown hair was closely cropped and he had the lean, rawboned build and face of a dirk blade. His office was painted white, sparsely furnished with huge battle maps on the walls. The space had the brass spit-and-polish feel of a cruiser's gun room.

Parnell braced. "Army Lieutenant John Parnell reporting as ordered, sir."

"Stand easy, Lieutenant." Stapp withdrew a gray envelope from a drawer and placed it on top of the desk. "Your SMT just came through. No need looking at it now, I'll fill in the high points." He rose and moved to one of the wall maps. It was a naval topographical map of the Ryūkyūs chain, with a smaller one of Okinawa Shima and its surrounding islands.

Using a pencil for a pointer, he indicated a group of small islands lying about fifteen miles southwest of Okinawa. "This is Kerama Retto," he explained. "Eight islands in the group, all with rocky terrain." Shifting the pencil eraser to one of the islets, he said, "This is Kuba, the second smallest of the group. Mile and a half wide, two long. You'll have battle maps and aerial photos of it with your SMT. That's where you and your men are headed."

He returned to his chair, went on, "There are several secret *Akatsuki* in the Kerama Retto. Those are small Jap raider units that use speedboats to make night suicide runs on our shipping. They're called Q boats. Not really high speed, just flimsy plywood eighteen-footers that can barely make twenty-two knots. But the damned things are loaded with explosives and maneuverable as hell.

"Unfortunately, they're hidden during daylight in caves and camouflaged pens. And the Japs constantly move them around. Since we're never sure of where they are at any one time, we haven't been able to hit their bases with air strikes. But during the *main* invasion, we'll have PT squadrons to intercept any sorties from Okinawa.

"Unfortunately, Kerama Retto's a different situation. On L minus six, we're invading the Kerama. Five battalions of the army's 77th Division and one of our BTLs will land on four of the islands in order to set up fleet bases for the main invasion. Intelligence reports estimate there could be as many as two hundred Q boats operating in these waters alone.

"But the PTs won't be here for these landings, so we've gotta put men on the ground to stop them from hitting Admiral Kiland's Task Group 51.1. Ordinarily, Underwater Demo Teams would handle this kind of op. All but Teams 12 and 13 are already committed to the Hagushi

Beach landing zones on Okinawa. These two will handle the bigger islands. You and your men'll take care of Kuba.

"Incidentally, ID codes are in your packet, along with your radio's presets. To bring you up to speed for now, they'll be Flyswatter 4 for the overall op, Roundup for your barrage assignment ship, and Honeycomb for the Kuba's ABCO. Yours is Blue Fly." The term ABCO stood for Assault Beach Control Officer.

Parnell shifted slightly, frowning. "I don't understand something, sir. For the last week, we've been undergoing sniper training. If we're demo, why the training?"

The colonel shook his head. "You won't be going in as demo. The concentration of Q boat bases on Kuba's along the rim of a nearly landlocked bay called Koniro-wan. It's on the south end of the island and connected to open sea by a narrow, quarter-mile-long inlet. When our assault ships hit Kerama Retto waters, those boats'll come out of there like bees out of a hive. It's your job to bottle up the sons of bitches with sniper fire."

Oh, yeah, Parnell thought. Shooting at speedboats running down a water course with his men laying in hot fire that'll expose their positions like goddamned flares. He said, "I assume we'll be firing incendiary rounds, sir?"

"Of course. So be ready to lay in ordnance and then quick-move to other firing positions."

No shit.

Colonel Stapp went on, "Zero in on their bow sections. That's where their primary six-hundred-pound explosive charges are. They also carry twin depth charges mounted on either side of the midships. Weather says it'll be a near quarter moon, not all that much light. But the boats run without mufflers, so you'll be able to clearly see fire from their exhaust ports.

"You'll be able to call in naval fire missions after 0500. But understand, you'll be low priority on the mission roster. Don't depend on getting an assignment. Also, you'll be using map coordinates instead of precise target blocks. If you get fire at all, it'll be time-on-target, so be well clear."

"How do we get there, sir? And what's our insertion point?"

"You'll be transported by sub, the *Stingray*, *SS* 134. She gets under way at 2345 tonight. She's berthed outboard in a three-pod at Dock 1-F West. Your insertion point's marked on your TMS maps, at the mouth of the Konirowan inlet. Nearby is an old Nip freighter that went aground yeas ago. Use it as your initial ICP."

There was a soft knock on the door. The colonel called, "In," and his sergeant major entered.

"Excuse me, sir," he said. "Fleet Op's requesting our TM-30 again, sir."

Stapp grunted, thought a moment, then said, "Get Major Hollands to clear it first."

"Aye-aye, sir." The noncom left.

Stapp returned to Parnell, went right on, "Your TMS also has your necessary ciphers and frequency presets. Take note of one thing, that particular stretch of coast always has strong currents in and around the inlet. Remember that going in." He studied Parnell a moment. "Questions?"

"Where do we draw gear, sir?"

"I'll send one of my men with you. Draw anything you figure you'll need."

"Yes, sir."

For a moment, a tiny frown crept between Stapp's eyes. He seemed to be debating something inside his head. Finally, he retrieved a yellow intelligence memo sheet and handed it to Parnell. "I hate to give you this right now, Lieutenant. But, frankly, the damned thing's been trailing you for over a week."

Parnell scanned it. *What!* He read it again, very slowly. Its point-of-origin was U.S. Third Army headquarters in Nierstein, Germany. From the number of relaying units, it had indeed chased him all over hell. The main message read:

> *Be informed that Colonel James R. Dunmore was killed on 4 March 1945 outside Oppenheim, Germany. While conducting intelligence operations near the Rhine River, he and his unit were taken under intense enemy fire. Although struck by shrapnel, Colonel Dunmore was able to personally carry two of his badly wounded men to safety before he himself was fatally hit by enemy mortars.*

There was a short addenda:

> *Sticks was a close personal friend. I will miss him. I have recommended he receive both the Distinguished Service Medal and the Silver Cross for his outstanding service to his country and for his splendid actions in the face of deadly fire. But more important than friendships or medals is the truth that he was a damned fine and brave soldier.*

It was signed by General Patton himself.

Parnell lowered the message to find the colonel watching. He quickly braced. "Is there anything further, sir?"

"No, Lieutenant. Good luck."

Outside, he sat in his jeep for several minutes. A dozen duece-and-a-halfs pulling 75mm caissons thundered past, throwing up a thin cloud of coral dust. He looked out over the massive staging depot. All the machines of war coming together. *Another goddamned day, another goddamned hill.*

He thought about Colonel Dunmore. *A close personal friend.* He should feel more pain, he thought, the sorrow of a lost comrade. Then why didn't he? He had had a deep affection for the colonel, more, a respect. A good man, a *damned* good man.

Jesus. The reality of the situation struck him. How far had he gone, how much of himself had he lost that he couldn't even mourn with proper intensity? A sudden recollection came to him, something an old Frenchman had once told him in Normandy, the man having fought in the First World War, having seen the trenches, saying to him that it was, in the end, all futile and meaningless.

Yeah.

He lit a cigarette, kicked over the jeep's engine, and pulled away. He'd already decided not to tell the rest of the team about Dunmore.

2230 hours

The captain of the *Stingray* was Lieutenant Commander Burl Vanderstel. He was thirty-one years old, looked like the movie actor Jimmy Cagney, and boasted the strongest coffee in the fleet. Now seated with Red in his stateroom sharing a cup, he said, "I hear you boys did a helluva job extracting those POWs, Parnell. I figure it must have gotten a bit close at times, huh?"

"At times," Red said. He took a pull of coffee. It was sharp as gunpowder.

All in all, Blue Team had been able to get out thirty-seven prisoners, three lost on the way and three drowned after the side-wheeler took the close-in hit from the Jap frigate's long gun.

A day after the pickup, they, Farnsworth and his Filipinos and the prisoners, were landed at the newly constructed Hundred Islands Naval Base in Lingayen Gulf. The POWs, helping each other carry off their wounded, came slowly down the submarine's gangplank, grinning in the sun, shriveled, yellow-skinned men who had left a great deal of their lives back there in the Luzon mountains, yet grinning now, almost on the verge of hysteria.

He and his men were ordered back to detached duty with the 37th Division until further orders reached them. The division's headquarters had moved from Lingayen

Gulf to a Catholic convent in Panay on the outskirts of Manila.

Soon after, Red was told to report to a Captain Skip Cowell, the division's intelligence liaison with the Marine Corps. Cowell informed him that Blue Team had just been assigned a new task mission. He had no further details, he said, but Parnell and his men were to be flown to Saipan as soon as transport was arranged, and begin training with a special ops team from the First Marine Division.

Parnell now asked Venderstel, "You anticipate any problems getting us in?" The sub captain's stateroom was small, white, compactly constructed with flawless beading in the joiner welds, undersized utilities. It smelled of Aqua Velva aftershave and steel paint, and the soft hum of machinery sifted through the bulkheads.

Venderstel shook his head. He had very blue eyes. "No. In fact, we'll be able to close the beach to within a couple hundred yards. All these Ryukyu islands have steep offshore declines. The southern end of Kuba drops to five hundred fathoms in less than a tenth of a mile."

"How long to get there?"

"Four days to reach watch position. Then we'll sit off until moonset, give you guys a lot of dark going in. Moonset's scheduled for 0332 on the twenty-fourth."

"Colonel Stapp mentioned bad currents."

"Yes, the South China Sea's notorious for heavy tidal shifts. When you add the narrow inlet, you've damned near got a bore situation when the tide changes."

Parnell grunted. "We'll also have a quarter moon."

"Right."

"That means spring tides."

Vanderstel nodded. "Yeah, but you'll be inside the twelve-hour lunar interval. Besides, we'll lay to upcurrent, shouldn't be too bad." He tilted his head slightly, gave Parnell an eyebrow-lifted glance. "One thing, though, stay the hell outta the water if you possibly can. When you've got depths like those and strong tidal currents, there's gonna be some badass pelagic jacks feeding that zone."

"Jacks? You mean bonito fish?"

"Hardly." The captain chortled. "I mean sharks, man. Blues and great whites."

"Oh, right."

The captain finished his coffee and stood up. "Well, time to go to work. Stay and have more coffee. You want to spice it, there's a couple bottles of scotch in my foot locker."

"Thanks, sir. But I think I'll check my men."

The team was being berthed in the forward torpedo room, bunks up on top of torpedoes, big, long black tubes that glistened like polished ebony in the overheads. Parnell himself was bunking with the boat's XO, a lieutenant commander named Stan Forty.

Wyatt, Cowboy, and Smoker were playing spit-in-the-ocean poker on a blanket spread on the deck of the torpedo room. Sol and Weesay were asleep in their bunks. The team's gear lay on bunks and against one of the bulkheads, everything cased in plastic bags from which the air had been sucked: Thompsons and the Springfield sniper rifles, ammo and grenade canisters, explosives and setup gear, walkie-talkies, a larger radio transceiver, binoculars, three days of D-rations, and medical supplies.

Parnell stood outside the watertight door, watching for a moment. Then he caught Bird's eye and gave a slight nod. Wyatt tossed in his cards, rose, and came over, then gripped the door's brace, and slipped through, feet first. "Lieutenant?"

They moved down the companionway a bit and paused beside the door to the radio room. "Everybody set up?" Red asked him quietly.

"Yes, sir."

"How they doing?"

Wyatt turned slightly as if to spit, came back, running a finger along the edge of his left ear. "They're jumpy, Lieutenant."

"I know. Ain't we all?"

"Gettin' hurrahed by them Sandpounders di'n't help none." From the radio room came splurges of intercom talk, beeps, and rings.

Parnell stared at the overhead for a moment, then said, "I'll see what I can do." He turned and headed for the CIC, returning in a few minutes with one of Vanderstel's bottles of Johnny Walker Black Label. When he handed it to Bird, the sergeant's thin mouth curved up in a smile.

"It'll take us four days to get to our IP," Parnell told him. "See everybody gets as much rest as they can. Don't let 'em get too noisy. And none of that booze for the swabbies."

"Right, sir. Thanks."

At precisely 11:33 P.M., the USS *Stingray* disconnected her power cables and loosed her lines. Backing slowly away from her pod berth at Dock 1-F West, she maneuvered around and moved slowly along the Tanapag Harbor roadstead under steaming lights.

The night was calm with just a hint of a southern breeze, the ocean flat and dark under the new moon that sent a faint, shimmering line across the surface. A half mile beyond the roadstead, the sub's up lights abruptly went out and the distant clatter of her dive klaxon sounded.

Soon, she disappeared beneath the surface, leaving only a gentle disturbance that danced with moon glow for a few seconds and then vanished.

Chapter Sixteen

Kuba Island, Ryukyus Group
24 April 1945
0351 hours

The *Stingray* lay two hundreds yards off the coastline, black, rugged silhouette of rock cliffs with white streaks of beach at their bases. From the sub's position, the square angles of the grounded Jap freighter showed against the eastern stars. It was canted sharply to port and had run much of its hull onto jagged tumble rock below the cliff line.

Vanderstel had the sub idling on its batteries, just holding station in a four-knot current. Her deck was awash so Blue Team could deploy their Goodyear SSA-89F life raft without having to work over the side of the hull. The ocean had a slight chop, which sent wavelets against the base of the boat's sail, the skipper and his two lookouts up there.

The sub's XO was overseeing the launch, his forward torpedo room crew assisting Parnell and his men in loading out their gear, their raft snugged in tight on double lines. They could hear the soft rush of waves landward, more a washing than surf, as they surged across the tumble rock amid the sharp calls of shearwaters and bitterns up among rock crevices.

One by one, the men boarded the raft, Parnell the last to leave the *Stingray*. First he and Forty shook hands; then he turned to salute the stern and then the captain, finally climbing into the raft. The torpedo men cut them loose, the raft sliding along the foredeck a few feet before drifting out into free water.

With Parnell steering, the others began paddling toward the shore. The current swept them along powerfully, Red guiding the raft so it cut diagonally across it, holding the moonlit silhouette of the freighter as a landing point.

Astern, they could hear the *Stingray's* props surge up as she slowly moved away. Then there was the churn and hiss of venting air and the sharp slap of water against metal as the sub began her dive. In a few moments, she was gone, leaving only the sound of ocean distance and beach surge and the birds.

They struck the freighter at the stern. It was an old ship with a counter stern and a single-plate rudder, typical of merchantmen of World War I vintage. It stank of rusted plating and oil seepage and bird shit, large patches of guano disfiguring its surfaces like dirty snow. The tip of the three-blade propeller stuck above the ocean's surge, draped with seaweed.

They heaved a hook line over the fantail and the men went up hand-over-hand, slipping over the transom railing onto the after-house deck. Their gear went up next, followed by Parnell and Weesay and then the raft itself. Partially deflating it, they stowed it and the rest of the gear in the small after house.

Inside the compartment, now dimly lit by their small tunic lights, were stacks of empty oil drums. Rusted Japanese Army food cans and broken ceramic jugs of *shochu*, an Okinawan beer made from sweet potatoes, were scattered about. In a corner lay a small pile of calcified human excrement. Affixed to the forward bulkhead was a spiral ladder that led up to a docking bridge and an emergency steering wheel. Rats scurried in the dank, foul-smelling darkness, their nails scratching on the tilted deck.

Parnell checked the time: 0421. He called a meeting, the men huddled around him, down on one knee. "We'll split into two three-man teams," he began. "One here, the other in the main wheelhouse. One man on security at all times. When daylight comes, everybody stay where they're at, don't show yourselves on deck. Those off watch, get some rest. Stay off the radios unless some bad shit's coming our way, then click code." He looked around at shadowed faces. "Everybody on the same page?"

"Yes, sir," they murmured quietly.

The watertight gear satchels were broken open and they began assembling and loading their sniper rifles, and setting out hand grenades and explosive satchels. The walkie-talkies and main assault transceiver were unbagged, their batteries checked and hooked up. Parnell picked Sol and Cowboy to go with him to the amidships watch station and they left.

Wyatt and his crew immediately began setting up the main radio, a compact, short-range SCR 200 FQ unit with preset frequencies for the Group's Bombardment Assignment Ship, a destroyer-transport ship named the USS *Scribner* code-named Roundhouse, and the Kuba ABCO, *Honeycomb*, extending their reel antenna up through the docking bridge hatch.

Meanwhile, Red and his crew headed for the wheelhouse, crouched below the top of the bulwark, darting between deck fittings and ventilation intakes and grabbing hold to keep from sliding down the salt- and guano-encrusted deck. Their movement spooked resting seabirds, which took to the air amid raucous cries.

Reaching the midhouse, they quickly went up to the bridge deck. Its railings had weather cloths between the stanchions. All were tattered and black with rot stains. The starboard door to the bridge house was made of thick mahogany wood and hung crookedly from a single sealed brass hinge. They stepped over it and entered the bridge, the space surprisingly small, stinking of rat feces and old wood and rust.

It had been stripped, the wheel box gone, the tarnished, brass-hooded binnacle housing in front of it empty. Beside it, the engine-order telegraph stand was minus its order plate and setting handles. All the pennant and chart slots had been rifled. In the forward bulkhead were three encased windows with bolt seals running completely around them, their glass opaque with salt scum.

Red took the first watch. Kaamanui and Fountain withdrew through an inboard door looking for some place to sleep. On the bridge, Red deposited his walkie-talkie into one of the empty pennant racks, then stepped back onto the starboard bridge wing and looked out at the island.

He sensed a faint lightness to the dark now, so subtle it might only have been his imagination. Still, he could clearly see patches of white beach off both the port and starboard beams. The ship had apparently flung nearly a third of its overall length aground.

To the right, a cliff climbed steeply up about a hundred feet. Beyond its rim the stars were scattered across the sky, looking sharp and clean. To the left was a long stretch of beach. He could smell the drift of foliage from the land, a dry, summery scent.

He returned to the bridge house, stood listening to the dead, metal silence of the ship. Then he cleaned the salt scum from the windows and leaned against the forward bulkhead, peering out at the island, waiting for dawn.

Down in the bowels of the ship, it was like moving through ancient steel ruins, the bulkheads sweating moisture, everything coated with oil and accumulated dirt. Weesay and Smoker went slowly, looking around. Too keyed up to sleep, they had decided to explore the vessel.

They had started in the after house, going down a narrow, barrel ladder-way into a carpenter compartment where there were old, scoured wooden benches and emptied shelves. The deck was littered with wood shavings that looked like shriveled leaves. There were also four coils of huge chain, the links black with rust.

Forward of the carpenter compartment was a stowage area with empty sea chests and bulwark shelving and two upright sections of cast-iron piping braced in with metal straps bossed into the bulkhead. Everything else had been taken out, even the electrical circuit boxes and conduit piping.

Next was a machinery room. There was a small diesel donkey engine geared to a capstan drum, parts of the engine stripped off. Pressure pipes made of metal matting ran overhead from which rats' eyes gleamed down at them like scarlet-orange agates floating in the dimness.

Smoker threw a large bolt at them and shouted viciously, "Y'all's lucky I can't shoot, ya goddamn worthless plum-suckin' little fucks."

They worked their way down into the ship's shaft alley, a low, dome-arched tunnel that went off beyond the reach of their lights. In the center was the propeller shaft running through heavy foundation braces. It was two feet in diameter, polished black steel formed into sections with perfectly milled flanges fitted and bolt-sealed. In between the coupling joints were big spring bearings, looking like huge white doughnuts, their paint faded and stain-scoured. The tunnel smelled of scorched metal and overheated gear grease and red lead paint.

Something shiny caught Weesay's eye, on the underside of one of the bearings. It looked like grease that had leaked from the seal casing. It sparkled as if containing tiny shards of yellow glass. It was actually lubricating oil mixed with Babbitt dust, a metal alloy lining bearings.

He scooped some up on the tips of two fingers. It felt slippery, like graphite. As Smoker bent down to look,

Laguna turned and playfully wiped two streaks of the oily mess across Wineberg's cheeks. "Now chu one *real* Mo-hawker, *meng*," he said, laughing.

Smoker jacked backward, his expression gone stone hard in the faint light. "Wot ya'll think you're *doin'*, ya fuckin' little prick?" he yelled, his voice reverberating hollowly down the shaft tunnel.

Weesay drew back, stunned. "Hey, take it easy, *meng*."

"*Goddammit*." Smoker viciously wiped his face on his tunic sleeve, still glaring at his companion.

"I was just playin', for Chris' sake," Laguna said.

Wineberg closed his eyes. Then he inhaled deeply, slowly, calming himself. Finally, he opened his eyes, saying, "Yeah, y'all're right, man. Jesus, I'm sorry." He shook his head, puzzled. "I don' know what the *hell's* a-matter with me lately. I'm flat pissed at ever'thing, all the time."

Laguna straightened up. He nodded. "Yeah," he said. "Ever'body gettin' like that. Chu know why? It was them marine assholes givin' us all that doggie shit."

Smoker chortled mirthlessly. "Yeah, I guess so. Man, I like to tore one of 'em's head off. Would have, too, the lieutenant hadn't stepped in."

"Hey, was same with me, *meng*. I almos' knife that gunny, Oldfield."

Wineberg looked around and sighed tiredly. The close steel overhead, the stench, the feel of trapped time, of entombment, had suddenly become repugnant to him. He turned and let go a knot of phlegm at the big driveshaft. "Come on, Chico," he said. "Let's get the hell outta here."

They came just before the first glow of dawn, the sky still dark and the bigger stars showing in the west, four small, flickering lights looking like big fireflies in a line. They suddenly appeared at the rim of the cliff.

Parnell had been hunkered down below the bulkhead having a cigarette, his palm cupping its glow. When he rose, there they were. Remaining in a line, they began to descend along a pathway in the cliff.

He retrieved his walkie-talkie and tapped the transmitter switch three times: *something approaching*. Then he held down the receiver switch. Two clicks came right back, the other watch post acknowledging.

He put his binoculars on the lights and immediately made out four men, Okinawan natives, each with a small paper lantern at the end of a pole that he held close to the ground ahead of him. Parnell suspected what the lamps were for, to scare off the snakes. His TMS had mentioned that the islands had highly venomous snakes called *habus*.

The men were all small, barely four feet tall, and dressed in striped kimonos tucked up on the upper arms and below the groin. They wore grass sandals and conical straw hats and every man had a coil of rope over his shoulder with a large hook attached. The only weapons he could see were long, slender-bladed knives strapped to the poles.

He keyed the radio, said, "Fishermen." Two clicks came back.

He watched them for a long time, the sky slowly gathering dawn light. First, a deep grayness that gradually faded into a soft yellow-reddish tint that coated the top of the cliff. The Okinawans had crossed past the grounded freighter and gathered near where the narrow inlet broached into the sea.

They began casting their rope lines out into the water, then hauling them back, letting the big hooks wrapped with seaweed trail just under the surface. As the light got stronger, Parnell could see just how strong the current was. It ran along the shoreline, forming dimples and little swirls.

Occasionally, a sudden flurry would erupt and a school of flying fish would burst out of the water and go gliding for nearly a hundred yards, their pectoral fins looking like dull silver in the dawn light. Big dorsals and tail fins often appeared, cleaving lethally through the water and sometimes making explosions in the surface as sharks fed.

The fishermen finally hooked a small white-tip shark, about five feet long. All the men instantly grabbed the same line and heaved in unison until the fish was dragged completely up onto the rocks, its jaws snapping loudly, the body twisting and thrashing at the end of the line. One man killed it quickly with a knife thrust into the top of its head.

It was fully daylight by the time the men strung up their white-tip onto one of the poles and left, two men carrying the pole on their shoulders. They went back up the cliff face, laughing. Within a few minutes, they had disappeared beyond the cliff's rim.

At 0630, Sol relieved Parnell, and Red went aft. Small compartments lined the main companionway, most with their doors missing. He chose one and went in. Apparently, it had been the captain's stateroom. It was dim inside with only the light from a single dirty-glassed porthole.

Everything usable had been taken from here, too. The deck, covered in worn linoleum, was littered with empty food cans, several broken sake bottles, and shredded straw wrapping. A crumpled woman's kimono lay near the bunk alcove. It was made of a silky material. Beneath it was a red undervest. A chart desk was built into the bulkhead next to the sleeping alcove.

Parnell gathered up some of the straw, scattered it over the empty bunk, and lay down, using the stock of his Thompson as a pillow. He closed his eyes and felt the fatigue thicken in his body. Yet it was more than a physical drain. It was a deeper, mental exhaustion. *Bad, bad,* he thought, *the men antsy, on edge, running on nearly expended adrenaline. No goddamned way to start a mission. Watch out.*

He shoved his mind from that, allowed it instead to drift aimlessly. Images came, vanished. He listened to the chatter and squealing of the seabirds, the dark, sequestered chirp of rats. Abruptly, a face appeared, with it the sensual smell of a particular female's flesh. And Anabel Sinclair was there, beside the bunk in his mind's eye: flooded in sunlight, laughing, behind her the wildflowers of an English moorland that ran down to a misty sea. He felt an aching surge rush through him like fulminate.

Oh, Christ, don't walk that ground.

His eyes shot open. He lay staring at the dirty light pouring through the porthole, felt the metal enormity of the ship all around him. It seemed suddenly possessed of some dark fume, like an echoing melancholy at its own slow, inevitable decay.

He never did fall asleep.

Two hundred miles southeast of Okinawa, Rear Admiral Ingolf N. Kiland's Western Islands Attack Group, TG 51.1, steamed across a flat sea under the new sun.

It consisted of nineteen large transports, a screen of destroyers and destroyer escorts, eight destroyer transports, some carrying UDTs, twenty-six service and auxiliary vessels, and a flotilla of forty-one LSTs, LSMs, and LCIs.

Accompanying them was the Bombardment and Fire Support Group made up of the cruisers *San Francisco* and *Minneapolis* along with the battleship *Arkansas*. There were also three "jeep" or escort carriers, the *Marcus Island*, the *Savo Island*, and the *Anzio*. These would supply the Flyswatter 4 landings with air cover. The Task Group had been at sea for five days now, having sortied from Leyte on 19 March.

At 1000 hours, blinkers suddenly began flashing and signal flags hoisted aboard Kiland's command ship *Mount McKinley*. Within minutes, smaller groups of ships began veering out of formation.

First were the radar picket destroyers who were to dash ahead and form a watch blockade around the Kemara

Retto as protection against Japanese air attacks. Next, the minesweeper flotilla left, steaming northwest so it could approach the islands from the south. Its task was to sweep the channel choke points between them. It was accompanied by the two destroyer transports carrying the Underwater Demo Teams who were slated to go ahead of the landings and survey the beaches.

Over the next two hours, the other TG elements would move ahead and to the flanks of the main group to form a protective shield. These would include the big bombardment gunships, the escort carriers, and their screening destroyers and patrol frigates.

It was now only a matter of hours before the prelanding naval salvos would start hurtling in from the sea to initiate the opening of the conquest of the Ryukyus.

The day seemed endless, everyone sluggishly cleaning weapons and unsuccessfully trying to grab sleep. By noon, the interior of the ship was extremely hot from the sun, heat fuming off the outer bulkheads, making the interior compartments thick-aired and stifling.

In the late afternoon, Wyatt went forward to meet with Parnell. He had to work his way through connecting tunnels and hot, cavernous, pitch-black holds stinking of bilge water and heaped with rusted cables and rotting dunnage.

He emerged into a small mess room connected to a crew's pantry on the second deck of the amidships house. Nothing was left in either compartment except bolt holds in the deck where mess benches and tables and a stove had once been secured.

Parnell and Kaamanui were on the bridge when he reached it, both men standing near the port wing doorway, listening. The faint sound of engines came drifting in from somewhere to the east, revving and then fading off. Parnell glanced around, held up one finger for silence. Gradually, the engine noise faded off completely.

Bird frowned and asked, "Q boats?"

Parnell nodded.

"They ain't comin' out *now*, are they?"

"I don't know," Red said. "Doesn't sound like they're moving, just running up their engines." He glanced out from under the overhead at the sky. The afternoon was well advanced now, twilight already beginning to soften the horizon to the east. The bow of the ship threw a huge shadow of itself across the beach.

"It'll be dark pretty soon, in about two hours," Parnell said. He pulled his map case from his tunic and squatted to spread out the TMS maps and aerial photos of Kuba Island onto the bridge deck. Sol and Wyatt hunkered down beside him, all three studying the material.

Finally, Red said, "Okay, we'll go in in three teams. Sol and I will go straight east for the lake. Hopefully we can spot out some of those boat positions and figure barrage coordinates. Wyatt, you'll follow the inlet up to here."

He pointed out on the map where the inlet broached into the main body of the lake. There the southern side of the inlet curved downward, while the other side protruded farther out into the lake itself. The accompanying aerial photos of the inlet showed light-colored, treeless ground along both banks and low bluffs forming the shorelines.

"Set up your sniper positions right along there," Parnell went on. "Two men to a position. But stay within sight of each other. I don't figure these boat outfits'll have heavy offensive ordnance, probably just service crews with a few mortars and MGs. Still, be ready to move, back and forth. Don't let the bastards home to your rounds."

"What's our rally point?" Bird asked. At that moment, Cowboy came sleepily onto the bridge. Without a word, he came closer and also squatted down.

Red checked the map and photos for a moment, then indicated a block of rocks that lay about twenty yards off the lower side of the inlet. "RP's right here, opposite this rock island. Now, as soon as the Qs try to break out, Sol and I'll head straight back to it and hit any boats that get by you. Don't withdraw to us unless it gets too hot. Or until I whistle."

"One thing, Lieutenant," Cowboy asked. "Jes' how do we take on these boats? Should we lay volleys on 'em, or fire at will?"

"That's up to you, do whatever it takes. Just be sure you don't get fixed and held up by counterfire. Remember, your tracers're gonna light you up like goddamned neon signs."

"What's the emergency fallback point?" Kaamanui asked.

"Here, the ship. This old tub's like a bunker. Hell, we could bastion ourselves here if necessary. At least until forward elements of the landing battalions probe out this far."

He checked his watch: 5:28. Once more he lowered his head to see beyond the overhand, up at the eastern sky. "Those TG gunships are scheduled to reach their fire zones around midnight, and the main landing bombardment slated for 0400. We don't know what Jap air recon capability is. So, there's no telling when the incoming invasion armada will get spotted and these Qs ordered out. I just hope the pricks don't start sending their boats out while it's still daylight. They do, we'd have to taken 'em on from here."

Sol grunted and Wyatt said, "Once they break out of that inlet, it'd be a bitch snipin' 'em off in open water."

"I know." He fell silent, considering. Then: "Get everybody up here now. If we *do* have to take 'em from here, we'll hit the bastards from the port bulwark. It'd give a clear field of fire up to the mouth of the inlet. And those gunwale plates are great defilade. To cover our ass, Wyatt, take one man and set up a fire position right at the inlet mouth. They come out, slow 'em up."

"Yes, sir."

Parnell sighed. "Well, I guess that about covers it. Anybody got anything else?"

No one said anything.

"Oh, I almost forgot," he said, catching himself. "The TMS says there's a good chance we'll run into venomous snakes on these islands. I guess they're bad enough to be mentioned. They're called *habus*. And they like thick grass and trees."

Wyatt cursed softly. "Ain't *that* all gawddamn cozy? Fuckin' *tree*-climbin' fangers."

"Just stay upright as much as possible when you move in the dark," Parnell said. "Your boots'll protect your legs. Watch overhead branches and double-check your prone positions before you hit the ground." He began folding up his maps. "Okay, start bringing everything up."

The men rose and silently trooped back into the after companionway. Parnell replaced the maps and photos in his case, stood, and peered out through the starboard wing door. The eastern horizon, coated in reddish orange haze, seemed terribly far away, remote even. The onshore breeze that had been gentle throughout most of the day was now picking up as the sun lowered. It blew through the bridge, carrying a coolness and the smell of salt and distance.

He lit a cigarette, automatically cupping it despite the light and expelling the smoke toward the deck so it wouldn't give away his presence. It felt hot and raw in his throat. He turned to face the incoming breeze. The core of its coldness touched his face, a gentle but suddenly clammy sensation, as if in its origins lay dark and dangerous shadows.

Oroku Peninsula, Okinawa

At that exact moment, thirty-one miles away in a shore battery bunker on the very tip of the southern peninsula of the island, SNFL Lieutenant Yasio Sacabe sat perfectly still, his legs curled under him, his buttocks resting on his heels, and entered the final phase of *kenshin ni sennen surushi,* his act of dedication to death.

The compartment was his sleeping quarters, located on the same level as the main firing room that contained the twin 200mm defense guns of *Yon-Tamaru* or Gun Mount 4 of the Naha Harbor's Special Base Force Artillery unit. It was spare, five-foot-thick walls of cement, dark moisture stains, and the odor of fungus and crotch.

As prescribed by ancient ritual, he had removed its few furnishings and laid down exactly three tatami mats onto the stone floor. At their head, he placed a small *kami-dana,* or personal altar. Before it lay a white pillow with a bright red sun crest on its face. Across the crest was his great-grandfather's sheathed *tachi* sword and his *waki zashi,* a shorter sword, both traditional weapons of the ancient samurai.

Next to the pillow was an opened metal fan, a ceramic *cha-no-yu,* or ceremonial teapot, which sat over a small charcoal burner, and a cup containing green tea powder and a small rice-straw brush. There was also a copper bowl of water and three incense sticks from which thin strings of perfumed smoke rose into the air. Sacabe's only attire was a *fundoshi* loincloth and a *meiyoshi* or suicide headband with a similar sun crest centered just above his eyes.

For the past hour, he had been deep in *zazen* meditation, focusing his mind onto nothingness, void of all the mundane cares of existence. Within such a mind state, he could achieve *honsho* and *oyomei gaku,* the release of his true and pure and uncompromising warrior character where even death became as light and insubstantial as a feather.

He sensed he was there, immersed in the sweet headiness of *giri* and *on,* duty and obligation, so exhilarating and profound, it was too deep to understand. No matter, for the first time he felt cleansed of the burden of dishonor he had brought upon himself by failing to fulfill his Toro mission for General Yamashita. Now he was reborn.

It had been agony to watch those *ganji* prisoners slip from his grasp, the enemy raiders killing all but two of his *hara guntai* during that final rush of the steamboat. And these two were wounded. His heart had been impregnated with horror. In fact, he had contemplated committing seppuku, ritual suicide, right there on the bank of the river.

But he'd hesitated. To die with no one to witness his ultimate sacrifice would be futile, leaving his dishonor intact. No, it would be far better to return to battle, to reengage the enemy, and win back his honor and his eternal soul.

Shooting the two wounded men, he headed southeast, and reached Santiago in three days. From there, he continued on to General Yamashita's headquarters in Baguio, shocked by what he saw on the mountain roads between the two towns: endless lines of retreating Imperial Japanese Army units, some of the soldiers devoid of equipment, starving, their fighting spirit gone.

It was just as bad at Fourteenth Area Army HQ, the place in the advanced stages of panic. Apparently, Yamashita's forces were crumbling all along the front. Many regiments and even brigades had been scattered and driven into smaller and smaller pockets. Most units were so depleted of men and material, they were no longer functional except as banzai fodder.

Rumors were also rife that Yamashita himself had been killed. That wasn't true. But many of his high-ranking staff officers *were* dead, killed in American air strikes or while inspecting the front. Among them had been General Nagai and Colonel Kurisaka, two of the coconspirators in the general's secret gold-hoarding plans.

That news pleased Sacabe. Since Nagai had sent him on the Toro mission, and since the whole thing had been so secretive, it was likely no one would even know of his failure. He had at least regained his chance to fight again.

But not here, he decided. The news of the complete slaughter of his beloved Special Naval Landing Forces in Manila had so jolted him it had projected an uncontrollable wish to die among his own kind, his SNLF Marines: *karera wa kyodai desu,* those that were like his brothers.

He devised a plan, using the still powerful fear of the Kempei-tai. Stealing a Secret Police officer's uniform, he quickly obtained one of the nearly-impossible-to-get travel vouchers, and, the following morning, left Luzon aboard one of the few supply aircraft that were still operating in and out of the Philippines.

It landed at an airfield south of Naha, the capital of Okinawa. Sacabe immediately went to the headquarters of the ten-thousand-man Third *Konkyochitai* or Special Naval Base Force of SNLF Marines assigned the duty of protecting this essential harbor and its surrounding entrenchment and bunker systems.

He was fortunate. The SNBF was commanded by Rear Admiral Keizo Ota under whom Sacabe had once served as an intelligence liaison officer. He presented himself to the base senior intelligence officer, explained that he had been on a special assignment for the Fourteenth Area Army on Luzon until his unit had been overrun and destroyed. He had, he recounted, hidden in the mountains for over two months before he was able to escape aboard a stolen fishing boat. The officer believed every word and eagerly assigned him command of Gun Mount 4.

This was one of four powerful 200mm or eight-inch gun emplacements that constituted part of the system of shore batteries that guarded the western approaches to Naha Harbor. These particular casements were located deep within a sea bluff at the northern tip of the Oroku Peninsula on the bottom side of the harbor.

Each gun was mounted on a rail car pedestal that could be retracted after each firing series. The entire installation was honeycombed with levels, galleries, rooms, and vertical crawl tunnels, all drilled or blasted out of pure rock and protected by cement and steel foundations.

The gun embrasures themselves were also protected by massive steel-and-cement doors that could pneumatically

close to withstand aircraft attack and most indirect enemy
naval fire. Following traditional Japanese Artillery Theory,
each casement was also totally self-sufficient, able to maintain a siege for several days. . . .

Now Sacabe opened his eyes. The room rang with the silence, disturbed only by the soft hiss of the incense sticks.
He bent and washed his hands in the copper bowl. Again
and still again, the ritual purification, or *harai*.

Next, he prepared the tea, pouring the heated water
into his cup and gently stirring with the rice-straw brush
until the green powder was completely absorbed. He
gently set down the brush and lifted the cup with both
hands, turned its face to the east, and sipped, three times,
each time making audible sounds. He placed the empty
cup before the altar.

The final step had arrived. He picked up the open metal
fan and slipped it under one knee. Then, swiftly, he leaned
forward and drew the *tachi*, the long sword, its blade whispering against the sheath as it cleared. Gripping it
two-handed, he held it forward and up before the *kami-
dana*, the glowing tips of the incense sticks casting red dots
onto the polished brilliance of the blade.

He felt himself again flush with the infusion of *munen*,
the state of no thought. Eyes tightly shut, he solemnly murmured the ancient incantation of the samurai warrior
whenever he drew his sword, "*Kirisute gomen.*" It meant *The
right to cut down and leave.*

Now the rituals had been fulfilled. He was prepared for
death.

Chapter Seventeen

2132 hours

Parnell glassed the opposite shoreline of Koniro-wan Lake. Through the binoculars, it looked as still as a sheet of black steel bisected by a shimmering path of blue-white light cast by the quarter moon. The perspective gave the bluffs that rimmed it the look of a continuous line of clouds lying along an ocean horizon.

They had left the freighter just after eight o'clock, waiting that long for it to get completely dark. The sun had slipped off the western end of the world an hour earlier, yet its light lingered in the sky for a long time.

One by one, the men lowered themselves down the side of the old ship, assembled among the rocks, and quickly moved off, jogging along the beach, sand now, fine and white and hard-packed, still bearing the tracks of the Oki-nawan fishermen.

The night was alive with moderate gusts of wind from the sea. In the still intervals between, they could smell the land, dry and brittle, like corn scrabble in the middle of August. The land beyond the cliffs near the ship was flat, slanting down to the shoreline. It was filled with scattered stands of spindly trees, low, more like thickets. Their contorted branches had tiny leaves and looked like networks of roots protruding upside down out of the earth. The rest of the landscape was thickly covered with dry grass that snapped in the wind.

At the very edge of the inlet, the beach petered out and there were piles and small plateaus of black rock that extended out into the water for about twenty yards. It was pockmarked with tidal pools that glistened in the dim moonlight like overturned metal pie pans.

Parnell and Sol left the others at this point and cut directly cross-country toward the lake. The grass and trees were full of furtive rustlings in the wind gusts. Parnell was lead, his sniper rifle and Thompson slung across his back, twin bandoleers of spare clips, his harness hung with grenades, and his walkie-talkie clipped to his belt. Kaamanui was similarly geared plus having the transceiver tucked under one huge arm.

The land was gently rolling, low hills with rock outcroppings like dark islands that were still sun-warm to the touch. A half hour later, they topped a slight ridge and were able to the see the entire Kuniro-wan a half mile away. In the moonlight, it looked like a desert lake, completely surrounded by low bluffs.

They made the shore at a low promontory, the edge of it twenty feet above the water. The rock was solidified igneous lava, full of sharp points as if the molten material had landed in thousands of droplets that created little explosions that immediately hardened. Down below, the water was dark and slightly polished by moon glow and had the look of great depth.

Parnell lowered his glasses, asking, "You see anything, Horse?"

"Nothin', Lieutenant. But them bluffs is full of cave holes. That's where them Qs are, for sure."

Parnell started to say something but there was a sudden rushing sound. Both men dropped to the ground, their Thompsons swinging around into firing position, safeties clicking off. A hard, rasping flutter came, and a large white egret lifted above the edge of the promontory, its wings working slowly up and down, almost agonizingly as it reached for altitude. Then the bird caught a slight updraft off the cliff face and rose rapidly and went skimming over them, its vague moon shadow racing across the ground.

Red watched it climb higher into the sky. It crossed the quarter moon, outlined for a moment, looking skeletal, its wings almost transparent, like a crane in a Japanese painting. Something touched his mind, a thought, a bit of trivia: *Isn't the crane the ancient Oriental symbol for Death?*

He lifted his binoculars and began another sweep of the opposite shoreline.

Bird and the others had moved swiftly up the south shore of the inlet, following the edge of its bluffs, which now and then dipped down to small, isolated strips of beach where tiny black crabs scurried and clicked as the men came down.

The water of the inlet looked calm, but Wyatt noted little swirls and dimples of current in the moonlight, the swirls elongated toward the ocean. That meant the tide was running out. He knew that if the suicide boats came down the inlet any time before dawn, their speed would be boosted by this tidal pull. So, he and his crew would have to damn well fast-track and get off their rounds quicker if they hoped to blow the bastards. He passed on the word.

When they reached the point where the inlet broached into the lake, their side of the shoreline formed a slow curve to the right, the bluff here only several feet off the water. They could hear the current sucking past partially submerged rock outcroppings just off the shore.

He set up the first sniper position between two boulders, everybody first stamping their boots to chase off the snakes. It was a good site, giving a clean, 180-degree field of fire along any point of the inlet. He left Cowboy and

Smoker there, while he and Weesay moved back down to
set up the second firing position, this one beside a tree into
which they carved muzzle braces.

Then they waited.

Gradually, the night began to give up its hidden sounds:
the soft popping of the wind as it struck pockets in the
earth, sounding like snapping sheets on a summer afternoon clothesline; the faint cries of seabirds; the low, almost
imperceptible undertone of the ocean.

High over them on both sides of the sky, the stars were
bright and slightly misty, which made them seem to jiggle
if he looked at them directly. Nearer the scimitar of the
moon, only the brighter ones shone clearly, appearing far-
scattered, as if they had been flung off the moon itself.

He looked at his watch, tiny glowing hands indicating
nearly eleven o'clock. He leaned his head against the
trunk of the tree, barely a hand's span thick. The bark was
rough and smelled of peppermint. He looked out at the
inlet, picturing fast boats coming by, his mind automatically calculating distances, trajectory arcs.

But something else hovered on the edges of his mus-
ings. The team. As he'd told the lieutenant, the men were
antsy. He'd seen it coming, yet he'd never quite been able
to pinpoint the precise moment it had begun or its exact
cause.

Had it been since Samar? Luzon? Or, was it further back,
all the way to Germany? Whatever and wherever, it had
now become a deep-down anger and a bone-weariness,
something usually hidden by the stolid silence of a combat
vet. But now it revealed itself in spurts and flashes, like
the undercoating showing through a paint job.

He shook his head, turned, spat, resettled against the
tree. *Stupid and wasteful bullshit thoughts, these.* After all,
when *wasn't* a soldier tired and pissed? No, these were
good men, *fine* soljers.

For a moment, the thought possessed him as to what it
would be like when the war was *over* and they'd no longer

be at his side. They weren't *professional* soljers like he was, thirty-year men. So, they'd go back to their own worlds and lives.

Bullshit. He didn't like *that* line of thinking, either. Sure, this particular group of men had come far together, shared a soldier's existence. That was supposed to bond them for life. But was *anybody* bonded for life? Shit no. He snorted derisively at his own stupidity. Comrades came and went, for a soldier, separation had no significance.

Still, *this* time, he couldn't quite make himself savor that particular rationale.

The minutes eased past him, became an hour. He felt sleepy, blinked his eyes, drove it away. He thought about how sweet a cigarette would be, dismissed it. He glanced over at Laguna, the younger man's head down on his chest. Wyatt found a pebble and bounced it off Weesay's head. Laguna's face jerked up, alert.

"Wake up and piss, Chihuahua," Wyatt said, chuckling.

"What?" Laguna said, squinting at him. "Shit, *meng*, I no was asleep."

"I was jes', checkin', then."

Weesay growled disgustedly.

Several minutes later, the Jap planes came over. They had no lights and flew in tiers of Vs, their engine exhausts spitting blue fire like bullets nicking off steel. They were headed southeast. Holding ragged formation, they crossed the moon at about five thousand feet, Zero fighters, at least sixty of them. Momentarily backlit by the moon's gloss, they appeared like a child's drawing of planes, crude and narrow-winged.

"Fighters," Weesay said softly.

"Naw," Bird corrected. "They more'n 'at, some of them fuckin' kam-ee-kazis, suicide planes. I guess that strike force's been spotted." He turned, spat. "Well, she's about to run into some hard shit."

They watched the aircraft until they were out of sight, their engines slowly fading off. The night once more folded down onto itself like an animal curling in for sleep. *Won't be long now,* Wyatt thought. He ran his fingers over the bolt of his Springfield to make certain it was locked snug. He clicked off the safety, then unshouldered his Thompson, checked it, and laid it beside him.

For the first time, he felt the tingling in his fingers begin.

At precisely 0028 hours, the air search radars of TG-51.1's picket destroyers registered the approaching Japanese planes, sixteen miles out.

Suddenly, the night was filled with bells and buzzers as each ship went to General Quarters. CICs frantically began running plots, radio circuits crackled as stations called to report Manned and Ready. Skippers darted from their bridges to the Control Rooms to fight their ship from its data-dense gear, ships' gun mounts and turrets began probing and weaving, their black muzzles like insect antennae.

The Japanese aircraft closed, passing slightly westward at about six thousand feet. When they were five miles out, fifteen Zeros broke from the main formation and began to drop altitude. The others continued on, obviously intending to go for the larger ships of the Task Group.

For several minutes, the fifteen fighter planes circled the picket destroyers, staying out beyond their gun range, like Indians riding around a wagon train, waiting for the perfect moment to attack. Then, abruptly, four planes broke out of the circle and began a long glide, boring in to make their suicide run.

At eight thousand yards, the ships' five-inch guns opened up on them, slamming out rounds with dull *ba-rooms.* Their fiery tracers lashed out in red curves that faded to hot points of light and then seemed to hover as the incoming planes flew into their cones of fire. On the kamikazes came, dropping lower and lower until they were barely skimming the ocean.

Aboard the ships, range director dials spun down rapidly and Mark 14 fire directors homed to the incoming targets. Then the 40mm guns began firing, staccato *a-whomps,* and the night sky flamed brighter with tracers streaks. At two-thousand yards, the 20mm guns lit off with their frantic, near-machine-gun rapidity. Yet still the Jap planes drove in, seeming to fly right down the line of tracers.

Then one Zero was hit. It burst into flames forward, then began cartwheeling, over and over before hitting the sea and exploding in a huge ball of orange fire. Another got to within a hundred yards of a destroyer before getting blown apart, showering the American vessel with flaming debris.

In rapid successtion, the two remaining kamikazes broke through the storm of gunfire. One crashed the bridge of the destroyer *Littrel* and blew it apart. The second dove into the forward deck of the *Cooper,* the explosion literally lifting its hull completely out of the water from the forward five-inch turret to the bow.

Meanwhile, three minutes after the attack on the picket destroyers, the main Jap suicide formation ran head-on into the two upflights from the carriers *Anzio* and *Marcus Island,* F4U Corsairs, and F4F-1 Wildcats. They struck from above, diving through the enemy formation. Moments later, the eastern sky bore flaming lines as Nip planes plunged toward the sea.

Yet many still got through the air cover and attacked the screening and bombardment ships. Two Zeros exploded almost simultaneously onto the afterdeck of the *Savo Island,* carrying all the way down through the lower hangar deck. Another struck the frigate *Delano,* which sank within minutes with a loss of 132 men. A destroyer and another frigate were hit, but their damage control and repair parties managed to keep them both in the battle.

It raged on for thirty-seven minutes before the last kamikaze plane was shot down by the fighter cover.

Licking its wounds, the Task Group continued toward Kerama Retto, the choppy sea shimmering and dancing in colored light from the still burning *Savo Island*.

0158 hours

"Here they come," Parnell said quietly.

A Q boat had suddenly popped into view, just there as if from nowhere, moving slowly at first, the engines not even audible yet, then rising as the boat picked up speed, bow lifting, leaving a white wake like a chalk line on the black surface of Koniro-wan.

Parnell and Kaamanui were already adjusting the butts of their Springfields to their shoulders, taking a dead sight on the boat, far out, crossing toward the center of the lake. Abruptly, a second boat appeared, from the farther end of the lake, this one already in top-speed regime, on the step.

The sound of the engines spooked the birds that had been feeding along the base of the bluffs. Now they cawed and squealed and lifted up into the night sky, the moon low above the western horizon now. The birds looked like sheets of paper blowing in the wind, wheeling.

The first boat neared, three hundred yards out, cutting across their position to head for the entrance of the inlet. Red followed it with his scope. It bounced in and out of the oval lens, dim out there, the white streak of its wake the only thing of real brightness. He had to keep sliding ahead to reacquire the boat itself.

Suddenly there was a roaring nearby. *Jesus!* The sound rolled up the bluff and burst into the sky, engines winding up, screaming. Then came a third boat, less than a hundred yards away, almost directly below the promontory. It had obviously exited from a cave almost directly below them. Right behind it came a fourth boat.

Up this close, they looked clumsy, the bulbous bow like a radome nose, and the twin depth charges on either side of the cockpit looking like big black balloons tethered to the hull. The engines sounded louder than the speed of the crafts would indicate. They bounced and slammed, the *whomps*, woody sounding, bouncing off the face of the bluff and then counterbounding.

"I'll take the first one," Parnell called, his cheek already against the stock of his rifle. This boat was so close the dimness of the night made no difference. He fixed on the wide, cottonlike strip of its wake, bright as moonlit snow, eased the rifle gently forward, past the two pilots hunkered down behind the cockpit windscreen, then a tiny bit more, and he homed onto the bulbous bow.

There.

He held the sight picture, moving with the boat. Inside the oval lens, the vessel jerked and lunged, but the oval itself was steady, locked. He inhaled, let it out, inhaled again, eased out some of the air, all this happening within seconds. As he held the last layer of air in his lungs, his finger gradually pulled, pulled.

The Springfield's discharge and recoil were a surprise, as they should be with a good marksman. The stock jolted against Parnell's shoulder and the incendiary tracer streaked out of the muzzle like a fireball, pure white, sundering the air and leaving the stench of cordite and burnt phosphorus sweeping over him.

He saw the round tear out the coming of the cockpit, saw one of the pilots get violently hurled to the side. The Q boat was abreast of him now, turning, almost directly below the bluff as it crossed his field of vision.

He'd already slammed in another round, the rifle's butt back to his shoulder. He found the boat in his scope instantly, so close it filled it. He could see the head and shoulders of the remaining pilot, the man turned this way, his body riding the dipping, lunging craft.

His second round hit home, the tracer line going right into the boat's bow. There was a fractional second, and then the vessel blew apart in one gigantic explosion that formed an orange-white-red ball of light that lit the closer shoreline, exposing birds in midflight.

The concussion hurled across the water in an invisible energy wave like a tsunami. It flashed over the bluff, past them, making their ears hurt, bending the grass. Shrapnel and pieces of the boat sailed upward, peaked, and arched back down again, trailing smoke.

There was the sharp, clean crack of Sol's rifle right beside him, then another explosion, the big Samoan scoring on his first bullet. The second concussion came rushing, too, but not as strongly. It swept by, chasing the other.

Kaamanui looked at Parnell, grinned. Red grinned back.

Smoker and Cowboy, in their advanced position at the curve of the inlet entrance into the lake, watched the two boats go sky high. *All right!* Their fighting blood was up full now, triggering off at the first crack of a rifle, the first explosion.

They turned their attention to the other two boats, creaming across the water, closing with the inlet. Wineberg put his scope on the first one, the other trailing about two hundred yards back, angling in to get on the leader's stern. Both boats were partially lit by the flames from the initial explosions, flickering and shadowy, but it was easy for him to pick out their contours.

The two Jap pilots were standing in the cockpit, their heads turned to look at the wreckage of the other boats, debris floating out there with flames licking up and more debris coming down, making little pinnacles in the water.

Come on, you little sumbitch, jes' a bit closer.

He locked his breath, relaxed, pulled off. The tracer round went out like the spark hurling along a line of TNT powder. And the suicide boat disappeared in a violent explosion of water and smoke and fire, six hundred pounds of TNT going up, *Jesus,* loud as hell this time, like thunder, rumbling and rolling.

He whooped, yelling joyously, excitedly, "Got y'all's wish to die, di'n' ya, shit face?"

Cowboy had also fired but missed. He cursed and quickly fired again. Another miss. Jacking in a third round, he glanced at Smoker, his face tight, angry. He swung back, lifted his rifle, sighted up once more, and threw out another round. This one blew his boat all to hell.

"Score four," he shouted.

"Whoa," Smoker yelled back. "Here come more a'the bastards."

Across the lake, three Qs had suddenly appeared, all emerging from the same bluff face, sweeping out fast, forming up in an offset line, the after boats hurtling over the expanding V wake of the lead boat.

The echoes of the explosions had hardly riffled away, fading up into the sky, when a mortar round exploded sixty yards beyond the edge of the bluff. Both men hit the ground. Slivers of metal went slashing over their heads, sounding like mad bees going past at supersonic speed.

"Time to move," Smoker bellowed.

He and Cowboy lunged off the ground and headed farther along the edge of the inlet, keeping to the rim of the bluff, running bent over as another mortar came in, the click of its fuse audible just before it blew up in the water thirty feet from the base of the bluff.

Within another minute, a third mortar round hit, farther to the left of the first two, the Nip gunners not very good, putting their ordnance in without a bracketing pattern. Several machine guns had opened up, too, Japanese green tracers arching over the lake. But the gun positions were too far away, forcing the gunners to elevate their weapons past seventy-five degrees. This put the rounds in along a high trajectory with a narrowed target zone.

Still, Wineberg and Fountain knew they had to move, the possibility of heavier mortars coming in, the shooters able to reach out and walk their rounds right over them along the bluff line. Or perhaps machine gun suppression fire from somewhere closer in. As they ran, they heard the sudden chatter of Thompson fire, familiar cracks of American M3A frag grenades. Parnell and Kaamanui were engaging ground troops farther along the bluff line.

Four more boats had abruptly deployed out into the lake, all coming toward the entrance to the inlet, their wakes converging. The Americans quickly set up again, this time on a small ledge below the top of the bluff. As soon as the boats came within decent sniper range, Cowboy got the leader, and Smoker the next one in line. The two remaining ones bore in and were blown apart by Wyatt and Weesay. The powerful explosions, coming so close together, made it sound as if the entire area were being attacked by heavy bombers.

More fiery debris floated out on the lake, looking oddly like fishermen's torches on the water. The odor of spent explosives and cordite and the sharp, poisonous stink of picric acid and benzene from the mortar rounds lifted up into the breeze.

Cowboy and Smoker moved back to the top of the bluff and went halfway back to their earlier position, just in case the lieutenant and Sol needed security.

Earlier, Parnell and the big Samoan had moved back from their promontory, trying to locate the cave from which their two Qs had come, expecting any moment to run onto Jap soldiers climbing up onto the flat ground. Every few yards, they'd stop to listen. They could hear what sounded like machinery. But what it was precisely, and where it was coming from, was hard to decipher, their ears still ringing from the boat explosions.

Then about a hundred yards south of their promontory, Nips began appearing, the two catching glimpses of their silhouettes against the burning lake debris, approaching in single file between rocky boulders, running hunched over.

They opened on them. The Japs counterfired instantly, but it wasn't heavy, merely a few rifle rounds that popped and burned past. Then a stick grenade came sailing, rising for a moment into the fading glow of moonlight. The two men were already flat on the ground hiding their eyes against the flash when the thing bounced into the grass twenty feet and tumbled noisily against a rock. There it fused out, a dud.

They rose, jerked their own grenades from their harnesses, and pulled the pins. Cooking off for three seconds, they hurled them into the darkness. Both blew up in the air above the Jap soldiers, nearly drowning out the blast of the first enemy mortar round.

A few seconds later, the remaining Nips jumped up and ran back down the side of the bluff. Red and Sol followed them to the rim and began dropping more grenades over the edge. The explosions were muffled, some going off in water.

Parnell shouted, "Sol, set up a cross-fire position, farther south."

Kaamanui rolled to his feet and sprinted off just as the shotgunlike reports from Springfields came farther up the bluff line, followed by the quick explosions as the four new suicide boats were taken out.

A thick silence came then, as if it were a blanket fallen from the sky. As always, its suddenness following so close on the heels of exploding ordnance, it seemed deeper, more substantive than normal silence. The way the switching off of a bright light makes the immediate absence of light appear darker than dark.

Parnell, his heart pounding wildly, blood hot in his temples, probed the silence. He could only hear the ringing in his ears. Then that began to taper off, replaced by the frenzied cries of water birds coming from all along the lake bluffs and up in the night sky.

A minute passed. Another. Still another. Nothing moved but the birds. Parnell took out his binoculars, scanned the far bluff line. The moon was almost gone now. It left nothing but undifferentiated darkness on the opposite shore.

Five more minutes dragged by. The Japs had not attempted to come up onto the flat ground again. But Red was getting antsy anyway, his combat instincts putting up red flags. At last, he curled his tongue against his teeth and gave a loud, single-note whistle.

A few moments later, Sol soundlessly appeared beside him.

"I don't like this," Parnell said. "I'll bet my ass the slant-eyes're putting out patrols to skirt the lake. Then they'll rush us in strength."

Kaamanui nodded, said, "That's what I figured, too, Lieutenant. They'll probably also come at us from both sides of the inlet."

Parnell grunted. He inhaled, sucking the air through his teeth. "Well," he said, "we better meet the bastards unified. Let's go."

They moved off, running without caution, the hell with the goddamned snakes, their boots slapping on volcanic rock, warning enough.

0229 hours

Twelve miles south of the Kemara Retto, blinker lights and coded TBS traffic flashed throughout TG 51.1's minesweeper flotilla. Immediately, the group began breaking into four detachments, each veering slightly away toward their assigned sweeping zones. Boatswains' pipes screeched through loudspeakers, and, "Now hear this. Now hear this. Stand by to train out trailing gear."

Meanwhile, twenty miles to the east, the Bombardment and Support Fire Group was already maneuvering into assigned firing stations. Within the PFC and EGCP

rooms aboard the *San Francisco* and *Minneapolis* and farther out aboard the battleship *Arkansas,* computers were
already calculating target pictures of their assigned barrage sectors.

On the firing decks, turret-handling crews, all dressed
in hooded, fireproof coveralls, began loading High Capacity shells into the ready racks as powder cars shuttled loads
of silk explosive bags up from the magazines. The ships'
skippers throughout the entire Task Group had already delivered their traditional before-combat speeches. Last-
minute prayers had been said.

Now the time for battle drew inexorably closer.

Red and Sol reached Cowboy and Smoker first, softly
calling out, "Blue," which was immediately countersigned
with "Fly."

Parnell squatted beside Fountain. "Where's Wyatt?"

"Yonder about fifty yards, Lieutenant."

"What's the count?"

"Six Qs," Cowboy said, a grin in his voice. "This here's
like shootin' goddamn fish in a barrel."

"It's about to get harder. The Japs're moving into fire
positions to protect their boats. From here and over
there," he said, pointing to the opposite bank. "Then
they'll rush us and send out the suicide boats all in a
bunch."

He paused for a moment, thinking, evaluating his men
to decide who were the best three marksmen. Easy choice:
Bird, Fountain, and Wineberg. He said, "We keep the
three teams. But now one shooter, one security. Smoker,
you're sniper here, Sol on security. I also want trip wires
back there in the grass.

"It'll take the Nips at least thirty minutes to get around
to this side of the lake. But watch your back from now on.
There are caves back on this side. Troops've already tried
coming up to level ground. Sure as hell, they'll try it again.

So, pick out good defilade that will still give you a wide-angle field. And stay put unless it looks like you're gonna get overrun. If you have to, drop back to the next position in line. If it's necessary, we'll overbound all the way back to the sea. Just don't leave any position uncovered."

The men nodded in the darkness.

Red slipped the walkie-talkie from his shoulder, handed it to Kaamanui. "Sol, you take the 300. Give me the transceiver." The big Samoan did. The lieutenant turned to Fountain, slapped his arm. "Let's go." They trotted off.

Bird was examining a dead snake when they reached his position, Weesay countersigning them in. Wyatt had his tunic light cupped in his hand studying it. The snake was four feet long, the color of clotted cream with brown streaks across its top. It had no head. Wyatt had felt it sliding over his boot in the dark, Laguna said, and had simply snatched it by the tail and snapped it like a whip. The force of the snap had instantly torn off its head.

Red chortled, impressed. "Hell, fella, I thought you didn't like touching the damned things."

"I don't. But right about there, I figured it was either me or him."

Parnell quickly reviewed his deployment plan. Bird agreed, the Japs *were* being too quiet now, something *had* to be up. The lieutenant then assigned Cowboy and Weesay to hold this position, Fountain as shooter, Laguna as cover.

He squinted out at the grassy land behind them, not much to see out there except shaking branches that flicked with light like skeletons' bones in the fading flames coming from the lake.

He came back. "Place your grenade wires in a semicircle in the grass. Maybe fifty yards out. Expect the Nips to come from that direction. If the shit gets too hot here, withdraw to the next position down the inlet. But, again, don't leave anybody extended out farther than you are. Whistle, yell, whatever, just let 'em *know* you're moving."

"Okay, sir," Cowboy said.

He and Bird then moved on down the inlet and set up the last position, on the upside of a small strip of beach. It had good rock cover and clean fields of fire, both on the inlet waters and back across the flat ground. They quickly laid trip wires, four of them, using Wyatt's grenades and going slowly through the grass, shoving sticks ahead of them to flush the *habus*. Then they returned to their position, locked and loaded, and sat silently watching the stars, listening to the night, and waiting for the killing to begin again.

The time was 2:57.

Eight minutes later, one of the grenade trip wires went off, up there near Sol and Smoker. The blast seemed isolated in the silence. Until it exploded, the night had been filled only with the rustle of grass shifting in the breeze and the little ticky clicks of tree branches. Even the birds had quieted down into their usual soft, piping twitter. Yet everybody knew, *sensed* that the enemy was already out there.

Parnell and Wyatt both went tense, listening, straining, catching the thuds of the grenade shrapnel as it slowly fell to ground in the grass. Red frowned, trying to project his thoughts to his men up the line: *Don't open up. Not yet, not yet.*

Nobody did.

A second grenade went off. Just before it blew up, there had been a startled Jap cry, the man obviously the one who had tripped the wire, and realizing it with shock, cursing maybe, but too late. This one sent metal parts zinging out like flat stones skipping across a pond. Then the silence folded down again, covering the ground as if two great, invisible combers had just rolled through, cutting off all sound.

Again, no one fired.

More time elapsed, nobody moving, just sitting there tensely listening for the tiniest sound, the least rustle, ping, or clank that would give away an enemy. Nothing. Abruptly, a piercing scream exploded from the grass, a wild thrashing, the scream breaking and a Jap voice crying out, "*Habu! Habu!*" There was the thumping of sandaled feet running through the grass and the voice rose sharply into another shriek, which quickly devolved down into a whimpering.

A muffled pistol shot came. The whimpering stopped.

Small birds suddenly came whirring noisily over their heads, wings going with such terrified energy the men could feel the downdraft as they rocketed past, the tiny things driven from cover by the wild screams and thrashing. They disappeared into the night above the inlet.

Parnell turned and looked at Wyatt, lifted his chin toward the flat ground: *Snakebit*. Wyatt nodded, turned, spat.

Slowly, the night became quiet again. The air, sifting up off the inlet's surface, was cool, full of oxygen as the tidal current aerated it. Now and then came a sucking sound as some large fish created a swirl of turbulence as it fed.

0317 hours

The birds again warned them, like sentinels, disturbed by movement on the opposite side of the inlet, plovers suddenly crying their rusty-hinge squeals and gulls squawking and lifting off. Then the men themselves could hear the Jap soldiers taking up positions along the opposite bluff, the faint tinkle of their equipment, a furtive murmur of voices.

Parnell felt himself coming up to it completely now, his body going into that thudding-yet-relaxed mode of combat. All the long minutes of waiting, knowing the enemy was out there now, setting, getting ready for the attack.

He automatically checked his Thompson. And, as always, liked, *relished,* the good solid feel of it in his hands. A few feet away, Wyatt had shifted his body, getting comfortable in the prone position, his sniper rifle strap looped around his arm, adjusting himself, making him and his weapon one.

The engines started again at precisely 3:22. They revved and faded from spots on the other side of the lake, sounding in the distance like English motorbikes, some coming in louder than others. First two, then more joining in, as if the drivers were restless, had had enough of the waiting and wanted to hear the starting gunfire and get the damned race going.

From his position, Parnell couldn't see the bulk of the lake, only the north shore and the curve where Smoker and Sol were located. And all of that only vaguely in the darkness with only the faint, collective glow of starlight to show contours.

He eased himself up onto one knee behind his boulder and faced toward the flat grassy ground. He studied it in the darkness, staring so hard things began to move in his vision. When they came in strength, he knew, they'd come fast. He *must* stop that initial rush, halt it in its tracks, or he and Wyatt would be overrun.

He slipped two spare clips from his belt pouch and slid them between the fingers of his left hand, then rechecked the weapon's safety. The engine sounds abruptly began to climb in volume and tone, the whining of each individual engine going harder now, yet all of them combining to become a single wild scream as the Jap Q boats made a concerted run for the inlet.

Smoker tried to keep his mind focused on the inlet, the goddamned Jap Q boats headed his way, out there leaving streaks in the lake. At least twenty of the sumbitches, making for the entrance to the narrow strip of water to the ocean like flies homing to a four-day-old corpse.

He snuggled in against the stock of the Springfield, smelled the familiar scent of gun oil coming off the wood, off the receiver metal. In the scope's oval lens was nothing but blackness. He swung the muzzle of the weapon out toward the center of the lake, and there they were again, their exhaust pipes spitting fire. He could hear the pound of their hulls as they came bounding.

When the Japs in the grass began their rush, their screams damned near jolted Smoker right off his weapon. *Jesus Christ!* He hadn't expected so *many* screams, his ears picking out at least twenty distinct voices. They sounded like Civil War gray bellies coming down on Gettysburg positions.

From behind him, Sol immediately opened fire, throwing traversing bursts out into the darkness. Bullets *whinged* and *whanged* and went sizzling past, others impacting, taking out chunks of volcanic rock. Suddenly, he realized the damned things were coming from the *other* direction, too. The Japs across the inlet had begun firing now, pouring rounds all along the bluff, not specific-target firing, just laying in grazing fire.

He twisted, still holding the Springfield strapped to his arm, and hauled out his sidearm, a big 1911 Colt .45. He boomed off an entire clip toward the grassy flat ground. A grenade trip exploded out there, the quick flash showing two bodies sailing. For a fraction of a second, it had also silhouetted three Jap soldiers running straight at them, their long bayonets glistening, firing and screaming, bent over, their squat, bowed legs caught in stop action.

More grenades went off, farther to the right, down where the second sniper position was set up. The machine guns from across the inlet kept chopping away, making the tinny sounds of 6.5mm rounds, but focusing tighter now, homing to the American muzzle flashes.

The next seventy-eight seconds went by in a wild, banging clamor of small arms fire. Finally, it began to taper off. Sol and Smoker stopped firing and frantically tried to search the grassy ground, their bodies thundering with adrenaline. No more rounds seemed to be coming in from there now.

The enemy banzai charge hadn't carried to the bluff line. For a moment, Smoker was shocked. *Our undirected fire couldn't have killed them all.* Then it dawned on him. The stupid fucking Japs, obviously not combat savvy, had charged directly into the kill zone of their *own* machine guns coming from the opposite side of the inlet.

Suddenly, a single enemy soldier loomed out of the darkness, growling as he lunged forward. Both Wineberg and Kaamanui swung to face him, firing. The muzzles' discharges lit him up for a nanosecond, his bloody face contorted, his uniform filthy, his rifle in stiff thrusting position with its absurdly long bayonet held forward, the oiled metal reflecting their discharge flashes.

Smoker's finger tightened to blow off another round. He caught a movement and realized Sol had intercepted the Nip. He heard the two of them struggling for a moment in darkness, those intense, animalistic grunting and straining sounds of men trying deliberately to kill each other. The Jap screamed once more, then stopped. A moment later, Sol rose and wordlessly returned to his position.

From across the inlet, the volume of firing abruptly intensified. Smoker could pick out four distinct machine guns working. Their bullets tore and sheared off the top of the rock line. He hunkered down, pressed tightly against the back of the boulder he'd chosen as his sniper position.

The firing slowed. He inched his head up, lifted his rifle, and scoped the lake. The flames of a boat's exhaust pipes leaped into his lens. It was less than two hundred yards away. Directly behind it was another boat, and a third slightly off to its right, the whine of their engines intermittently audible between the chatter of the Jap machine guns and isolated pops of Arisakas.

As he watched, the two trailing boats moved forward, flaring to the leader's flanks, like a tank squad protecting its lead tank. Within a few seconds, they had achieved an abreast formation and were coming on fast.

The three boats entered the inlet still abreast. For a few seconds, the Jap suppression fire stopped totally, the Nip gunners apparently reloading for the heavy shoot when the Qs actually got deeper in, knowing the enemy snipers would go for them then. The sound of the boat engines was funneled between the inlet's bluffs, echoing, making them sound like a dozen high-speed boats coming.

From the upper curve of the south bluff, Wyatt saw a tracer round lash out, knowing it was Smoker getting in the first shot. The bullet's burning phosphorous left a stencil of white light that held for a second on his retinas, then slowly faded. Dead-on, the round created a massive explosion, its light as bright as a sun for a fractional second, then turning various colors, reds and yellows and oranges, all clothed in dense smoke while blue gasoline flames rushed outward cross the surface of the water.

The sound of the blast was horrific, six hundred pounds of TNT letting go so close. Bird had instinctively ducked as the concussion slashed over his head, coming around his rock like an energy wave, sucking at his clothing, his face and ears. As it passed, he lifted up slightly for another look and caught sight of one of the flanker boats swerving sharply, the bottom of its hull showing in the firelight.

Then it, too, exploded. This time the blast heaved water and debris and fire upward at an angle, toward the opposite shore. It immediately set off small fires in the grass over there.

One second . . . two . . .

Wyatt had jerked his Springfield to his shoulder, no need for the scope this time, and fired by instinct as the third boat came hurtling through smoke, fishtailing, throwing spray off its prop, the pilot trying to work his way through the fire and chunks of debris all around him without dropping speed.

His first shot missed. *Shit!* Another sniper's bullet, Cowboy's, slashed a line through the smoke, but it also missed. By now the boat was past Fountain's position, a little over a hundred yards from Bird. He rolled the bolt of his rifle, brought up another round, rammed it home, locked, lifted, and fired, all in one smooth, connected movement.

Bull's-eye!

The third boat exploded less than seventy-five yards away. The thunder of it smashed across the inlet, up and over the rocky bluffs like a hurricane wind. Scattered fires lit up out in the grass behind them. Now the night was full of light and the sizzling sounds of flaming debris and dry grass igniting.

Farther off came the sounds of more engines homing to the inlet.

He glanced at Parnell, saw the lieutenant's narrowed eyes glistening in the firelight, that stoic grimness saying, *We're in some deep shit here, partner.* Then the Jap machine guns opened again and the air was filled with hot chunks of metal tearing up the landscape.

0343 hours

"Roundup, this is Blue Fly, do you copy? Over," Parnell calling to the Flyswatter 4's bombardment Fire Mission Assignment ship for the third time. He flicked the mike button to receive and dipped his head, listening. Static riffled through the loudspeaker, almost drowned out by the racket all around him.

Over the past five minutes, the team had destroyed two more Qs and driven off several others, the pilots veering before they reached the kill zone of the narrow inlet, filled with explosion debris and oil and gasoline flames. Now they were circling out on the fringes of the light, waiting for their ground troops to take out these blasted enemy sniper positions.

Again: "Roundup, this is Blue Fly. Do you *copy*? Over." More static, swirls of sound lifting and sinking like wind gusts.

Then: "Blue Fly, this is Roundup, go ahead."

"Roundup, request fire mission. Flyswatter 4 designate Kuba. Urgent. Over."

"Blue Fly, stand by."

Close beside him, Bird threw another Thompson burst across the inlet. Instantly, a volley of rounds came slamming back. Rocks chips flew. One sliced across Red's neck. He felt blood slide down into the collar of his battle tunic.

Let's go, let's go.

"Blue Fly, negative on your FM call. Over."

Parnell furiously keyed: "Why, for Chris' sake? *Over.*"

"Blue Fly, status CB is minus sixteen, over."

Goddammit, sixteen fucking minutes before the bombardment begins. He jammed his thumb down on the key. "Roundup, I say again, urgent you comply. Suicide boats involved. TOT absolutely essential. Over."

There was a long pause, then: "Blue Fly, stand by."

He felt Bird tap his shoulder. He swung around. Wyatt yelled over the firing, "Them Japs is startin' to swim across the inlet, Lieutenant."

Rear Admiral Ingolf N. Kiland had been an outstanding linebacker at Annapolis although he only stood five feet nine. His initials being IN, everybody naturally nicknamed him "Iron." He was in the *Mount McKinley* CIC when he was notified by a communications lieutenant that an urgent fire mission request had just been received by Roundup.

He swiveled his bull neck around to glare at the young officer. "What's that?" he demanded.

"It's from a special op unit on the island of Kuba, Admiral."

"Doesn't the son of a bitch know the schedule?"

"Apparently it's quite urgent, sir. He says suicide boats are involved and requests a TOT fire."

The senior officer grunted, squinted his chocolate-brown eyes thoughtfully, murmuring, "*Renrakus*, huh?" He glanced up at one of the bulkhead clocks: 3:45. His jaw muscles hardened, relaxed, hardened.

This was not an easy decision. If he authorized a fire mission now, a full fifteen minutes before the scheduled commencement of the bombardment, it could possibly throw confusion into the entire invasion schedule. Officially, he had the option to *extend* his barrage according to circumstances. But his operational battle plans did *not* give him the authority to *begin* it before the specified time.

Still, those kamikaze had badly wounded his Task Group. He knew they were gearing up to hit him again. If he had to contend with goddamned suicide *boats*, too, his battle casualties would be unacceptable. No, he couldn't allow that possibility. So, he thought, *let's get creative.*

He thought a moment longer, then turned his head and snapped, "Authorize Scribner to assign the mission now. On my specific order. The man wants TOT fire, give it to him. Also, notify all ships to be advised that we are extending our BFS time by fourteen minutes. At the *beginning* rather than the *end*."

A slight frown of surprise creased between the younger officer's eyes, which instantly disappeared. He wasn't able to conceal the tiny lift of one side of his mouth, however. The admiral, noting it, glared and bawled, "Well, god-dammit, move your ass, Lieutenant."

"Yes, sir," the man snapped, whirled, and dashed off.

* * *

The Jap soldiers had stripped off their uniforms and were jumping into the inlet, farther down from the boat wreckage where only fingers of burning fuel and debris had been pulled down by the tide. They came across holding their weapons over their heads, one-arming it, kicking furiously against the pull of the water.

Back on the bluff, their machine-gunners kept up suppression fire, constant long bursts, which would be putting massive heat strain on their barrels. They were obviously inexperienced, probably service troops pressed into a combat role and not familiar with passing off bursts in order to create continuous fire.

Whenever there *was* a slight pause, the Americans laid in their fire on the swimmers, bodies rolling, heads suddenly disappearing as fields of water geysers exloded all around them.

Then the sharks came. Drawn by the tumult and sound and then the blood, they'd hurtled in from the ocean, big blues and white-tips, caught up in feeding frenzy, thrashing and snapping at anything and everything within reach.

The screams of the soldiers was horrible, the shrieks from ancient terrors that even overrode those of battle. Frantic, many turned and tried to regain the opposite shoreline. A few others actually reached the south side of the inlet and scrambled up onto rocks, only to be met by Thompson fire.

So intense and loud had been the fighting, Parnell hadn't heard his radio. Now as he stopped firing and watched the sharks and men in the water, appalled even here and now in the midst of slaughter, a loud burst came from the loudspeaker: "Blue Fly, Blue Fly, this is Roundup, come back. I repeat, come back."

He scrambled around and swept up the mike, keyed: "Roundup, Blue Fly, go ahead."

"Blue Fly, your FM is approved. Relay target coordinates, over."

He had dropped his map. *Shit!* He slapped the ground until he found it, down there with all the spent shells. He flicked on his tunic light, fixed its little beam onto it. After a moment of study, he keyed: "Roundup, Grid Zebra-set, map reference 124 Baker. Coordinates 28 point 41 north, 127 point 01 west. Suicide boats, scattered. HC only on TOT. Commence fire immediately."

"Copy that, Blue Fly. Advise you vacate area. Stand by."

He hunkered down close to the radio, static riffling, sounding like rain on a tin roof. Seconds dragged past. Another volley of Thompsons cut loose, the enemy soldiers still screaming down there in the inlet. Then he picked up another sound, the boat engines whining up again.

Vacate the area? Just like that, asshole? Jesus Christ, come on.

A different voice suddenly came through the radio's speaker, the radioman aboard the assigned gunship: "Salvo, Blue Fly." More long, drawn-out seconds droned by, disappearing into the air. Had he heard the big gunship? No, wishful thinking.

Then he *did* hear a familiar sound, a rushing, intense sonance far up in the air. He swung around, saw a brace of four shells arching across the southeastern sky, balls of fire that seemed to leisurely drift up there like huge stars trailing fire that had somehow formed into a line.

"Splash, Blue One."

The missiles struck just off the center of the lake, the explosions powerful, telegraphing their horrendous vibrations through the water. The ground shook violently. Huge white columns of water rose into the air as concussion waves raced out in expanding circles that swept over the bluffs and flat ground, bent trees and grass, sucked away the air around Parnell's face for a moment, then slammed it back.

For the next ten minutes, brace after brace of eight-inch High Capacity shells from the cruiser *Minneapolis* crashed into the waters of the Koniro-wan and its surrounding shoreline. Blue Team hugged the ground as the world exploded around them, their bodies shaken and jolted, ears gone numb, minds desperately hanging on through the most terrifying of all battle circumstances, a barrage, this one composed of their own ordnance raining out of the sky.

At last it was over.

By now the first salvos of the main bombardment had started, their shell braces traveling northwest toward the other invasion islands of the Kerama Retto, arching high across the heavens in their slow, methodical, deadly journeys. Both sides of the sky now flashed and flickered, the rumble of the guns like thunder from dual lightning storms far out on a plain.

Slowly, Parnell and his men emerged from cover like stunned mice crawling out of holes, out into a silence broken only by the hiss of burning debris and the wild calls of terrified birds. The shelling had caught most of the Q boat fleet out there on the lake. Any survivors had fled back to their caves, as had the remnants of the Japanese troops across the inlet. Now only Blue Team held the field.

All through the day, they remained in their positions along the bottom side of the inlet, listening to the sporadic sounds of battle drifting in on the wind, and later watching as elements of TG 51.1 battle groups steamed through the Kuba Channel. The faint screech of boatswains' pipes lofted over the water and signal blinkers flashed, the ships' battle flags snapping in the wind.

Just at twilight, two Q boats appeared and attempted a frantic dash for the inlet. Smoker got the first, Parnell the second. Then it was night. The sky came alive with stars, which burned with an odd yellow tint from the dust driven upward by the naval bombardment. Out in the channel, the ships' lights looked like those of Coney Island carnival boats a helluva long way from home.

At 0532 hours of the following day, 16 March, figures appeared a mile away, soldiers coming through the gray dawn light. It was an advance patrol from C Company, Second Battalion, 305th Infantry Regiment of the U.S. 77th Division conducting final mopping-up operations on Kuba Island.

Chapter Eighteen

1 April 1945
Easter Sunday

L-day. Allied weather forecasters had predicted a beautiful day. They were absolutely correct, the day arriving with the temperature a comfortable seventy-four degrees F, a light swell out of the southwest, and no coastal surf. Visibility would be several miles with only a slight smoky haze, and sunrise was set for 0543 hours.

Within the first hour after midnight, the over thirteen hundred ships of Vice Admiral Richmond Turner's TF 51 Joint Expeditionary Force had achieved their prelanding positions off the Hagushi Beaches of Okinawa Shima. This was a ten-mile-long stretch of open beach located on the lower western side of the Zampa Misaki Peninsula near the midpoint of the island.

Assigned to carry out the initial assault were units of TF 56's Expeditionary Troops and Tenth Army under the overall command of Lieutenant General Simon Buckner. These included four divisions: the Seventh and 96th Infantry Divisions of the army's XXIV Corps, and the First and Sixth Marine Divisions of III Amphibious Marine Corps.

The first Americans to touch Okinawan soil, however, had been men from Underwater Demolition Teams 1, 2, 3, and 5. Dropped by fast boat a mile from the beach at 2100 hours the previous night, they had conducted reconnaissance of the Hagushi Beach from the 6 ½ fathom limit to the high-water mark.

They took soundings, marked out approaches with buoys, tested beach sand for resistance to weight, located beach obstacles to which were laid demo charges, which were all connected to a single command detonator for simultaneous triggering just before the landing craft came in. Their collected data was then radioed back to the control ships.

Meanwhile, everyone in the invasion armada simply sat and waited. Then at 0406, Admiral Turner aboard his flagship USS *Eldorado* signaled the order, "Land the landing force." Immediately, troops began loading onto their amphibian tractors and landing craft. There they'd remain on hold until the actual launch at 0630, after which they'd circle in position until the final order came to head landward.

As the first solid but gray light of dawn began to appear in the eastern sky at 0505, the preinvasion bombardment began. Organized into six groups, the Gunfire and Covering Force included the battleships *Texas, Maryland, Arkansas, Colorado, Tennessee, Idaho, Nevada,* and *West Virginia;* the cruisers *Tuscaloosa, San Francisco, Minneapolis, Birmingham, Wichita, Pensacola, Biloxi, Salt Lake City,* and the ill-fated *Indianapolis;* along with numerous destroyers and escorts.

Salvo after salvo pounded the beach along an eight-mile-long, thousand-yard-deep strip, the new day thundering with sound and fury. The gray sky was filled with the smoke contrails from outgoing missiles and shells and crisscrossed with rocket vapor lines. Dense black smoke rose boiling over the landscape as more than twenty-five rounds would eventually strike every hundred square yards of the bombardment zone.

Since the offshore waters were so deep, and because all earlier intelligence data had indicated the Japanese possessed no heavy coastal batteries in this area, even the battleships were able to close the shore to within two thousand yards and pour in big-gun fire with unbelievably massive destructive power.

The only real response by the enemy was quite feeble on land. However, at sea the ships of the invasion force were struck by a moderately sized kamikaze attack. Here, for the first time, the Japanese used a new flying bomb, the MXY-7 Ohka or Cherry Blossom bomb.

Flown by a suicide pilot, it was released from a Mitsubishi twin-engine bomber and carried a twelve-hundred-kilogram warhead. The Allies would come to nickname it the *Baka*, which meant "fool" in Japanese. Fortunately, every kamikaze plane and over fourteen *Bakas* were destroyed before they could inflict any really serious damage to the U.S. ships.

After two hours of blowing hell out of the Hagushi Beach the big gunships lifted their fire farther inland. Dozens of LCIs immediately closed the shore and opened up with their three-inch, 40mm guns and rocket racks. At precisely 0815, H-hour, control craft pennants were lowered, signaling the eight assault waves to begin their four-thousand-yard run to the beach.

Meanwhile, an American diversionary feint on the coastline fifteen miles south at Minitogawa, code-named DG-Charlie, was mounted by the Second Marine Division. Its purpose was to force the Japanese to reroute reinforcements intended for the Hagushi Beach battle zone.

But the tactic didn't fool the enemy. Once more kamikazes were encountered, coming from a secret airfield at Yonabaru on the east coast. Unlike the strike during the primary landings, this one would eventually result in more battle casualties than those incurred during the entire main invasion. A transport ship and an

LCI, both heavily loaded with troops, were crashed and exploded, killing over three hundred Marines and wounding nearly seven hundred others.

This was an ominous precursor of things to come. Between 6 April and 10 June, ten major kamikaze attacks would strike the U.S. Navy's fleet elements off Okinawa. Over twenty-two hundred aircraft launched from fields on Taiwan and Honshu would manage to sink twenty-eight American ships and damage 225 more with the accompanying horrendous loss of life.

But for now, on Hagushi Beach the enemy resistance on the ground continued to be almost nonexistent. As on Peleliu, the Philippines, and Iwo Jima, the Japanese had withdrawn from the coast into prepared defensive lines deeper inland.

At two in the afternoon, heavier landing ships began beaching, carrying in support troops and more Sherman tanks and heavy field artillery units. By nightfall, over sixty thousand American soldiers and marines, would be ashore in a beachhead of fifteen thousand by five thousand yards, with a casualty count of 28 dead, 27 missing, and 104 wounded.

As the days passed, these totals would rise drastically.

7 April 1945
1321 hours

Standing on the fantail of the escort carrier CVE *Anzio*, Parnell was eating an ice cream cone from the ship's service locker, vanilla, delicious as hell. For the past nine days, ever since they'd arrived aboard the vessel, he and his men had seemingly been unable to fill their bodies with enough food, good, solid navy mess: sirloin steaks, French fries, biscuits, butter, fresh coffee, and ice cream.

After being relieved on Kuba, they'd gone into detached status with the 503rd's intelligence section to wait for further orders. Then, four days later, they were transported by LCI to the escort carrier, which was stationed out in the channel between Kuba and a group of islets called the Kansen Gurupu. Since then, they had had the run of the ship with no duties assigned.

That night the *Anzio* had linked with the ship train of Turner's TF 51 JEF for the landings on Okinawa. It had been quite a sight, Red and his men out there in one of the flight deck gun galleries viewing the bombardment and the assault waves going in. All with a strange sense of displacement, seeing all this massive movement of men and equipment and firepower while they themselves took no part in it, merely spectators this time around.

Now the carrier was forty miles out in the East China Sea on antisubmarine duty, the ship on around-the-clock air operations, continuous recoveries or launches of F6F-5 Hellcats on search-and-destroy flights against prowling Japanese subs. Much of it was done in heavy rain squalls.

Parnell had enjoyed the freedom to wander all over the vessel, along endless steel corridors full of vents and piping, poking into detail sections and tiny offices and gear rooms, down in the engine spaces, climbing up hundreds of hatch ladders, and finally getting the hang of those damnable light locks, U-shaped locks that allowed men to pass quickly from belowdecks without opening watertight doors or letting light escape.

He especially liked the flight deck, the handling, loading, fueling, and armament crews in their green and yellow and blue and red jerseys and helmets hustling about with frenzied precision. Huge elevators coming up from the hangar decks with their wing-folded Hellcats, which were then spotted and armed. Klaxons going off and bullhorns blasting and the gruff, thunderous voice of the Air-Control Officer issuing his succinct flight op orders.

All of it being carried on in a rainy ocean wind that whipped across the vast open deck, heavy with the rich, salty-sweetness of the sea and the sense of tropical sunlight and softer breezes just beyond the horizon.

He'd been assigned sleeping quarters with the assistant Air-Plot Officer, a wisecracking lieutenant commander from Miami named McGoldrick who never seemed to lose at the nightly poker games in the officers' wardroom. The rest of the team was below in the crew's quarters, cramped space with four-decked bunks.

Now a detail was at work in the fantail section, the area wide open to the sea and the men in their blue dungarees and white Dixie Cup hats. There was machinery and huge refueling drop lines that curved down through the deck to pump rooms below, and a retractable jury boom, everything spotless and painted white or gray.

From up above him, he heard the bullhorn go and then the ACO's voice boom out, "Heads up. Clear the deck. Clear the deck." The carrier was preparing to either recover or launch a flight.

Parnell leaned over the cable railing. He could feel the heavy rumble of the ship's engines coming through the deck, watched the huge props leaving a wide wake of turbulence astern. It trailed off into the distance like scar tissue on the surface. Abruptly, it began to turn glassy. He glanced up, noted the stern ensign above him shifting its direction. The carrier was coming around into the wind.

"Sir?" a man said behind him. He turned. A young sailor snapped to attention, saluted. "Lieutenant Parnell?"

"Yes."

"You're wanted in Air Op, sir. Lieutenant Commander Tennes."

"Commander Tennes? Who's he?"

"Platoon leader for Underwater Demo Team 6, sir."

UDT. He inhaled, let it out. *Here we go again.*

He looked down at his cone. He hadn't finished it, yet it seemed to have suddenly lost its allure. He flipped it over the cable rail, turned, and followed the young sailor back into the ship's interior.

* * *

Frank Tennes was leaning against a door frame in the AP room aft the Control Bridge, the compact area filled with sailors and squadron officers working over radio gear and dead reckoning tracer plotting boards fitted to bulkheads. Dressed in his officer's tans with the sleeves rolled up over muscular arms, he looked like a sun-browned Yale tight end, his brown hair boot-camp short across his scalp.

He spotted Red in his army fatigues, pushed off the door, and came over. "Parnell?"

"Yes, sir."

"Commander Frank Tennes." He glanced around, came back. "Let's go find some place to talk."

Parnell followed him down a ladder and into a corridor just as a loud *bong-bong-bong* began to sound, followed by the ACO's call, "Pilots, man your planes." Down the corridor, pilots in their tan flight suits, tight flying caps with goggles pushed up, and yellow Mae West vests came scrambling from a side compartment.

Tennes and Red reached it as the last man ran out. Tennes peered inside, then turned to Red. "Let's go in here. It's private enough now."

It was the Pilots' Ready Room. It had leather chairs, blackboards and weather charts, Take Off Estimate boards and plane insignia charts, along with posters bearing recognition signals, attack plans, and Time Trees attached to bulkheads. It was cool from the air ducts and smelled of chalk, Mae West rubber, and the acrylic odor of the shark repellant bags attached to the vests.

They sat. Tennes offered Parnell a cigarette, lit it for him, then his own. He took a deep drag, blew the smoke upward, and looked at Red. "How are you and your men doing?" he asked. His speech was clipped, his eyes an odd bluish green.

"Fine, sir."

"Well, we've got a bit of a problem here. I need your crew."

Parnell nodded, waited.

"I know you people've been through a lot of combat," Tennes said. "You deserve a rest. But you're also experienced in clandestine insertions and heavy demo work. I understand you took out a German shore battery in Normandy. True?"

"Yes."

"That's exactly what we need done here." He went on to explain. After initially encountering very little resistance on Okinawa, XXIV Corps units had run into heavy concentrations of Japanese defensive fortifications, deep bunkers, and cave systems south of the beachhead.

He stood up, motioned Parnell to one of the bulkhead maps of the island where he pointed out an area due south of the American beachhead and eight miles east of Naha Harbor. "These underground works form a solid, cross-island wall right there. It's called the Shuri Line. It's anchored at an ancient castle that's now HQ for the Nip 62nd Division. Tenth Army intends to bisect the island at that point to isolate the northern enemy units from those in the south.

"So far, it's been a bust. One major assault by the 27th Infantry's already stalled. The area's been pasted with field artillery and even air strikes. But most of the bunkers haven't been penetrated, they're too damned deep. Now Nip registered artillery's tearing hell out of Buckner's troops down on the plain. If he continues trying to punch through the Shuri, his casualty lists'll go through the roof and his push south will lose essential momentum." He shrugged. "So, he's asked for *naval* fire to neutralize those bunkers and tunnel systems."

He paused to take a drag, his eyes studying Parnell. "That presents a different problem." He now pointed to Naha Harbor on the map, fourteen miles south of the Hagushi Beaches. "Right there on the southern curve of the harbor are four big-gun batteries, each with two 240mm coastal cannons along with smaller AT automatic how-itzers. The big guns move on rails.

"Across the channel, right there, is a group of small off-shore islets, the Keise Shimas. There are three similar gun mounts there. We've tried everything to take out the sons a' bitches, but so far no dice. Would you believe it, those damned guns are *British* made?

"In any case, our big gunships'll have to steam through the Naha Channel to get within accurate range of the Shuri Line. The channel's only six miles wide, very little maneuvering room. So, if those batteries open on them while they're in such restricted waters, they'll knock 'em out by detail. And kamikaze strikes will hit 'em, too. NavTel says there are at least two suicide squadrons at camou-flaged fields east and south of the harbor."

Parnell nodded. "That means those batteries'll have to be taken out individually," he said. "On the ground."

"Exactly."

"What about the kamikaze?"

"Before the bombardment, heavy carrier air strikes will hit the harbor, the airfields, and certain positions along the Shuri."

From overhead came the ACO's booming voice again, blasting through steel bulkheads, "Stand by to start engines."

"How many men in the insertion force?" Parnell asked.

"For the Naha Harbor guns, twenty-one of mine and the six of you."

Red narrowed his eyes. "How come us, Commander? Why isn't this a full-up UDT op?"

"It nearly was. But we've only got part of three teams left in this zone." Tennes squashed out his cigarette in a chair ashtray. "The rest are either running beach recons farther north on the Motobu Peninsula for upcoming landings, or staging in the Palaus for insertions on Honshu Island in the Japans.

"There's also another point. UDT operations are essentially beach and shoreline. Our main demo work's with beach obstacles. To be honest, we're not all that sharp on structural demolition. Particularly in disabling very heavy field guns. Each of my squads will have a single heavy demo man go in with it. That still leaves me one gun short."

"Is the jump-off time set?"

Tennes had to wait while the call "Start engines" came down, immediately followed by the rising roar of Hellcat Pratt & Whitney XR-2800 Double Wasp engines up on the flight deck. When it faded, he said, "Not yet. Sometime over the next forty-eight hours."

"What's transport?"

"Submarine. To and from."

"I'll brief my men and be on call, sir."

"Good," Tennes said. "It's John, isn't it?"

"Call me Red."

"All right. We'll have a short briefing in twenty minutes in the captain's emergency quarters. That's directly below the con bridge. Bring your noncoms."

"Yes, sir."

"Forget the sir. From here on in, I'm just Frank."

"Right."

"Three naked ladies," Weesay said triumphantly, turning over his hole card, the queen of hearts, giving the others his big Zorro grin. "Hey, chu *payasos* never had a chance." He nodded at Cowboy. "Even with them two big bullets *you* got showin', Roy Rogers."

"Whoa, little fella," Fountain came right back. "Don't be countin' your goddamn money yet." He flipped his hole card over with a fingernail. It was the ace of spades. "Now I got me *three* bullets, Chihuahua."

"Well, shit," Smoker said disgustedly. "That's the fifth straight pot the sumbitch's taken."

"Don't worry about it," Wyatt said, his dark eyes twinkling. "Kid New Mexico's time is right around the bend."

The men were playing in the alleyway between stacks of bunks. It was stuffy and hot, constant sound coming out of the bulkheads. They all had their blouses off, sitting cross-legged on a cream-colored navy blanket, their suntanned forearms and faces contrasting with the whiteness of the rest of their upper bodies. The only one not playing was Kaamanui, who was asleep in his bunk. Their gear and weapons hung from the bunk piping.

They'd been playing for an hour, five-card stud, spit-in-the-ocean, and low-ball. At first it had been a penny-ante game. But then they moved on to larger coins, finally to dollar bills. A decent little pile was in the center of the blanket, which Fountain now gleefully raked toward himself. Some of their back pay had finally caught up with them just before they left Saipan. Now each man had several hundred dollars on him.

But now everybody was looking at Laguna, who was, in turn, staring darkly at Cowboy's hole ace. Even his face had gone a little pale down under his tan and Hispanic color. Finally, Cowboy said, "What's the matter, Chico? Y'all look like somebody stuck a pipe up your ass."

Weesay didn't answer, just kept staring at the ace of spades. There was a sudden rumbling roar from high overhead, one of the catapults working. The sound faded, as if it had been swallowed by the hull of the ship.

At last, Laguna looked up, frowning. "What?" he said.

"I said, what the hell's bitin' ya?"

"Nothin', nothin'."

"Then go ahead and deal the cards. It's your turn."

Laguna slowly gathered the cards, began to shuffle them, gazing emptily at the blanket. Then he stopped abruptly, stood up, pocketing his money. "I don' wanna play no more," he said. He began pulling on his blouse.

"Where the hell y'all goin'?" Smoker asked.

"Get something to eat." Still buttoning, Weesay turned

without another word, went quickly down between the bunks, and ducked through a doorway.

The others exchanged glances. Cowboy leaned over and picked up the deck of cards. He slowly shuffled them, looking first at Smoker, then at Wyatt. "I think ole Chico jes' had hisself a spooky joe."

Smoker nodded. "He sure as hell acted like it." Bird just frowned. Cowboy finished shuffling, lightly slapped the deck onto the blanket for Wineberg to cut, then began to deal. The three of them watched the cards going out, their eyes following each one that spun out of Fountain's hand.

A *spooky joe* was a barracks term for a combat soldier's premonition. Anything might trigger it: a sudden insight, a feeling, a sound, a flashing vision, even a certain smell, the thing coming quick and mostly momentary. But its effects could linger for days, this stunning, ominous glimpse into the future. It could shake a man to his soul.

"What y'all figure set him off?" Cowboy asked.

"Was your hole card, what else?" Smoker said. "The ace of spades, the Death card."

Wyatt grunted, shook his head.

Two sailors coming off a work detail suddenly came through the doorway, one angry, bitching, saying, "I mean, how the hell was *I* supposed to know he wanted Skilowsky on the drum? Tell me that. What am I, a fucking *mind* reader?"

He reached the men on the blanket and stopped to glower impatiently down at them. He was tall, basketball-player slender, his Dixie Cup hat on the back of his head, showing cropped blond hair. "Je-sus Christ," he barked. "Can't you dog-faces play some place else?"

Cowboy stopped dealing. The three of them looked up at him, Bird having to turn his head around to do so. For a long moment, they simply stared, a flat, darkness suddenly in their eyes.

Then Wyatt said, very quietly, "I think y'all better simmer

down, boy. Less you fixin' to start somethin' y'all ain't gonna finish."

The young sailor instantly flushed at his low, lethal tone. Behind him, his buddy's head tilted to the side, the sudden expression on his face saying, *Oh, shit, you asshole, you're messing with killers!*

For a tiny part of a second, the first sailor's eyes touched Bird's. Then they cut away. His facial skin went from flush to pale. Mumbling a muted "I'm sorry," he turned and headed back for the doorway, shoving his buddy ahead of him.

Bird watched them go. He finally turned back. "Come on," he said, his voice still very low. "Deal them sumbitches."

Before Cowboy could comply, Parnell came into the compartment. He came big-shouldered between the bunks. When he reached Kaamanui, he slapped him on the leg. "Look alive, Sol. You and Wyatt come with me, we got a briefing."

Bird rose, reaching for his blouse. Kaamanui slipped off his bunk and began pulling on his shoes. Fountain and Wineberg watched, expressionless. Finally, Cowboy asked, "Where we goin' *this* time, Lieutenant?"

"Okinawa," Parnell said.

Cowboy began putting away the cards.

The *Anzio*'s emergency captain's quarters were sparse, merely a built-in bunk, a power phone panel, a small desk and chair. Through a port-side door was a small conference room with a mahogany table but no chairs, shelves containing rolled-up maps, and ocean and theater zone charts on the bulkheads.

Tennes and his men were already assembled. His 2IC or Second in Command was a navy lieutenant, the other four men chief petty officers. All were husky and suntanned and except for the commander wore gray 511 tactical jump coveralls with the UDT shoulder insignia showing a Popeye-faced frog with a cocked sailor hat and a cigar and carrying a stick of lighted dynamite.

Tennes quickly introduced everyone. The 2IC was Phil Gabany, the CPOs Tony Barnardo, Ken Bays, Gene Querry, and Mike Terhune. He spread out a large map of Okinawa on the table and began running through the details of the mission, everybody standing around, arms crossed, listening.

He began by showing the exact positions of the four Japanese coastal gun batteries. "They're encased in the face of a 150-foot-high cliff line that runs along the very tip of the Oroku Peninsula, a place called Kakibana. Each battery's far back inside the cliff, about midway between the upper rim and the ocean The guns are mounted on pedestal rail cars that can move back and forth after each firing series.

"The installation is protected by what the Nips call Special A fortification material. That's outer walls of at least eight feet of rebared concrete. It'll withstand just about everything except direct sixteen-inch fire. The gun embrasures are protected by heavy armored doorways called *ni kagi o kakeru*. They're also made of steel and cement, run pneumatically, and automatically close when the guns are retracted.

"The individual batteries are about three hundred yards apart, with bunkers and trench systems in between. Some of the entrenchments are actually dummies, but everything's wired, even the phonies. This type of fortification network is called a *kogeki chikujo*. That's important. It means it's basically *offensive* in nature and completely self-sufficient. Magazines, personnel, supply, the whole shebang. Could actually withstand a month-long siege."

"How do we breach it?" Parnell asked.

"Good question," Tennes said. "The offensive nature of the thing's the key. Jap battle theory's based on the attack. The little bastards *hate* defensive warfare. As a result, they've never designed their bunkers and accompanying trench systems for it. That's how we'll get in, through the communication trenches, which connect separated emplacements. All of them lead directly to entry points into the main structure."

One of the CPO's, Terhune, asked, "What's the overall time frame?"

"We'll have exactly four hours after insertion to neutralize the batteries and get back to the shore for pickup. The air strikes'll come in against adjacent airfields precisely at 0400. This allows the bombardment ships to enter the channel and open up by first light."

"What're our target assignments, Frank?" Gabany asked.

Tennes turned to Parnell and his noncoms. "Red, since you people're the most experienced in heavy demo work, you'll take the number four mount. It's the closest to the harbor entrance and has the widest traverse angles and field of fire.

"Your code name's Strawberry 4. I'm S-1, Phil's S-2, and Mike's S-3. The overall operation's called Gallant. Our delivery sub is the *Triggerfish*, code Hunter. For any reason you need to call in fire missions, the operational assignment ship's the destroyer *Hollenbech*, code Bull Pen." He smiled. "I know, I know, the guy who chose that code name obviously never got himself a piece of ass in Honolulu."

The men chuckled. A door opened in the outer room. Hearing it, Tennes leaned back to have a look, then snapped into a brace, shouting, "'Ten-*tion*." Everybody braced. It was the ship's skipper, Captain Glenn Montgomery. He looked around the doorsill, smiled, and said, "At ease, gentlemen, at ease." They relaxed. A moment later, he left, calling back, "Carry on."

Tennes bent and picked up a briefcase from the deck. He opened it and began passing out small, waterproof map envelopes along with AP-23 lithographs to each of the men around the table.

"The map covers your individual target zone to a quarter

mile inland. Including *estimates* of the adjacent bunkers and trenching scheme. There're also updated aerial shots of the same area. Your AP-23s show the general interior of similar Jap gun installations that were found on Saipan and the Palau Islands. Study them and then work out your postentry movement plan. Just remember your particular casement may not be exactly like these.

"There's not a helluva we know about specific operational schedules or routines in these batteries. But here are a few items. The outside bunker guards change every six hours, at twelve and six. There's very little night patrolling in the bunker-and-trench system. Use that. But, again, watch out for changes and keep tight security discipline." He momentarily paused to shuffle through his notes.

CPO Bays utilized the pause to ask, "Do we swim this one, Commander?"

Tennes shook his head. "No, the shark danger's too high in these waters. We'll use standard SIP."

He immediately turned to Parnell to explain. SIP stood for Submarine Insertion Procedure, he said, in which each team or squad physically exited the delivery sub through the vessel's forward escape trunk, along with their gear-packed rafts, which were automatically inflated as they ascended.

"About your gear," he went on. "Each man brings only personal weapons. Everything else is sealed in your raft. Including a small SCR-450NZ radio unit for the squad leader. It's a new development that transmits and receives on preset VHF frequencies. All op codes and call signs are taped to the housing.

"After task completion, all the rafts will rendezvous offshore at the approximate drop-off point. The *Triggerfish* will have released a small radio buoy that'll periodically emit a locator beacon signal. Its frequency is also taped to your transceiver. Once together, we'll attach lines and transmit our presence to the sub. Things are likely to be hot as hell ashore by then so she won't surface. Instead, she'll snag our line with the periscope and tow us out far enough for it to safely come up. If the Nips lay in too much ordnance, however, or send out aircraft, we'll immediately return to the beach and wait for the next night's pickup."

Parnell was thinking, *Return to the beach and wait for the next night's pickup. Just like that, matter-of-fact. Back into highly hostile ground with a lot of pissed-off Japs who would by then know precisely where we are.*

It was obvious everybody else was thinking the same thing. But, like him, their faces showed nothing, each man an old hand at this business of placing himself directly into harm's way.

Tennes closed his briefcase. "Questions?"

Parnell said, "Any idea when we jump off?"

"No specific time yet, still just a forty-eight-hour window. Weather forecasts do look good, though, a rain-free period of at least two days. As of now, you're on thirty-minute alert. When you're notified, assemble on the forward hangar deck for final briefing." He lifted his briefcase, turned to his 2IC. "Phil, show Red and his men where to draw their gear. Particularly silencers, if they don't already have them."

"Right."

"I suggest you all remain here awhile, get familiar with each other and do a little round-robin Q and A. I know each side can teach the other a few helpful hints."

Everyone came to attention. Tennes left.

At the very moment this briefing was being held, 472 miles to the northwest, the last important battle between U.S. Fleet units and ships of the Imperial Navy was also taking place.

During its initial dominance of the southwest Pacific Ocean, the Japanese Navy had been one of the finest among seagoing nations. Included in its arsenal of ships were two of the largest superbattleships in the world, the

Musashi and her sistership, the *Yamato*. Both were 870 feet long, ran 73,000 gross tons with 16-inch armor plating throughout, could travel at a swift 28 knots, manned by 2800 officers and men, and carried the massive firepower of a main battery consisting of nine 460mm or 18.1-inch guns.

The *Musashi* had already been sunk during the battle off Samar in late 1944. Now, in a last gasp attempt to destroy the Okinawa invasion fleet, the *Yamato* had been dispatched from the Japanese Inland Sea on 6 April. In truth, she was on a suicide mission, her oil bunkers holding only enough fuel to reach the Ryukyus but not return.

Accompanied by a small consort including the light cruiser *Yahagi* and six destroyers as part of her Surface Special Attack Force, she had quickly cleared away from the approaches to the Inland Sea and turned west-northwest in order to swing around and attack the American naval units off Okinawa from the west.

She was first sighted by two patrol aircraft of VPB-21 out of Kerama Retto just after dawn of the seventh. They trailed her for nearly two hours but had to break off because of their own fuel situation. Then at 0830, a Marauder from the carrier *Essex* again fixed her position. Immediately, TG 58, patrolling the waters west of Okinawa, swung about to intercept the battleship, sending its fast-attack carriers and their cover ahead as vanguard.

The main battle began at precisely 1232 when the *Yamato* opened up on the rapidly approaching Americans. She was instantly counterattacked by carrier air strikes that would eventually involve over 350 aircraft. During the next two hours, the super-battlewagon would be hit by ten torpedoes and three midship one-thousand-pound bombs and go dead in the water.

At precisely 1423, she would go under, leaving only 269 survivors. The cruiser *Yahagi* and three destroyers would follow her to the bottom. It was a great U.S. victory and the death rattle of the Imperial Japanese Navy.

Tragically, another end was drawing close, one that would elate the enemy but bring shock and stunned grief to the rest of the world. At exactly 0430 hours of 13 April, Okinawa time, Admiral Turner's command ship *Eldorado* would receive a jolting message from Naval Headquarters, Atlantic at Norfolk, Virginia.

Within minutes, it would be broadcast from the loud-speaker of every vessel standing off the Okinawan shore: "*Attention! Attention! All hands! President Roosevelt is dead. Repeat, our supreme commander, President Roosevelt is dead!*"

Chapter Nineteen

The night was clear, filled with stars, the end-phase moon not yet risen. A slight onshore breeze came in from the southwest, and the sea had long-reaching swells with smooth, rounded tops in which the stars' reflections glistened like tiny lights under the polished black surface.

The delivery submarine, USS *Triggerfish*, lay still, silent, like a wounded whale come to the surface for oxygen. Only the top of its sail, its periscope sleeve, and its antenna poles were visible, facing into the long swell that would come into it gently, rising, then pass on as silently.

The captain, Commander William Halbert, Tennes, Parnell, and two lookouts were on the sail bridge. Standing there inside the steel parapet gave Parnell the feeling of movement as the swells moved by. A faint vibration of machinery came up through the deck.

Halbert and Tennes were glassing the shoreline, the UDT commander's face like Red's and the rest of the insertion team smeared with a mixture of fuel oil, canned milk, and powdered egg to prevent skin shine. Okinawa-Shima lay five hundred yards to the east, a dark bulk against the stars. There were no lights anywhere, not even to the left where Naha Bay cut into the land. They could hear the cries of seabirds, the sound of surf, not heavy or booming but subdued, the swells coming into the land easily out of deep, reefless water without combing.

Tennes said softly, "She looks clean enough, Bill."

Halbert grunted. "You're lucky those swells aren't coming in with power. It'd be touchy as hell landing if they were big rollers. You ready?"

"All set."

Halbert squatted and knocked lightly on the bridge hatch. Instantly it opened, pitch-black down there. A balloon of internal air blossomed, smelling of diesel fuel and electrical wiring and the coolness of ventilation. A man quickly exited the hatch and stepped onto the sail bridge. It was CPO Tony Barnardo of Team 1. He was to be the scout swimmer who would go over the side to retrieve a line on one of the rafts as it emerged from the sub's forward escape trunk. He was shoeless.

The captain leaned close to the open hatchway to say quietly, "Release the rafts. Insertion force, stand by to deploy."

Parnell glanced toward the bow of the boat. Several seconds passed. Then a slight pressure bubble broke through the surface above the front of the vessel, creating a sound like water running through a pipe. A faint hissing came from under the water as the first raft automatically inflated itself once it exited the sub's escape hatch. It popped through the surface. Then, one by one, the others came up, too, rectangular objects of blacker black out there, lifting gently on the swells.

Barnardo climbed over the parapet, waited for a wave top, then dropped lightly into the water. Breaststroking, he swam to the first raft, took hold of its painter, and headed back, towing the others, all attached and swinging slowly, following.

Tennes replaced Halbert beside the open hatch. The

captain moved to the parapet and peered over, watched as Barnardo got the first raft against the side of the sail. He turned, said softly to Tennes, "Start 'em up."

The UDT lead officer called quietly down, "Team 2 debark."

Men began climbing out, members of T-2, which would act as leadoff squad until the entire insertion force closed the shore and separated, each team heading off for its own target zone. Each man was dressed in a black, close-fitting cotton jumpsuit, head wrapped in a black bandana like a medical cravat, and black coral booties, tennis shoes on his feet.

Each carried his own weapons. Most were Thompsons and sawed-off Ithaca Model 37 twelve-gauge pump shotguns with factory-flared duckbill muzzles and double-ought buckshot or slugging shells capable of blowing through an engine block or a steel door and M3A1 Browning .45-caliber submachine guns called "Greaseguns."

In addition were individual sidearms in black shoulder rigs, boot and belt K-Bar knives, and harness belts with pouches of spare ammunition clips and fragmentation grenades and taped-together bundles of high-tensile aluminum climbing pitons and carabiner buckles.

Up and over the parapet they went, without a sound, dropping down into the first raft, Barnardo down there holding it steady against the sail. Quickly, they completed their loading, cut the line, and moved off. Next came Team 3 while Barnardo brought in the next raft in line. Swiftly, it too was loaded and cut loose.

Tennes called down, "Team 4 debark."

First came Bird, then Fountain, Laguna, Wineberg, and Kaamanui, disappearing over the parapet. Parnell felt Halbert's hand clap him on the shoulder, *Good luck*, and then he too went over the combing and down into their raft, dropping onto the unsteady rubber bottom, the men already with paddles in the water.

Sol cut the line and they eased away from the sub, the

black square of its sail and periscope and antenna uprights silhouetted against the stars for a moment before disappearing against the backdrop of the Okinawan shoreline.

The four rafts formed up into a flared formation with the 2IC's raft in the lead and headed for land. From behind came the soft rumble of venting air from the *Triggerfish* and the surface disturbance created by the ocean slipping up and over the sail as the submarine sank stealthily back into the sea.

Ahead lay the cliffs. They paddled steadily, silently on, rising and falling gently on the swells.

Weesay was having a tough time holding back the memory of the spooky joe, the damned thing punching right into his mind repeatedly, despite how much he tried to focus on what he was doing: pulling his paddle silently through the water.

Ever since Cowboy's Death card had come up, he'd been wrestling with the significance of it. *A presagio,* a portent of what lay ahead. Like when he was a boy in the tough streets of south L.A., instinctively sensing things coming at him, bad shit. Yet such warnings had always given him the edge, made him just a flick faster, expecting it. All his life, he had been a solid believer in instinct and premonitions.

Yet, this thing had thrown him. First off, what was it telling him? Whom did it apply to? There were four men playing in that game. Although Fountain had drawn the ace of spades, that didn't necessarily mean it was about him. No, they'd all been within the aura of the card, the thing covering the *entire* game like a stinking black cloud. So, who, then? And what could he do to deflect it?

Then there was the other side of the coin. Maybe it hadn't really been a sign at all. No, he discarded that quickly, his beliefs way too deep to ignore such an open warning. Okay, so it *was* coming and *somebody* was going to be in serious shit. But did it make any difference who? Any of them or him? Either way, it would be the same.

These men were his *familia*, for God's sake, his real *hermanos*. He certainly loved and respected them as such with his having fought at their sides for so long, the past, *his* past with its connections and relationships and kin foundations, had all but vanished. These particular men were now part of himself. He knew they would willingly die for him, and he for them.

Jesus y Maria, why must *any* of them die *now*? he wondered. Since the very beginning, the team had lost two men, Kimball and Cappacelli. Then Sol was badly wounded in Italy. Weesay swore. Hadn't *that* been enough payment to *Dios*? Instantly shocked by his own indiscretion, he quickly retracted his question, took his right hand off the paddle, and hurriedly crossed himself.

Perdoneme! Madre de Cristo, only a fool questions God!

In all the combat he'd seen, Laguna had always been afraid. So much death, so bloody, so random. Yet he had known that that very fear had given his mind and body the ability to move faster, to think and react with more swiftness. That was one of the first things a combat soldier learned in order to stay alive: *use the fear.*

There had been something else, too, a feeling, no, more than that, a *certainty* that nothing would ever really happen to himself. Or, by extension, to any of his comrades. When those others were lost, it had badly shaken his belief system. Yet it could not be totally abolished since it was part of the very fabric of human survival.

In reality, the whole thing was foolish, *estupidio*, even. But it was necessary. It rendered to a soldier a sort of irrational immunity, made him go forward instead of freezing. After all, what man would be *willing* to go to his own death? Without such self-delusion, he'd lose the ability to function amid the horrors of war.

And that chain of thought had brought him right around in a circle. With that sense of invulnerability suddenly stripped away by the spooky joe, Laguna was discovering that he had lost his ability to handle its absence.

He cursed with frustration, then anger. *Focus your mind, el culo. Moment by moment.* With an effort, he forced his body to respond, falling back into the rhythm of the stroke: pulling, lifting, swinging, dipping, pulling . . .

The line of rafts was now within a hundred yards of the shoreline, the ocean going into the rock debris at the foot of the cliffs with a louder, tumbling crashing that seemed to telegraph vibrations back out to them. There was also the quieter hiss of surf running up stretches of beach, and they could actually see patches of white sand in the dim starlight. Without a signal, the rubber boats began to separate.

Blue Team moved parallel to the shore, the men in a rhythm now, pulling in sync. The raft slid smoothly through the water, enough weight in it to prevent the bottom from popping with each forward spurt.

Minutes moved past in tune with the high cry of gulls and shearwaters. The men could sense them up there, soaring, shadows crossing the stars. Occasionally, one would appear out of the darkness, gliding past the raft just above the water, its head turned, curious about this large object coming in from the sea.

Twelve minutes later, they felt the shoreline receding away, sensed it as the beach sounds changed, the land curving eastward as it formed the bottom side of Naha Bay. They followed the curve for another four minutes. Then Parnell signaled that they head in, tapping shoulders of the men directly in front of him and them passing it on. They turned and went directly toward a narrow line of beach.

A swell lifted them and rode them up onto a long, slanting stretch of sand. As the water was then sucked back, the raft was deposited lightly onto the beach. Before it could slide back down on the film of returning water, they leaped out and hauled it farther up beyond the surf line.

The area was covered with thick clusters of seaweed that smelled like crab shells and iodine. Tumble rock and portions of shelving jutted away from the base of the cliff, which began about forty yards farther inland, the higher sandy spaces covered with growths of sea grass and sedge. There were remnants of barbed-wire fences here, the posts rotted and the wire merely loops of rust. Also antilanding boat log pilings that were still bound with disintegrating steel cable. The rock shelves near the water were dotted with tidal pools that stank of dead fish.

They carried the raft up into a formation of rocks, jagged volcanic breccia, all of it splotched with seabird guano that was gray white in the dim light. Using arm and hand signals, Parnell ordered Bird to reconnoiter the right, Cowboy the left. Silently, both men disappeared into the darkness.

The others now swiftly began to unpack their gear, everything air-sealed in plastic bags that had then been strapped to the double seats of the raft. Opening the bags, Parnell and Sol distributed the ammo and explosive kits, specific items going to preassigned men. Each demo kit held ten thirty-two-ounce cartridges of British PE 808 or ten kilos of U.S. C-3 plastique explosives wrapped in wax paper. The odor of the PE 808 had been transferred to all the canvas satchels and made them smell like warm marzipan.

In other gear bags were the comp charges and detonators, (CE)TNT and number 27 Mk fuses, along with rolls of detonating cord containing PETN cores that gave a 21,000 ft/sec detonation velocity. There were also grenade launchers that could be fitted to the Ithaca twelve-gauges and operated on the high-low pressure system to take up recoil; two collapsible bazookas with two rounds each; and one M1-SI-2 flamethrower, a smaller version of the M1. It weighed forty-seven pounds, had a small pressure tank, two gallons of fuel, and was capable of shooting out a tongue of flame for thirty yards. There were also climbing ropes with high-tension pitons and carabiners, along with Parnell's radio unit.

Once the raft was emptied, they hid it among the rocks. A moment later, Wyatt returned, squatted close beside Red to say softly, "No sentry posts that way, Lieutenant. The cliff drops right down into the sea, almost sheer."

"Bad?"

"We'll be able to make 'er, but she's gonna be a bitch."

Red cursed. He tapped a nearby chunk of rock with a bent forefinger. "We'll have to free-climb. This volcanic rock's too brittle for pitons."

When Cowboy returned, he had better news. No sentry posts on the left, he said, and he'd found a pathway that looked like it went all the way to the top of the bluff. It was littered with empty food cans, used fishing spools, and chunks of smelly bait. Nip soldiers had obviously been using it to come down to the ocean to fish.

Parnell nodded, pleased. "Okay, let's move. Cowboy, up on point. Sol, you and me on drag."

Forming into single file, they moved along the beach in the direction from which Fountain had come, going swiftly, weighted down with gear, their weapons locked and loaded and shoulder-slung for quick action.

Parnell was the last in line, Kaamanui with the flamethrower strapped to his back directly ahead, then Smoker. The pathway was narrow, a foot wide, sand and tufts of sea grass, the rocks on both sides luminescent with bird shit. It wound back and forth in easy switchbacks, climbing steadily.

The sea breeze was more brisk up here, everything in darkness save for the stars, pinpoints of glistening ice way up. Close to the hundred-foot level, they could make out the Jap gun position's embrasure forty yards to their left, a big black rectangular opening in the wall of the cliff. The *ni kagi okakeru* firing doors were closed. They detected the odor of rusty metal, the fishy smell of pneumatic oil and cement. A line of birds, small gray shapes in the dark, was perched on the bottom lip of the embrasure.

Close to the top, the path abruptly disappeared into a narrow fizzure in the cliff, a lava coulee that was covered over with a flow mantle that formed a slender tunnel. The walls were little more than a foot and a half apart. Cowboy halted them while he scouted through, having to squeeze sideways, pushing with his knees and palms along the rock walls.

It took him ten minutes to return, passing the word back to Parnell that the tunnel was about forty yards long. Beyond, the path continued on to the upper rim of the bluff. But, he said, the damned thing was way too narrow for the larger men to pass through.

Red studied the mantle rock above the coulee. It was nearly sheer but marked with darker streaks, indentations in the face. He knew this kind of rock, ancient, calcified magma, dangerous as hell to climb since it was terribly brittle and could give way without warning. He checked below the path, the rock forming an overhang down there. He signaled Smoker to pass the word back up the line: he and Kaamanui would go over the coulee tunnel and meet them on the other side. Wineberg nodded and moved off.

He leaned close to Sol, pointed at the rock. "Watch this shit," he whispered. "It breaks easily." Then he quickly unwound one of the climbing lines and tied a bowline, which he slipped over his shoulders. Sol also fashioned one for himself, tying it down under his flamethrower harness.

Looping the spare length of line onto his own harness, Parnell started up, moving very slowly, first up and then sideways across the cliff face. It had a jagged surface, filled with craggy knobs and spines that cut his hands and the soles of the coral booties. In some of the crevices was ball-bearing gravel that made him slip. He hugged the face tightly, feeling for handholds, gingerly shifting weight, and inhaling the acidic smell of the rock, vaguely like lye soap.

Around and above them, the seabirds kept up a continuous squawking. Some occasionally dropped down to have a closer look, only a few feet from the rock face. Then they'd lift into a straining soar, their wings making a rushing sound before they disappeared back into the darkness like ghost birds.

Suddenly, Parnell heard two other, deadlier sounds: the cracking of rock followed by the tumbling rustle of pebbles bouncing down the slope. His heart went cold. *Sol just slipped from the cliff face!*

He braced himself. A fraction of a second later the safety line jacked taut, thrumming, as Kaamanui's full weight hit the end of it. The horrendous shock nearly heaved Parnell from his precarious position. His entire body automatically countered it, shoving back hard and holding, *forcing* himself to cling to the rock.

He could feel Sol swinging back and forth at the end of the line, could hear the rattle of larger stones tumbling down the slope. Now and then the weight would ease off slightly as Kaamanui reached the end of his swing and was momentarily nearly weightless. Then it would come on again as he swung back, increasing until he hit the bottom of his arc.

Parnell was growling inside his distended throat, knowing that he couldn't hold on much longer, his arms burning hotter and hotter, his fingers slipping. The line swung far to the right, paused, started back. At that precise moment, the loop of his bowline slipped, snapping, down over his upper right arm. As the line swung back the other way, it twisted a bight around the shoulder. A fiery bolt of pain shot through his right shoulder as Sol's full weight violently wrenched it downward.

He felt something seem to crack and his entire arm went numb, leaving the blast of pain in his neck and upper back. Fighting against it, teeth gritted until they hurt, he still held on, the line swinging, pausing, swinging again, once more fully weighted.

Then it abruptly went completely slack. Kaamanui had regained footholds. Red slumped back against the rock, panting viciously, face drenched in sweat, heart racing wildly. He tired to lift his right arm. He couldn't even feel from the biceps down, the thing hanging loosely at his side.

Sol reached him. Red waved him past, pointed: *go on, go on.* The Samoan shifted the line and crawled past him. Then, by keeping the rope in tight against his chest, he literally pulled Parnell along behind him, both men struggling, fighting the rock. Stabs of white pain kept exploding in Parnell's shoulder and up into the back of his head. It seemed to make his skull palpitate and buzz.

They reached the other side of the tunnel, the others already through, waiting, dark shadows kneeling. Red immediately sat down and began squeezing his shoulder. He felt a peculiar swelling of flesh and bone there, a discordant out-of-placeness. He swore. He'd dislocated his shoulder socket.

Sol and Bird knelt beside him examining the injury. They, too, knew right away what it was. Kaamanui quietly said to him, "We gonna have to pull that back into place, Lieutenant."

"Yeah," Parnell said.

Sol stretched his arm out straight, which missiled another shock of pain into him, along with the peculiar sensation of bone grinding against bone. The feeling made it seem as if he could actually feel the contours of the shoulder's rotator cuff. Next, Kaamanui placed his left foot under Parnell's armpit for leverage. He paused to let Red brace himself, then heaved back on the arm.

Another explosion of pain erupted like incandescent fire. But Red also felt, down under it, the joint snapping back into place. He released his breath. Most of the pain had vanished. He cautiously tried to lift his arm, the area throbbing now. It worked, although still a bit awkwardly. He flexed his right hand. It felt numb, as if his fingers had fallen asleep. He worked them a moment, then pushed himself to his feet and signaled the men to move out again.

Six minutes later, they reached the rim of the cliff. It was 0126.

The ground stretched away into the darkness bristling with lethal things. The team held to the pathway, secure ground. At least for a while. Parnell pushed the faint numbness in his hand out of mind and narrowed down his concentration.

He could feel the others focusing, too, into that familiar energy triggered by the presence of the enemy, right *there* now, the knowledge that the shock of battle and killing was only seconds away creating that mysterious coming together as a single unit. Each man knowing, so automatic now after years of functioning side by side, what was in the others' minds, a certainty of their moves and reactions before they were even performed, communicated through some telepathic magic, now everyone suddenly functioning within the same speed and tempo regime, all of them clicking as one.

Directly ahead, just barely visible, was a line of barbed wire: a single apron system with five-foot poles spaced every ten feet. Thicker accordian wire was spaced between the poles with horizontals running across the anchor wires and tangle-foot tripping wires like broken debris on the ground. The fence curved out of sight, concave-shaped toward the edge of the cliff.

Beyond the wire, back from the rim about fifty yards and faintly silhouetted against the lighter background of the land, were spaced pillboxes and small bunkers, each forming a low dome above ground like the cap of a mushroom. They'd been placed so their weapons could utilize complex fields of fire, both against an enemy coming over the cliff and one approaching from inland.

The rest of the land had been cleared of vegetation to deny cover. It possessed a wet, sweet scent signature like sugarcane, probably from timber sap leaching out of the logs used to build the bunkers. The earth itself was a sandy loam, filled with volcanic gravel and still quite wet from the recent rains. It contained thousands of bits of silica. Their tiny facets were like minute shards of black mirror glass that reflected the star glow, made the ground look like a glittering Liliputian city at their feet.

Parnell slipped forward, keeping to the trail. He reached Bird, squatted. Silently, he motioned for him and Weesay to scout. The two men moved forward along the path. In an instant, they were swallowed by the darkness.

Now among the enemy, Wyatt had lead off, the best scout in the team. He moved very close to the ground, going slowly as he approached the ege of the barbed wire. He knew soldiers in a defensive position often laid trip wires along used pathways, placing the traps after dark and then retrieving them once it became light.

As he progressed, he kept moving his head from side to side in a slightly circular motion, peering out from the sides of his eyes to pick out light from a continually changing perspective. *There!* He'd just spotted a tiny flick of reflected light, like the quick flash in a person's eyes just after getting clocked with a fist.

He slowly scanned to the left, back to the right, and saw the shape of a piece of bamboo staked into the ground beside the path. He reached out and gently ran his hand along it, felt three wire loops protruding from the side. He grunted. These were the suspension, safety, and support stays for a grenade booby trap.

He examined the thing with his fingertips and then disgustedly shook his head. Tricky, this one. There was no way he could disarm the unit without triggering the grenade's fuse. He leaned back and drew out a strip of yellow cloth from his tunic pocket and marked the trip wire, tying it very gently.

He turned to touch Weesay's shoulder, pointed at the knot. Laguna nodded. For a moment, Wyatt's stare lingered on his companion, the camo paint exaggerating the hollow blackness of his eye sockets. Weesay had been unusually quiet since the card game. But, as Bird stared, he seemed to be all right, once more fixed into that calm tenseness of a veteran.

He swung back, lightly stepped over the marked trip wire, and continued along the path. Soon, he reached the edge of the barbed-wire apron and paused again. It stretched across the path, loosely secured. That meant it was obviously opened each day and then rehooked each night.

He bent very close to examine it. He could smell the rusted metal, could make out its pattern, immediately seeing that the whole thing was scant and had been sloppily set up. Couldn't hold a goddamned candle to those complex patterns of Kraut wire he'd encountered back in Europe, he thought.

Frankie Trota had been right about Jap wire. He'd told him they rarely constructed barbed-wire lines in the islands because the Nip army was essentially an offensive one, and also because Japan was never able to supply its outlying troops with adequate rolled steel.

Wyatt felt over the ground until he found a tuft of grass. He broke off a reed, moistened it with his saliva, and touched it to the bottom wire strand to test for electricity. There was neither spark nor buzz. He reached out and checked the next horizontal, then the third, and finally the bracing wire and loop of concertina.

Still nothing.

He quickly cut the apron and concertina wires, and he and Laguna moved through. They stopped to listen on the far side. Here, the ground had been freshly dug up, like a field after spring plowing, the soil lumpy and wet. It was littered with worms that had come to the surface for the night's air and moisture. When he stepped on them, they gave off an odor like turpentine.

A quick thought shot through his mind: *snakes*. He drew back his lips, showing teeth, an old habit when combat was near. Then he spat, a soft hiss. *Fuck the gawddamn snakes*.

He heard the faint sound of machinery from somewhere and picked up the odor of cut wood, the damp, faintly rotted smell of sandbags, and even the soft scent of Japanese machine-gun oil in those moments when the sea breeze died.

They crossed the bunker line between two pillboxes that were spaced about sixty yards apart, watching for odd indentations in the earth, signs that antipersonnel mines were below. They didn't find any.

Again, Bird wasn't totally surprised. Frankie had also instructed him about how the Japs disliked using ground mines. All except the big Model 96 antitank bomb, which had distinctive lead pressure horns and electrolytic fluid fuses. But he knew such mines would not be in this kind of terrain, nor would the simple weight of a man trigger one.

They struck a zigzag trench with the edge banked with sandbags. It was three feet deep and had tin sheeting staked along the walls to keep the sides from caving in. There were slats of wood on the bottom, and telephone wire was tacked with U clips into the far side wall.

Lying flat on the upper ground, they watched and listened. Several minutes passed. Nothing moved. Finally, Bird crawled over the sandbags and dropped lightly down into the trench, Weesay right behind him. The floor slats were also covered with worms. Stepping gently, toe-to-heel as if traversing jungle, they moved northward.

The ditch cut back and forth, the wooden slats made of bamboo halves that felt spongy under their feet and squeaked softly. They passed three side ditches, very narrow and obviously leading out to individual one- and two-man foxholes that had been positioned behind the bunker line in order to cover any dead zones in their fields of fire.

A noise. It was out of place, a muffled clacking. Quickly, both men slipped up and back over the sandbags and went flat to the ground. As they lay there, the thunderlike rumble and flashes of an artillery barrage suddenly opened up east of them: Japanese 75mm pack howitzers and 105mm field guns discharging along the Shuri Line. Almost immediately came American counterbattery fire, the deep-throated reports from M1A1 155mm mountain howitzers.

A Jap soldier appeared in the ditch, walking with his head up, watching the artillery display. He carried no weapons and wasn't even wearing shoes, only wooden clogs that had created the racket on the bamboo slats they'd heard before the barrage.

Each time a new artillery salvo-stream cut loose, or a series of impacts came, the entire area would be lit up for a few seconds, exposing the two Americans hugging the ground out there in the open. But the Nip soldier was too preoccupied with the fireworks to notice. So, they watched him pass, less than four feet from the trench, the flashes etching his round, Oriental face with bursts of light.

They moved back a few yards and waited. Several minutes went by. At last, the Jap soldier came back, this time carrying a small can that seeped steam, probably tea, him and a buddy on guard mount getting thirsty. The artillery exchange was still going as they checked him past, hearing the sounds of his clogs down under the thunder of the guns slowly fading away.

Bird checked his watch: 0239. *Time to move.*

They reentered the trench and continued north. The sound of blowers grew stronger. Two minutes later, the trench abruptly became a small crawl tunnel. It was formed of a line of oil drums with their bottoms cut out and dirt piled onto the tops. Wyatt peered into the darkness, listened, then quickly slipped inside.

It was twenty feet long, slanted slightly with sand on the bottom that scraped loudly under his knees. The drum stank of fuel oil and Japanese soldier body odor, an acidic scent like vinegar. The tunnel opened onto a set of stairs that went down into the ground. It was an entry port into the coastal gun redoubt. There were no lights on the stairs, yet a faint, bluish illumination faintly tinted the lower steps, coming from deeper in the structure.

Stealthily, Bird studied the stairwell, the cement archway above it, and the dirt and sandbags along both sides. There didn't appear to be a sentry anywhere. He finally turned and made a clicking sound with his tongue, twice. In a moment, Laguna was behind him. They continued observing quietly for a few more minutes.

Finally, Wyatt placed his palm on Weesay's arm, *wait*, moved from the tunnel, and quickly slipped down the stairs. The risers were high and made of chiseled stone. The walls and face had cracked holes and showed that the archway had been made of layers of coral stone and steel bars and then covered by two-foot-thick coats of cement.

Ten steps beyond the arch was a platform, then another set of stairs leading farther down and to the left. He followed it. The air quickly turned thick, heavy with a feces odor like uncleaned toilets. At the bottom, he found a direct-fire and blast barrier that ran from wall to wall except for a narrow squeeze space at one end. The wall was two feet thick and had rebar tips protruding from its inner side. Five feet beyond was a second DFB barrier.

He cautiously looked through the second squeeze-way. A larger tunnel continued deeper into the rock, fading off into darkness. It was barely five feet high, with a domed ceiling and lined with small blue lights spaced far apart in the overhead. There were old drill marks in the walls and explosion burns that looked like splashes of charcoal dust in the pale blue light.

Wyatt returned to Laguna. The earlier barrage fire had tapered off, now only occasional, almost inaudible bursts of heavy machine-gun fire far out. He signaled Laguna to turn back. Within six minutes, they were back at the outer perimeter fence.

Wyatt squatted and took out his tunic light. Holding its lens cupped by his fingers so that it was visible only from directly ahead, he flashed twice, paused, flashed twice again: *come ahead.*

A minute later, Sol loomed out of the darkness, behind him the rest of Blue Team, coming in.

An hour earlier, signal lights had begun blinking aboard Admiral Turner's flagship *Eldorado,* holding station in the midst of the vast invasion armada that lay off the west coast of Okinawa-Shima. Soon, specific ships within the fleet began turning out of their assigned watch positions to head southward, toward assembly areas ten miles north-northeast of the entry to Naha Channel.

In the vanguard were the vessels from TG 52.7 Reserve Motor Minesweepers Group. Following them came the big gunships of TF 51.3's Bombardment Force, designated Two Tak: six battleships and five heavy cruisers along with their screening destroyers and frigate escorts of Destroyer Division 120.

Next came the ships of TG 52.1 Support Carrier Force under Rear Admiral C.T. Duryin. These had been drawn from TF 51 Amphibious Support Force and included the escort carriers CVE *Makin Island, Fanshaw Bay, Lunga Point,* and *Natoma Bay,* whose aircraft would provide air cover for the barrage ships.

Directly behind these were seven more escort carriers, the *Laguna Point, Saginau Bay, Sargeant Bay, Marcus Island, Rudyerd Bay, Tulagi,* and *Wake Island.* Flights from these vessels were to launch air strikes against the enemy land targets just prior to the beginning of the bombardment.

Both carrier groups were being screened by thirty-five destroyers and frigates from Destroyer Division 91.

By 0158 hours, the leading minesweeper flotilla ships prepared to launch trailing gear in the approaches to Naha Harbor. Meanwhile, the bombardment ships had already reached their assembly point farther north and were now positioning themselves into barrage steaming formation. Once this was achieved, they would all swing into big 360s, holding until the order to initiate entry into the channel came.

Aboard the air-strike CVEs, Ready Rooms were already alive with early briefings, pilots going over short-term weather forecasts, flight in-and-out plots, air maps, and updated intelligence on how much AA fire and enemy fighter intercepts they might encounter over their secondary targets of the Naha Harbor wharf facilities and the airfields at Naha Ichi and Oroku south and southeast of the harbor, and their primary targets, the Japanese positions along the Shuri Line.

Below in hangar decks, F6F-5 Corsairs, F4U-1D Wildcats, and SB2C Helldivers were being given their last-minute engine checks in preparation for the call to bring them to the flight deck for spotting and arming.

On Okinawa itself, forward elements of the U.S. XXIV Corps' 96th Infantry Division, drawn up in a static line for the last two days, had begun dispatching patrols to probe the ground just below the enemy bunkers on the Shuri. Accompanying each patrol were two FOs or forward observers, officers, and senior noncoms from the First Marine Division. They'd be calling in the naval fire and relaying damage assessments.

For the last thirty-six hours, the Japanese, using artillery units from the crack 62nd Division and the 63rd Brigade, had been sending over periodic harassing fire, right down onto the 96th's line troops stretched out below them on the Yonabaru Plain, a barren landscape with little vegetation. This made it a deadly business for anything moving there, even in darkness. Often, the Nip artillery and grazing machine-gun fire would catch patrols and companies, forced to shift, out in the open.

But by 0230 hours, many of the probing patrols had settled into observation positions facing the Shuri. Some were less than two hundred yards from the enemy artillery entrenchments, the big guns hidden behind escarpments with only their muzzle flashes and smoke rings blowing from the embrasures visible for a flashing second. Now these advance patrols silently waited for daylight.

Lieutenant Sacabe had watched the spider for twenty minutes. Fascinated, he lay on his straw *shindai* in his cell-like sleeping quarters located on the second level of the battery mount. The room was cold, a stone cold like a sepulcher. The rock walls were padded with asbestos sheets, and the room itself was stark, containing little furniture: his sleeping pad, a low, floor-desk, a sitting tatami, a single lightbulb strung from the rock ceiling, and a portable *toire*, or toilet, made of *matsu* wood with a canvas bag that was emptied each morning by his orderly.

The spider was brown with reddish eyes. It was called a *nameru*, because it devoured its victims by sucking out their intestines. The insect had worked rapidly and efficiently spinning a web, an intricate orb with perfectly symmetrical spirals and cross spokes. As the last stitch, it now strung out a vibration thread that would signal it whenever prey became entangled.

Sacabe beheld the completed structure. It crossed a corner, a meter wide, the silken threads sparkling in the light as the current from the air vent made it shift and sway slightly. The Japanese believe a spider's actions can foretell the future. So the lieutenant had observed this one with particular intensity, the thing continually performing a singularly unusual move. Whenever it completed a spiral, it would always return to the central orb or nest cluster.

As if it were its home.

Earlier, before observing the spider, Sacabe had
abruptly awakened out of a dream. He looked at his clock.
It was exactly three o'clock in the morning. He felt a cold
chill: the Hour of the Monkey, a death omen.

The dream itself had been of samurai, dark figures on
horseback moving through a moon-shadowy landscape in
deadly slow motion, only their plumed helmets and leather
curissas and pike points catching stray moonbeams, their
horses snorting frost smoke. In the far distance, he could
see a many-roofed *shiro*, a castle, pinioned in full moonlight. All else was clothed in moon-dappled purple, the
color of mourning. In the dream, he had wept with a
strange mixture of sorrow and ecstasy.

As he brooded, it now all became clear to him: the far-
off castle, the samurai astride their warhorses, the spider's
return to its hub, the Hour of the Monkey, all of it combining to summon a portent of what lay ahead. A homecoming,
his homecoming, back to the beginnings of himself, of his
essence.

He was about to die.

As this realization engulfed him, he felt a surge of heat,
like a fire on a freezing day, like the sweet, roiling release
of orgasm. He stared up at the web. His mind basked in
the warmth, floated on a sudden peacefulness. There was
neither terror nor retreat, only the tranquility of *oyomei
gaku*, the magnificent light of *giri* and *on*, duty and obligation, for which he had prepared himself.

At last, he rose and quickly dressed in the coldness of
the stone room. Then he stepped out into the main gallery
of the battery casement. It was silent save for the whir of
the air blowers, and a peculiar hum, so faint it might not
have actually been sound at all, seeping from the stone
walls.

This particular *kageki chikujo* had been built in 1927. It
was composed of three stories, all large chambers dug or
blown from the sheer rock of the cliff face. Connecting the

individual levels were vertical tunnels and horizontal shafts with rope ladders or rock or steel steps. Many single-man tunnels reinforced with steel oil drums led directly to the outside where machine-gun and rifle ports allowed crossing fields of fire against ground enemies.

The second level contained the main firing room with its two huge 240mm or eight-inch coastal guns mounted on individual rail trucks. Directly above the gun gallery was the ranging-and-sighting room with twin two-meter-base H&R rangefinders and a Model 115 computing director, which calculated target/trajectory convergence and windage, and computed the types and loads of the rounds. These were then brought up from the powder magazine, which lay far below on the third level. Over the ranging-and-sighting room was a smaller gun gallery with a dual-mounted, rapid-firing 40mm AA/AT auto cannon.

All the rooms and galleries had ceiling support posts of dense ironwood or *casuarina* timbers and stringers bound with steel staples. The gun ports or embrasures were also extremely thick-walled, eight feet of reinforced cement, back-packed with four feet of sand. Huge sliding doors called *ni kagi o kakeru* were four feet thick, made of rolled carbon-tempered steel sheets that sandwiched together layers of cement. The entire face of the gun mount could actually withstand indirect big-bore AP and HE fire, and direct siege artillery up to 175mm.

The inner walls continually exuded moisture from the porous igneous rock of the cliffs. This runout drained into shallow troughs in the slanted floors and was pumped out. But they always smelled foul, like sewers, the odor pervading the whole installation. Because of the constant moisture, all exposed metal was usually rusty, and the walls were disfigured with fungus colonies and the green stains from dissolved olivine veins that webbed the shaft faces.

Within the big structure were also barracks, a radio room, mess quarters, supply compartments, water tanks, and repair shops. The Tokubetsu Konkyochitai, or Special Naval Force Marine contingent, that manned the gun mount totaled forty-eight men, not including Lieutenant Sacabe and his second-in-command, Ensign Gunichi Fusata, a slender man but a savage fighter, and his burly chief warrant officer, Yoshige Ugaki.

Still in his mood of quietude, he now wandered about looking at things, listening to sounds, inhaling the foul air, which was thickened even more by the odors of en-closed humans and the fartlike pungency of their pickled diet.

Yet, he was aware that the stillness was also rife with specters, invisible thunderheads that lent augury. In his mind, images shifted, from delicate *tokonatsu* blossoms in moonlight a-sparkle with dew, to the memories of child-hood persimmon cakes, to the sound of the fragile pluck of a zithern in an autumn mood.

These then clashed with the darker but sweeter thoughts of the violence of war, and the exquisite, groin-aching sense of soldierhood and honor and death, all mantled in Bushido splendor.

He entered the main gun casement. Ensign Fusata had the night gun watch. On seeing his battery commander, he shouted and everyone braced in their tropical white cotton shirts and half breeches, their Naval Landing Force anchor badges on the fronts of their helmets. All were members of the Third Special Base Force from the Sixth Yokosuka SNLF, many very young replacements.

Sacabe continued to stroll about, contemplating things, touching the weapons and the cold brass of rounds stacked in their ready ammo racks. The two big guns were spotless, gleaming in the overhead light, British Model 38 Coastal Vickers cast in the midtwenties, their barrels eigh-teen feet long and a deep blue black that held filmy temper patterns like brown smoke impressed into the metal.

Each had interrupted thread breech blocks and hydropneumatic recoil systems encased in two cylinders directly above the barrel stem. The breech itself was connected to an electric firing panel that received targeting data from the ranging directors. The guns' field of fire could cover a seventy-seven-degree traverse arc and a forty-three-degree elevation/deflection angle, and when operated by a good four-man crew, it could launch eight two-hundred-pound AP or HE rounds per minute before being retracted behind its blast gates.

He paused beside Fusata. "How is everything?" he asked.

"Excellent, *Chui-san*. We have just completed an SSN." The initials stood for *Shimyureto Suru Ni* or Simulated Firing 2.

"Good." He turned, gazed into the ensign's eyes. "They are coming, Gunichi. Very soon."

"*Hai, Chui-san*." Fusata allowed a tiny smile to touch the edge of his lips. "It will be pleasant destroying them."

"Are you prepared to die?"

"Of course, my Lieutenant. That will be an even *more* gallant pleasure."

Sacabe nodded, pleased. "*Hai*," he said.

Turning, he climbed the spiral staircase that led up to the targeting room. From there, he gazed out through its viewing ports, only a deep blackness out there with stars like silver pinheads. Afterward, he descended all the way down to the powder magazine and walked among the wooden crates of rounds, listening to the rats scurrying in the shadows.

He was inspecting the mess quarters when a radio runner found him, the *senin-no,* or second seaman, snapping stiffly to attention before reporting. "Sir, we have just received an alert message from Shimaikomu." *Shimaikomu* meant "lock away," the code name for the *tsushin-rentai,* the signal regiment of Admiral Ota's headquarters at Tomi-gusuki, a suburb of Naha. He handed the lieutenant a teletype sheet.

It was yellow and the teletype keys were worn and made faint impressions. It read:

TT/0202//Z400:CC-3

From: Command Section (TE-L3)
2nd S/T Regiment
To: all units

Attention: double red alert . . . large enemy flotilla nnw
coordinates 1375-0798 . . .
have commenced minesweeping operations . . . attack/
landings imminent
Coordinates 1244 thru 1123 . . .
Initiate plan orange 4 . . .
Our beloved Emperor expects each man to do his duty. . . .
Acknowledge code zx-33

LOG: ////333
TE-L3
Shosa KK Yoshiga

Sacabe read it twice, his mind clicking, saying: *They are here.* Nearly trembling with anticipation, he broke into a run, the radio runner following close behind. Forty-three seconds later, the rasping surge of the alert horn came, echoing and reechoing through the galleries and shafts and tunnels of Coastal Mount 4.

It was 0340 hours.

Chapter Twenty

Once more flashing signal lights began transmitting command orders throughout the ships of the American air strike and cover groups. Immediately, all eleven CVE carriers began turning into the wind. Up went their battle pennants and the twin black balls that signified launching operations were now in effect.

At precisely 0350 hours, each carrier deck became a scene of organized chaos amid the thundering roar of engines and the blowing, booming slam of catapults as plane after plane was hurled forward to lift up into the night sky, their exhausts throwing back tongues of orange fire.

Once aloft, the aircraft quickly assembled into their designated mission groups, the air crackling and alive with radio cross talk as flight leaders positioned their planes into the staggered altitude layers assigned for their specific targets. Those from the four air-cover carriers, however, immediately climbed to fifteen thousand feet and formed up into a standard umbrella overwatch with flanker aircraft swinging far out along the periphery.

But they weren't the only force preparing for air engagement. On secret aprons of the Naha Ichi and Oroku Ichi Airfields, volunteer Japanese pilots of the 951st Air Group, a Kamikaze or Tokko Special Attack Force, were already assembled at rigid attention for their farewell ceremony before takeoff. Beyond them in the darkness and brisk sea wind, their Zeros and Mitsubishi G4M "Betty" twin-engine bombers with their loads of MXY-7 manned rocket-propelled bombs called Bakas sat waiting, their engines warmed and their bays and wing brackets armed with high explosives.

By this point in the war, there were very few tactical Japanese air units still on Okinawa, primarily only remnant squadrons of the Sixth Air Army and the Imperial Japanese Navy Air Force. Then in late February, most of these were withdrawn to Kyushu and Formosa, to be consolidated into the First Air Army under the single command of Admiral Soemu Fukanaga.

Its new mission, code-named Operation Ten-Go, involved conventional massed air strikes against enemy naval targets south and southwest of the main Japanese islands. Also included were kamikaze attacks, code-named *Kikusui*, which meant *floating chrysanthemums*.

Only four Tokko AAF squadrons had been left on Okinawa, at secret fields primarily in the south. Now two of them prepared to engage the incoming allied ships. Braced, the pilots in their flight suits and goggles with their *meiyoshi* or suicide scarves around their throats listened intently to the closing words of their individual base commanders who, for the last time, whipped them into a frenzy of patriotic excitement.

Each would then be given a glass of sake. After drinking the rice wine, he'd break the glass and stomp the shards into the gravel with his flight boots, a symbol that he would not be returning. The assemblage would then shout three "banzais" with their arms raised in salutation like Roman gladiators. Some, so caught up with emotion, would openly weep with gratitude to have been chosen to carry out this sacred mission for emperor and motherland.

At a final command, the pilots would sprint to their air-

crafts, singing an ancient samurai battle chant. Within
minutes, the *Kikusui* leaders would begin their rollout,
their engines gunning up and cracking open the silence.
Once aloft, the entire contingent of eighty aircraft would
assemble into separate attack groups at eight thousand feet
over Naha Harbor and turn northwest.

The Jap gun entrenchment stank like dog shit, the odor
seeming to come out of the stone walls, seep through the
overheads. Blue Team had been moving through the
humid, smelly air ignoring it, focusing instead on sounds:
the burring hum of air blowers, some other, unidentifi-
able machinery, everything exaggerated by the stone
enclosure. . . .

It had taken them very little time coming through the
wire and bunker line. They reached the zigzag trench and
then the crawl tunnel before the gun casement's entry
point at 0340. Since all the assaults on the four batteries
were to be coordinated and carried out at the same time,
0345 hours, they still had over five minutes to kill.

Parnell huddled with Wyatt and Sol and went over the
lithograph of the interior of the Jap gun emplacement, pin-
pointing where they were and what they could expect
inside. Apparently, this entry point was one of six, this one
facing south. There were only two large openings, the
others merely ladder shafts to the top of the entrenchment.

The lithograph showed that at the end of the corridor
Bird had explored was a machinery room that contained
the air blowers. Directly below it was a machine shop for
manufacturing and milling, a supply warehouse, the main
powder magazine, and a stairway running down to them
on the third level.

On the same level as the machinery room but deeper
into the installation were located the crew's sleeping quarters and mess, a radio room, and the senior officers'

quarters along with water tanks. Close to the commander's room was the back entrance to the main gun compartment. Its schematic showed shell hoists to the magazine, ready ammo racks, and firing computers.

Above the main gun room, in a sort of half-level, was the ranging-and-targeting space from which the gun directors below received their shoot-data. This area was small and contained radio consoles, height-and-range finders, target-speed and course-angle calculating gear, temperature and wind-correction scales, and big, double Model 89 10cm spotting binoculars. Directly above *it* was an even smaller space containing a 47mm rapid-fire Bofor-like weapon.

The three men went meticulously over their Insert and Attack procedure, whispering close to each other just outside the crawl tunnel and using their cupped tunic lights. They again spotted a lucky advantage. According to the lithograph, the entry tunnel they would use ran to a corridor intersection just outside the main firing room. Most of the other crew rooms and machinery spaces were at least seventy-five yards from it.

If they could reach the gun room without being discovered and take out the on-duty watch crew, they might be able to set up their timed demo charges on the gun breeches and actually exit the installation before anybody even knew an enemy had penetrated the casement at all.

They also knew there were a helluva lot of ifs in that scenario.

One last watch check showed 0345. Forming a single line, the team penetrated the entryway and quickly passed beyond the explosion walls. There they paused, everyone watching Parnell. He gave the search-and-kill hand signal, a palm-down cut, then a chop into the other palm.

Silently, swiftly the men had moved forward up the dark corridor, the blue overhead lights reflecting off the tiny facets of silicates in the walls. They looked like tiny diamonds in a cave. Bird was on point, then came Smoker and Weesay as flankers, and Parnell, followed by Sol and Laguna on drag, all in bounding overwatch formation, thirty feet apart except for Wyatt, who was fifteen yards out front. . . .

They were a quarter of the way in when the Jap alert gongs and buzzers went off. It was as if a wave of electricity had just charged the air around them, energy rolling past. They'd been discovered! Everybody hit the stone floor, weapons focused ahead and to the rear.

Shouting Japanese voices echoed under the raucous sounds, the tramp of boots, the slam of metal doors. After a moment, Parnell came to his feet and dashed forward, bent over and moving lightly, soundlessly. He dropped beside Wyatt.

They listened intently, watching the head of the corridor, a semidarkness study in blue. The alert noise continued. They could feel its vibrations coming through the stone, which gave the rebound a peculiar hollow tone. Twenty seconds passed . . . thirty . . .

Parnell said, "I don't think it's us."

Wyatt nodded. His eyelids were slits, deep inside his dark eyes, both catching the blue light and glinting oddly. "Sounds to me like jes' a gen'ral alert. They musta spotted them incoming navy ships."

"Damn it," Red said softly. He considered. His heart was banging away in his chest, not fully backed off over the Jap alert. Should they pull back and wait, come in a little later? Or go ahead, breach the gun room before the Nip crews got set up? No choice, no choice.

He tapped Wyatt's arm. "We hit 'em."

Bird nodded, rose to one knee, Parnell, too, looking back. The others were only dark, blue-etched shadows on the stone floor back there, their weapon barrels making blue reflections. He held up his hand, flat, made a cutting motion: *continue SOP.*

* * *

Sacabe was glassing out the main gun mount's embrasure, a three-by-ten-foot-wide port directly in front of the big gun rails. It had cobwebs in the corners, the thing cut out of stone and now coated with salt. A cool ocean breeze ruffled the collars of his white shirt.

From behind him came the steady whine of the chains in the shell hoist, which was now bringing up fresh ammunition: long, two-hundred-pound AP and HE rounds capable of punching through ship armament up to heavy cruiser class, and battleship main and secondary turret armor. The gun's loading crew stood, waiting for the hoist platform to halt so they could grip the shells with block and tackle gear and then swing them to the ready shelves. They all wore black coveralls with hoods and flash goggles.

They worked efficiently, no wasted motion, the slam and clank of the hoists and tackle gear filling the big stone room. Like the embrasure, the room itself had been blasted out of solid rock. It was 150 feet deep, sixty wide.

The walls contained timbers blocked and then covered with liquid cement, which would produce a flexible concussion-proof bulkhead. The surface was then packed in asbestos padding to prevent leakage, the padding encased in thin aluminum sheeting, which made the entire compartment look as if it were constructed of stainless steel.

The twin rail tracks ran from the embrasure to the back of the firing room, each end with bumper stops made of two-by-six ironwood timbers. The guns were pedestal mounted, their barrels eighteen feet long with two sleeve seams. To compensate for the barrel length, there were equilibrators built into the pedestal, and each gun was moved forward and backward on its rails powered by a cable-and-pneumatic drum system.

A radioman now approached Sacabe with a second radio message. He braced, handed it over. The lieutenant scanned it, going right for the core. *Ni-ki ga tsuite iru . . . red back . . . all coastal mounts unr enmy raid-frce attack . . . ppare agnst insertion attempt . . . reinforce disptchd . . . excute stan yellow/orange 3 (Pos assign 3400mm/Z code).*

Sacabe smiled. *Now they come to me.* He began barking orders, everything going into total lockdown, bellowing to his telephone talker to alert all noncoms that enemy raiders might attempt to penetrate the entrenchment and that they were to reposition their men into a defensive perimeter to protect the main gun and magazine compartments.

From beyond the room's steel doors suddenly came the single crack of an Arisaka rifle. Sacabe's head snapped around and every man in the firing room froze. There was a slight pause, then everyone was moving again, the lieutenant himself bounding for the door.

As he reached to slide back the door's retaining arm, there was another Arisaka muzzle burst. A third. This last seemed to draw into its fading pulse the quick, staccato hammer of an *American* automatic weapon. It sounded deep and rich compared to the other.

They are here!

Bird had run into two Jap marines at the junction of the main corridor and a small, secondary gallery, the Nips just there, coming into sight running, one with a rifle, the other with a Model 96 light machine gun, which he carried by the handle. Fortunately, it didn't have a clip inserted.

All three men stopped dead still and stared, shocked, at each other in the blue light. In the silence, the steady whirring of the blowers suddenly changed pitch, going up in sound, the things automatically adjusting to the increased volume of polluted air coming from all the sudden activity throughout the installation.

Wyatt was the first to move. He sprang forward, his hand dropping to pull his belt knife. His lunge carried him across the six feet between him and the Nips. Then the soldiers were also moving, the rifleman swinging up the muzzle and his right hand rolling the bolt open and back, bringing up a round, then jamming it forward again. In the intense stillness, it made a sharp, hard crack.

Before he could fire, Bird slashed out with his knife, a sweeping horizontal backhand cut. It sliced right across the Jap's eyes. Clear fluid and then blood spurted from both eyeballs as the Nip gasped, a shuddering inhalation. He threw up his hands and his body fell back against the wall. But he didn't scream.

Instantly shifting his own weight, Wyatt reversed his swing, rotating the knife handle, and came back along the same attack line to cut the wounded Jap's carotid. This time the blood *blew* out and onto his jumpsuit. The man's rifle clattered to the floor. As it hit, it fired off. The blast exploded loudly through the confined corridor as the bullet slammed into the ceiling and ricocheted off, sounding like a wounded puppy.

By now, the second Nip marine had abandoned his empty machine gun and immediately engaged Bird with his bayonet, the thing first sliding hollowly, metallically from its sheath as the man's round Oriental face went stiff and pale and fixed in the blue shadows.

Wyatt swung around to face him and the two circled in that silent, deadly dance of mortal combat. Bird still held his Thompson in his left hand, up in high parry position. Despite the rifle firing off, he still didn't want to use his weapon. The Japs would instantly identify it as enemy. Hopefully, they might have thought the rifle shot had merely been an accidental discharge.

The only sound was the soft shuffling of their shoes on the floor and the hiss of air exiting their nostrils. The Nip lunged, his arm extended full out. Wyatt parried the bayonet with the barrel of his weapon. It made the high ting of steel on steel. He started an underarm attack but the Jap recovered too swiftly.

They continued circling, Wyatt grinning an icy smile at his opponent now, his teeth terribly white in his black, grease-smeared face. For the next fourteen seconds, each moment seeming isolated, an eternity unto itself, they lunged and parried and reset, only to lunge again.

The Jap was very fast, moving the tip of his bayonet in front of his body, back and forth, like a man scything weeds. Bird watched it, right, left, gauging the timing. Suddenly, dropping low, he drove forward, moving in under the protective shield of his Thompson.

The Jap countered quickly, swinging his bayonet back before it had completed its arc. The slightly mistimed movement threw him off balance. As he recovered, Wyatt slashed out, his knife opening the Jap's left forearm.

There was another moment of mutual quick movement and the two men merged, grappling, slicing at each other. Blood flew off the Jap's wounded arm. His bayonet cut into Bird's shoulder, a sting only, an instant of hotness, then gone.

As the Nip pulled his arm back, Wyatt came up under it with his weapon. Twisting the Thompson, he slammed the barrel into the marine's forehead. The shock threw the man's head backward, exposing his throat. Bird put his knife up to the guard into it, twisted and cut, slicing until the blade was free.

Silently the man dropped like a slab of lead.

Wyatt inhaled, straightened. His head buzzed with blood. He reached around to explore his wound. A Jap rifle went off. He felt the bullet strike the back of his left thigh, violently hard, as if someone had just hit him with a pipe. He actually felt the slug pass through his tissue and exit from the front of his thigh. It blew open his coverall trousers, the cloth opening like a flower petal that spewed tissue.

He heard another Arisaka shot. *Tinny-soundin' sumbitch.*
The bullet whipped by, not close. He didn't care. There
was another Jap round. Then came the quick, throaty *thru-
uuuup* of a Greasegun, bullets slapping through the air
over his head, himself falling down toward the stone floor
and his head buzzing, with a powerful burst of dizziness.
He hit the floor hard and lay there crookedly.

The dizziness vanished. In its place came a feeling that
his skin was shaking. No, it was the floor, very faint,
tremulous. He heard a distant rumbling, and then the
sharper cracks of things exploding far away.

They had come in extremely low, skimming the ocean
to avoid the Japanese radar, the attack flights from the
American carrier force over the dark sea so close the back-
wash of their props sent up a mist that made the stars
shimmer.

After assembling high over their separate ships, the four
main attack squadrons designated by their target code references, X, Y-1, Y-2, and Z, had headed inland, each on a
different heading. X Target was the Naha Harbor itself. Y-
1 and Y-2 referred to the double airfield strikes southeast
of Naha. The last, and perhaps tactically most important,
was Z Target, the positions along the Shuri Line.

The total number of aircraft involved was ninety-two:
twenty-three four-man flights, each with its own flight
leader and call sign. The flights were then assigned to their
individual target ASs or Attack Squadrons. For this particular operation, itself coded Quad Red, each AS was then
referred to as Q Red followed by the call sign of its AL or
attack leader.

X Target squadron was first to make landfall, the great
bulk of Okinawa-Shima looming up out of the star-scat-
tered darkness. Its AL was Commander Jerome "Jazz"
Delahousse.

He immediately keyed his radio, called, "Q Red Lancer One, break, break." Now, the entire AS broke into its separate flights, flaring, the flights themselves falling into staggered echelons.

By then, Delahousse and his three flight mates had already crossed over the causeway that linked Naha with the Oroku Peninsula and were swinging wide turns over the two-mile-long inner loch of Naha Harbor.

From each aircraft now dropped two flares, the combined illumination covering the entire harbor and its extensive loch system in brilliant white light. In it, the incoming attack planes looked pale, like children's models hung on threads, their props creating whirling light ghosts as they pulled up, turning, and then started back for their initial strafing and bombing runs.

The air was now alive with radio cross talk, pilots shouting, calling out info: "Q Red Pieman Three, ship cluster starboard two clicks." "Triple fuel tanks eleven o'clock." "Stallion Two, watch it, watch it! Ack-ack dead ahead."

The Japanese machine-gun counterfire sent tracers skyward, peculiar bluish green balls of light that sailed leisurely upward, while the AA fire made sudden bursts of red and green and blue light, their debris showering down like curling, smoking confetti.

Again the echelons of aircraft came sweeping back across the target field, still looking like toy planes under carnival lights, their .50-caliber wing guns and 20mm nose cannons banging away now and trailing lines of dark smoke.

Bombs began tumbling away from them, somersaulting for a few seconds and then hitting, making dust scars in the land and hurling water geysers among the lochs, the things on delayed fuses so they wouldn't explode too quickly and take out the delivery aircraft. The explosions came with that shocking suddenness and outburst of energy, expanding in a flashing, widening circle amid the fleeting moment of light and deep, rolling, sundering sound of HE ordnance.

But missed by the attacking aircraft, a convoy of eight trucks had just crossed the causeway between the Naha lochs and the upper part of the Oroku Peninsula. Aboard was a double company, 243 men, from the Japanese 44th Mobile Infantry Brigade, which had been ordered to engage a reported enemy insertion force at the four coastal batteries that guarded the approaches to the Naha Channel.

Things were coming very swiftly now, the sound of more Jap soldiers converging on the firefight, the sounds of bombs and ack-ack fire coming faintly through the stone walls, the even fainter roar of aircraft.

Parnell had come up just in time to see Smoker cutting loose with his Greasegun, standing over someone down— *Oh, Christ*—firing at two Nip soldiers kneeling inside a dark side alley, already engaging. He focused on the downed man, a dark shape on the floor. He rushed to him, knelt. It was Wyatt. He turned and looked at Parnell, his eyes full of blue rage.

"Bad?" Red asked tightly.

"Through and through."

Smoker came up, then Weesay, pausing for a fraction of a second to make certain Wyatt was all right, then sprinting on, going for the two dead Japs' position, to cover that alleyway and the gallery above it.

"Where?"

"Left leg. *Goddammit!*"

Parnell was already cutting away Bird's trousers, exposing the wound. The front of the thigh had been ripped open, a jagged gash, the sides flapping, globular with fatty tissue, blood black as ink dripping. He unwound his battle scarf and quickly formed a battle tourniquet, asking, "Can you move the leg?"

"Hell yes." Bird waited till the lieutenant had bound and tied the wound; then he forced himself to his feet. He took a step, limping, turned, and looked at Red. "Let's finish it, sir."

Parnell eyed him for a moment, noting that Bird was still a little shaky. Then he saw the rage come again into the man's eyes, deep and cold and hard, and Bird putting those killer eyes on him now and saying, "That gawddamn *lith*-o-graph was dead wrong, Lieutenant. Things ain't where they supposed to be."

Red examined the situation, his mind working at ultra-high speed, clicking through estimates, possibilities, positions. *Shit, shit!* The volume of noise was increasing, Jap voices yelling, the tumble and rumble of wheeled weapons, the whole goddamned gun mount forming to counter them.

He turned, looked back down the corridor, Sol and Cowboy back there on one knee, holding position, securing their rear. Up the other way Laguna and Wineberg were at the corner of the intersection, their heads and gun muzzles swinging, checking high and low space. After a moment, Smoker took a wire from his jacket and began to lay a booby trap in the intersection.

We gotta hit 'em fast, Parnell decided, *right into the gun mount.*

Then again, what if it isn't where the lithograph says it is? He scanned, nothing but dark walls and blue light and the hard solid shadows of his men, their heads turned, waiting. *Okay, think, think.* The mount *had* to be on the cliff side, *that* way. The picture says the mount's at the end of this corridor. Same way. Or is it? No goddamned time to sort things out. *Gotta move!*

He whistled, twirled his hand, then slapped it into his other palm and pointed straight down the corridor:

everybody key on me for coordinated thrust straight ahead. Then he was on his feet, the others, as one, also coming up into a crouched position and moving forward, Bird leaving a blood trail, the soft slap of their boots lost in the rising sound and clatter inside Gun Mount number 4.

By comparison, Sacabe's mind was tranquil, despite the raging of his blood and the firing and shouting that came from beyond the main gunroom door. He listened to it coolly, certain his noncoms were handling it properly, good Imperial Marines killing this foul, sneaking enemy that had dared come against them.

A lance corporal from the targeting room abruptly come plunging down the narrow ladder-way from the ranging-and-targeting room and hurried to him. He was heavily muscled in the shoulders and had a blue-black birthmark on his face that had the shape of a dog's face.

"*Chui-san,*" he blurted, "we are receiving updated targeting data from Tomigusuki. They are sighting enemy ships now *within* the channel."

Sacabe nodded. "Gunship class?"

"No, honored sir. These appear to be minesweepers."

Minesweepers, he thought, the gardeners of battle, clearing the field. *Soon the enemy battleships and cruisers will come. Then we'll discover who is to die.* Good. He told the targeting lance corporal, "Initiate your data into the directors immediately. And stand by for firing sequence."

"*Hai, Chui-san,*" the corporal said and dashed away.

Sacabe shouted an order. It was repeated, twice. Within seconds, there was a heavy humming, and then the great *ni kagi okakeru* armored doors began to slide along their runners, rumbling, solid steel wheels squealing. As they cleared, a sudden wave of cool, salt-laden air came into the room.

The lieutenant opened his mouth with another order.

But he was cut off by a sudden sharp, sundering crack that came from the outer corridor. The heavy steel entry door buckled but did not rupture. White smoke blew through the bottom seam and chunks of cement from the door frame went whirling through the air.

Sacabe froze, stood there in his sea-green uniform over white shirt and glass-shiny black boots and gaitors and scowled indignantly at the door. One of his men had been standing close to him and a long sliver of cement and rebar had struck him in the top of the head. It took his helmet and most of the top of his skull with it and now blood gushed from it as the marine fell across the yoke plate of the port gun, then slid down, leaving a thick smear of blood on the polished metal.

Some of his blood had also sprayed onto Sacabe's uniform. The lieutenant dipped his head and looked down at it, the stuff fleshy red and as raw-looking as a sliced pomegranate. He touched it with the tip of his finger, lifted it to his nostrils, sniffed. It had the scent of rose *gekido saseru*, the incense sticks he remembered from childhood.

This seemed to trigger a violent, raging burst of energy in him, his mind, body suddenly coming fully alive, no longer in the doldrums of resignation. He whirled around and started screaming orders, his high-pitched voice cutting through the sounds of fighting that still banged and burst and rumbled from beyond the doorway:

"Battery, achieve barrage positions and commence loading procedures. When armed and locked, stand by for rapid firing . . . Security, assemble full *shubitai* here and prepare for counterattack . . . Wireless, contact the *chikus* to execute SS-1 . . . Demolitions, prepare for *jisatsu buki* . . ."

On and on he bellowed, getting his big guns ready to open on the intruding enemy ships, positioning his men within the installation, calling for reserves from the defensive bunkers to consolidate his strength within the main entrenchment itself, the so-called SS-1 maneuver, or *shujinchitai sakusen,* and finally bidding his demolition section to prepare small, personnel explosive charges for the possibility of a suicide charge.

Each order was repeated, everybody jumping and moving wordlessly. The two chiefs-of-the-gun, both sergeants, and their four-man crews snapped into action around the big howitzers, first throwing switches to activate the shell-lifting hoists, then using double levers on the pressurized air tanks that operated the pneumatic positioning rams that would shove the big guns forward to their firing positions.

Both pedestal cars began to move, these steel wheels only whispering on their rails. Within fifteen seconds, their forward buffer plates struck the end-stop bumpers that halted the cars. Overhead, the shell feeder trays, suspended by cables from the stone ceiling and resembling jointed, half snakes, automatically swung with the guns and as they stopped neatly fitted themselves into the yokes of each weapon's lower shield plate.

Moving with practiced precision, both firing crews cracked open the breeches and swung the blocks back. The lead loader closest to Sacabe then stepped back on his loading board to receive his first two-hundred-pound missile, its brass casing shining like gold in the brilliant overhead lights.

It rumbled noisily, coming down the tray chute. The secondary loaders guided it into the breech face and then the lead loader stepped forward again and, using his weight and a long padded stick, rammed the shell home. There was a loud click as it locked in. He withdrew the ram stick. The instant it cleared the block face, one of the secondary loaders slammed the breech bolt shut and twisted it into lockdown.

Remaining at his firing position beside the gun's slide trunnion, the chief-of-the-gun threw up his hands and shouted, "Mount One armed and ready for sequence." A second later came the call from the starboard gun's COG, "Mount Two armed and ready for sequence."

Sacabe turned to the two operators seated at the automatic director panel in the back of the firing room and shouted to them to initiate the firing sequence. They immediately took electronic control of the two big cannons and began feeding in the ranging and firing data from the targeting room overhead. It, in turn, had received target-positioning radar fixes from the main SNBF Artillery Command Unit headquarters at Tomigusuki.

The two long-gun barrels were now jutting out through their embrasures. As the director's data fed in, they began to move slowly in unison, their positioning motors whining as they quickly responded to the preset arcs and azimuths and began to search out the coordinated horizontal-vertical target-lock-in-point for this initial firing.

At last, they fixed into position. The senior director operator called out the weapons' status. Sacabe stepped up to the left embrasure and glassed the darkness at the end of the rectangular tunnel of cement. Nothing out there yet.

He turned back. The gun room had fallen into a hush now, all the crews and security and panel operators waiting, listening to the suddenly vanished fighting sound from outside the compartment.

Sacabe smiled. The intruders had been vanquished. He raised his arm for the order to commence firing. Everyone covered their ears. The arm came down. There was the horrendous muzzle blasts from the two big guns, the sound so dense it filled the room like a fluid as the double explosive flashes burst forth light as white as lightning.

Both weapon pedestals instantly slammed backward along their tracks, the guns in recoil. Then they were slowed as their pneumatic ram systems automatically countered the violent reaction, absorbing it, along with the hydropneumatic suppressor tubes mounted on the breeches, both causing the rail car to now ease to a complete halt. Within a few seconds, the pneumatic positioning rams pushed it forward again into firing position.

Now the loading crews leaped forward, each man again moving with that skilled precision. The entire room was filled with explosive residue, misty, stinking like burning creosote. The barrels of the guns gave off a wispy heat vapor that made the inside lights shimmy.

At that instant, the doorway to the outer corridor blew half off its frame as a missile tore through it, creating a huge, jagged-edged hole in the center. The missile continued across the room trailing sparks and smoke and smashed into the opposite bulkhead. Its main AP charge exploded, filling the entire space with a dense cloud of hot gasses and stone dust and cordite that made the overhead lights go as dim as if seen through Victorian smoke-glass, within it the shadowy figures of the firing crews darting and shouting.

Shaken by the tremendous explosiveness of the two big Jap coastal guns, their horrendous blasts like double acoustic images of each other that shook the ground and walls and sent dust raining down from overhead, Cowboy had hardly felt the two bullets enter his spine.

They had felt like only a shove in the back. His finger had been pulling the trigger of his bazooka just as the guns went off, the shock transferring down through the nerves of that finger to send the AP rocket right into the entry door of the firing room.

He turned then, still crouched, intending to cut back to the corner of an intersecting tunnel. But his legs suddenly felt odd. He stumbled and fell onto his face, the bazooka tumbling away, noisily now since all firing had stopped and the echoes of his own weapon and the much larger explosions had quickly faded off, going deep into the stone walls.

He lay with his mouth open on the cold floor, near the

small, shallow drainage groove, the thing oddly not stinking now. Someone was yelling close by, cursing in Spanish. Weesay, he thought, good ole Chico giving the slant-eyes shit. He smiled at the image.

Then his mind shifted and began sending out sensory probes, signal flashes questioning the parts of his body and fielding the nearly instantaneous responses, nerve impulses transiting at atomic speed.

Nothing was coming back from his legs. . . .

Blue Team had hit the assembling Japs head-on, putting all their firepower down the corridor, saturating the corners and intersecting galleries with ordnance. Bullets hurled stone chips, made little sparks in the blue light, their gun flashes throwing illumination like welders' torches seen in a smoky foundry.

The initial enemy convergence had been momentarily shattered by the Americans' charge, most of the Nips retreating, others in their green uniforms that looked Wehrmach gray in the blue light suddenly dropping in that deadweight way as they were hit, crumpled bodies strewn all along the corridor.

The team's frontal attack had carried it to within forty yards of the main firing room, into an area that was a kind of central intersection where several smaller corridors and tunnels converged along with the entrances to smaller rooms and vertical tunnel shafts that went up and down between levels.

The fleeing Japs quickly regrouped, turned, and came back, yelling and firing in counterattack, their Arisakas and Type 100 submachine guns making ear-piercing claps of sound in the confined tunnels of stone. Again, the Americans opened on them.

A hot firefight erupted, bullets cutting the air, men screaming, bellowing. One of the Japs leaped at Bird, tried to embrace him. Wyatt kicked him off, back against a wall. The man instantly exploded. He had been strapped with a bomb. Flesh and bits of bone and skull were hurled onto Bird's clothing, his hands, weapons, face. Cursing wildly, he turned to face another opponent.

Parnell had signaled Sol to bring his flamethrower into play. But the nozzle had malfunctioned, the big Samoan down on one knee knocking it against a wall, slowly, calmly cursing it. One of the bazookas fired off then, Smoker and Wyatt laying it in, the rocket crashing into the steel door that led into the main gun casement. It seemed to jump with the impact, yet it held. Slowly, the firing tapered off as the Nips again withdrew.

Another Jap exploded. His head went hurtling past Cowboy's shoulder, spinning, blood from its neck making a twirling fan. He winced. Then Parnell was whistling. Fountain turned, saw the lieutenant pointing at him, giving the bazooka sign, a bent right arm with the left wrist crossing over the right.

He immediately swung the weapon off his shoulder, snapped it open, and went to the one-knee firing position. Weesay had moved up beside him and now pulled an AP round from his ammo canister. Cowboy lifted the weapon and settled it onto his shoulder, the metal cold and smelling of Cosmoline. It jiggled slightly as Laguna loaded the three-pound rocket. He heard it click into place and then felt Weesay's "Ready" tap on his shoulder.

He sighted through the thick smoke, the blue wall bulbs looking like moons showing through a heavy overcast, the door square finally coming into view through the peephole. He held it captured and locked his breath, his finger gently pulling, pulling . . .

Now everything went *totally* silent, not a single sound seeping through. Cowboy frowned. *What the hell? I been shot in the ear?* It was nonsense. He tried to move his right leg . . . couldn't. His left . . . nope. *Well, goddamn!* He felt a surge of panic come up into his chest like a spray of icy water.

He blinked. At least his eyelids worked. *Funny, funny.* He focused, saw Weesay's face staring down at him, saw his mouth working, his features contorted, his hands pulling at him. Then he was moving, no sensation of it coming through. And the realization came to him that he was going to die in this place. It took his breath away.

Oh, Sweet mother of Christ Almighty!

He saw a bullet slam into the dark wall beside him. He was no longer being moved. Laguna was kneeling beside him, then Parnell, both looking down at him darkly. And beyond them, the stone walls with their little blue calcite stars shining so damned beautiful.

A memory snapped into view in front of his mind's eye: a frosty night up in the Apache Peaks of the Peloncillo Mountains in southwestern New Mexico, himself riding the high country . . .

He stopped. *No, no memories.* He recalled something someone had told him, that just before you died, you remembered the happiest place you had ever been. *No,* he ordered himself, *I won't allow the memory.*

He couldn't stop it. It came as clearly and as purely as if he were there again, looking at the same scene as he had so long ago: *snow pockets under the trees and the rocks etched with snow like streams of white fat and the sky so powerful with splendor it might have been electrified, and—*

He was suddenly very thirsty. Again, he tried not to think or remember. Was it getting dimmer? He looked out from his eyes, saw only the darkness, the shapes of the others' heads now like black paper cutouts against the stars. And then the stars themselves began to disappear, one by one.

Oh, Christ, not yet . . .

Well, shit.

And then they were gone.

Fountain's death electrified them, the men looking at each other, their eyes gone silent, cold, dense, transmitting shock and then anger, all of it happening within seconds, Parnell looking back at them, his own face telling them without words. He picked up Fountain's body.

Then they were up and charging again, eating up ground, their voices bellowing with rage through the corridors and channels and crawl tunnels, the Japs going down, turning, running, scattered little shits fleeing in that gimpy, bowlegged scramble and bullets striking with that thudding, wet impact.

They reached the main gun room door, Parnell first. Without altering his motion, he hurled a grenade through the opening and then threw himself to the side, the others behind him going to ground, too.

The grenade went off with a muffled crack. Smoke blew through the door frame. Before its echoes could recede, two more frags went sailing through the opening and almost immediately exploded, the explosions so sharp they created feeling needles that penetrated their eardrums.

They headed for the doorway, again Parnell leading off, the body of Fountain slung over his shoulder, going to the right once he cleared, sweeping his Thompson from right to left, back. Weesay was next, moving to the left, firing. Finally, Bird and Sol and Smoker surged into the hot, explosive-smelling, oily-smoky room firing directly ahead.

Yells, screams filled the space. Japs began to appear out of the smoke, their features contorted, uniforms powdered with explosion dust, lunging at them, bayonets out, knives, firing as they came, the flashes of their weapons like little flicks of snakes' tongues.

Both sides met, merged, firing, cutting, slashing. The Americans fought with a frigid, silent intensity, giving no quarter, slaughtering with an efficiency garnered from four years of killing.

A Japanese officer flailed away with his sword, screaming Japanese obscenities. Someone shot him in the arm. The sword fell behind the breech of the port gun. He fell also, sideways, as if he had lost his balance. He disappeared behind the gun.

The Mohawkers reached the opposite wall of the gun room, turned, and came back. But the Japanese gun crews had so thinned by now that the few who were left cut and bolted, out into the corridor, their officer up and leading them, his arm hanging limply.

Parnell, his eyes blazing, whistled: *converge on me.* The others came, their black jumpsuits bloody, everybody in that terrible killing place in his mind, thoughts going at high speed, their blood now thoroughly saturated with the hot violence of combat.

"Sol, the door," Red rasped, pointing. "Get that damned blowtorch working. Weesay, check the overhead crawl tunnels. Wyatt, you, me, and Smoker'll lay in the demo charges. Then we take the upper room and blow the smaller gun."

The men immediately obeyed, turning to their assigned tasks. But each paused for a tiny, still moment to look down at Cowboy Fountain's body, lying limply against the closer howitzer's pedestal truck where Parnell had rested him, looking as if he were only asleep, but not asleep, something of him no longer there, his body slightly deflated in repose.

Aboveground, the Nip support troops couldn't wait to get off their trucks and down into those big gun mounts, to start killing *Amerika-jin,* the dogs whose pilots had nearly killed them just now. Meeting and joining them, converging like ants on mounded ground, were soldiers from the defensive line bunkers and trench holes, these also aware now of the raiders down in their gun casements, all jumpy now, watching over the cliff edge, expecting more enemy to show up.

Quickly, as noncoms bellowed orders, sections of men

deployed along the trench lines toward their assigned attack targets. Meanwhile, two of the trucks continued along the road, carrying the rest of the troops to the farthest entrenchment on the bluff line.

At Mount number 4, seventy soldiers formed into two attack columns and cautiously approached the entry points and crawl tunnels. Their equipment and weapons made little metallic collisions in the brisk near-dawn wind off the sea.

Suddenly, a violent explosion sent shock waves through the entire point, the ground shaking so hard soldiers were knocked off their feet. From the farthest outmount suddenly came a great column of orange red light that was hurled skyward. It was clothed in rock dust and chunks of lava and calcite and sandstone and ordnance blowing upward. Then a second shock wave rocketed by, carrying the intense stink of explosions mixed with the odor of burnt stone and shattered rock, oddly smelling like warm bread.

The soldiers stopped, many dropping into squats, watching the fiery column climb, knowing that a powder magazine had just been blown up. The enemy raiders were indeed here. After a moment, the soldiers rose and continued heading underground.

Parnell, Smoker, and Wyatt worked rapidly, setting up the demo charges on the big 240mm coastal cannons, placing the cartridges of PE 808 and C-3 plastique in offset positions so the blasts would create a scissors cutting effect on the tempered steel of the breeches and barrels. They worked the soft, brown yellow puttylike explosives holding their breaths, slit-eyed, since the stuff caused splitting gelignite headaches when inhaled.

Every charge was linked to a main ring of PETN detonating cord in a straight series so they would all go at the same time, the men using individual 45mm fuses of fulminate of mercury and a single number 10 Dupont capacitor-discharge blasting machine.

Then Smoker and Wyatt crawled through the embrasure, pulling themselves on their elbows over the stone to set grenade loops inside the eight-inch muzzles to split them open, and more C-3 plastique on the barrel sections to crack the seams.

Parnell checked his watch. It was 0439 hours.

At precisely 0438 hours, the battleships and cruisers of TF 51.3 Bombardment Force had swung out of their time-delay circling and quickly realigned into their assigned positions within the barrage steaming formation.

High up in the masts of the gun ships, senior gunnery officers were already spinning up their gyro-synchronized MK 38 Mod 2 range/finder/director units in the ships' PFC or Primary Fire Control stations, while the Forward Gunnery Computer rooms far below were readying their "selsyn" or self-synchronous systems to receive the designated assignment target-sighting instructions.

In the gun turrets themselves, firing crews were completing their preloading task charts, their ready ammo racks filled, powder hoists and carts loaded, as each turret phone man called in "Manned and ready" reports to the ships' CICs, everything now running on Commence Bombardment minus twenty-two minutes and holding. Gradually, the big ships began dropping speed, going from fifteen to eight to four knots. By the time the signal to begin their salvo runs came, they'd be moving at a mere two knots per hour.

Suddenly, the radios in bridges all through the TF exploded with, "Bridge, CIC, bogies spotted . . . Targets bearing 143 . . . Speed 180 . . . Closing rapidly." More bells and buzzers went off while bridges and CICs began jamming their phone lines with orders and status reports: "Control, aye, tracking." "All guns air action port. Air action port." "Range five ought double ought . . . Range four five double ought . . ." "Commence firing, commence firing."

Aboard the screening destroyers and escorts, captains' orders sent the vessels into flank speed, the ships darting and slicing through the ocean to achieve positions as protective shields along the flanks of the barrage ships. Searchlights began probing the sky and 40mm and 20mm gun turrets slued around in automatic control from the directors, then opened up, *a-whoomp, a-whoomp, a-whoomp,* their rounds sailing in that leisurely lethal arching into the night sky.

The American air strikes on Naha Harbor and the two airfields to the south had caught many of the Japanese Tokko Special Attack Force aircraft still on the ground. Of the original ninety-three, almost half were destroyed on the runways and in their revetments. Of the remaining planes that did manage to lift off, nearly half of those were quickly shot down. But that still left a deadly force of over thirty aircraft.

Now they savagely hurtled themselves toward the big ships of TF 51.3 and the escort carriers that had already swung into the wind to begin recovery operations of their returning air strike planes. The entire sky quickly became a mass of tracer lines and cannon arcs, air bursts, the explosions and fiery trails of struck Japanese suicide planes falling like massive shooting stars, their tails of orange and white and red stark against the ever so faint gray sheen of the approaching dawn.

It was a lonely battle, Weesay fighting it by himself up there on the spiral staricase to the upper range and targeting room. He had managed to get one grenade into the space before the Japs up there slammed and locked the hatchway. The jolt had nearly knocked him off the stairway, the whole thing shaking from loosened bolts and the wrought-iron railing itself old and rusted. He was carrying Cowboy's bazooka now along with his slung Greasegun.

When the grenade went off, it blew hot gases through the three holes in the hatchway. Shielding himself on the ladder, he glanced below, Parnell, Wyatt, and Smoker busily working their demo charges onto the big gun breeches.

He cautiously returned to the metal hatch and shoved the muzzle of his Greasegun through one of the holes and gave a short blast. It felt odd, the gun holding perfectly recoiless, as if it were locked to a firing stand. He stopped to listen, heard only the soft ticking of hot metal.

Without volition, the image of Cowboy Fountain leaped into his thoughts. *Madre de Dios!* It seared his insides like fire, Cowboy gone, dead. Over the past four years, Weesay had seen so many dead people, some only the remnants of human beings. Many had touched him, but only momentarily. All the others had merely been there, part of the landscape.

But here his brother had died, a horribly, terribly different thing. *This* death filled him with a wild, thundering rage that prompted him to destroy things, *Jap* things, to open up with his weapons and kill every goddamned slant-eyed son of a bitch that there ever was.

Feeling such intensities, he again rammed his muzzle into a second hatch hole and literally emptied the weapon, hearing the bullets whining off upper walls and bulkheads, no countering fire coming back, the smell of explosive and cordite sifting down the stairwell like a pall.

Then, nearly somersaulting, holding to the shaky rail, he kicked at the hatch. It didn't give. He kicked it again. It still wouldn't move. Cursing, he reloaded and laid in a five-round burst along the edge of the hatch. Rock slivers flew, metal sang and tanged. He kicked at it one more time. It slammed open and back.

An Arisaka round struck the edge of the hatch. It made a funny, leady sound, as if the slug had simply mashed into the harder metal. Another came. A Jap voice yelled something. Weesay jerked another grenade from his harness, pulled the pin, let it cook off for three seconds, then heaved it.

The second explosion again shattered the silence. But this time it seemed to go on and on, getting larger, expanding with a deeper, richer sound until he realized that something *else* had just blown up, something far away, its vibrations and shocks coming through the stone of the installation. He glanced down, saw Parnell and Bird look at each other, then return to their demo charges.

He moved up the end of the stairway, just below the hatch, and listened. Still nothing coming from up there. With a lunge he shoved himself through the hatch. The room was filled with smoke. Equipment lay scattered. He saw a body. Its left leg was missing, the trousers deflated, lying flat, as if the leg had been sucked out of it.

A Jap soldier sat against a wall. He looked as if he had been hurled against it. His head was bloody. He did not move. Beside him, a two-meter-base height and range finder lay on its side, the barrel sighter cracked, lens fluid seeping from it like yellow blood. A small speed and course-angle calculator had been completely blown apart, and there was the three-foot-wide metal circle of a powder-charge temperature and wind scale lying near the hatchway.

Another hatchway opened slightly in the ceiling near the back wall. He spotted a gun barrel came through the crack. It fired at him. The bullet actually made a pathway through the smoke, like a sharp object cleaving water, and struck the edge of the range-finder, ricocheting off.

Laguna ducked below the hatchway again. Swinging his bazooka off his back, he snapped it open, retrieved the last round from his musette, loaded the weapon, leaning in to hear the locking click, then swung it up onto his shoulder. He lifted slightly, easing the end of the firing tube through the crack in the hatch. Pausing just long enough to shout, "Check, tennis ball going," he aimed and fired.

The rocket made a horrible hissing-rushing-slamming sound in the confined room. It struck and went completely through the hatch in the ceiling, blowing the metal edges out like flower petals. A fraction of a second later, its core charge blew, made a ringing sound that seemed to travel endlessly, then finally fading, like the continuing resonance of a tuning fork in the stone.

He crawled through the hatch and lay amid floating smoke and explosion stench, with it the raw odor of sundered flesh, a hot, mushy stench. The 40mm cannon gun crew were all dead, scattered around the weapon in various positions and states of sundering.

Stepping through pools of blood, he quickly shoved two grenades into the gun's breech and blew off its sliding wedge and swing-aside bore block. Next, to be absolutely certain the Nips couldn't use the weapon again, he jammed a round into the breech backward, then crawled out and blew the muzzle open with a cartridge of 808 and a number 11 safety fuse with a slow, two-foot-a-minute flash rate.

Afterward, he stood surveying the death and destruction he had made and felt unsatisfied, unrevenged.

SNLF Lieutenant Yasio Sacabe sat against a stone wall and watched himself bleed. The blood looked like crankshaft oil seeping from a broken transmission in the blue corridor lights. He felt no pain. Instead, there was a glorious rush of emotion, *nekkyoteki*, rapturous as orgasm. His blood was flowing for his emperor. He trembled at the exquisite sensation of glory this rendered to his thoughts.

Finally, he turned and looked at his men, most of them squatting against the wall, their eyes white in the blue light, their legs restless, as if they were impatient to die. In his mind, that's what they thought, his own thoughts mingling, becoming a single entity, undeniable.

The time had come, *his* time, *their* time. He rose. His arm felt like nothing. It dripped blood onto his dusty gaiters and boot tops. His men rose with him. They looked at him wordlessly, him looking back. Their faces seemed so stark, so warrior-like in the methylene blue aura: *Kabuki* samurai, *No* theaterlike savagery.

Each withdrew his own *meiyoshi* death pennant, slowly unknotting it, its cloth grimy from such long pocket storage. Stoically, the soldiers untied them, rolled them onto their palms, then banded them and tied them around their foreheads, the *kanji* characters outward so that the Shinto gods would recognize their sacrificial souls when they approached the sacred *toriis* of death.

Now they reloaded and charged their weapons. Men took grenades from their harnesses, all naval issue, Model 3A incendiary units looking like Popsicles loaded with phosphorus and carbon disulphide, and Model 33T stick fragmentation grenades, big blowers containing five ounces of lyddite explosive, the men removing the brass caps, then tying the string loops to their fingers so that when they snapped their arms down and released the grenade, it would trigger off in three seconds.

Sacabe paced slowly, his arm limp, his Model 94 8mm pistol looking like a cheap toy in his other hand, face hard, blue-glossy, cheeks trembling with nearly hysterical fervor. His entire body pounded with the exquisite ecstasy of impending *seppuku*. He experienced a flashing, purifying sensation of complete oneness with his men, marines all, standing there waiting for his order in that glorious patience of sacrifice.

The moment hummed with emotion. From far off came

the faint rumbling and growling of combat from Naha Harbor and the Shuri Line deeper inland. Then Sacabe's arm shot upward. The men in a single voice gave a shouted "Banzai!" the collective sound of it primeval, frightening in its savage volume. Again. Once more.

Then Sacabe leaped forward and charged through the blue light, down the corridor toward the main firing room, his men following in a rushing, hurtling, screaming clot.

Parnell crouched with the Dupont blasting machine, a little thing, barely big enough to cover his left palm, but heavy. He glanced back at Smoker, just now climbing out of the second gun embrasure where he had placed charges.

From above, he had heard Weesay engaging whoever was up there, feeling discomfort, the little Mex all by himself. At that moment, Wineberg gave him the raised fist sign: *all charges hooked up and ready.* Red pointed him toward the spiral stairway that led up to the ranging and targeting room. Smoker darted to it and started up.

Meanwhile, Bird had been checking the charges set up on the closer gun. Now he too turned, signaled that he was finished, and backed out of the way. At the main doorway, the blasted metal still seeping wisps of smoke, Sol watched them over his shoulder, his flamethrower apparently fixed, the nozzle pointing through the doorway, its fuel tank looking absurdly small on his broad back, clownishly out of proportion.

For one single, stunning, motionless moment, Parnell took it all in, every tiny image of the room, the walls, the Japanese guns, the director panels, the shattered bulkheads, the bodies, the air, the smells. But mostly he beheld his own men, caught in one eternal iota of time that was instantly branded into memory: Wyatt and Sol and Smoker and dead Cowboy and the absent Weesay, their presences gathered and frozen forever in this single time and single place, like live creatures captured in amber.

The moment ended. His hand started to twist the blasting machine handle. Sol gave a shout. He swung around. And all hell broke loose.

The screams of the banzai charge came up the corridor and through the ruptured door frame sounding like the screech of leopards, its shrillness bouncing off walls, convoluting, piercing. Then the firing, a single, voluminous volley, at least a dozen weapons going off, and bullets tearing through the remnants of the doorway, the frame, slugs hot-zinging into the room, thudding into walls, pinging off metal.

Without consciously realizing it, Parnell rose to his feet, found he was yelling, answering the Japanese challenge, flinging it back at them, "Come on, you sons a' bitches," Wyatt bellowing, too, then Sol growling and the sudden rushing sound of his flamethrower going, like high-pressure water blowing out of a narrow spigot.

The thick orange-yellow tongue of fire shot through the sundered doorway and down the hall as a wave of scorching air blew back into the room, Kaamanui standing with his big legs braced, holding the nozzle, still yelling.

The banzai shouts turned to screams with barely a difference. More rounds came through the door. These were answered by Smoker's Greasegun, *thrrrrruuuuppp*, the rounds going out so fast they made one continuous sound. Red moved up and threw bursts past Kaamanui until his bolt locked back on empty.

There was a pause. Parnell again dropped into a squat, shouted, "Fire in the hole! Fire in the hole!" Bird went to the floor as did Sol, who had just finished a second burst of fire, the nozzle dribbling flames for a moment as he, too, crouched.

The big gun charges went off with a hard, punching, cracking explosiveness. Chunks of metal hurled about.

Concussion waves crossed and recrossed between the walls, which thrummed as the sound of the blast ricocheted and rebounded like bullets. It abruptly dissipated, the echoes disappearing through openings, swallowed by open space.

The air seemed to hum. The Americans rose. Two Jap soldiers lunged through the doorway, charging hard, firing their submachine guns. Parnell saw Sol rise to meet them. On his right, Bird moved in to engage. There was a hollow, *shushing* sound and again the flamethrower threw out a tongue of fire.

Both enemy soldiers were engulfed. The liquid flames dripped off their bodies like water, the men screaming and twirling and thrashing as the cloying, hot stink of burning flesh and burnt fuel fumed up off their bodies to fill the room.

One man dropped heavily to the ground. He tried to crawl away, as if he were seeking a hiding place. Red could hear him burning, his skin popping and crackling like kindling. The Jap lifted his head. The flames had eaten away half of his facial tissue, the under bones now burning.

At last, he dropped flat and lay still, only the flames rampant on him, like feeding things. The other man had turned and disappeared back into the corridor, leaving an oily plasma drifting and lifting in the heated air.

Earlier, as he led the charge, Sacabe had stumbled over one of his own men who was killed in the first skirmish. He went down hard, striking his knee, a jolt of pain momentarily making his entire right leg go numb. His men rushed around and past him, screaming, firing, the ends of their *meiyoshis* fluttering. Their faces shone with fanatical ardor and their eyes were flat, staring robotically.

Then the flamethrower hit them, striking like a blazing wind. Its tremendous heat enveloped them, swept down the hall and over Sacabe. He could actually feel the cooler areas within the cloud that were created by his men's bodies that took the full thermal force of the weapon. The charge immediately disintegrated, men turning away from the horrendous firestorm. Others stopped, shielding their faces, turning, crouching, fleeing.

Sacabe stood up. The air around him swirled with flame-created currents. A loud blast came from the firing room. He heard things strike the walls, saw a blossom of smoke blow through the side of the sundered door.

As if picking up the expanding energy of the explosions, his body seemed to absorb it. It rang in his head. Again he felt that surging rush of unquenchable yearning to kill the enemy in that room.

He saw two of his men rise from behind the corner of the intersection where they had dived for protection. Now they charged through the doorway. A fierce firefight erupted for a few seconds. There was another outburst of flame and screaming, an ungodly sound. He saw one man engulfed in flames turn to run. A moment later, he fled past the lieutenant, the flames hissing, his face blackened like charcoal, and his body trailing a peculiar mist.

The lieutenant started forward. He did not have his pistol. His arm still did not function. He paused to look down at one of his men, dead, the corpse smouldering, seeping a ghastly stench. Another body lay beside it, this one untouched by fire. The back of its head had been shot away.

Sacabe knelt, lifted the corpse's hand, and quickly slipped the grenade and its igniter ring from it. Retrieving a second grenade from his own belt, he came to his feet already moving. He was only thirty feet from the firing room. He saw the door frame burning now, too, creating a rectangle of fire, the metal of the door itself flickering blue and white and red as burning flamethrower fuel drained off and dropped to the floor where it made tiny conflagrations.

He pulled both grenade rings and leaped forward, giving full vent to his voice, not speaking words but merely an outburst of air from his chest, the focusing of all his being into the center of himself called *kiai*.

He leaped through the doorway. A huge man in dark clothing was directly ahead of him. He had a tank on his back, the tubing and firing nozzle of a flamethrower in his hand. To the side was another man. Sacabe saw them in stopped motion, both looking at him, then bringing their weapons up and firing.

He felt the bullets before he felt the unbelievable pain of the flames. For a brief moment, he thought he flew, his body's reaction to the pain so violent it had thrown his entire brain's sensory balance into malfunction. Then the pain came again, a huge, engulfing, covering wave. He heard himself screaming, his legs still moving, fire all around.

The big man in black rose, holding the nozzle of his flamethrower at him, the flames stopping, then coming again, Sacabe hearing the rush of it, feeling the flames, liquid fire, white hot, and again the sensation of flying. He flung out his left arm, saw that the two stick grenades were also on fire, and there was the big man, four feet from him.

He propelled himself at him, felt his huge bulk, heard him cursing, growling, large as a montain bear, smelled his clothing, smelled his own flesh burning, and the pain flashing again into enormous heights, beyond feeling, into numbness.

Both grenades exploded and then the flamethrower fuel tank blew apart. But Sacabe heard only a double click and then there was nothing.

Parnell saw Kaamanui's right arm and shoulder blow off his body, the stump whirling and twirling like a boomerang sailing through the air, trailing droplets of blood and bits of tissue and shards of metal. The sight froze him. He watched the slow-motion tableau unfold amid the blood mist, felt his own body jerk and draw back.

The Jap officer had taken the full force of the grenades directly in the face and chest. The blasts had gouged out his upper body like a deseeded pumpkin half and hurled him back against the slanted door where he slumped, his lungs and lower jaw a mass of hamburger.

Parnell moved then, lunging forward and down onto his knees. He touched Sol's sundered body. Blood gushed from his massive, grotesque wound, dark, dark red. Kaamanui turned his head. His face was sliced from shrapnel, his eyes glassy. He looked at Red, Parnell yelling, "Oh, Christ Jesus, hold on, Sol, hold on!"

Then Wyatt was there, the two men looking at each other, both their faces blank, the enormity of the thing too much to express. Parnell had his aid kit open, fumbling with the syringe, Bird's hands unrolling bandages, compresses. The outflow of blood from Kaamanui's body was slowing now, already covering everything, a sea of blood, smelling hot and raw.

He sagged. His big brown face seemed to shrink slightly, as if some of the air beneath its surface tissue had seeped away. Parnell's eyes closed, opened. He gently touched Sol's carotid artery. Nothing.

Oh, God, two gone.

Smoker came up then. He stood and looked and looked. Then he snapped around and went out into the outer corridor. Parnell heard him begin firing. Bird lunged to his feet, turned, and went out, too. More firing came.

Parnell felt only cold. *Here they come again.* He unslung his Thompson, stepped over Kaamanui's body, and pushed through the doorway. Wineberg and Bird were shooting the already dead Japs, the corpses jerking and jumping as the slugs went in. Some were mere lumps of blackened clothing and flesh and the bullets flushed off small puffs of ash.

He walked over to a Nip's body. The man's face wore a scowling expression, as if someone had just insulted him. Parnell put the muzzle of his weapon against the corpse's forehead and fired a three-round burst. The man's skull blew apart and the bullets made hard thuddings against the stone floor. He then moved to a second dead soldier and fired into him until his weapon was empty.

Now there was a sudden silence. Gun smoke and fire stink drifted, the blue corridor hazy, like a smoky slaughterhouse, parts of bodies scattered, blood in black pools and channels on the stone floor. The three Americans prowled about but did not look at each other.

The sound of boots suddenly cracked through the silence, men running. A Japanese voice came, hollow sounding, calling out, "*Shinpo suru, kono yarikata. Oisogi, chikusho!*"

0444 hours

Everyone aboard the big gunships of CTF 51.3 was preparing himself for the show to start, bracing his body for the jolting thunder of the weapons going off, the heavy recoils that could actually heel and rock the huge war vessels. It was just now coming up to Commence Bombardment minus fifteen.

In PFC stations throughout the armada, senior gunnery officers had already completed transmission of their final prefiring range/windage/roll-and-pitch data reports on all designated targets, along with their assignment of initial turret firing sequences. Now they slowly glassed the dark mass that was Okinawa-Shima with their light-gathering binoculars, peering through their stations' armored slits.

The sky had a soft luminousness now, faint but strong

enough to just barely silhouette the mountainous outline of the island. Five miles to the southeast, a weak glow fused up into the cloudless sky, coming from fires created by the air strikes on Naha Harbor and the airfields farther south. Even fainter light issued deeper inland and occasional explosions as the X-Target fighters assigned to the Shuri Line continued their bombing and strafing runs.

At the same time, aboard USS *Hollenbech,* the *Bull Pen* operators and the Strike Force's bombardment CMAO or Chief Mission Assignment Officer, Commander Terrance Sayre, were the busiest people in the fleet, constantly fielding updated reports from the Air Intelligence section of the CVE *Savo Island.* They were responsible for collecting and interpreting all after-action reports from the returning air-strike pilots so as to adjust existing firing data when necessary.

Sayre was a cigar-chomping, red-eyed officer who never seemed to sleep. He spoke with a rapid Boston accent, forbade the slightest deviation from protocol, and when beyond hearing was referred to by his men as Donald Duck for his squabbly voice when he got excited.

Now, pacing the *Bull Pen* operations room, he was hailed by one of his radiomen. "Sir, I'm picking up a fire mission request."

Sayre's head snapped around. He glared at the young sailor.

"It's coming from code reference Strawberry 4, sir," the radioman said.

"Goddammit." Sayre hurried over. "What the hell's the *matter* with the idiot? We're still fourteen minutes from CB."

"He's calling for smoke, Commander."

"Smoke? The son of a bitch wants *smoke?*"

"Yes, sir."

Sayre drew back his lips, showing teeth. "Put him on LS."

The operator obeyed. A roll of static washed through the speaker, then Parnell's voice, rising but still faint in midmes-

sage, ". . . astal battery. Grid set double two-zero-niner. Willy
Peter only. Commence firing for two minutes, over."

"Mission denied," Sayre snapped.

"Sir?"

"Goddammit, mission *denied*. Log his call and put him
into the rotation. We'll assign him when we come to him."

"Yes, sir," the operator said. He turned back to his panel,
keyed: "Strawberry 4, you are negative for FM. Status for
CB is now minus fourteen. You will be placed in rotation.
Stand by for recall. Do you copy? Over."

"Godammit!" Parnell bellowed. "Not *again!*" He felt a
core of rage so heated even its periphery seemed to burn
a hole in his heart. *Idiots! Lousy, fucking stupid idiots!*

He stared at the stone floor. Bloody, littered with explosive debris and stone dust, chunks of human tissue, metal.
Beyond the doorway, he could hear Wyatt, Smoker, and
Weesay out in the corridor wiring grenades in the intersecting tunnels.

Laguna had scurried down from the upper rooms once
the firing started. When he passed Kaamanui, the side of
the huge Samoan's body truncated where his arm had
been, his jumpsuit in tatters and his blood like thick paint
on the deck, Weesay's face had gone stark and pale. He
paused for a moment, then moved quickly through the
doorway.

Beyond the men, the sounds of the fresh Japanese
troopers had diminished throughout the complex of stone
tunnels and climb-ways, only single words coming, even
the running tramp of boots gone, the Nips creeping, probing, moving cautiously now.

Parnell's mind, racing at breakneck speed once over the
shock of Sol's death, had quickly formulated an escape
plan, the best he could come up with. They were in serious
trouble now, he knew, with two men gone and the remain-

der of the team isolated within an impregnable fortress that was rapidly filling with enemy soldiers.

The possible, no, the *probable*, outcome was obvious: He and his men were going to end it here. That last hill, that final mission was about to be concluded.

Thinking that, he was swept by a wave of sorrow. Not fear, not even anxiety. Just this deep sense of utter regret that seemed to pool down in his groin, made him ache with an inexplicable, inexpressible sadness. He and these men had traveled so far, not just in war, nor together, but back beyond that, each one in his own, individual past and hoped-for life that, in a few moments, he would be relinquishing.

The radio speaker burst out again: "Strawberry *4*, do you *copy*? Over."

Red keyed: "Bull Pen, Strawberry 4. I copy, all right. Now *you* copy. I want an air strike on this site immediately. I say again, *immediately*. Coordinate grid set is double two-zero-niner. Bunker line. HE or Willy Peter. Over."

There was a deliberate pause. He keyed. "Bull Pen, Strawberry 4. Move your ass, buddy. I want *acknowledgment*, over."

"Strawberry 4, stand by."

"Bullshit, stand by. Acknowledge, goddammit."

His team began coming back through the doorway, first Weesay, then Wyatt and Smoker, their harnesses devoid of grenades. Silently, Bird positioned himself and Smoker at the door. Weesay moved to the base of the spiral stairs to guard against attack from above.

A half minute went past. Parnell again keyed, speaking with quiet, cold fury: "Bull Pen, acknowledge, you son of a bitch."

"Strawberry 4, we are attempting to coordinate your AS request. Stand by."

Red looked up from under his eyebrows, saw Bird and Wineberg watching him over their shoulders, both kneeling beside the sundered door, beyond the corridor deep in smoky blue twilight. Smoker already had one of the bazookas up on his shoulder, loaded. Both men's eyes were hard and flat, saying a great deal, saying nothing.

Parnell had intended to bastion here until he could call in a smoke barrage topside. After dropping explosive charges down the gun mount's shell hoist and booby-trapping the ready ammo, they'd exit through the gun ports, taking the bodies of Kaamanui and Fountain with them. They had a good chance of reaching the beach inside the smoke.

But now that was impossible because of some dumb-ass martinet of a fucking assignment officer. And even if he *were* rotated into the barrage sequence, it could be up to an hour before his mission call was assigned. They could never hold out that long.

But then it had occurred to him that an *air* strike was a completely different matter. It was controlled and assigned by the Air Wing Commander, not the bombardment's CMAO. If he could get his AS accepted, fighters could be over the Oroku Peninsula in little more than eight minutes.

Once more, the radio speaker blew a burst of static. Then: "Strawberry 4, this is Bull Pen. Your AS request is now on hold. Repeat, AS status is hold. You are advised to maintain watch this frequency for recall. Also monitor two-one-point-two-niner. Do you copy? Over."

Status is hold. They were on their own.

Wyatt and Smoker silently turned away and Parnell angrily tossed his radio mike aside, paused for a moment to look out the gun embrasure, ocean out there. Its inner cement bulkheads were explosion scarred. He could feel and taste the sea wind sifting through, cool and salty and clean against the stink of gelignite and cordite fumes and burnt flesh. The faint gray aura of approaching dawn thinned the darkness.

He turned, whistled. Wyatt and Smoker turned. "How many demo charges you got left?"

"Two kilos of C-3," Bird answered.

"Smoker?"

"My wad's gone, Lieutenant."

"I got one kilo," Laguna called from the spiral stairs.

"Okay, light 'em up on timers. Six minutes. Wyatt, you take the magazine hoist. Weesay, lay charges to the shells in those ready ammo racks. Everybody, toss your ropes over here."

The two men shrugged out of their rappelling lines, flung them to him. Then they quickly moved to their demo positions and began setting the charges.

Bird's was an easy set, his two kilos of C-3 fused off with MK 27s on a windup timer detonator. But Laguna had it more delicate, having to wire up a series of chunks of C-3 placed directly onto the base detonators of the long 240mm shells, the things stacked like fire logs in the big steel ready racks. He used his last (CE)TNT fuse on the first ball, then linked all the others with detonating cord and completed the circuit to a command detonator running off a small battery timer.

Smoker had also thrown his rope to Parnell, then reshouldered his bazooka and once more took up a security position at the side of the door, staring out into the corridor.

At the embrasure, Red swiftly uncoiled the lines. They felt slick in his hands, made of nylon fibers and sisal cord with test strengths of half a ton. He anchored their ends: two to a gun carriage axle, one to a manual elevation wheel, and the last to a still intact recoil tube bracket of the port gun.

Just as he completed the last double hitch, there was a sharp explosion from one of the connecting corridors as an M3A frag booby trap went off. Its reverberations echoed, receding and surging and receding again as they passed through the convoluted network of levels and stone passages.

Silence.

A second explosion, a man's scream. A single Arisaka round zinged through the space in the doorway and slammed into the opposite wall. Then came a small, hollow, metallic sound, like something striking a helmet.

"Grenade!" Smoker yelled and dropped to the floor. So did everyone else. The Jap grenade struck the outer side of the door and bounced back into the corridor. There was a brilliant sun-bright white flash, the thing a phosphorus stick. The surge of the fire blew a wall of heat and pure white smoke into the firing room.

A second grenade came sailing through, this one clearing the space between the doorway and frame, black, a foot long, with rounded head and handle similar to a child's rattler, turning circles in the air.

"Grenade!"

In reflex, Parnell was already moving toward it. It reached the apogee of its flight, started downward. He leaned toward it, shifting his weight, his legs slightly bent and lowered into a perfect football kicker's stance. With absolute precision, he booted the grenade right back through the doorway and into the corridor. There was another dazzling flash. This one sent separate streamers of smoke arching and spewing into the room.

Into the fading echoes of the second explosion came a voice, isolated, low-pitched, eerie with an otherworldly monotone to it. Like an Indian medicine man calling to the spirits, or the droning wail of a professional mourner in Sicily or Morocco. It rose from its initial guttural sound, strange wordings within it, climbing and climbing to a culminating scream that made the hairs on the back of Parnell's neck rise.

Then more Japs charged the firing room.

Now it was all there again, that sudden, shocking explosive sound and fury of close combat. Bullets crashed through the doorway. Screams rode the air like missiles. The leading Japs rushed to the door, bunching, jostling together, forced to converge onto the single opening into the room, their long, slender, dark bayonets probing like pikes.

They were answered by the Americans' counterfire, Thompsons and Browning Greaseguns hammering in that steady, deep-throated thunder, a single Ithaca twelve-gauge going off like a rapid cannon.

Then Smoker's bazooka fired. Its backlash was like a dragon's breath. The rocket flashed out, immediately struck a Jap trooper full in the chest. It blew completely through him, lifted and carried him along in its violent path. A full second later, it exploded far down the corridor.

Right behind it came another burst, then another, two more booby traps going off, those that had been set up on the dead Jap bodies. Chunks of human flesh slapped against the doorway mushily, shot into the room. There was a slight pause as the enemy charge began to falter. Then it disintergrated completely, the Jap marines turning and running back into the smoky, fiery, stinking, bloody blue light of the corridors.

"Let's go, let's go," Parnell bellowed. The firing room was so thick with smoke and explosion drift, it made the men appear like ghostly apparitions moving, and the gray-white stone dust that had quickly adhered to their face paint gave them the appearance of ghouls awash in blood.

Outside, the Japs were starting to regroup. Officers and noncoms shouted in that perpetually outraged tone of the language, and from various parts of the gun battery came other voices as more soldiers rushed toward the center of fighting.

In the main firing room, however, there was silence

again, disturbed only by the sharp metallic clicks of carabiners as Parnell, Bird, and Weesay cinched up their
rappelling lines, looping them around their shoulders,
under their legs, everybody moving with methodical, cold-
eyed precision, knowing that the next few minutes might
very well be the last of their lives. Even the clogged air
seemed charged with that lethal thought like a plasma.

Four minutes, three seconds before the charges lit up.

The Japs hit them again, this time too quickly, without
enough men, the charge sloppy and disorganized. Again
they were turned back after a short, ferocious fight. This
time, Blue Team took more casualties, Weesay getting hit
in the ankle by a richochet, the wound bleeding profusely,
in a bad place for a compress wrap. As he moved, his coral
booties sloshed. Smoker took a round that creased his
head just above the left ear. It made his head ring and
stopped his hearing on that side.

Cinched up, Parnell and Bird picked up Kaamanui's
body. It was heavy as hell, the man weighing 253 pounds
when alive, now in that can't-get-a-grip-of awkwardness of
the dead. His blown-off arm socket was ghastly to look at,
his clothing saturated with blood, which had coagulated
and now glistened darkly in the bright fluorescent lights.

They carried him to the port embrasure and laid him
into it, between the gun barrel and the left bulkhead. He
rolled and flopped grotesquely and left black smears on
the cement. Weesay finally had to crawl in to keep him
moving to the outer edge.

Parnell glanced at his watch: 5:12.

Two minutes fifty-one seconds.

Jesus. He felt his whole body getting antsy, jittery, almost
hearing the ticking off of the time, the seconds skimming
through the smoky air and out the embrasure, gone. He

kept turning to look at the door, Smoker still over there on security watch.

He clapped Bird on the shoulder. "You and Weesay handle Sol. Drop fast. If we can reach the sand, we've got a chance as long as it's dark."

Wyatt's eyes held his for a moment. Then he wordlessly turned and climbed into the gun port, going forward on knees and elbows, the ancient soldier's crawl.

Red swung around. "Smoker, up here."

Wineberg came back, facing the door, stepping lightly, watching over his shoulder. Out there the Japs were starting to holler again, more officers and noncoms resetting their men, yelling, raging, whipping them on, determined that *this* time they'd *take* that *maimashii* gun position or *nobody'd* be coming back.

Hooking up his carabiner, winding the line around his shoulder, Smoker grinned at the lieutenant, his crazy-eyed smile like a demented jackal's. Blood coated the entire side of his head from the grazing wound. Then they picked up Fountain's body and also put him into the gun port.

Two minutes four seconds.

Red started to say something. From the corridor came that same, eerie, atonal sound, gathering guttural strength and then rising again until it was a skirling wail. Another wave of Jap soldiers stormed forward, firing, trying frantically, maniacally to break into the firing room.

Parnell swiveled, Smoker doing the same, both men already returning fire. He could hear Wineberg cursing, almost joyous, himself snarling and growling like an animal. From the corner of his eye, Red saw Smoker's Greasegun lock back. Instantly, Wineberg swung his Ithaca twelve-gauge off his back and began fast-firing, banging out big booming bursts, and the double-ought slugs slamming into the doorway, leaving plate-sized indentations.

Now his Thompson also locked back. Cursing, he

slapped at his harness, searching out a pouch with a clip left. All were empty. He tossed the weapon aside and pulled his handgun, the Browning 9mm Hi-Power, and started picking out targets, firing methodically.

Bullet holes like black bugs appeared on grimacing Jap faces, skin flew off as he switched from target to target smoothly, his mind caught in a steady, cold, still place that was as motionless as the sun, himself in it, in some strange way in total disregard of the zinging, popping, slamming bullets that hurtled past him.

It seemed to go on endlessly. Actually, it was only fourteen seconds. Then the Nip charge was halted and driven back. The bottleneck of the doorway had again defeated them, taken the momentum of their attack.

Another throbbing, ticking silence followed. Red turned, grabbed the back of Smoker's jumpsuit, and propelled him toward the mouth of the embrasure. "Go! Go!" he shouted. "I'll handle Cowboy. Drop fast."

Wineberg went, lunging into the gun port, crawling, skittering. Again Parnell checked his watch. *One minute forty-six seconds.*

He darted to the embrasure and slid himself into it, the cement aperture tight against his wide shoulders. He shoved forward, working his hips. The massive barrel of the coastal gun pressed against his right side, smelling like an old Victorian wrought-iron fence in a spooky house. The rest of the space held the odor of cement and stone dust and dried blood and the sea wind that whipped around the outer corners, making a soft, gentle, fluttery sound.

Beneath his body the other rappelling lines felt taut as cables. Yet he could also feel them shaking, the dropping movements of his men telegraphing through the fiber. He put his palm against Cowboy's back, pushed, pushed. It felt flaccid, a dead coldness coming through the material. Or was that imagination? He didn't think about it.

He reached the end of the embrasure, Fountain's left

leg already hanging over it limply. He held him and slid forward until he could look out, into space that was beginning to achieve substance. Far out, he saw the thin line of the ocean's horizon, a soft glowing demarcation that was interrupted by two shadows, islands of the Keise Shimas across the channel.

In the cramped space, Parnell had a difficult time setting up his rigging and positioning Cowboy's body just right so it would slip down onto his shoulders in a fireman's-type carry when he finally left the gun port and went out into space.

He finally got set. A gust of wind whipped in at him, made the cement dust on the bottom of the embrasure lift and whirl, stinging his eyes for a moment. He ducked his head under Cowboy's corpse and slowly let his legs go over the side.

The eerie cry came again. It sounded hollow and far away. *Here they come!* His forearm was close to his face, the light from the firing room dim out here, mostly blocked by the big 240mm's barrel. He saw his watch.

Thirty-nine seconds.

Then he was dropping, the full weight of Fountain's body on his shoulders suddenly, his feet against the cliff face as he dropped, almost bounding, shoving off and dropping and hitting and then shoving off again. The rope twanged with tension, his right hand feeding it through the carabiner, his leg feeling the burning, sharp tension of it around his leg and stomach, and now, suddenly, a sharp pain in his shoulder where he had wrenched it earlier.

He heard the banzai charge very faintly, a soughing, rushing, shouting sound. Muzzle bursts echoed. He looked down. Fifty feet below was darkness, save for wavy, vague, flitting reflections. He was over *ocean*.

Bullets started pinging and skipping along the face of the cliff all around him. He looked up. Japanese heads up there peering down, their rifles reflecting light, the muzzle flashes like small orange rings.

He felt and heard a round go into Fountain's body, a heavy, solid *thud*. Outrage burst through him. *He's already dead, you rotten little bastards.* He dropped another ten feet, heard *another* solid hit, close below him. He tried to look down, couldn't.

Fourteen seconds.

Suddenly a new sound blew into the air, a roaring big-engine noise that bounced off the cliff face. A huge dark shadow flashed overhead. He felt the wind of its passage slam down along the cliff, and caught the powerful smell of heated oil and hot steel in it. For one nanosecond, he saw exhausts ports roaring fire.

An aircraft!

There was a crashing, metallic sound, muffled by the rim of the cliff. Then an explosion. Dense white smoke immediately appeared all along the rim of the bluff, coiling and turning and flowing down over the face like a snow avalanche. Bits of sawdust rained down on him, stinking of titanium tetrachloride like ammonia.

The Nips instantly stopped firing and Parnell was plunged into a thick silence as the smoke continued to settle over him, closing out all sound. It stung his eyes badly, drew large teardrops from them, which cascaded down his cheeks and dripped from his jaw. He looked down, everything blurry.

His coral booties collided with the cliff's face again, his legs automatically bending to absorb the shock and propel him back out and down once more. He felt the rock tremble. Instincts triggered off and he closed down on himself, bending as tightly forward as he could, pulling in Cowboy's body tightly against his back and shoulders.

A pause, a breath, and then the Japanese gun emplacement blew sky-high.

For a violent, thunderous, deafening moment, Parnell

held to the rock face. It seemed to buckle under his feet, as if it were sundering into separate blocks. The rappelling line went completely slack. At the same moment, a powerful surge of concussion energy hurled him off the cliff, out into smoky space, his body turning somersaults, his arms still clinging to Cowboy's corpse.

Over and over he went and then suddenly plunged into water, going way down deep, night cool and black and filled with the sickening feeling of falling into depths that went all the way to the center of the earth.

Finale

Operation Iceberg, the taking of Okinawa-Shima, turned out to be the second costliest battle of the Pacific War, only overshadowed by the protracted campaign for the Philippines.

Nearly 8,000 American soldiers and marines were killed and over 31,000 wounded. In addition, there were nearly 25,000 casualties from battle fatigue and disease. The U.S. Navy, withstanding constant attacks by more than 4,600 kamikaze aircraft, sustained 9,780 casualties, along with the sinking of 36 ships and the damaging of 368 others.

On their side, the Japanese lost 106,000 men and nearly 8,000 aircraft, most from fields in Taiwan and Kyushu. Officially, the island would be secured on 2 July 1945, but mopping-up operations would extend well past that date.

Meanwhile in Europe, the war and the Nazi regime of National Socialism would come to an abrupt end at precisely 2:41 A.M., German double summer time, on 7 May 1945, when *Feldmarschal* Alfred Jodl, Chief of Operations for the German High Command, signed unconditional surrender documents in the city of Reims. At the same moment, *Feldmarschal* Wilhelm Keitel would undergo the same painful ceremony, watched by the baleful eye of Soviet Marshal Georgi Zhukov in Berlin, where, seven days earlier, Adolph Hitler and his mistress Eva Braun had committed suicide in the Führer's underground bunker near the Chancellery building.

Nevertheless, the Japanese, dominated by powerful military fanatics, were determined to fight on. Even to the "honorable death" of Bushido tradition, which would mean the complete annihilation of the entire nation.

Now the Allied focus homed in completely on the final conflict of the Pacific War, the invasion and conquest of the main Japanese Islands, which had been in planning stages for over eight months.

Initial landings would be made on the southern island of Kyushu at three specific points, the operation tentatively scheduled for mid-November. The tremendous amount of men and material for the undertaking was already being assembled in staging areas throughout the entire Pacific, many of the ground divisions, air groups, and naval-support ships having been shifted from the European Theater.

Everyone expected it to be a bloodbath of horrendous proportions. The extreme difficulties and fanatical resistance encountered on Okinawa and Iwo Jima gave a powerful example of what could be expected when the Japanese homeland was invaded. Estimates of the dead and wounded were being placed at a million men, with at least three times that in Japanese military and civilian casualties.

But fate and science would intervene.

Early in 1941, a group of scientists headed by Albert Einstein had written to President Roosevelt stating that they believed a nuclear bomb was a theoretical possibility. At first, this generated little interest. Then Pearl Harbor came, and Roosevelt, coordinating with the British, immediately created a highly secretive and massively funded organization to build such a weapon. It was given the code name Manhattan Project.

The first test of this new bomb took place at the Los Alamos Research Center's Site S located in the desert fifty miles from Alamogordo, New Mexico, on 16 July 1945. The resulting explosion literally stunned everyone. It generated a heat core ten thousand times the temperature of the sun's surface, broke windows two hundred miles away, and cast into the stratosphere what would become the symbol of the atomic age, a huge mushroom cloud that flashed green and deep purple and orange.

The ability to release such awesome power prompted the chief scientist of the project, Dr. Robert Oppenheimer, to softly utter a quote from the *Bhagavad-Gita*, "I am become Death, the shatterer of worlds."

President Harry S. Truman, Roosevelt's successor, now issued a final demand for unconditional surrender to the Japanese government in a speech following the Potsdam Conference of the Big Three. The Nips contemptuously dismissed it. With no further options, Truman okayed the use of the new weapon.

At precisely 8:15 on the morning of 6 August, the first atomic bomb to be used against a human enemy was detonated nineteen hundred feet over the city of Hiroshima. Carried there by a B-29 named the *Enola Gay* from the 509th Composite Group of the Twentieth Air Force, the bomb released the explosive power equivalent to thirteen thousand tons of TNT.

In the blink of an eye, eighty thousand Japanese were killed and thirty-five thousand wounded, most of whom would die within a year from radiation poisoning. Also, sixty-two thousand buildings were completely destroyed. Then on 9 August, another B-29 named *Bookscar* delivered a second bomb to the city of Nagasaki, this one with the force of twenty-two thousand tons of TNT. An additional seventy thousand civilians instantly died.

That was enough for Emperor Hirohito. On 14 August, despite violent reactions within the Imperial Japanese military, he exerted his power and forced the government to accept the unconditional surrender terms. Finally, on the morning of 2 September, the formal surrender ceremonies took place aboard the American battleship USS *Missouri* in Tokyo Harbor, marking the official end of World War II.

USS General John Pope T-AP 110
20 April 1945
0310 hours

The sparks from Parnell's cigarette made a tiny comet's tail down to the ocean. Exhaling its smoke, good Lucky-Strike-Green's-gone-to-war smoke, he drew in the sweet freshness of the night and the sea.

Under his hospital slippers, he felt the steady, gentle tremble of the ship's deck, a good, solid, nonwar feeling. High overhead, the stars were majestic. As always. It struck him now that in all the years of war he had looked up at these same stars, perpetually so remote and coldly uninvolved, so unceasingly tranquil. There seemed to be some sort of symbolic lesson in that thought, he decided. What was it? He shrugged. It didn't matter.

The *General John Pope* was now five days out of Saipan, headed for Pearl Harbor, which lay another twelve days away. Parnell was at the starboard weather deck railing of the vessel, which had once been a fast transport but was now a converted hospital ship.

It was totally white and there were spotlights shining on its huge red crosses painted on the hull and top deck. Like all hospital ships, it always steamed without blackout and broadcast its position in the open every fifteen minutes so the enemy would know precisely what it was.

Parnell, Bird, Laguna, and Wineberg had been brought to the ship by the USS *Triggerfish* late on the morning of the raid against the Japanese coastal guns, the sub easing close beside it as it lay at sea anchor five miles off Okinawa-Shima. They were hoisted aboard in a litter sling, along with four wounded UDT men and the bodies of Sol Kaamanui and three of commander Tennes's team. That evening, the ship departed for the Marianas.

All four Japanese batteries on the Oroku Peninsula had been destroyed. But like Blue Team, the navy frogmen had taken heavy casualties. CPO Terhune's Strawberry 3 was completely wiped out, and Tennes's Strawberry 1 had lost four men, including the commander.

Two days from Okinawa, Smoker Wineberg died of his wounds. Rock debris and metal shrapnel from the explosion of the Japanese casement had nearly torn out his spine. Parnell himself had also been similarly wounded in both legs and the buttocks, as had Laguna.

Red spoke to the ship's captain, requesting Wineberg and Kaamanui be buried at sea. It seemed appropriate. Sol had always loved the ocean, and Red recalled that Smoker's favorite place on earth had been New Orleans, which sat at its edge. The request was granted.

The ceremony took place at sunset, the two corpses sewn into canvas shrouds, the last stitch of which by custom looped through the dead men's noses. They were carried to the railing feet first, draped in the national flag, its stars at their heads. The sailor bearers wore white leggings and neckerchiefs. The ship's chaplain read the short service and the committal and three marines fired off a single round for each man with M1A3 carbines and then the bodies were allowed to slide into the sea.

Two days later, the *General John Pope* anchored off Saipan. The worst of the wounded were transferred to the big naval hospital on the side of Mount Tagochau, each man with his helmet on his chest, containing his meager belongings. Other walking wounded from the hospital were brought aboard until the wards were filled again and the ship prepared to sail for the Hawaiians.

Before it left, Parnell received a radio dispatch that contained orders from the Department of the Army in Washington, relayed through CVE *Anzio*. Due to the death of Colonel Dunmore, it said, the Mohawkers and its single

506   *Charles Ryan*

active unit, Blue Team, had officially been disbanded as
1 April 1945. He and his men were to report to the P/
section at Schofield Barracks, Honolulu, ASAP, for proce
ing and reassignment.

Someone came up beside him, Wyatt, on crutches. H
wounded leg was thickly wrapped in bandages, the wra
pings stenciled with his dog tag numbers and the kind
wound he'd sustained. The two men stood silently for
long time, listening to the ship sliding through the sea.

Finally, Bird asked, "You think we gonna be in on the b
one, Lieutenant?"

"I don't know. Probably."

"Ain't gon' be the same goin' back on the line witho
them boys."

"No, it won't."

They fell silent again. Parnell did not like to think abo
that part. It made him feel uncomfortable, as if he had fo
gotten to do something important, or had failed
accomplish something he should have. But now with tl
night's tranquility and the closeness of Wyatt Bird, he l
his mind replay it.

Three of my men down this time. Five out of eight. Kimball
Africa, Cappacelli in Italy, now Sol, Smoker, and Cowboy. A
don't forget back there in Europe, the colonel. Six out of nine.

He turned to Bird. "Colonel Dunmore was killed la
month. I didn't want to say anything before."

Wyatt made no comment. He merely hissed through l
lips and looked down at the dark sea, his face expressio
less in the light reflected from the Red Cross spots.

Parnell's thoughts expanded, recaptured those wild m
ments from the instant he felt the cliff of that Jap gu
battery start to go, and then the crazy, whirling plung
things hitting him feeling numbing and cold and the sti
of smoke and explosion dust and then the impact into t
sea. It had torn Cowboy's body from his grasp, only hi
self going down deep into pitch-black water not knowi
where the surface was, his mind racing, knowing he was

ocean now and, even amid the chaos and confusion, the ancient terror of sharks had come at him like lightning bolts.

He had finally worked his way back to the surface and found that the carrier fighter's smokescreen had descended completely over the ocean. He rose and fell gently on swells, heard the hiss of small surf close by. Frantically, he began searching for Fountain's body, feeling a peculiar flabbiness in his legs and buttocks as he kicked, hunting through the darkness and screaming despairingly in his throat.

He was eventually picked up by Wyatt and Weesay in their raft, which had Kaamanui's corpse resting crookedly between the seats. All three attempted to find Cowboy, but it was useless. Around them, the dawn light coming down through the smoke was quickly brightening.

Then Commander Gabany's raft came in with the remnants of the frogman strike teams. The commander ordered that they abandon the search for Fountain. They tied the two rafts together and quickly moved seaward, Gabany radioing the sub to come get them while the smokescreen cover still lingered.

Wyatt silently pushed back from the railing and moved away. Parnell lit another cigarette. Other wounded men passed along the spotlight-shadowed deck like silent, struggling ghosts, obviously unable to sleep below in the dim, blue-lit wards, wanting instead to be topside, in the open.

Parnell's thought pattern shifted. He looked far out, the horizon out there, faint, dark on dark. It seemed suddenly so unattainable, as if the slow passage of the ship might never make its contact as it perpetually receded beyond reach. The image triggered a sense of regret, of loss, of impossibilities.

It came with an utter sadness, too. Like the men he had known and fought with and watched die, had he himself died as completely, too? The part of himself he had slowly seen disappear as he passed through the evolution of a soldier? If he were to survive the coming, final invasion, could he ever go home again, recapture what he had once been? Or, like the horizon, would it forever elude him because he had simply come too far?

DON'T MISS CHARLES RYAN'S
EXCITING WWII THRILLERS

LIGHTNING STRIKE
ISBN 0-7860-1564-0

For their inaugural mission, the Mohawkers are sent to
the African coast ahead of the Allied invasion to take out
a battery of railroad-mounted artillery. Led by the relent-
less Lieutenant "Iron John" Parnell, the misfit unit of
soldiers must fight their way past a corps of hardened
French Foreign Legionnaires who are out for their blood,
outwit an enraged Luftwaffe colonel, and grab the guns.
Surrounded by enemies who'd gladly end their first mission before it begins, the boys know there's no room for
mistakes—and they'll have no mercy for anyone who gets
in their way.

THUNDERBOLT
ISBN 0-7860-1565-9

Two days before the Allied invasion of Sicily, Lieutenant
John "Red" Parnell and his Blue Team are put ashore for
a high-risk mission—to find and rescue a powerful Mafia
capo who can aid the Allies in taking the island. But a
bloody war erupts between Mob strongmen and Blue
Team is sucked into it, fighting against bloodthirsty
mafiosi armed to the teeth by a brutal German Waffen-
SS officer, Captain Karl Keppler. Obsessed by his hatred
for Blue Team and their partisan guides, Keppler grimly
continues hunting them throughout the invasion of
Salerno, through the bloody guerilla fighting on the
Volturno River and the great Liri Valley, to the final,
deadliest event of the Italian campaign, the assault on
Monte Cassino.

STORM FRONT
ISBN 0-7860-1566-7

Deep in occupied France, Lieutenant John "Red" Parnell and his Blue Team are conducting raids with the Resistance when they receive new orders. Rommel is to be arrested for conspiracy in the plot to kill Hitler. Their mission: escort an American officer to Rommel's HQ, to see if the Desert Fox will join the Allies before his downfall. But a traitorous double agent in their midst alerts the Gestapo, and the squad and their French comrades are captured. Tortured in the hellish eighteenth-century keep of Carpentras, Parnell and his men escape, only to learn of a Nazi plan to kill Eisenhower. Now they must stop the assassins on the eve of the Battle of the Bulge—and fight for their lives when they are surrounded in the isolated stronghold of Bastogne.

About the Author

Charles Ryan served in the United States Air Force, as a senior section airman and munitions system specialist in the armament of the 199th Fighter Squadron based at Hickman AFB, Honolulu. He attended the Universities of Hawaii and Washington, and has worked at numerous occupations, including judo instructor, commercial pilot, and salvage diver. He's written for newspapers in Honolulu and San Francisco and magazines, as well as being the author of ten novels. Ryan currently lives in northern California.